PRAISE
THE SHELL HOUS.
MYSTERY

'A cleverly plotted and thoroughly enjoyable book about dark deeds in beautiful places.'

—Elly Griffiths, author of the Ruth Galloway series

'A total delight.'

—Sarah Winman, author of *Still Life*

'Exquisitely written, set in Cornwall, great characters, and a gripping plot. Who could ask for more?'

—Jill Mansell, author of *Promise Me*

'This beautifully written cosy coastal mystery packs a real punch! With wonderfully atmospheric prose and twists and turns aplenty, the plot will have you riding a wave of suspense long after you've turned the final page. If you love Cornwall, you will adore this book.'

—Sarah Pearse, author of *The Sanatorium*

'Suspenseful, twisty and unputdownable . . . Loved it!'

—Claire Douglas, author of *The Couple at No. 9*

'Clever, plotty and compelling.'

—Jane Shemilt, author of *Daughter*

'If you're looking for a new favourite cosy crime series, here it is!'

—Libby Page, author of *The Lido*

'Engaging and enjoyable.'

—*Daily Express*

THE
ARTS TRAIL
KILLER

ALSO BY EMYLIA HALL

The Shell House Detectives Mystery series

Women's fiction

THE
ARTS TRAIL KILLER

Emylia Hall

THOMAS & MERCER

Text copyright © 2025 by Emylia Hall
All rights reserved.

Published by Thomas & Mercer, Seattle

www.apub.com

Amazon, the Amazon logo, and Thomas & Mercer are trademarks of Amazon.com, Inc., or its affiliates.

ISBN-13: 9781662521799
eISBN: 9781662521782

Cover design by The Brewster Project
Cover illustration by Handsome Frank Limited – Marianna Tomaselli

Printed in the United States of America

Dedicated to the memory of my mother-in-law,
Hazel Etherington (1946–2024)

Prologue

The killer can't sleep. It's mild for April, and the window is wide open. There's a crescent moon overhead, precise as a cut. Stars are sprinkled in every corner of the sky, with just the faintest lick of wind to keep things fresh.

A lovely kind of night.

Perhaps the people of Porthpella can't sleep either. *A village gripped by fear*: that's what the papers are peddling. And it's true that, coming on for midnight, there are more lights on round here than usual. A collective attempt to keep the dark away, with landing lights, security lights, a lamp left on in a sitting room – *just in case*. As if a low-wattage bulb is going to thwart an axe-wielding maniac.

Not that an axe is the weapon of choice.

The Arts Trail Killer. That's the cut-out-and-keep headline.

The killer is tempted to write a letter to the editor. To add a note, worthy of an exhibition catalogue, because while any work of art must speak for itself, a few lines of context never go amiss.

> *The artist and the murderer have much in common. Strength of conviction and a singularity of vision. The confidence to pursue one's own inspired agenda, in the face of societal opposition. Sometimes we plan with excruciating attention to detail, make intricate sketches*

in advance, commit to painstaking preparation before careful execution. Other times the process is instinctive and reactionary, where feeling, not thought, guides the hand. I have taken both approaches in my time and the end result is the same. The end result is unarguable. Though courts of law, and academic discussion, might protest otherwise.

The killer smiles, pleased by the analogy. The letter will never be written, of course, because it would cause a sensation and that's not the intention.

It never was.

The intention was pure. Simple. Heartfelt. But, somehow, it became something else, so the letter to the editor requires an additional point:

One of the greatest things that an artist and a killer have in common is knowing when to stop. That moment of stepping back, surveying the work, and declaring 'enough', because both know that one more touch will ruin it.

Only here the paths diverge, because this killer can't seem to – now, how should we phrase it? – *put the brush down.*

Outside the window, the night glitters as if everything is fine. But in people's homes, the lights stay on, because they know better. Or they fear worse.

Tomorrow's headline will read: *Arts Trail Killer Strikes Again.*

1

Two days earlier

Ally is in her studio, trying to see it through the eyes of a stranger. She takes in the whitewashed walls and grey stone floor, the salt-smeared windowpanes and sand-crusted ledges. The light beams in straight off the Atlantic, and this morning, after weeks of rain, it's luminous.

The Porthpella Arts Trail begins tomorrow, and Ally is all set. Her pictures are hung: intricate and vivid collages made of plastics brought in on the tide – here a sun-bleached bottle cap, there the thong of a flip-flop – a bid to make something positive out of sad reality. Her favourite piece shows the crescent of the bay, the island lighthouse, the undulations of the dunes. It's a view she's recreated many times, but because her raw materials are ever-changing, so too is the result. It's displayed on the oceanside wall, so standing back one sees the view twice: in salvaged form, and in real life.

In previous years, Ally took part in the Arts Trail week in a small way, with just one picture on display at the Bluebird gallery, but after the success of her solo show last summer, Sunita persuaded her to fully commit. The only catch? The hallowed walls of the Bluebird are to be the sole domain of celebrated guest artist

Harrison Loveday. And if Ally's admittedly quite ancient memories of Harrison hold, that's nothing less than he would expect. Indeed, Ally is surprised Harrison is gracing the Porthpella Arts Trail with his presence at all.

Could you open up The Shell House for the week? asked Sunita. *It'd be a wonderful venue, Ally.*

The idea with the Arts Trail is that artists exhibit their work in their own homes and studios. It's a more intimate experience than a trip to a commercial gallery, and surely part of the draw for visitors: legitimised snooping in the houses and gardens of total strangers. Ally can't help but feel wary of this.

It's true that her life has undergone a sea change these last few years, but the one constant has been her home, her sanctuary, The Shell House. Before her beloved Bill died, Ally had everything she needed here: the beach as her back garden; the endless possibilities of the shoreline; the ever-shifting ocean bringing a sense of fulfilment and occupation. But Ally is now a detective who's helped solve four major murder cases, with numerous smaller investigations unfolding in between. And it's all thanks to Jayden, in her opinion. The Fates and Furies brought them into one another's orbit two years ago, with life-changing consequences. Including the new group of friends by whom she's now surrounded.

While Ally's life has opened up in ways she could never have imagined, she's not quite ready to throw the doors of The Shell House wide. But her studio and garden? To this, she's agreed. The wobble she experienced on seeing the listing in the Arts Trail programme – the photograph of her lean-to studio; the blue weatherboard of the house in the background – was only momentary. Which was thanks, probably, to Gus, who reassured her thus: *You've been rubbing shoulders with the murderous and meddlesome for the last two years, Ally. How much trouble can an Arts Trail crowd be?*

But they should all know by now that, in Porthpella, trouble comes when you least expect it.

◆ ◆ ◆

Ally checks her watch. She can't wait to see Jayden. And his baby son. Porthpella's newest resident is just one month old, born in the wettest March on record. Spring was slow to arrive this year, but Benji Weston was bang on time. Unlike Cat and Jayden's firstborn, Jasmine, who came early, just as they were deep in their first case.

'Al!'

Ally's face breaks into a smile. She is always so happy to see Jayden. And with Benji curled in a sling at his chest, it's a double treat.

'Jazz is with her granny. She was cross about not seeing Fox. It's been a while, right?'

And it has. Since Benji came along, the Weston family have hunkered down. Perhaps serendipitously, no new cases have come their way; crime in these parts is lying low too.

'Coffee?' asks Ally.

She leans close to look at the perfection that is Jayden's little son. His rounded cheeks and long lashes. His tiny, immaculate hands, with mother-of-pearl fingernails.

'Coffee would be amazing,' says Jayden, his mouth splitting wide with a yawn. 'There's a reason he's out for the count now.'

Her friend looks exhausted, dark scoops beneath his eyes.

'You know you didn't need to come down and see me today,' she says, squeezing his arm.

'No, it feels good to get out the house. For Cat too. I told her to have a bath. Enjoy the quiet.'

'How is she?'

Jayden hesitates. 'It's always full on, these first weeks, isn't it? It was the same with Jazz. I guess we just forgot. We'll get through it.'

He looks down at Benji; kisses two fingers and rests them on his dark curls. Jayden looks as transfixed as if he's seeing him for the first time. Ally remembers Bill always being affectionate with Evie as a baby, but somehow with restraint. The love just spills out of Jayden. It's one of the special things about him.

'If I can ever do anything,' she says, 'you will tell me, won't you? Babysitting or . . . anything. It must be quite the step change, with two . . .'

'Right? Two is somehow like . . . six. I don't know. But thanks, Al, we're all good.' He sucks in a breath. 'Hey, how's the prep going for the Arts Trail?'

'I think I'm ready. The opening party's tonight and Sunita said you and Cat are invited. Are you coming?'

Jayden rubs at his jaw. 'Yeah, Cat's not really up for it.'

'Well, that's understandable.'

'I guess. It's not like her though. Plus, Sue said they'd have the kids, but . . . Benji's still kind of fussy with the bottle. And we're both so tired, we'd probably just turn up and go to sleep in the corner.' He grins. 'Is Gus going with you?'

'He is,' says Ally. 'I think he's mostly excited about seeing inside Island View House.'

Island View is a vast Victorian house just outside of Porthpella. Built just below the curve of the coast road, it has – as the name suggests – an enviable view. From the sloping tropical-plant-filled garden, the pepper-pot stem of the island's lighthouse looks close enough to touch. The owners, Gideon Lee and Connor Rafferty, are a decorative artist and a sculptor, and Porthpella's answer to an art-world power couple. They also head up the Arts Trail committee, along with Sunita, and this evening they're opening their home to launch the event in style. Drinks on the terrace, if the rain stays away.

And right now, the sky is as blue as a newly washed blouse.

Ally has lived through enough spells of bright and dark to know that the weather is rarely an omen for what the day has in store. Havoc is just as likely to appear out of an unblemished sky as one that glowers and weeps. But perhaps it's human nature to look out at a morning like this – a cornflower-blue sea, white-tipped waves chasing one another into shore, the sand glinting gold – and feel promise. And with the day set fair, all bodes well for the Arts Trail party at Island View House.

'Yeah, I thought Cat would be tempted by seeing the place too.'

And he sounds vaguely mystified. In the last two years, Ally has come to know Jayden's different faces. Always ready with a smile, his default setting is upbeat. But she also knows that, sometimes, good humour takes a force of will.

'Are you worried about her?' she asks gently.

'Worried? No, no. When you're tired, everything's just a bit harder, isn't it? A bit bleaker.'

'You know, Evie struggled with postnatal depression after Sam was born. I think it's rather a natural reaction to the demands of it all, actually.'

Ally watches him carefully as she says it, but Jayden just shrugs in response.

'Yeah, I hear you. A night out could have been good for us both though.'

But the party itself is likely to be little more than a lot of arty types glugging wine and quietly trying to outdo each other. Not Jayden's style. And not hers either, really. Ally has never been one for crowds.

'You won't be missing anything,' she says. 'It'll just . . .'

But her next words are lost as a trio of herring gulls – beefy creatures, with beaks like blades – fly screaming overhead. Seagulls are a constant soundtrack here, but every so often their cries are so explosively loud, so human in their pitch, that even the most habituated of coastal dwellers are stopped in their tracks.

Jayden nods to the sky. 'Yeah, that lot beg to differ, Al.'

And just like that, Benji wakes and wails.

2

When Saffron designed Hang Ten, she made it so that she could see the sea from behind the counter, so no matter how busy she is frothing milk and serving brownies, she can always look up. Drink in all that blue. The added bonus? A wave check is always on. If perfect sets start rolling into the bay, then she flips the sign to 'Gone Surfing' and grabs her board. From workplace to playground in seconds.

Today is the first time Saffron wishes she had a different view. A different sea. A two-dimensional one, in fact.

No sooner has she finished swooshing a heart on the top of a flat white than another customer is at the counter. The Easter holidays can be busy, but this morning is crazy. It's the rare blast of sunshine and blue skies coming after weeks of rain; everyone wants to be out in it. And something good from Hang Ten is the cherry on the cake.

'Mango and coconut smoothie? Sure!'

While Saffron is all smiles, she longs to be outside, watching the wall of Broady's surf school. Seeing what Milo Nash is doing, and whether that wave of his can get any more beautiful.

She looks to the door, and suddenly there he is.

Milo's baseball cap is on back to front, and for once he's not wearing the mask he uses when he's painting. His grey t-shirt looks tie-dyed, smudged with all the colours of his spray cans. Saffron plants a straw in the smoothie; delivers it to the table with an extra kick in her step.

'Hey,' she says, turning to him, 'how's it going?'

'Yeah, good.'

The first time Saffron met Milo Nash he was shyer than she'd imagined, considering the boldness of his work. But maybe that's how it goes: the spray cans do the talking. Three days ago he started with a bare wall, and now it's a blissful beachside scene, with one enormous wave set to break; the kind of wave that fills even the gnarliest surfers with terror and awe and desire. But unlike in real life, the face of the wave is dotted with people, everyone smashing it: kids, oldies, grins wide, dropping in like it's the easiest thing in the world. And the most okay thing too.

Broady was uncertain when he saw the direction that the piece was going in. *Kind of sends the wrong message. Surf etiquette is key in the ocean. You know what the next scene is, Saff? Broken noses, broken boards, and a whole lot of fighting and tears.*

But not in Milo Nash's world, where waves are big and beautiful and shared out like cake.

'How much do you have left to do?' she asks.

'It's basically there.'

'It's looking incredible.'

He grins. 'Cheers. And I'll take a coffee, please.'

She makes it on the house.

This time last year, Broady's surf school was operating out of a makeshift hut beside Hang Ten. Now, thanks to a small business grant and the input of a local investor, that makeshift hut is a custom-built cabin, with high beams and wide windows. Saffron and Broady spent the winter in a beachside shack in Hawaii, but in the downtime Broady was finalising permissions and Zooming with the designers and contractors. While her boyfriend was busy both on the water and off it, Saffron was sadly neither. A stupid slip on the way to the beach left her with a sprained wrist, costing her weeks of surf time. She's never been good at staying on the sidelines, and for all the beauty of the place, she felt weirdly occupation-less. And very gutted. Especially after it had been such an emotional decision to make the trip in the first place. Then, at the end of January, just as her wrist was mending, Broady said he needed to fly home to oversee the build, so Saffron came too – with the uncomfortable feeling that she was trundling in his wake. Two months later, the surf school is fully up and running. And Milo Nash, West Cornwall's hottest street artist, is adding the finishing touch.

Milo's work is usually unsolicited – patches of concrete in need of a little love and colour – but the pay packet clinched it. One of Broady's occasional surf buddies fronted the cash: an ex-public-school boy busy styling himself as a patron of counterculture. Broady was stoked but Saffron's more sceptical. Jonty is fine in the sea – nothing blasts away a person's hot air like a slap in the face from a wave – but on land he's a pain. Saffron doesn't love the thought of him bragging that he owns a bit of the oceanfront.

'Oh hey,' she says, holding up an Arts Trail programme from the stack on the counter. 'You're in here.'

Milo rolls his eyes. 'Well, they're public spaces.'

A Milo Nash walking tour, from Porthpella's chippie to the skatepark to the newly minted Mahalo Surf.

Mahalo. 'Thank you' in Hawaiian. Saffron suggested the name on their first starlit evening in Waimea Bay as they lounged beneath the palms, the sound of the sea a freight train in their ears. It was before she hurt her wrist; before the trip lost its glow. *It's given us so much*, she said to Broady then, her voice full of love. *I mean, it's given you so much.* Because the surf school isn't a joint venture. If it was, she wouldn't have taken Jonty's cash. Or maybe that's just her post-Hawaii grumpiness kicking in. Yet again.

'You didn't agree to it?'

He shrugs. 'What's there to agree to? If they want to tell people where to see stuff, then . . . whatever.'

'It's good to get the exposure, isn't it? There are some big names exhibiting this year. This guy Harrison Loveday . . .'

'Not big names in my world,' grins Milo. 'They wanted me to do some pieces to sell, but that's not what I do. A gig like this . . .' He gestures towards the surf school. 'Someone's paying for it, but it's still public art. It's for anyone to enjoy, not shut up in some rich person's house, you know?'

Saffron looks down at the page. The photograph of Milo shows him leaning against a brightly painted wall, his arms folded. Half of his face is obscured by a mask.

A leading light in the UK street art scene, Milo Nash seamlessly blends positivity and rebellion.

She holds it up. '"Positivity and rebellion", huh?'

'Yeah, that's me.' He pops an Instagram-worthy peace sign – then flips it. 'Can't you tell?'

Saffron laughs. 'So, does this positive rebel want a cookie to go with the coffee?'

'Hey guys.'

Broady. He's in his wetsuit, hair salty and tangled from the ocean, and stands with his feet planted wide. It's his 'I've got something to say' pose.

'Milo, mate, I know I keep going on about it, but all those people on the wave. I've got this image of chaos in our bay. No one respecting the rules, you know?'

'I thought rules were for ordinary sports,' says Milo.

'Unwritten rules. Etiquette.'

'Etiquette? Now it sounds like polo. Or croquet.'

'I can't teach people not to drop in on someone else's wave if they see something different painted across my surf school.'

'It's just art, Broady,' says Saffron. 'It's representative. Togetherness in the ocean. Share-the-love vibes.'

'What she said,' says Milo.

Broady seems unconvinced. 'People are literal though.'

'How about I add a line? "No surfers were injured or angered in the making of this work."'

'Yeah, that'd help.'

'Mate, I was joking.'

'It's beautiful,' says Saffron. 'You're overthinking it, babe. Plus . . . you saw the original designs, right?'

Broady frowns. 'He's added people.'

'Creative fluidity,' says Milo. 'Talking of, I've got moves to make. Saffron, thanks for the coffee. And the cookie. You're a sweetheart.' He claps Broady on the shoulder. 'Don't sweat it, bro. It looks great.'

As the door swings closed behind Milo, Broady turns to Saffron. His face is stormy – and that's rare.

She goes for lightness. 'No one's going to steal your waves, babe.'

'It's a commission. You're supposed to do what the client wants.'

'I don't think Milo works like that.'

Broady sends her a look she can't quite read. 'Tell me about it. Hey, don't feel like you have to give him free stuff, by the way. He's getting a good fee out of me.'

Out of Jonty.

'I always give the people I like free stuff. Oh, and Mullins.'

Broady grunts. 'Constable Mullins would nick Nash if he could.'

A couple of summers ago Porthpella awoke to an infestation of seagulls. The side wall of the village chip shop was completely covered in them – a spray-painted riot of wings and beaks and stolen chips. The owners, Jim and Babs, couldn't decide if they loved it or hated it. But then it became a talking point, and sales went up too. They decided to love it – and didn't press charges.

'He'll be done today, anyway,' says Broady. 'Then from tomorrow we'll get the Arts Trail crowd coming through. Flog them some surf lessons.'

'Hand out some of those surf rule books too.'

But by the look on Broady's face, Saffron's joke falls flat.

3

As Jayden walks along the dunes, his feet are heavy in the sand. Back in the West Yorkshire Police he was on shift work, so he knows about all-nighters. The difference is, when he got in at first light back then, he'd close the curtains and crash.

He turns his face to the onshore breeze, hoping it'll wake him up.

'Breathe it in,' says Ally, beside him.

Jayden yawns, his jaw creaking.

Benji is still grumbling. After the rude awakening by the gulls, he wouldn't settle, so Jayden, Ally and Fox are out walking. Jayden thought about messaging Cat, thinking she might find it funny: we need to incorporate seabirds into this kid's sleep training. But he stopped himself, because what she really wants is a break from remembering she even has a baby for a couple of hours.

The birth started like Jazzy's, but then took a turn. Benji's heartrate was dropping. He wasn't shifting. The words *emergency caesarean* flew around the room and Jayden saw the look on Cat's face: pain on top of pain. As she explained it later, *I laboured for ten hours, Jay. It was all for nothing.* He's tried to understand it, but how could it be for nothing when their perfect boy is the result?

When they first got home from the hospital, Cat crept into bed, doubled over with pain from the operation. Jazzy was crying, *Benji hurt Mummy*, and Benji was crying just because. That night,

Jayden felt like he had to grow a foot taller. He made Trini corn soup for them all. He picked daffodils from the mud outside the cottage and put them in a vase on Cat's side of the bed. He gave Jazzy her bath while Cat fed Benji, laid on extra bubbles, stuck foam letters to the tiles saying *I love my big sis*. And when the girls were finally asleep, he settled down with his boy in front of *Match of the Day* – Benji's head beneath Jayden's chin, heartbeat to heartbeat – and the two of them fell asleep too.

That first night was both mania and magic.

The thirty nights since have had a bit of both. The current status? Cat's back on her feet; her scar healing well. Jazzy loves her little brother – most of the time. And Benji is the best baby boy Jayden has ever set eyes on. Sure, he's turned them all upside down and back to front, but that's the deal, right?

And spring finally feels like it's here now. Everything's better with a bit of sunshine. That's what he told Cat this morning and she didn't disagree.

Though she didn't agree either.

Jayden knows she's been rocked by this. He knows that she's not getting the sleep she needs; that even when the kids are down she shifts and turns fretfully. He just doesn't know what he can do about it. Ally mentioned Evie having postnatal depression: is that what's going on with Cat?

Before they moved to Cornwall, after Jayden left the police, he was flattened by grief. Cat carried him then. Jayden's never admitted it, but the experience reshaped their dynamic: in his eyes, Cat became the strong one. She'd always been tough – a farmer's daughter, growing up vaulting fences, running into winter seas with her surfboard – but overnight she grew epic. And she held him together, when nothing else could.

But whereas it was death that undid Jayden, Benji is life. Roaring, beautiful, brand-new life.

'So, the party tonight,' says Ally, 'there'll be a familiar face there actually.'

'Oh yeah?'

They pause as Fox investigates a rabbit hole. He noses at the entrance more from muscle memory than excitement, then pads on.

'Harrison Loveday,' says Ally. 'Many moons ago, I was at art school in Falmouth with him.'

'And who's Harrison Loveday?'

'The big-name guest for the Arts Trail. Sunita described him as the feather in their cap. But he's more of a turkey cock, in my opinion.'

Jayden raises an eyebrow. 'Is that some countryside expression that I'm not getting?'

'Back then he had rather a big opinion of himself, anyway,' she says with a low laugh. 'Half a century ago, or thereabouts.'

'A lot can happen in half a century, Al.'

'Agreed. But I must confess to having done a little sleuthing.'

'Wouldn't expect anything less. Go on then, what's the dirt?'

Ally tells him that after Harrison Loveday's spell at Falmouth, he moved to London. He went on to have an illustrious career as a portrait artist, represented by a high-end gallery, his work loved by celebrities.

'He lives in Tuscany these days, in a palatial villa. There was an interview with him in *Homes and Gardens* magazine. Rumour has it that he hasn't been back to Cornwall since he left Falmouth.'

'And that's his crime?' Jayden laughs.

He's only half-joking. As much as Ally is a live-and-let-live kind of person, if someone gives Cornwall the cold shoulder, she'd probably have a hard time understanding it.

'He was always just so big for his boots. Talented, and that success has clearly been rewarded, but . . . Oh, it's hard to explain.'

Jayden narrows his eyes. It feels like there's a bigger story here.

'Not to do with him taking your spot at the Bluebird, then?'

'Wholeheartedly not,' says Ally, her cheeks pinkening. 'I'll give you an example. He's a portrait artist, but it seems his specialism is . . . self-portraits. My goodness, I must have seen fifty different versions of him over the last few days.'

'That many, huh?'

And it cracks Jayden up, the thought of Ally putting her investigative powers to use like this.

Maybe she needs a case as much as I do.

'Oh goodness . . . Talk of the devil. Jayden, I think that's him.'

She points towards Sea Dream, the huge glass-fronted house in the dunes that used to belong to Roland and Helena Hunter – the epicentre of their first case, two years ago. It was sold not long after and is now a luxury holiday home. *For a change.* A tall man in a white cricket jumper and wine-red trousers is standing in the driveway. He looks like a South Coast yachting type – and prosperity lights him like a beacon.

'Is it him?' says Ally to herself. 'I can't be sure . . .'

'Whoever he is, he's got company,' says Jayden, as a bright white BMW storms down the track and the man throws up his hand in a wave.

'Driving too fast,' mutters Ally.

'Typical emmet.'

Emmet being the Cornish term for a tourist – meaning 'ant' – and Jayden's grumpy father-in-law's favourite word. Two and a half years in and Jayden's not sure what his own status round here is. Lucky that he doesn't actually care then, hey? Growing up with a black mum and a white dad, he's well used to people trying to put him in boxes. And he's equally used to ignoring them.

They watch as the car skids to a halt and a woman glides out. She's probably mid-fifties. Leather boots, leather trousers, leather jacket; a curtain of long red hair. Harrison holds out his arms and the woman steps into them. They kiss.

Fox picks this moment to bark. As the two break apart, the man looks in their direction, but if it is Harrison Loveday, it's unlikely that he's been googling Ally Bright because he shows no sign of recognition. He says something to his companion, then strolls towards the house with his hands in his pockets. The woman watches him for a beat, then goes to the boot of her car and pulls out a small suitcase.

'You could help me,' she calls out. 'Harrison! Where are your bloody manners?'

4

It was Gina who found the place in the dunes, so when she suggested to Harrison that she stay there too, he went along with it. Actually, that's not quite true. Harrison never just goes along with things. He performs a mental calculation to ensure that the numbers are firmly in his favour. In this instance, Gina Best will be a distraction; someone to keep him warm on the cold coastal nights. So long as she doesn't get in the way of what he really wants from the trip.

The trouble is, Harrison has forgotten how *much* Gina is. It's probably been eighteen months since he saw her in the flesh, though their phone and email contact is ongoing. It has to be. Gina is the owner of the Dashwood Gallery, his sole representative on these shores. And she knows her stuff, he'll give her that – she's been in the business for more than thirty years.

Just now she hurled herself from the car and into his arms with the vigour of a racehorse attacking a fence. And now that Harrison comes to think of it, there is something rather equine about Gina, with her strong teeth and flowing mane. A thoroughbred, obviously. Admirable, in a lot of ways, but she can't help champing at the bit. She's got a sharp kick too, when she wants.

'The non-Gentleman of Verona,' huffs Gina as she drags her case over the threshold. 'I see Italy continues to do nothing for your civility.'

'I'm a four-hour drive from Verona, darling.'

'Well, you're a lot further now. How does it feel to be on Cornish soil again?'

Gina has the capacity to be provoking, but this time it's an innocent question. She's always been obsessed with the Cornish element of his biography, wanting to style him as some sort of descendant of the Newlyn School, which he's strongly resisted. Three years in Falmouth? That's a footnote on his CV at best.

'Sand not soil,' he says. 'And it's itchy.'

'Too early for a drink?'

He checks his watch performatively. 'Never too early. Though I mustn't forget to hang the damn work.'

As she smiles, he can count her teeth. Her lipstick is a fiery orange. Her hand goes to her throat and she fiddles with one of her abundant necklaces, heavy silver chains that lend her a faintly piratical air. Harrison suspects she's going for coquettish, and at fifty-eight, she doesn't quite pull it off. Mind you, he suspects she wouldn't have at twenty-eight either. In his humble opinion.

'The *Sunday Times* are interested in a piece.'

'For the office wall? Nice of them.'

'A feature, Harrison. They love the angle that you've come home.'

Harrison rolls his eyes.

'A return to the remote corner of the world where your genius was born. Reconnecting with your roots. That sort of thing.'

'Gina, I was born in Saltash. Barely over the Tamar. I spent three poxy years in Falmouth, then double that unlearning everything I was taught. My parents are long buried, and I have no friends here to speak of.'

21

'No old flames, then?'

She's casual, but the need in her voice is obvious.

'No old flames. Otherwise, why do you think I'd agree to stay with you in this flat-pack beach house, like any other tourist?'

Gina's nostrils flare. *See – equine.* 'It's a cutting-edge build. A highly desirable luxury rental.'

'It's paint-by-numbers. And as I keep telling you, the Cornish connection is neither here nor there.'

'But it's an angle we can exploit for publicity.'

He snorts. Joining her in the stables.

'I hardly need to *exploit* anything.'

She tips her chin, eyes glittering. Her elaborate earrings swing like pendulums.

'So if Cornwall is neither here nor there, then why accept, Harrison? This Arts Trail. This backwater.'

He gestures to the wide windows, the surf rolling into the bay; the fizz of white water on sucking sand.

'Backwater? I think you'll find it's the oceanic frontline, Gina.'

'Alright, but why on earth would you say yes? When you finally deigned to tell me, I couldn't quite believe you'd gone for it.'

He's been wondering when the question would come.

Harrison turns away from her, his mouth hardening. In the depths of his head, he can hear his father's voice: *Don't you turn your back on me!* Harrison was belligerent even as a toddler, by all accounts.

Gina's right, of course. The Porthpella Arts Trail is far beneath him, even with the moniker of Guest Artist. To stick with the equestrian analogy, his presence in Porthpella is akin to Red Rum turning up at a donkey show.

Harrison squints at the blue water, the silver-green marram grass waving in the wind. The two people with the yappy dog are specks in the distance now, all but swallowed by the landscape. He shudders to imagine the many butchered versions of this view that must exist; amateurish daubs of paint on canvas, peddled in the kind of souvenir shops that pass as galleries round here.

'Gideon Lee asked me nicely. And is paying me nicely too.'

'Okay. He's well regarded as a contemporary decorative artist. His needlepoint is very competent, it's true. Fantastic use of colour.'

'Well, there you have it.'

'You said he was a friend of a friend?'

'Marco Pellegrino.'

A colourful chap, with a tattered but rather grand studio off the King's Road. There was a time when Harrison cared for parties, and Marco always threw good ones.

'You could have cobbled together some existing pieces for the show – any old Harrison Loveday would have been a coup. But instead, you've created new work.'

'Dabblings. They hardly took long.'

'Did Gideon request the Cornish focus?'

'It would have been churlish not to.'

'So, it is both a here and a there.'

'God, you're pedantic, darling.'

Encounters – that's what he's called the exhibition. *Seven portraits of the Duchy.* A fisherman in luminous oilskins, a beautiful young flower farmer, a salt-wet wild swimmer, a prosperous developer, an ex-military rough sleeper, a feckless teen with a hoodie and a skateboard – and an artist. The last is a self-portrait, obviously: Harrison as a young man. They're faces conjured from his imagination, though the notes for the exhibition suggest that memory has played the greater part.

Objectively, Harrison knows they're not his best work. And that's because they don't need to be. He's not here to catch the eye of an art collector; he's in bed with enough of those already. No, he's here to catch the eye of someone who he suspects doesn't know their Degas from their Disney, who probably thinks Caravaggio is a pizza topping.

And whose fault is that?

Meanwhile, Gina's lips are twitching. She wants to say something else but, for once, she appears to think better of it. He wonders what thoughts are buzzing round that busy brain of hers. No doubt they'll spill out later, a few drinks in. Gina is not the kind to let things lie. To appease her, he gives her a little of what she wants to hear – the same sort of tripe he'll offer up to the *Sunday Times* too, should they come calling.

'I don't know, perhaps I'm getting old, Gina. Perhaps I'm getting sentimental. But that's a hard thing to admit.'

The words trip from his lips – they're empty, hollow – but nevertheless they leave a distinct taste.

He turns back to the view and strikes a thoughtful pose. People do that, don't they? Stare out at the sea and wonder what life's all about. You see them along the seafronts of any dreary coastal town, plonked amidst the chip paper and polystyrene cups; hands folded in their laps, eyes on the water. The most basic individuals coming over all existential – though they wouldn't know the word for it.

Perhaps I'm getting old. Perhaps I'm getting sentimental.

That's a hard thing to admit.

Out of the mouths of babes and battle-worn artists.

Harrison thinks of the text message he sent earlier. The ones before that too. Are these bite-size missives really falling on deaf ears? He still hopes the show might serve as a carrot; his new work a lure. God, he's pathetic. A man like him shouldn't have to grovel for attention, for connection, for bloody anything. Especially given the gesture he's made; the one his solicitor put the ink on just last week.

Not that Harrison likes to contemplate his own mortality, but as soon as he made the decision, he felt a wash of emotion. Was it his own generosity that moved him? Or something else? Some instinctive, deep-buried acknowledgement of what had been lost?

Because there isn't anyone else.

There really isn't anyone else.

For all his connection with Gina, professional and personal, she's utterly expendable.

But Harrison has no intention of declaring his plan. He rather likes the idea of the grand reveal, down the line and after the fact.

Or is it because I'm afraid that, even with this almighty gesture, it won't make the blindest bit of difference?

Beyond the windows of this dratted house, the sea cares for nothing. Harrison is inconsequential. His head buzzes. His eyes mist. Somehow, his heart throbs on.

'Darling,' says Gina, her voice sweet and cloying as cheap limoncello, 'it happens to the best of us.'

And she's beside him, her arm around his waist like a pincer.

'You mustn't be afraid to show your vulnerability, Harrison. Not to me.'

Inwardly, he rolls his eyes. But by the way Gina flinches, perhaps it's outward too. She steps away from him.

'Fine. Let's go with that party line of yours,' she says. 'Cornwall? Neither here nor there. But seeing as we are here, shall we have that drink?'

5

Sunita stands in the quiet of the Bluebird, surveying Harrison's pieces. Now that the artist has left, she can take the time to really absorb his work. It was one of the quicker hangings she's experienced. She imagined him to be a perfectionist, in addition to the baseline characteristic: one of those privileged white men of a certain age who stride in with assumed authority. Perhaps his casual attitude was also to do with the alcohol on his breath; a pre-lunch gin and tonic or two could well be de rigueur in Montepulciano.

Harrison Loveday wouldn't have been her first choice of guest artist for the trail, but Sunita does admire his work. Five years ago, she saw a painting of his in the National Portrait Gallery and was transfixed. The subject was an elderly woman, with a floppy sunhat and a glass of wine in her hand. And she was laughing, as if she knew the secret of life itself. Sunita is fifty-two and hopes to have at least thirty more years on this earth. How she'd like to be that twinkly-eyed woman basking in full sun, one day. Perhaps on a last tour, taking in all the places that have mattered to her: the sway-backed bungalow in Plymouth where she was born, with the view of the grey and restless Sound and a devastatingly beautiful magnolia tree; her paternal grandparents' villa in Kuala Lumpur with its garden full of red hibiscus and the high-pitched squeak of tawny yellow sunbirds;

the Madrid apartment where she stood on a crumbling balcony and her first boyfriend went down on one knee and produced a ring that caught the day's dying rays and threw them back in pink and gold. And Porthpella, of course. Her final resting place? Perhaps.

All of these thoughts – this cascade of memory and possibility – provoked by a single painting, on an otherwise unremarkable afternoon in the capital. So, when Gideon proffered Harrison Loveday's name as a candidate, Sunita made appreciative noises.

Strictly speaking, Gideon should have officially cleared the invitation with both her and his partner, Connor, the other member of the Arts Trail committee. But Gideon's natural spontaneity meant he didn't observe the etiquette, and by then it was too late: Harrison had been sounded out, Harrison had accepted, Harrison was on board.

Sunita looks up as the doorbell clangs and Gideon surges in.

'Oh! It's done already? It looks . . . fantastic.'

The disappointment in his voice is palpable. But whether it's down to missing out on Harrison in the flesh, or the quality of the work, she's not sure. Sunita suspects a combination.

'He was in a bit of a hurry,' she says.

Gideon makes a noise of agreement as he leans close to the first painting.

'So I see,' he murmurs.

Sunita feels for him. It was Gideon's idea to draw in a big-name artist as a guest for the trail this year, and while she could see the benefit, she did worry that it might make the other exhibitors feel demoted. A *here's someone to show us how it's really done*-type flavour. That, at least, won't be the problem.

Gideon goes up to each painting in turn. He studies them with his hands folded behind his back, peering closely at the canvas. Then he steps back, and tilts his head, as if to open up a new perspective.

'I thought they'd be a bit bigger,' says Sunita, tactfully.

With seven small paintings, in a room that typically holds twenty or more, it does look a little airy.

'The colours are wonderful though,' she says. 'The backgrounds really pop.'

Gideon stops in front of the last picture: a teenager with a skateboard under his arm, the upper part of his face obscured by his hoodie. His chin erupts with acne, his lips are caught in a snarl.

'I don't like this one. There's a nastiness about it.'

'There is, isn't there?'

'There's an inherent judgement. As if the skateboard and the hoodie alone are markers of . . . depravity. You could of course argue that's deliberate, a depiction of the way that some aspects of society regard others, but the trouble is . . .' He steps closer; squints. '. . . the execution isn't up to snuff.'

'I thought the same of the fisherman. His eyes are . . .'

'Dead? Dead as the eyes of the mackerel at his feet. And the . . .' He checks the title of the next picture. 'The flower farmer. All heaving bosoms and armfuls of blooms. It's bawdy. I don't mind bawdy, but . . . it's cartoonish.'

'The daffodils are beautifully done though. Gideon? Gid?'

He slowly turns. His handsome face is pale and crumpled.

'Oh God, he's phoned it in, hasn't he?'

'I mean, the fact that it's new work is great.'

'He's only gone and phoned it in.'

'His hallmarks are there. I think you can tell it's Harrison Loveday. Don't you think? Just . . . looser.'

'Looser, but not impressionistic.'

'No.'

'Careless, in fact.'

Sunita shakes her head. 'A little. In places.'

'Harrison Loveday? Harrison Bad Day,' says Gideon, then holds his hand to his mouth.

Sunita can't help laughing. 'It's too late to amend the programme with that, unfortunately.'

Gideon turns from the pictures and flops down in a chair. He crosses his long legs.

'I couldn't believe our luck. I mean, I didn't really expect him to say yes. Then I kept thinking he'd probably cancel. But show up with inferior work? No, I didn't consider that option. I credited him with more integrity than that.'

Sunita nods, but Gideon's view of artists has always been rose-tinted, as if the decision to hold a paintbrush or spin a potter's wheel is immediately elevating. Sunita has spent too many years as a gallerist not to know that creative people do not necessarily equal nice people. In fact, in her experience, egos are often eggshell-thin, and entitlement rife.

'Oh God, look who it is,' says Gideon, stepping to the window. 'She's going to love this.'

Sunita joins him, watching the young woman exit White Wave Stores and march across the square. Her head is down, her fawn coat tightly belted. Her dead-straight hair, the colour of weak tea, hangs like a cape at her back.

Lara Swann: only daughter of legendary contemporary artist Billie Swann, and now a full-time resident of Porthpella after moving into her elderly mother's vacant holiday home, a grand old house called Westerly Manor. Lara submitted work for the Arts Trail and, unfortunately, talent was found to have skipped a generation – though their carefully worded rejection was a lot more diplomatic and kindly than that. Nevertheless, Lara didn't appreciate the knockback, and her return email to the committee said as much. Her subsequent three emails also said as much, with quite some spirit.

In the end they agreed not to reply. *Best let sleeping dogs lie*, said Connor – and, as always, Gideon listened to him. But if that was Lara in repose, Sunita would hate to see her at full throttle.

She doesn't look far off it now. There's a fierce energy propelling Lara's stride across the square. For a moment she looks like she's heading towards the gallery but then she swerves at the last minute, and instead takes the path to the beach, arms going like pistons.

'I don't like making enemies,' says Gideon. 'I wonder if we should invite her this evening. Extend the olive branch.'

Sunita shakes her head. 'I think that would make her feel worse. Anyway, she's not the only artist we turned down. She's just the only one who made a fuss.'

'Well, quite.' He turns back to the space, the work; the unremarkable paintings of Harrison Loveday. His face sags. 'They're not *bad*, as such.'

'No, they're clearly competent.'

'Competent. Yes. Come to the Porthpella Arts Trail and behold the wonderful competency of our star attraction!'

Sunita thinks a change of subject is wise.

'So, tonight. I'm looking forward to it.'

'I wish Connor was. He's in one of his "I hate people" moods.'

'That's unfortunate timing.'

'Oh, he'll rally. He'll be charm personified later, and no one will be any the wiser. How was he, by the way? Harrison? It's years since I saw him in person.'

Sunita ponders her adjectives. Gideon is disappointed enough without her adding to it with words like *nonchalant* and *superior*.

'Energetic,' she says. 'Very confident, of course. All smiles.'

And Harrison *was* all smiles. But then the part of her and Gideon's conversation about dead eyes flits back into her head.

'He made a point of saying he was looking forward to the party later,' she adds.

'Did he?' Gideon's face lights up. 'We'd better make it a night to remember then.'

6

'I've brought a torch for later,' says Gus, patting the pocket of his jacket.

Ally imagines the two of them walking home under a starlit sky. An ancient memory surfaces: the narrow streets of Falmouth by night, arms linked, singing. *Shh, people are sleeping!* Then: *But not us, Ally, not us.* She brushes it away and thinks of Gus again.

Gus, who she didn't see a lot of this winter – not by their usual standards, anyway. First there was her six-week trip to Australia, staying with Evie and the boys. Then the race to get her pictures ready for the Arts Trail upon her return. With the detective work quiet, Ally's art has consumed her. Meanwhile, Gus was doing the same at All Swell, though sifting through words rather than ocean plastics. He messaged her when she was in Sydney: It's the last push! He's finally close to finishing the detective novel he's been working on for the last two years. She glances at him now as they crest the hill outside Porthpella. There seems to be a particular spring in his step this evening.

They are firm friends; of this she is confident. But the possibility of there being more between them seems to ebb and flow. After Gus's terrible injury last summer, Ally was stunned by the intensity of her feelings. And it's true that they drew closer because of it. But just as she was moving forward, as if she might be ready for more, Gus stepped back. It was the end of a hard case and there was a storm brewing outside. They were cosy by the fire. The words she said come back to haunt her sometimes – *you'd be more than welcome. To stay, I mean* – because his answer was unequivocal. *Ah, now that's very kind. But . . . I'll be grand.*

A door held open. A threshold not crossed.

It made Ally think she'd read him wrong. But then she's so out of practice at reading anyone, that's hardly a surprise. Since that night, there've been walks along the coast path. Suppers. The splitting of a bottle of wine. The sorts of things that they now have the joy of calling usual, rather than occasional – but with the simple sturdiness of friendship. Their lives rub happily alongside one another, but you wouldn't call them inextricable. Sometimes Ally still detects a certain current in the air – a tingling quality; like the feeling before a storm – but then it's as if Gus resets himself. Steps back again. And not that she's counting, but if anyone's to make a move, it's Gus's turn now.

'A torch? Good thinking,' she says. 'Though I don't know how long we're expected to stay.'

'Past sunset, surely.'

Which is around eight o'clock this time of year. After the swamping dark of winter, the newly light evenings feel incredible at first.

'Look at that,' she says, stopping.

Because it doesn't matter how many times she's seen the view, it demands attention.

The water is denim blue, fraying to white where it meets the beach. The island lighthouse is close enough to touch. She can see the undulations of the dunes; the slanted rooftops of Porthpella. Beyond, the sky and the sea go on forever.

'No one's luckier,' says Gus.

And they meet in a smile.

33

There. One of those moments.

'Look,' says Gus, 'that's it, isn't it?'

He's pointing to the gable of a house, just visible over the next stretch of cliff path. They take the narrow track leading up to the back gate. It's festooned with fairy lights, and they step through it into the most beautiful subtropical garden. Burly palms and handsome banana trees, a blaze of early rhododendrons and late camellias, succulents of every shape and form. As they emerge from the shrubbery, the house comes into view and the sound of conversation and light music drifts over on the breeze. Perhaps fifty people are gathered on the terrace. They walk up towards it, the emerald-green lawn springing beneath their feet.

Gideon Lee stands a good head and shoulders above everyone else. He wears a bright flower-patterned shirt underneath his smart jacket and has a natural gravitas: the shimmer of the host.

A waitress – a girl in a white school blouse – proffers her tray of sparkling-filled flutes.

'Or there's cocktails at the bar,' she says. 'Mai Tais.'

Ally and Gus take champagne; their thanks are met with an indifferent smile and the girl drifts on.

'You said you've met Gideon?' says Ally.

He's one of the most talented, and commercially successful, artists that Ally knows. A needleworker, his intricate tapestries depict fruit and flowers and sea creatures in jaw-dropping colours. He's published a book on the topic. Even had do-it-yourself kits made up, sold in craft shops up and down the country.

Gus swallows. 'Cor, that's a nice drop, that is. Gideon? Yes, I've met him. Only in passing though. And never Connor. That's him, isn't it? In the khaki shirt?'

Gus nods to a man on the fringes of the group, with cropped blond hair and a bemused expression. A woman in a purple dress is gesturing with her glass, while her other hand keeps settling on

Connor's shoulder. His lean and muscular frame makes him look as if he's ready to run.

'Connor Rafferty's a brilliant sculptor,' says Ally. 'The heir to Hepworth, some say. That's one of his.'

In the middle of the lawn there's a sculpture of a broken seashell: the spire and whorls of a whelk, the twisted inner stem planted in the grass. It's resin and metal and looks at once delicate and immovable. Behind the piece, Ally can see the studio. It's a low stone building, and with its red-tiled roof and canary-yellow painted shutters, it's a work of art in its own right. Visitors will love nosing inside it, seeing how a textile artist and a sculptor create side by side. Soft twists of coloured yarn and wool contrasted with heavy hammers and razor-sharp chisels. From tomorrow, their studio will be open to the public, but for now the doors are closed.

'So, go on then,' says Gus. 'Which one's my temporary new neighbour?'

On the walk over, Ally told him how she and Jayden saw Harrison Loveday at Sea Dream. How moons and moons ago she and Harrison were at art school together in Falmouth.

'There,' says Ally. 'In the middle. Blue shirt.'

He's holding court, of course, a circle tight around him, including the red-headed woman who arrived at the house. It strikes Ally that Harrison is rather birdlike, with his beaked nose and feathered hair. He used to wear a long black coat, always open and flapping, and fly around campus like a jackdaw.

'Want to go and say hello?' asks Gus.

'I'm not in a hurry.'

'Fine by me. Who else here is an artist? Just so I don't put my foot in it.'

Ally eyes the group. 'Well, most people,' she says, 'and their partners and friends. Oh, that's Donald Crosby. He's a landscape painter. Did an interesting series of the mudflats at Hayle for last year's trail.'

They were melancholic, searching pieces. And, according to Sunita, Donald was melancholic when they didn't sell. He's with Sunita now, their heads bent together, deep in conversation. His half-moon glasses are up on his forehead, and he's rubbing at his stubble as if he's trying to get rid of it.

'I think I spoke to him in The Wreckers once,' says Gus. 'He's got a boat, hasn't he?'

'Several,' says Ally. 'He restores them, I believe.'

'And I recognise the lady in black and white next to him. A teacher, isn't she?'

'Pamela. She was, but she's retired now. An art teacher and a potter. She lives in a barn conversion just outside of Porthpella. I think it was controversial at the time.'

Ally can't remember why. Possibly something to do with planning permission? Pamela's been living there for twenty years or more.

'Well, that I have to see. Any good? The pots, I mean. Not the conversion.'

'Very good. I think she always does well on the trail. Though good sales aren't always an indicator of good quality.'

'Gotcha,' says Gus with a wink. 'It's a decent earner, is it, this trail? Maybe I should have a crack. I'm sure I could rustle up a watercolour or two.'

'Shh, Gus,' says Ally, biting down a smile. 'They've actually tightened up the application process this year. And there are a few noses out of joint, according to Sunita.'

Principally, a young woman called Lara Swann. Sunita told Ally that Lara sent a string of rather vicious emails after being knocked back, but they must have made amends, because Ally is sure she glimpsed Lara's distinctive long, flowing hair in the crowd just now.

'Well, no one likes being rejected,' says Gus, his voice suddenly a touch mournful. 'Speaking of . . . I'm now firmly open for business in the disappointment department. The novel's off my desk, Ally.'

'You finished it? Gus, why didn't you say earlier?' She raises her glass to him. 'Congratulations!'

He touches his glass to hers, but the gesture lacks verve.

'I sent it off to eight agents at nine o'clock this morning, and by three o'clock I'd already had my first rejection.'

'But they can't have read it that quickly?'

'Exactly. So I don't know if that makes me feel better or worse.'

Ally gives him her most encouraging smile. 'Seven still to go. Lucky seven.'

'Oh, and more besides. It's a numbers game, that's what I've heard. Still . . . rather a dent in the ego, that first one. Rather cruel too, I think, not to at least give me the weekend labouring under the misapprehension of hope.'

But he says it wryly and Ally squeezes his shoulder.

'Gus, you should be very proud.'

She knows just how much this novel means to him. It was why he came to Porthpella: to write. Initially booking a three-month stay, in the wake of his divorce, and then never quite leaving.

'Do you know, I am, actually.' He frowns suddenly. 'Ally, sorry, but there's a chap over there who can't stop staring at you. It's rather odd. Do you know him?'

'What chap?' she says, turning.

'Um, the one who's walking this way.'

'Who? Oh.' And Ally feels a bolt of something extraordinary. A sudden fizzing, from her fingers to her toes. 'My goodness,' she says, in barely more than a whisper.

My goodness.

7

Gina Best loves a good party, but she'd hardly call this that. A parochial gathering of self-important amateurs: that's more the size of it. And, inexplicably, Harrison is among them.

She takes a glug of champagne and wrinkles her nose. Correction: sparkling wine.

She knows there's more to why Harrison is here than he's letting on, but she's also confident that he'll spill the beans later, after hours, when she has him at her mercy. At a pivotal point in romantic proceedings, she'll go for the jugular: *Why is an artist of your calibre really slumming it in Porthpella?* And until Harrison gives her his honest answer, she'll do some withholding of her own.

Harrison is of huge importance to the gallery. And he's of importance to her on a personal level too. Who knows what the latter says about her, but the truth is Harrison is a game Gina likes playing.

'You're drinking quickly,' he says to her now. 'Thirsty girl.'

His voice is goading.

'I'm bored out of my brain, darling,' she says, her tongue spiked as a serpent's.

'There are some half-decent artists here, actually. Not least our hosts.'

And she can't tell if he's being sarcastic. He often is.

'I've never cared for needlework. It makes me think of Granny Ethel. And Connor's sculptures are a little Neanderthal-man for my tastes.'

'These walls have ears, dear,' says Harrison, gesturing to the full terrace.

'And I want yours. Listen,' she says, leaning close. 'I've been invited to a friend's wedding in a month's time.'

'At your age? Good God. What is it, third marriage? Fourth?'

'I have a plus-one. And would you believe it, it's in Italy. On your patch.'

'Oh, how original. I expect it's in a castle, is it?'

'It is. Beautiful castello, an hour's drive from you. Vineyard too, obviously. Glittering pool. I'd love you to come.'

And she's laying herself bare here, using that word, *love*. It sounds more than it is. Good God, she doesn't *love* this man. Does she?

'Not a chance,' says Harrison, with the kind of casual cruelty that Gina should be used to by now. 'Here, what's my glass doing empty. You'd have thought—'

'"Not a chance"?' she cuts in. 'That's your response?'

He flutters his eyelashes, in a manner that is, she thinks, quite mocking. 'I'm no good at weddings, Gee. You know that.'

'But for me . . .'

'Like I said, I'm no good.'

Gina feels, suddenly, a surge of exasperation so powerful she wants to smash something. Her fingers pinch the stem of her glass. She's hunting for a retort when a little round man in a cheap polo shirt accosts Harrison and starts prattling about being a fellow oil painter. She grits her teeth and plasters on a smile. *No matter.* She'll bide her time, then she'll either tell Harrison exactly what she thinks of his unbending nature, his continual rudeness – or she'll try a different approach to the invitation. Butter him up, the way she knows he likes it.

The thing is, when it comes to Harrison, Gina can never quite walk away. An onlooker might say that's to her detriment; that it will, in the end, be her downfall. But here's the good news: she's every bit as bloody-minded as he is. And her devotion, nonsensical as it is, is her choice.

Gina watches Harrison for a second, pretending to be interested in this little local, then lets her eyes drift seaward; not admiring the view, but planning her next move. Grace or grit? She can do both. How much does she really care about Harrison coming to this wedding with her? Well, it's not the hill she'll die on, put it that way, but it might be fun to push it. Just like, later, she'll push the question of why Harrison's really here in Cornwall at all.

8

Raymond Finch.

The name pinballs around Gus's head as he walks to the bar. He thinks of that hand of Ray's clapped into his own. *Good to meet you, Gus.* Then those tractor-beam eyes back on Ally. And Gus standing by, all the while trying to figure out, as blasts from the pasts go, where this one sits on the Richter scale.

Ally turned to him. *I haven't seen Ray for, gosh, half a century?*

Forty-seven years, Ally, Ray corrected.

Awfully precise, Gus thought.

It was the look on Ally's face that did it. She seemed, as she spoke to Ray, as if she was lit differently: as if she'd stepped into a patch of sunshine. This was the point at which Gus, noticing Ray's glass was empty, suggested drinks. He'd intended it as an easy, expansive gesture – as if here on home-ish turf he was akin to a host – but as Gus now ploughs his way towards the bar, he regrets it. *I hear they're serving Mai Tais*, said Ray. And they are. Only, the world and his wife seem to want one, and the chap behind the bar appears to be an extraordinary, and unhurried, perfectionist.

Gus shifts on his feet and glances back down the garden to where Ally and Ray Finch stand talking. Ray is leaning an arm against a tree and Gus winces as he thinks of the sitting-on-the-sofa trick, the old stretch-and-yawn. Meanwhile, in front of him, the bar queue inches forward painstakingly. Gus plants his hands in his pockets and rocks on his heels.

'All I'm saying is, I think you're being extraordinarily selfish.'

A low voice, hissing beside him. Gus stiffens, at first thinking it's directed at him.

But it's the red-headed lady, talking to none other than Harrison Loveday. She empties her champagne glass while Harrison ignores her, tapping out a message on his phone with one hand, his drink held in the other.

Gus looks away; no one likes to be observed being ticked off. And anyway, Gus is being selfish too, isn't he? No wonder those words landed. Why shouldn't Ally reconnect with an old friend out of the blue? It's wonderful. Lovely. Great stuff. Et cetera.

To his side there's another snapped exchange, and Gus shuffles forward, ignoring it.

'Mai Tai, sir?'

Finally.

'Three, please,' says Gus.

He turns to look back towards Ally and Ray, intending a wave, a triumphant thumbs up. *Drinks incoming!* But the crowd has shifted, and he can't see them anymore. Meanwhile the irritated exchange behind him rises to a mild kerfuffle, and Gus thinks, *Is this what art parties are like? Decorum out the window.* He hears a violent retching sound. Suddenly there's a shout of alarm; another voice overlapping it. The people around Gus are shifting like pebbles, and as he turns a channel opens. He sees Harrison Loveday fall to his knees. Gus exclaims; he can feel his mouth gaping, in a cartoonish expression of shock.

Someone cries, 'Gina!'

And it's Harrison, down on all fours; his mane of hair flying. And Gus can see now that it's the red-headed woman lying on the ground beside him. He has a sudden vision of a lion bending over a gazelle. But then Harrison yells, 'Someone help!'

Time slows.

The woman's legs are scrabbling, her hands grabbing at her throat as she convulses. One of her shoes – a sharp-heeled stiletto – slips from her foot.

'Help her!' Harrison yells again, and Gus moves forward on autopilot.

Because he's been here. He's been that person felled. Then, Jayden was his guardian angel. But Jayden's not here. Only Gus is here.

Gus and fifty other people.

Fifty people who all now seem to be moving at once, in varying states of ineptitude. The potter, Pamela, crying out in a high-pitched whine. The landscape painter, Donald, muttering, 'Dear God, dear God.' Connor Rafferty calling out, 'Give her some space,' at the same time as doing the opposite himself.

'Let me,' says Gus, elbowing his way through. Because he knows this moment.

He crouches beside Harrison, his heart skittering in his chest. *But let me what?*

The lady on the ground has stopped moving. Her head has fallen to one side, her curtain of hair drawn across her face.

'Is she breathing?' he says, 'We must check if—'

But Gideon, the host, is ahead of him. In a sunflower-bedecked shirt and with an air of beatific calm, Gideon presses his fingers to her wrist, holds his face close to hers.

Then he takes a deep breath, crosses his hands and starts chest compressions. Counts.

Suddenly, Gus can't watch. He stumbles back to his feet and pushes through the crowd. As he rounds the corner of the house there are fairy lights in the trees, and fairy lights dancing at the edge of his vision. He leans against the smooth white wall and steadies his breathing.

She looked so very dead, that's the trouble.

9

Mullins is trawling through images of convicted burglars when the call comes in. He's spotted someone who he's pretty sure is the brother of a girl he went to school with. Cassidy Stark: she was five-foot-nothing and wore pink trainers when you weren't allowed to wear pink anything; her laugh was machine-gun fire. Mullins thought she was silly and brilliant. Going by his mugshot and his rap sheet, Hayden Stark is only silly.

'A sudden death at Island View House?' He spins on his chair. 'Okay.'

Detective Sergeant Skinner is there too, shrugging his suit jacket on. 'Fifty-eight-year-old woman drops dead at a party? Come on, Mullins.'

They purr along the coast road, the sea spanning out before them. They pass two wetsuit-clad surfers who press their boards into the brambles as they pass, and a young woman jogging, her long hair flying behind her.

Mullins turns to look at her as they pass, a thought half forming.

'Go on then. Tell me what you know,' says Skinner. 'And make it snappy.'

Mullins is jolted back. 'Party to mark the start of the Porthpella Arts Trail,' he says.

'I've seen the posters. How many in attendance?'

'Around fifty. Victim's a gallery owner from London. Gina Best.'

'And the organisers?'

'Gideon Lee and Connor Rafferty. They live at Island View House.'

Together, Mullins almost adds, but then he supposes that's obvious.

'Connor Rafferty,' Skinner says thoughtfully. 'Why do I know that name?'

'Art fan, are you, Sarge?'

Skinner pulls a face. 'The wife was. Sorry, *is*. She's only dead to me.'

He bounces the car up over the verge as they see the crowded driveway of Island View House. Apart from its size, the house doesn't look like much from the roadside. Mullins goes to the door and takes hold of the elaborate whale-shaped knocker, but Skinner's already cutting down the side and into the garden. Mullins drops the knocker and follows. A woman in a purple dress looks startled at the sight of them.

'Can we leave, or . . . ?'

Mullins gets out his notebook. 'Did you see anything?'

She shakes her head.

'Give the constable your details,' says Skinner. 'Just in case.'

'Oh, thank God you're here.'

A tall man intercepts them just as they crunch over the gravel and on to the lawn. Given the circumstances, his cheery shirt strikes the wrong note. His face though? All pain.

'I've corralled everyone inside but one or two are getting twitchy. I thought it the right thing to do, I mean . . . she's just lying there, but . . . it didn't feel right to just carry on around her as if . . . ' He takes a breath. 'Sorry. Gideon Lee. I'm the one who called. It's all . . . well, it's a horrible shock. I tried, I did try to . . . kiss of life, but . . .'

Mullins sees Gideon's eyes glaze. He knows that moment himself: it's do or die. And this man stepped up, but the lady still died. He won't be feeling good.

Mullins holds out his hand and Gideon takes it. They shake.

'Good effort,' says Mullins. 'You okay?'

Gideon nods. 'Let me show you the . . . Gina. Gina Best. She came with Harrison Loveday. I'm afraid he's very upset, he's . . . They've worked together for a long time, you see. For years now.'

'Was Harrison Loveday with Gina when she collapsed?' asks Skinner.

'He was.' Gideon's hand goes to his forehead. 'He's our special guest. We're supposed to be looking after him. I don't know where he's gone now . . .'

And Mullins looks to Skinner. He won't like a sudden disappearance after a sudden death. But the sergeant's expression is deadpan.

'If you could show us the deceased,' says Skinner.

As they cross the terrace, Mullins takes in the place. The sea feels like a garden pond from here. He could bounce a tennis ball off the island lighthouse. And for once, the owners actually live in this big fancy gaff all year round; *it's a miracle.* Mullins turns to look at the house again and sees a row of faces at the window. The partygoers, watching their every move. There's a man with half-moon glasses, standing so close to the glass his nose is wonky. Further along there's a young girl in a white blouse, her hand over her mouth. And then Ally Bright. Mullins does a double take.

Is Ally a party guest? She must be. Unless she received the call too, and got here first? Which must mean there's more to this. Mullins gives Ally a nod, and she offers a quick wave in reply. There's no sign of Jayden.

'Mullins, get yourself over here,' barks Skinner.

The sergeant is squatting beside the body. Gideon stands slightly to one side, with his hands knotted, head dipped as if he's saying his prayers.

Mullins clenches his jaw. It's never easy, this bit. It's the blood that gets him; he's never liked blood – not as a kid when he kept getting nosebleeds, and not since he's worn the uniform either – but at least there's none of that here. Steeling himself, Mullins looks at the deceased, Gina Best. But he doesn't *look* at her. He wouldn't be CSI for a lottery win.

'Note the complexion,' says Skinner quietly. 'Red as a cherry.'

Mullins darts his eyes, enough to determine that, yes, her skin is pinkish. Okay, red.

He makes a noise of agreement. 'Sign of a heart attack, is it, Sarge?'

'I'd wager something a good deal more sinister.'

Mullins glances back towards the house. That lot still watching this? Apparently, yes. The windows, the garden doors, are crowded with even more faces. Art-crowd faces. Fancy glasses. Wayward hair. A lot of linen. Mullins refocuses on the sergeant. His eyes widen as Skinner bends close to the corpse and holds his face right up close to Gina Best's.

Mullins glances across to Gideon, who's watching the sergeant like he's something on TV.

Skinner sniffs. Not once but twice. Three times. Then he straightens up. His face is as grim as Mullins has seen it. And that's when Mullins knows that Skinner has something. Because his boss doesn't look like that around accidental deaths. Not even the really sad ones.

'Mr Lee,' says the sergeant.

'Call me Gideon, please.'

'As we arrived, a woman in a purple dress was leaving.'

48

'Oh, Claudia? Yes, she only intended to drop in.'

'To your knowledge, has anybody else left?'

Gideon shakes his head, gestures towards the house. 'No. They came for a party, and I suppose they're staying for one.'

Skinner's jaw tightens. 'No one leaves. Not a single one. Mullins, you've got something in the region of fifty statements to take. Including Harrison Loveday's. So, get him found.'

'But you'll be here all night,' says Gideon.

'We'll be here a lot longer than that,' says Skinner. 'Because this is officially a murder investigation.'

10

'What do you make of it, Ally?'

Ally turns from the window and looks into Ray's enquiring face. A face that, astonishingly, hasn't changed much in half a century. *Forty-seven years, Ally.*

His thick brown hair is speckled with silver. His face is lightly tanned, with well-grooved laughter lines. His eyes are the shade of the sea when storm clouds are coming – iron grey, with a memory of blue.

And she shouldn't be noticing any of these things when a woman lies dead.

Gina Best is her name. Harrison Loveday's gallerist. Harrison is, according to Ray, in the upstairs bathroom, attempting to collect himself away from prying eyes. And Harrison is the reason for Ray Finch being in Porthpella.

I heard he was coming back to these shores. I couldn't resist the trip, Ally.

'I don't know what I make of it,' she says, thinking it's rather a strange question.

Outside on the terrace, Skinner and Mullins are in close consultation. Skinner pointing, Mullins nodding. Beside them, Gideon Lee stands with his arms wrapped so tightly around his body he looks as if he's hugging himself; he keeps shooting nervous glances towards the house.

'Ah now,' says Ray, giving Ally an apologetic smile – did he read her mind? – 'here's where I confess to googling you. Let's just say I was . . . intrigued. Intrigued, but maybe not that surprised.'

'I don't know what on earth comes up if you google me,' says Ally.

'Jayden Weston comes up.'

'Ah.'

'And Rockpool House. Shoreline Vines. JP Sharpe. The Shell House Detectives . . .'

'And you say you're not surprised? Because I know I am.'

Ray shrugs. And it's a gesture she's seen before, many times, many years ago. The lift and drop of those shoulders. Next there'll be a half-smile.

'You were always curious. Enjoyed a puzzle. Plus, you liked reading Agatha Christie.'

The half-smile.

Ally laughs, then immediately stops herself, the sound of it all wrong. But when she looks around, she's surrounded by people having animated conversations. There's nothing like a death, apparently, to bring people to life. And to make them thirsty, she thinks, as the waitress proffers a tray of drinks.

Ray goes to take two glasses, but Ally declines.

'Well, a lot of people enjoy reading Agatha Christie,' she says. He probably imagines her detective work to be genteel; tricky little puzzles to solve. Not violence and fear. Not life and death. Her eyes move to the window again.

Skinner is on his phone now, and he's pacing the lawn, doing laps of Connor Rafferty's broken whelk. Mullins is carefully unspooling a roll of blue-and-white police tape. So far so standard, for a sudden death; she knows this much now. But there's something in their body language that gives her pause. There's an urgency in Skinner's step, even if it's only taking him in circles. And Mullins looks faintly awestruck, his eyes following the sergeant's every move. Gideon, meanwhile, has disappeared.

'But they don't all turn detective,' she says, turning back to Ray.

'You married a policeman.' There's a strange expression on his face suddenly. 'A constable in Falmouth.'

'I did. Bill.'

Ray nods. He looks as if he's about to say something, then changes his mind.

'We were married for forty-one years,' she says.

'I'm sorry he died, Ally.'

Presumably that comes up on Google too. As much as Ally has come to love the internet for their investigative work, it still feels strange to her, that certain details of her life are accessible to just anyone.

Not that Ray is just anyone.

'Thank you,' she says, just as she always does. And it's normally a full stop, this moment.

'Was it a happy marriage?'

She wasn't expecting that.

'Very happy.' Then, 'What about you, did you ever . . .'

'Oh yes. Yes. Twice. Divorced twice too.' He grins, rubs the back of his head. 'I guess I'm into "third time lucky" territory now . . .'

And if Ray isn't surprised that she's a detective, perhaps Ally isn't surprised that he's twice divorced. While Ray Finch was her first boyfriend, Ally knew she was a long way from his first girlfriend. At the time, she wondered if she was even his only girlfriend.

'I should check on Harrison again,' he says. 'I don't want to crowd the guy, but . . .'

'Ray, did Harrison say anything to you? When you first went to him?'

'Only that people are presuming an allergic reaction, but Gina didn't have any allergies. Harrison's known her for years. He doesn't understand it, Ally.'

Just then a hush spreads over the room like a slow tide. Gideon stands in the doorway. Thanks to his height, Ally can clearly see his face. He looks hollowed-out with shock; a different man from the one who herded them gently inside half an hour ago. Ally's inkling solidifies: the police are treating this as suspicious.

Gideon calls out, 'Has anyone seen Harrison Loveday?'

Ray clears his throat, but then Harrison suddenly appears behind Gideon. His face is flushed and his hair slick, as if he's stepped from a shower. He taps Gideon on the shoulder and their host startles. The waitress stifles a gasp.

'Here,' says Harrison gruffly. 'Who's asking?'

'I am,' says Skinner, filling the doorway. 'Would you kindly step outside, sir?'

Ray turns to Ally with one eyebrow raised. Then says, 'What about your mate Gus, what happened to him, anyway?'

11

Donald Crosby has given his statement. He's confirmed his name, address and telephone number. He is, apparently, free to go.

'Don't leave town,' the round-faced young constable says.

And he sounds like he's straight out of an amateur dramatics club. The thought makes Donald's lips twitch with a smile, which isn't at all appropriate for the circumstances, but he feels, in truth, slightly hysterical. And what does it matter, because the officer is already eyeing his next victim; he's not the most observant of individuals.

'Donald.'

Pamela. Her big eyes swimming with tears.

'I told them everything I could,' she says, kneading her hands. 'It's . . . it's just surreal. Horribly surreal.'

And Donald knows he should show compassion. It's a shock – of course it is. And they're hardly crocodile tears, for his friend is an emotional sort. But who is Gina Best to Pamela? That's what it comes down to. Only Gina's nearest and dearest will truly feel her loss. Any emotions among tonight's crowd are, surely, largely existential: the foul breath of the Grim Reaper coming too close for comfort; a brutal reminder that life can be snuffed out at any moment, which is something human beings seem to forget, from one death to the next.

The shock! The horror! When, really, it's the only certain thing in life: that we'll die.

He realises his face is breaking into an absurd grin.

'Donald?'

'I'm sorry.' His face aches with the effort of not laughing. 'It's the shock.'

A vivid memory lands, sudden as an apple dropping from a bough. Little Donald being told off by his father – *what for? Just about anything* – and laughter bubbling up inside him like he's a bottle of lemonade; noticing his little sister's horror-filled expression and the stopper coming clean off. An explosion of giggles. Then the clap of a slipper. Tears.

'Let's go home, dear Donald,' says Pamela, slipping her arm through his.

His legs feel weak as he steers her to the door, briefly thanking one half of their hosts, Connor, as they go. The man looks glad to be rid of them. In fact, he looks as if he wants to take hold of the whole house with his muscled arms and tip it on end; shake them all out.

'Take care,' says Connor. Then, 'I'm sorry.'

As if the whole thing is his fault.

'Please thank Gideon too,' says Pamela. 'It was a wonderful party, before . . . you know.'

As the door closes behind them, Donald glances back at the house. What is he expecting to see? A face at the window? *Wait! Is that Donald Crosby?* But the house gazes impassively back. The fact is, Donald is insignificant here. Just another partygoer. Just another witness – or not, as it happens – to the untimely death of Gina Best.

'Your place or mine?' says Pamela as she opens the car door. 'Because I don't know about you, but I need a drink.'

They go to Donald's. Tyres crunching over the gravel drive, nettles swishing the metalwork. As the security light flicks on outside the house, they sit in its yellow tint. As Pamela turns and smiles, her teeth appear yellow too.

'Do you know, I think I just need to go to bed,' he says.

'You don't want company? For a drink, I mean. Not the bed part. Obviously.'

But it's not obvious, because they've been there, done that, a few times over the years. Not with any definitions assigned. Nor with any expectation – or indeed, desire, if he's really honest – that it'll necessarily happen again. And that applies to both sides, he's sure. Of the two of them, Pamela is light of spirit, dynamic. If she's a butterfly, Donald is a mole. Workmanlike and retiring; no one's idea of a pin-up.

He shakes his head. His foolish nervous laughter is gone, replaced by an old familiar weight. All he wants is to lie down and draw a cover over his head; pinned by his own sorrows.

'Donald, how are you feeling?' Pamela asks, her voice loaded with concern.

He'd like to be accurate, for his own benefit as well as hers.

'I don't feel anything.'

She reaches for his hand, and he lets her take it. She squeezes his lifeless fingers, as if to find a pulse. Then slowly releases him. Pamela is disappointed, of course. If he were a different man, tonight's death might have given him perspective. *Let bygones be bygones.* Too flip an expression, but nonetheless it darts into his brain and bumps about like a full-bodied moth. But then again, if he were a different man, he'd never have let his words go this long unsaid.

'I'm so sorry,' she says. 'Tonight . . . It must have brought a lot back up. Even if, right now, the shock—'

'No,' says Donald, a little tersely 'Not really.'

Because something must sink in order to rise; to recede in order to be brought forth once more. And the 'lot' that Pamela speaks of has never gone anywhere. It's the clothing that Donald never takes off. Not a hair shirt – he has nothing to repent for, except, perhaps, inaction – but an almighty greatcoat: heavy as armour; protective of nothing.

Donald slumps from the car and drags his feet back towards the house. His heart is a stone in his chest.

'I'll see you tomorrow!' trills Pamela. 'The show must go on!'

And he holds up a hand in acknowledgement of her efforts. Because even though Pamela wears him out, Donald does appreciate her. On occasion he's thought of telling her that, but then Pamela's expectations might alter. And how can Donald bear the weight of anyone else's existence, when he can hardly manage his own?

12

'A murder at the Arts Trail party?'

He keeps his voice low, so he doesn't wake Benji.

Jayden lays a hand on the little man's back as he shifts into a sitting position. The TV is frozen with the image of a maverick LAPD cop following a suspect into a tunnel.

'Al, you're not serious?' he whispers.

'Are you sure you're okay to talk?'

'Sure. Just tell me if you can't hear me. Benji's sleeping, like, right on me.'

Ally fills him in on the details, a combination of what she knows and what she gleaned afterwards. Gina Best, Harrison Loveday's visitor – and a gallery owner – is dead.

'Jayden, we thought it was a seizure or a heart attack. People were shocked, but not scared. Then the police arrived, and the mood changed. Harrison Loveday spent most of the aftermath in the bathroom. They took all of our statements.'

'Okay, so Skinner must have seen something at the scene, or was told something, that made him confident it was a suspicious death.'

'But given the circumstances . . . Gus said one moment she was standing by the bar with Harrison, surrounded by people, and the next she was convulsing and then . . . dead. There was no blood, Jayden. No one fleeing the scene. Nothing out of the ordinary.'

'Allergic reaction?' he says.

'Harrison Loveday has apparently known Gina for years. She doesn't have allergies.'

Jayden runs through the scene in his head, his tired brain clunking into action. Of all the ways to kill someone, to do it in plain sight, as if everything's cool? But then for the police to immediately treat the death as suspicious?

'Poison,' he says.

He forgot to whisper that one, but Benji doesn't shift.

'Poison?'

'Got to be.'

Jayden's conviction feels misplaced. A poisoning at a party in Porthpella? That's wild. But you can't rule anything out.

'Toxins aren't my specialist subject, Al . . . but maybe they're Skinner's, if he's thinking that way without even waiting for any lab results. So, any arrests?'

'Harrison Loveday went off in the patrol car with them. But Gideon said he demanded that, said he wanted to make his statement in private. Is that usual?'

Benji whimpers in his sleep, opening and shutting his tiny, puckered mouth. Jayden wills him not to wake up hungry and start crying. Cat really needs her rest up there. She told him yesterday that the 'sleep when the baby sleeps' advice is just another way of making her feel like she's failing. *I can't even drop off when I'm supposed to, Jay.* Then he tried a joke about her being over-tired, like she's a fractious toddler. But the truth is Jayden knows that feeling: eyes wide and staring; mind racing, body aching with fatigue. Throw in the needs of a baby and a two-year-old, plus a body that's still bearing the ravages of childbirth, and it's bad news all round.

Jayden drops a gentle kiss on his son's head. Not *all* bad news, obviously. Benji's scalp is so warm, so sweet-smelling. He could spend a whole day kissing this boy's head, and if you'd told Jayden a thing like that before his daughter was born, he wouldn't have believed it. But how can these tiny, beloved creatures cause such chaos? Hand grenades, the lot of them.

'It doesn't feel usual,' says Ally, answering her own question.

'To be honest, if they've reason to suspect it's suspicious, then yeah, they'd take him in. How many people at the party, Al?'

'Around fifty.'

'And they took statements from everyone?'

'They did. It was just Skinner and Mullins initially, then reinforcements arrived.'

The Major Crimes team from Newquay, probably.

And there's something wistful in the thought. Is this why he's been binge-watching cop shows on TV this last month? Jayden left the police before he became a dad. And since Jazz was born, he's never wanted to go back to it – though he's had at least one serious offer – because the detective work with Ally has given him way more than he was getting in uniform. But this last month . . . He can't explain it. Or maybe he can: a combination of factors making him chew over his choices.

Maybe it's the pressure to be earning; bringing in a proper monthly wage. Jayden's a father of two now – which his father-in-law likes to remind him of frequently. Months back they decided to only take campsite bookings for after the Easter holidays. Cliff said it was short-sighted, but both Cat and Jayden agreed that, however much they needed the income, they wanted the family time more.

Maybe it's seeing Cat laid low after Benji's birth. The instinct to provide dialled up; his responsibilities intensified.

And maybe – though it's harder to admit – Jayden would like an unarguable reason, a non-flexible reason, to leave the house every morning. To take a shift that's professional, not personal. Because sometimes these four walls seem to be edging closer. Sometimes his broad shoulders ache a little too.

Yeah, that's harder to admit.

'Think there's a way in for us, Al?'

'I had to explain to a friend of mine that unless we're specifically hired, we don't get involved. Well, unless we want to.'

'And we usually want to, right?'

'It does feel very close. Doesn't it? The Arts Trail. The victim staying in the dunes. And, well, the Harrison Loveday factor, of course.'

Jayden feels a flicker of anticipation.

A new case.

'Our patch, for sure,' he says.

'This friend of mine, he's never been around a murder before.'

'Not many people have, Al. Thankfully.'

'He actually came here to catch up with Harrison Loveday.'

There's something in her voice that Jayden can't quite decipher.

'You don't suspect him, do you?'

'What, Harrison Loveday?'

'No, this friend. Does he know Gina Best too?'

'Goodness, no. *No.* Not for a second. He's . . . No.'

Jayden looks to the TV, the freeze-framed cop charging into danger. Meanwhile Jayden's so sunk into the sofa that his bones feel like they've melted. Benji is warm as a just-baked loaf. If he let his eyes flicker and close, Jayden's pretty sure he'd be asleep in seconds.

But he wants in. He's on the starting blocks.

Is it possible to split himself in two? Even without a case, his responsibilities are divided; sometimes being here for his wife and being here for his children feel like different things. And he knows who screams loudest. To say his daughter's amped up her demands since her baby brother's arrival – *Daddy, look at me! Daddy! Daddy, look! Me! Me now! DADATZ!* – is an understatement.

'What I'm wondering,' says Ally, 'is why someone would choose to do it so publicly. It must be that this was their best means of access to the victim. Which surely makes them a stranger – or at least not close to Gina. And it would rule out Harrison, because Gina was staying with him at Sea Dream. Unless it's a double bluff. Or deliberately . . . performative.'

'Interesting thinking, Al.'

Somebody seizing their best-possible opportunity, or a deliberately staged murder? Either way, it's majorly premeditated. Fast-acting poison is hard to get hold of.

'Unless the poison only took effect at the party,' he says. 'It could have been administered before. I don't think we should rule anyone out right now.'

'No, you're right, Jayden. We shouldn't. Just . . . Are you sure you have the time, or energy, to get involved? I don't want—'

'Al, I've got both,' he says.

Which might be the only lie he's ever told her.

13

Gideon finds Connor in the studio. He doesn't mean to creep up on him, but Connor's lost in thought and doesn't hear the door.

He's sitting hunched forward in a chair, passing a hammer from hand to hand, like a man plotting a heinous act – or having just undertaken one. But Gideon knows that's just his imagination revving up, because now that the house has emptied – the blue lights no longer strobing, the white-suited CSIs having tramped off – the horror of the situation is settling.

A woman murdered in their home.

A high-profile gallery owner – not that that matters. Harrison Loveday's representative – not that that matters.

Gideon feels his throat close, the sting of tears in his eyes. Island View House is a sanctuary. A creative, soulful space; a place for joy and love and art. Not murder.

'Conn?' he says.

And Connor turns, his own eyes red-rimmed. He keeps on passing the hammer, as an off-duty magician might shuffle cards on reflex. He knows Connor feels rooted when he holds the tools of his trade. Their studio is their mutual happy place.

Everything was primed for the Arts Trail opening tomorrow. More cynical visitors might imagine they set-dressed the studio for the sake of the trail, but walk in here any day and this is how you'll find it. Gideon's inspiration boards, with the initial sketches and the still lifes in gouache; reference material, clipped and stuck; and the bundles of yarn in a hundred different colours. The same for Connor and his sculptures; his silken stonework and shimmering bronze. The old French dresser, its drawers half-open and cluttered with tools, the rust-tinged biscuit tins from the 1950s holding vital bits and bobs, the bouquet of chisels in a jam jar. The big Cornishware jug in the window, always filled with whatever flowers are abundant in the garden. It's how they work. A visual cacophony. A delight in the journey as much as the destination.

For tomorrow, Gideon has ordered flagons of apple and rhubarb juice from an orchard along the coast. He's baked trays of delicate Brittany butter biscuits. He wants to share their studio, their garden, their hospitality, with anyone who cares to see it. And if they end up selling work too? Well, that's a bonus. Because for him and Connor – two artists who have the luxury of making a year-round living from their work – the Arts Trail is above all an opportunity to celebrate creativity in the community.

But now their venue is shut down. Police tape criss-crossing the terrace.

'I was alright and now I'm not,' says Connor.

Gideon pulls over a chair and sits beside him. Connor doesn't like fuss; if Gideon reaches for his hand, he'll bat him away like a fly. So, he tries for levity.

'It was all going so well too. Even Lara Swann didn't cause a drama. I thought she would, didn't you? My heart sank when I saw her come in. So much for invitation only.'

Connor barely grunts.

'Sorry,' says Gideon. 'Prattling.'

'The thing is, it's made me think of Meghan Phillips. Hasn't it you?'

Connor's voice is quiet, as if it's coming from another room, another place, altogether.

'Meghan? Good God. Yes, I suppose so. I hadn't . . .' Gideon takes a breath. *Stop prattling, Gid.* 'Yes. Of course.'

'Harrison was there that night too.'

Marco Pellegrino's studio in Chelsea. Marco had just finished a major exhibition, so he cleared out the space and in they all crowded. They danced until London's best attempt at a sunrise filtered through the fume-clogged windows. Well, Connor didn't dance; not his style. Nor were the drugs, not for either of them. So the two them were clear-headed when a young woman called Meghan Phillips died in the middle of the party. Gideon called the ambulance that time too, though it was already too late.

Was Harrison Loveday really there that night?

He can see Meghan's body lying on the concrete floor, pooled in the rose-gold light of that early morning. It must have been fifteen, sixteen years ago. How strange, that something so affecting at the time could fade to a distant memory. Because when Gideon looked down at Gina Best earlier, he saw no echo of the young woman in the Chelsea studio. He thought only of the chest compressions, the steady breaths; a process he remembered from school but had never tried on anything more than a dummy, crouching in a hall that smelt of boys' socks and school dinners.

He tried and failed. Beneath his hands, Gina died.

In the quiet space of the studio, Gideon sinks his head into his hands.

'Gid? The fact it's Harrison again. I think it's weird. That's all.'

But there's no 'that's all' about it. Because Connor's voice is as loaded as a shotgun.

14

Ally walks into the thinking room at first light. Over the bay the sun is just rising, but in this little room at the back of the house it's yet to find its way in. Here, objects lack definition, just as Ally's own edges feel blurred. She pushes open the window, the frame nudging the fronds of her garden palm. Cool air flows through, along with overlapping currents of birdsong: the electric cries of the swallows; the more distant wails of gulls. She breathes deeply, drawing it all in. Then she goes and sits in Bill's chair, the leather making a squeak-crunch sound as she shifts her weight.

The thinking room: it was Jayden who called it that, back in the autumn. Until the vineyard case, Ally hadn't shared Bill's office with Jayden. She hadn't shared it with anyone. But since then, it's become their base. The whorl within the shell. The whiteboard still bears the marker-pen traces of their last case. The list of suspects. The emerging patterns, questions, theories.

Ally finds a cloth and rubs at it, until it shines bright white.

She takes a pen from the desk drawer and writes *Gina Best*. Then she sits back down and stares at the name. She's wide awake and has been for hours. So many things rattling about inside her head.

Not least Gus. Gus, who was one of the first people to get to Gina, who was so close to her the moment she collapsed. She knows it will have affected him. When Gideon gently herded them indoors, she couldn't find Gus at first. When she did, he seemed folded in on himself, as if events had robbed him of some essential scaffolding. Beyond the trauma of the death, Gus would have seen the attempt to save Gina's life and felt the echoes of what happened last summer. Just as Ally did too.

Ray had no idea of such thoughts, of course.

Ray Finch.

His presence was unsettling in a different way. How strange, for Ray to once have been so important, then to have dropped almost entirely from her consciousness, only for him to walk back in decades later, fully formed. Ray was always more forthcoming than Ally – and the same is true now. He was unabashed when he confessed to searching for her on the internet. Though she's sure her connection to Porthpella wasn't a factor in Ray's decision to come and see Harrison Loveday's show.

The feeling Ally had as she saw him walking across the lawn, though. Her body recognised him before her mind. Did she gasp out loud? She thinks she might have done.

What must Gus have thought?

Ally looks to the window. Little by little, more light flows in. She refocuses. Along the dunes, she wonders if Harrison Loveday is back at Sea Dream.

'Someone at the party killed Gina Best,' she says out loud.

Even this simple statement holds uncertainty. Jayden's quite right: it's possible Gina was poisoned beforehand, the effects only striking on the terrace of Island View House. But from the meticulous way that their statements were taken, the energy in DS Skinner's movements, the cascade of white-suited CSIs, Ally thinks the police are erring on the side of the killer being among them.

A chilling thought.

So, who gave Gina a drink or a canapé? Surely the first focus will be on the waiting and bar staff. Gideon said the company came highly recommended; he merrily proclaimed as much at the start of the evening, before anyone had a reason to suspect foul play. Though *suspicious death* is the term being used in the early news reports.

Despite everything, the Arts Trail opens today. That was one of Gideon's questions to DS Skinner last night: should the show go on? Ally will be stationed in her studio, ready to welcome all comers. But her mind will be elsewhere – and buzzing with questions.

She doubts that Harrison Loveday will be at the Bluebird. Ally told Mullins that she and Jayden saw the way Harrison greeted Gina Best at Sea Dream. At the mention of their assumed relationship, Mullins raised an eyebrow. *Are you sure about that?* he said.

There's no mention online of a romantic connection between the two. Ally ascertained that much late last night. Ray had no knowledge of their relationship either – though, as he said, he and Harrison weren't close. *I'd drop him a line every couple of years, but it was mostly one-way traffic.*

Ally turns on her laptop and picks up where she left off.

Gina Best, a gallerist of some repute, was based in Mayfair. In an interview with Harrison Loveday, he said 'Gina has the best eye for talent in the business', which strikes Ally as suitably self-complimentary. They worked together for more than twenty-five years, Gina handling his Cork Street exhibitions and private commissions. Ally combs through a couple of articles on Gina. For a 'Day in a Life' feature for an art school, she talked about her Notting Hill mews house, her passion for both interior and garden design; no mention of a partner or children. In the various photos in which she appears – shoulder to shoulder with creative-looking people – she looks happy and popular; or certainly as if she understood how to appear so for the camera.

Ally clicks on to Gina's Instagram. She scrolls through her sporadic posts: lavish art books on coffee tables; a porcelain-neat

Siamese cat; the piazzas and colonnades of Rome. Ally can't tell who went to Italy with Gina in February, but she must have had a companion as there's a photo of her walking across an expansive square, her red hair bright against the slate-grey sky. Other photos from the trip are of numerous galleries, including the Caravaggios at the Galleria Borghese. Here, 'Idol' is the caption. Ally can see how Caravaggio might be cited as inspiration for the best of Harrison's work too. The fierce contrast between dark background and brightly lit figures; the hyper-real depictions of humanity.

Ally opens a new page, returning to the article where Harrison Loveday was interviewed at home in his Tuscan villa. Did Gina and Harrison see one another on her trip to Italy? Ally's mind keeps looping back to the same question: were they in a relationship? There was an intensity to their embrace outside Sea Dream yesterday. Ally didn't like the way Harrison then spun on his heel and left Gina with her suitcase. Did it hint at a more complicated dynamic? The fact that Mullins didn't know about the pairing, that's what gets Ally too. But people can have any number of reasons for keeping a relationship discreet. It's not suspicious.

But then again, in a murder investigation, isn't everything potentially suspicious?

Harrison Loveday is the person with the most tangible connection to Gina. Gideon's path also crossed with her once. Apparently, Ray's too, in a remote way. But of all the guests at the party, Gina probably knew the least people there.

Ally's phone buzzes with a message. *Ray.* In the hullabaloo of it all, she forgot he asked for her number last night.

Good morning. Not quite the reunion anyone would plan but terrific to see you anyway, Ally. I'll come by your studio today, would love to see your work. Going to check in with Harrison first.

She's mulling over a reply when her phone buzzes again.
Gus.

Ally, how are you? I'll be along first thing, if the show's still going ahead? Still reeling a bit here. Poor woman.

Ally puts her phone down and looks to the board. It immediately refocuses her. *Gina Best.* Already, after just a brief wander through the landscape of the internet, Gina has become more than a name. A woman who was passionate about her work. Who saw the beauty in the world – and was killed in front of their eyes.

Why? And in so determined a way?

Ally picks up her phone again and messages Jayden.

Gina Best was probably the least connected person at the party. Don't you think it's strange that the killer should strike then and there?

Just after she hits Send her phone starts ringing from a number she doesn't recognise. It's early still, and she answers with a hint of caution.

'Ally, love, it's Wenna. Something terrible's happened. Right outside my shop.'

15

It's early Saturday morning and the station has cranked into life. Mullins rocks back in his chair and chews the end of his pen. The Newquay lot – the Major Crimes team – are in the house. And making a big noise about it too. DS Chang, who he basically likes, is on maternity leave, and the rest of the team are a bunch of grey suits, as far as he can make out. Sporty backpacks and big watches. Solving crime – *major* crime – and still finding time to go down the gym, probably.

Skinner waits for the briefing room to settle down. He stands in front of the whiteboard, fiddling with his tie, his eyes occasionally flicking to DCI Robinson as if he's the teacher he wants to impress.

'Until we get the full toxicology back, we can't be sure, but initial indications suggest poisoning. At risk of sticking my neck out, I'd say cyanide.'

Cyanide. Not something Mullins knows much about – other than the fact that no good comes of it.

'Why? Two reasons. First, the deceased's complexion. Bright as ketchup. Second, I detected the scent of almonds. Both are consistent with cyanide poisoning.'

Mullins knows Skinner's chuffed with himself. The sergeant confided that one of his first cases as a young detective was a case of cyanide; some codger who murdered his wife out in the garden shed. Nasty business, Skinner said with a shudder, and Mullins could tell the memory was cut through him like letters in a stick of rock.

'Cyanide is lethal, fast-acting. And not easy to come by in the first place. Whoever killed Gina Best planned it in advance and executed it with purpose.'

'So why at the party?' throws out one of the Newquay lot.

'Access,' says Skinner. 'That's got to be top of the list. Gina Best only arrived in Porthpella yesterday and she intended to leave for the Big Smoke again today. That's only a twenty-four-hour window in which to strike. The party likely presented the best-possible opportunity. We're looking at a scenario where the victim ingested the poison, either through a drink or a canapé. CSI are all over the glasses. When Best collapsed, she smashed a couple.'

'How do we know Gina Best was the target?' asks the DCI. 'Waiters going round with trays of drinks, platters of finger food, it's possible that she took the poisoned item in error.'

But someone who picks poison as a murder weapon doesn't seem like the sort of person to leave things to chance, thinks Mullins. He's wondering about voicing this, whether it's okay to get a bit lippy with the DCI like that, when one of the Newquay lot gets there first. He snaffles Mullins's words just like they were one of those fussy little canapés held out on a silver platter.

'Agreed,' says Skinner. 'You go to the trouble of getting your hands on a poison like cyanide – toxicology pending, et cetera, et cetera – I don't think it's likely you'd get sloppy with the dispensing of it. The means, and opportunity, suggest that Gina Best was the intended victim.'

'Witness statements confirm that the cocktails were freshly mixed,' says Mullins, getting in there this time. 'Basically, if you wanted a Mai Tai, you got in the queue. If you're the killer, that makes it a better bet than the glasses of champagne that were going round. Though a couple of witness statements confirmed that one of the newbie waitresses was handing out glasses of champagne, rather than offering the tray.'

'So the newbie waitress is a potential suspect?' pipes someone from the back.

'We're not ruling anything out. The catering and bar staff are all under scrutiny. Company called Sundown Kitchen, based out of Hayle,' says Skinner. 'Now, listen up. A Mai Tai typically contains almond syrup, which, if you hold in mind the fact that cyanide can carry the smell of almonds, throws up an interesting question. Was the cocktail specifically chosen because of its aroma? The hosts designed the menu, Gideon Lee and Connor Rafferty, and apparently the Mai Tais were Gideon's personal choice. Now, we've got witness statements from over fifty-seven party guests, and the four members of catering staff. Out of everyone, there are just five people who claim an acquaintance with Gina Best. Two of them are Gideon and Connor. Though neither say they knew her well.'

'From the London arts scene back in the day,' says Mullins. And he quite likes the way it sounds. As if he knows anything about London, art, or any scene at all.

'Interesting,' says DCI Robinson, narrowing his eyes. 'Who are the others?'

'Harrison Loveday, Gina's client, had the most intimate relationship with her. A professional relationship for twenty-five years, and a more personal relationship on and off, though Loveday was cagey about that one. He didn't volunteer the information, but nor did he deny it when asked. The pair were staying together at Sea Dream, down in the dunes. Loveday made a fulsome statement here at the station. If he was faking shock, he was convincing. And Sunita Singh, owner of the Bluebird gallery, had a couple of email dealings in the run-up.'

'Tell us about the fifth person with a connection to the victim,' says Robinson.

'Raymond Finch. Artist, though not exhibiting on the trail. He's here as a visitor. Mullins, you took Finch's statement. Over to you.'

'Based in Suffolk,' says Mullins. 'He's known Harrison Loveday for years, and at some point he met Gina Best too. He can't remember when or where, but it was in London. He remembers that they talked about Harrison's work and Finch was struck by how enthusiastic she was. He wasn't represented by a gallery at the time, and he wondered if he should be. How it'd be nice to have someone in his corner. Bit dog-eat-dog by all accounts, the art world.'

'Strikes me Finch is a long way from home,' says Skinner. 'I shouldn't think the Porthpella Arts Trail typically draws an East Coast crowd.'

'Best part of an eight-hour drive, that is,' says one of the Newquay lot. 'On a good day. The in-laws live in Lowestoft. And if I'm headed in that direction, it's basically never a good day.'

Cue low-level laughter.

'But Raymond Finch couldn't have known Gina Best was also going to be here with Harrison Loveday, could he?' says Mullins.

'Judging by the statements, Loveday is a diva,' says Skinner. 'I think it'd be safe for Finch to assume a bloke like that is going to drag his entourage, such as it is, along with him.'

Mullins looks down at his notebook and writes the name *Raymond Finch*. Then adds: *Seemed like a nice bloke. Pally with Ally Bright too.* Which as far as Mullins is concerned makes for two ticks in the 'Not Guilty' column.

'Harrison Loveday, Sunita Singh, Raymond Finch, Gideon Lee and Connor Rafferty. We have ourselves a Fab Five: the only people at the party with any known connections to Gina Best. Next step is we need to look more closely at the deceased and see if there are any links, however tenuous, to other people who were there last night. Guests, catering staff, other artists in the vicinity. And we need toxicology to pull their finger out because if we're looking for a killer with cyanide as their weapon of choice then we've got a nasty piece of work on our hands. A very nasty piece of work indeed.'

Skinner rubs his hands together as he says it.

'What about Ally Bright and Jayden Weston?' asks DCI Robinson. 'Our famous Shell House Detectives. Ally Bright was at the party, wasn't she? I take it not in an official capacity?'

Skinner gives a bark of laughter. 'Official? That's generous, sir. No, she's got an exhibition as part of the trail. And the word is that Jayden's busy doing daddy day care. Those two won't be sticking their noses in, if that's what you're worried about.'

But Mullins fights a grin. *Don't count on it.*

The door to the briefing room swings wide, giving Carl the desk sergeant a bigger entrance than he maybe intended. He looks uncertain for a second, then coughs.

'Call just in. A report of vandalism outside White Wave Stores in Porthpella.'

There are titters from the Newquay lot.

'In case you hadn't realised. . .' begins Skinner.

We're working on a murder case, Mullins finishes in his head.

'No,' says Carl, arms folded, 'you're going to want to hear this.'

16

'Who'd do this?' says Saffron. 'It's crazy. It's awful. It's . . .'

'It comes with the territory,' says Milo with a shrug. 'Harsh, on day one, but . . .'

'Day one of the Arts Trail?'

Milo laughs. 'Erm, no. Day one of its existence as a finished piece. Here's where I should say something about transience. Beauty in the temporary. Right?'

Saffron stares at the wall of Mahalo. Milo's work – Broady's commission – is destroyed. The intricately gorgeous wave, the freewheeling surfers, the sunburst sky and gilded sand – all ruined. Two giant words are now sprayed across it in white: *WHO'S NEXT?*

Saffron saw it as soon as she pitched up on her bike this morning to open Hang Ten. She called Broady in tears. And then he called Milo Nash.

Saffron was surprised at the intensity of her reaction. It felt like a violation. Not just of their sun-filled patch of beach, the dreamland of coffee shop and surf school side by side, but of what Milo had made. She'd seen the care that went into it, the precision and the talent. It filled her heart right up. And now someone has wrecked it with stupid graffiti.

'Can you save it, Milo?'

He must have caught her emotion because his face softens as he shakes his head. 'Hey,' he says, 'it's only spray paint.'

And for a second, she thinks he's talking about the white lettering, like it's a material that can easily be removed. But he's talking about his own art.

'I've reported it,' says Broady, steaming round the corner, 'but apparently the police have got their hands full with a murder, so it's not exactly high-priority. We've never had vandalism at the beach before. Have we, Saff?'

Saffron gapes. 'Hold on, a murder? Where?'

'Island View House. It's up online. Suspicious death, anyway. Fifty-something woman, apparently.'

'But that's where the Arts Trail party was.'

Saffron runs through a quick roll call of anyone she knows who might have been there, and to her relief no fifty-something women come to mind. Sometimes she feels like whenever there's a crisis round here, she's in the thick of it.

She's still processing the information when Milo, looking pretty much unbothered, shrugs.

'There you go, guys. Worse things are happening. Hey, the tide's come in and washed it all away. See it like that.'

Broady eyes him sideways and Saffron can see he's wondering whether to take him literally.

'Anyone got beef with you, Milo?' asks Broady suddenly.

Milo laughs. 'How long have you got? Hold on, it's *your* surf school. Anyone against having fun around here? Or anyone against bringing capitalism to surfing?'

'Capitalism?' Broady blinks.

'He's teaching people to surf,' says Saffron, 'not stealing their money.'

Milo pulls a face. 'Not cheap though, those surf lessons. Hey, I'm joking. But someone out there might see it that way. Some gnarly old surf rider with his nose out of joint because you're bringing all these learner drivers to his wave.'

Maybe there's something in it. A surfer taking against the overload on this painted wave, writing WHO'S NEXT? as a snarky dig.

'I want to get who did this,' says Broady, his jaw jutting.

'You got CCTV here?' says Milo, but Broady shakes his head.

'Nor me,' says Saffron.

'Least Big Brother's not at the beach. Look, I'm sorry, okay? You paid good money. But getting the police on it? A lot of the time they see what I do as criminal damage . . .'

'This was a commission. On my personal property. And now it's vandalism.'

'Yeah, I don't think it'll be top of anyone's list though. Especially if there's been a murder. Man, they're not going to care if one of my pictures gets scribbled on. No one's sticking the blue lights on for that.'

Broady shakes his head; stuffs his hands in the pockets of his board shorts.

'But you know who will care?' says Saffron. 'Ally and Jayden.'

17

Jayden is walking the long way round. He's hoping Benji will nod off by the time he gets to The Shell House so he and Ally can get down to it. Go over the details of what happened at the party yesterday and see if they can find a way in.

I'll take little man out, Jayden said to Cat this morning. *Give you a couple of hours to hang out just with Jazz.*

And let him talk murder with Ally.

She wants to make cupcakes, said Cat. *I don't want to make cupcakes.*

You don't have to make cupcakes, babe. She just wants one hundred per cent mama-time.

One hundred per cent? Cat gave a humourless laugh. *I'm running on about thirty, I reckon.*

But as they left, Cat had a recipe book out, and Jazzy was busy emptying a bottle of sugar sprinkles over the sideboard. Jayden scooped up Benji, took the bottle, kissed both his girls – with a *you be good* for his daughter – then slipped away. Guilt nipping at his heels.

Outside in the fresh air, Jayden turns his face to the watery sunlight. Focuses his mind on the case.

Ever since Ally's message last night, he's been turning over the thought that Gina Best was an unusual target. She came to

Porthpella and was murdered in one of the most premeditated ways out there. Because poisoning is sneaky. The sneakiest of the lot, surely. Who here would do that?

In the middle of the night, Jayden combed the internet looking for Gina Best's name in association with any of the Arts Trail players. It wasn't long before *Connor Rafferty and Gina Best* returned a direct hit. It was obscure – they'd both taught at a creative retreat in Dorset eight years ago, and one of the participants wrote a blog about it – but tangible. Presumably the police already know. But if they don't? Maybe Connor Rafferty is worth talking to.

Jayden's nearing the foot of the big hill into Porthpella – the helter-skelter one with wild views of the bubblegum sea – when his phone rings. It's Ally. He lengthens his stride, one hand resting on Benji's warm back through the sling.

'Al, I'm on my way over.'

'Can you make a detour via White Wave? I'm supposed to be opening my studio in five minutes and—'

'Sure. What do you need?'

'Wenna rang. You know the big poster that's gone up outside the shop, showing the map of the Arts Trail with all the venues? Someone's vandalised it.'

'Right,' says Jayden.

But there's something grave in Ally's voice. He waits.

'It's rather a haunting message, given what's happened. Someone's written "who's next?" in big letters.'

'They've written "who's next?" on the Arts Trail map?'

'Wenna's reported it to the police. She heard about the death last night and thinks there might be . . . a connection.'

'Alright, I'll take a look.'

Probably the work of a local joker. Jayden says as much to Ally, and she agrees. But there's still that tinge of uncertainty in her voice.

'Wenna said it wasn't there when she locked up yesterday. It must have been done overnight or very early this morning.'

'Just as the news was breaking,' says Jayden thoughtfully. 'That's fast.' And now that uncertainty is in his voice too. 'Okay. I'm on it.'

He passes the outermost cottages and wide-windowed bungalows, the ones with grinning names like Happy Days and Ollibobs. On the face of it, Porthpella is Good Vibes Only. The square lies ahead, White Wave Stores on the far corner. Arts Trail bunting loops from the Bluebird to The Wreckers Arms, and as a lively breeze catches it, the flags flutter like trapped birds. Jayden checks his watch. It's quarter to ten. Sunita will be ready to open the doors to the gallery, though with a sombre air, probably. Has she seen the writing on the poster too? He wonders if Harrison Loveday will go straight home now, or if DS Skinner delivered his favourite 'don't leave town' line, like a self-important sheriff in some backwater. Which isn't that far from the truth. Skinner: grizzled cowboy meets middle management.

Before Jayden gets to the gallery, he crosses the road and heads to White Wave Stores. He can already see the community noticeboard; the space is almost totally taken up by the Arts Trail map. And right across it, in white letters a foot high: WHO'S NEXT?

'I wanted to pull it down, but Ally said I shouldn't,' says Wenna, appearing from the shop. She stands with her hands planted on her hips, ready to take on the world. 'Doesn't set the right tone, does it, Jayden? Not for my shop and not for this village. Course the police were hardly interested, but then I said, "What if it's a message?" – because we've all heard about the death of that poor woman on the news – and then the cops sat up.' She stops to take a breath. 'You see where I'm coming from, don't you? Course you do. I don't like it one bit. Here, is that that little fella of yours in that sling? Let me get a good look at him, I could do with a lift. Oh, isn't he a sweetheart?'

As Wenna is distracted by Benji, Jayden takes a closer look at the poster. The letters are spray-painted block capitals. They run the total width of the poster, obscuring just about every venue. Ally's place – The Shell House – is the outermost spot, and a white dribble stops just short of it.

'Who's next?' he murmurs.

'I don't know about you, Jayden, but that reads like a threat to me.'

He takes out his phone and gets a couple of photographs.

'Wenna, have you got CCTV here?'

'No, we haven't. We've talked about it, Gerren and me, but we never bit the bullet. Never felt we needed it. We can count on you and Ally though, can't we, Jayden? You'll get to the bottom of it.' Behind her glasses, her eyes are glittering wide. 'Because, best case, there's a miscreant running round Porthpella, making a mockery of our community. And worst case . . . Well, I don't want to think about that. Don't want to, but can't help it either.'

Wenna bustles back into the store, and Jayden takes one more look at the poster – the careful letters, that big, looping question mark – but there's nothing more he can get from it.

He crosses to the Bluebird. Outside the gallery there's a wooden easel with the Arts Trail poster showing the venue number – both are unblemished. Looking through the window, Jayden sees a tall man in a blue linen suit. Harrison Loveday.

Last night Jayden pored over pictures of the guy, read interviews and reviews, trying to build a picture of this man that Ally knows from years ago and clearly doesn't like much. This man whose gallerist was murdered yesterday. Who Jayden didn't think he'd see out and about in Porthpella this morning.

Harrison is in the space on his own, no sign of Sunita. Jayden pushes at the door.

'Morning,' he says. 'I know you're not open yet . . .'

'Come in, come in,' says Harrison. 'It's never too early for art.'

Jayden had a line ready about looking for Sunita, but he's not sure he needs it. Harrison saunters over to him, hands in his pockets, a half-smile on his face. His casualness is mind-blowing. *Gina Best who?*

'I'm told they'll go quickly, so if you see something you like don't be shy.'

Jayden nods along. 'I like them all, to be honest.'

And he's aware of Harrison watching him. It's the wrong way round, thinks Jayden. *I should be eyeballing you.*

'Day-tripper?' asks Harrison.

'No, I live here.'

'Do you really?'

And Jayden feels a flicker of irritation at Harrison's undisguised surprise. He's willing to bet it's not just his Leeds accent that's throwing him off.

He turns from the pictures and scrutinises the guy right back.

Harrison doesn't look like a man who's been through it, who's had the shock of his life – his companion dropping dead – then the police descending, calling it murder. Harrison looks, Jayden thinks, completely normal. Like he's ready to attack the day, flogging his art – which, by the way, isn't even that good – and making lazy judgements.

'Talking of living here, did you see the news this morning?'

Playing innocent.

Harrison rocks on his heels. Hands still in pockets.

'I tend to avoid the news,' he says.

Jayden waits. Harrison's not going to deny knowledge, is he? Because that would just be weird.

'I won't crowd you while you're admiring the work,' says Harrison, and he abruptly turns away.

Okay, very weird.

'What about the noticeboard out there? Did you see anyone vandalising that?'

'Does my role extend to neighbourhood watch, do you mean?' Harrison laughs over his shoulder. 'Well, I'm sorry to disappoint you.'

◆　◆　◆

As Jayden heads on towards The Shell House, he checks in on Mullins. It's been a slow burn, that relationship, but Jayden and Ally's last few cases have shown the constable that they're here to help, not hinder. Maybe Mullins has even surprised Jayden as much as the other way round. He reckons the guy's a bit of a softie, underneath his bonnet – though obviously Mullins can't resist flexing his muscles every so often, reminding them who's got the badge around here.

Jayden taps out a message to him.

Any news on cause of death?

The reply is instant.

Morning Jayden yeah I'm good thanks for asking how are you?

He calls him instead.

'Sorry, mate. I thought you'd appreciate me getting down to business.'

'Very cold, Jayden, very cold.'

'Well, is there? Cause of death?'

'It's suspicious, haven't you heard?'

'It's got to be poison, hasn't it? Ally was there . . .'

'I know she was there. I have her statement. She's one of about sixty suspects, as it happens.'

'You won't have got the toxicology yet, but the initial post-mortem . . .'

'Jayden, I haven't got time, mate. I'm on a murder case. And you know what, this time, we've got this.'

'You've got this?'

'With bells on.'

As Jayden nears The Shell House he can see the Arts Trail easel outside it, just like the one at the Bluebird. Ally is venue number 12, and for someone like her, who's basically an introvert, this is a big deal. There's already a cluster of people at the gate, brandishing their Arts Trail booklets. It's weird, seeing total strangers at Ally's.

'Mullins, I saw Harrison Loveday just now,' says Jayden, slowing his step. 'He wasn't looking very bothered considering his friend and gallerist has just died. Sorry – been murdered.'

Jayden can hear Mullins hesitate; probably cooking up his next wisecrack.

'Where did you see him?'

'At the Bluebird. Just after I saw the vandalised Arts Trail poster outside White Wave.'

'"Who's next?" you mean?' says Mullins, putting on a dumb voice. 'Some no-hoper having a bit of fun.'

As Jayden nears the gate, he becomes conscious of someone observing him: a man about Gus's age, in a leather jacket and with a sharp haircut. He tries to figure out the expression on the guy's face. How loud was he speaking just now? As the man turns and walks up to the studio, Jayden keeps his eye on him.

'You're not taking it seriously then, Mullins?'

'Would you?'

'I wouldn't rule anything out.'

'Nice bit of fence-sitting, Jayden. Over and out.'

Jayden pushes through the gate, the neon buoys swinging. There's a cluster of people ahead: two kids pushing at each other and a weary-looking pair of parents; a woman in an elaborate scarf with a Tate bag over her shoulder. He crunches down this path he knows so well, then stops. Through the studio window he sees the man again – leather-jacket guy, good-hair guy. Jayden watches as he walks straight up to Ally and kisses her on the cheek. With all the casual confidence of someone who's done it a hundred times before.

18

'Jayden,' says Ally. 'This is Ray. We knew each other many years ago, at art school.'

She makes the introduction without awkwardness – which wasn't how she felt yesterday at Island View House. What Ally can't fathom is whether that's the Gus factor, or whether she's already grown used to the idea of Ray Finch being, passingly, back in her life.

'Good to meet you,' says Jayden. Then, 'That was with Harrison Loveday too, wasn't it?'

There's something pointed in the way Jayden says it. There's also something pointed in the way he's looking at Ray.

Perhaps there's to be awkwardness after all.

'Ah, Ally's partner,' says Ray. 'Of the crime-fighting variety. Pleasure. And yes, with Harrison. Though he was a couple of years above us, wasn't he, Ally?'

Ally nods. 'He was. Ray, I told Jayden everything that happened.'

'Were you at the party as Harrison's guest, Ray?' asks Jayden.

'I was. Always made a good plus-one.' Ray grins at Ally.

'Harrison's out manning his show this morning,' says Jayden.

Ally frowns. 'Is he really?'

'I don't know how long that'll last,' says Ray. 'You saw him, did you, Jayden?'

'Yeah, I did. We talked a bit. Apparently, he was surprised I lived round here.'

Ally sends him a questioning look.

'Obviously I don't know him, but you'd never have guessed anything serious had happened,' Jayden goes on. 'Let alone—'

'Yes, well, that's Harrison,' cuts in Ray. 'Doesn't surprise me at all that he's out there putting a brave face on it.'

'Brave face? Like I said, I don't know him, but he was very . . . controlled.'

Ray looks to Ally. 'There's a label for everything these days, isn't there? When it comes to Harrison, well, "narcissist" is probably the frontrunner. I'm not sure how much he ever *feels*. And a situation like this – well, that's probably a bit of a godsend. Feelings can be bloody inconvenient.'

Ally's aware of the studio's numbers swelling. She sends a welcoming smile in the general direction of her visitors, but really, she wants to keep talking about the case. To batten down the studio hatches and head to the thinking room with Jayden instead; he's clearly interested in Harrison Loveday. And they haven't even got on to 'who's next'?

'Inconvenient?' says Jayden quietly. 'That's one way of putting it.'

'Ally, you probably want to do your thing,' says Ray. 'We're cramping your style here. So I'll see you later on. Seven o'clock?'

Dinner at The Wreckers. *A chance to catch up on the last forty-seven years*, Ray said. Ally was surprised to find herself agreeing without hesitation.

'Seven o'clock. Thank you for coming down.'

'Jayden, are you heading off too?' Ray asks.

'No, I'll stop here a bit.'

Ray throws out an arm, almost knocking the Panama hat off an elderly man in the process. 'Ally Bright,' he says. 'Beautiful. All of it. Your work, your studio, your view . . . All of it.'

As Ray strolls out, Jayden raises his eyebrows in comical fashion.

'It's a long story.'

'I'm here for long stories.'

'I'd rather talk about the case.'

Ally looks to a couple standing by one of her larger pieces. She catches the words 'It could work in the master bedroom, couldn't it? As a bold statement?' A different artist might go over, engage interest and nail the sale. But she turns back to Jayden.

'What did you make of the vandalism on the poster? Wenna thinks it's sinister.'

'And it's not like Wenna to jump to conclusions,' he says with a wry grin. 'If it's reffing the death at the party, someone acted very quickly. "Who's next?" Though it could be interpreted a different way, maybe. Graffiti is its own language, right? Insiders only. Except . . . this wasn't graffiti-style. It was just spray-painted.'

'Could it be as innocent as someone considering which venue they're going to visit next? You know, if they're following the trail, "Okay, who's next? Number 12." That sort of thing?'

Even as she says it, Ally doubts it. That kind of thought is unlikely to have someone reaching for a spray can. Meanwhile, Jayden's passing her his phone, showing her the photos. She takes in the words; her own spot on the map is just clear of the paint.

'It's provocative,' says Ally. 'I can see why Wenna called the police. What about when you spoke to Harrison, did he mention it?'

'He didn't want to go there. I tried to bring up Gina's death too. Really casually, like anyone would, and he shut it down fast. I didn't get a good vibe, Al.'

'I wonder if I coloured your view of him.'

'No, this view's all mine. I spoke to Mullins on the way down, by the way. They've got nothing on Loveday, or he wouldn't be strutting about the Bluebird, but reading between the lines, he's a person of interest.'

'He'd have to be,' says Ally. 'He's the only one who knew her.'

'The only one who knew her *well*. I've been doing some digging. There was someone else at the party who was connected to Gina Best.'

'You're going to say Ray. He told me they met at a party once. She extolled the virtues of good gallery representation.'

'She wanted to represent him, did she?'

'I think it was the other way round, actually. But Ray didn't pursue his art commercially, in the end. He went into teaching instead.'

Ally sees Jayden absorbing this information.

'So maybe there's sour grapes on Ray's side, if his work was rejected?'

'Jayden, Ray was with me when Gina Best collapsed.'

'But what about before?'

'Before . . .' Ally tries to remember. She was with Gus and then, all of a sudden, there he was. Ray Finch, walking towards her across the lawn. It was as if he came out of thin air. 'I don't know. But we all gave our statements to the police. And Ray was upfront about having met Gina once before. Were you thinking of somebody else? I presume Gideon had contact with her, as it was his idea to bring in Harrison Loveday.'

'Connor Rafferty knew her.'

Jayden shares his discovery: that Gina and Connor appeared on an artist-led retreat in Dorset eight years ago.

'Connor was a tutor, and Gina came and gave a talk. It was at some luxe country estate. One of the participants wrote a blog afterwards. Seems like Connor was all about the creativity but then

Gina came and gave a more ruthlessly commercial perspective on it all, which knocked the confidence of some of the participants. According to the blogger, Connor and Gina were a bit frosty with each other at dinner that night.' He holds up his hands. 'I know, it's not exactly juicy but . . . it's a connection, right?'

Jayden's phone buzzes and he pulls it from his pocket.

'Sorry, Al, I thought it was Cat. Oh, hold on, it's Saffron.'

He looks at the screen, eyebrows raised.

'And . . . she's got a case for us.'

He holds up the phone, and Ally peers at a photograph of a colourful mural. The words WHO'S NEXT? sprayed across it, this time in letters a metre high.

'That's the surf school,' says Ally.

'Same message. Someone's been busy.'

'But it's nothing to do with the Arts Trail this time. Is it?'

'They've specifically chosen this wall. And it's art, right?'

Ally saw the young artist working on it two days ago, as she was out walking Fox. He was wearing a full face mask and had music playing from a speaker. A splash of something different at the beach. She has a sudden thought, and moves to the table where there's a stack of Arts Trail programmes. She flicks through one and finds the page she's looking for.

'Walking tour of Milo Nash's street art pieces,' she says, holding up a double-page spread. 'A new addition for the trail this year.'

They look at one another. The hubbub of the studio visitors falls away.

'I'll call Saffron,' says Jayden. 'Obviously we're taking the case, right?'

19

Gus checks his watch. He wants to get to Ally's exhibition early, to show support, but something's holding him back. So Gus is still sitting at his laptop, resolutely staring at his inbox. Saturday morning isn't perhaps a classic time for literary agents to send acceptance or rejection emails, but nevertheless, he's poised. Gus is objective enough to know that his detective novel isn't likely to set the world on fire. It's solid, decent, but not necessarily remarkable. *Good God, like man like novel?* But the fact that it exists? Ah now, that is remarkable indeed.

In the gloomy days following his divorce, Gus resolved to finally settle down and write his book. This was his next chapter: Life After Mona. He took himself to Porthpella – no more than a pin dropped on a map – because it felt like the kind of thing a real writer would do. But the venture has exceeded all his expectations. To Gus, this novel is precious, because it's born of this place, and the people he's met here.

The person, probably.

At the thought of Ally, another name crashes back into Gus's mind, and he winces. *Ray Finch.* Because here is the inconvenient truth, and at least part of the reason why Gus is lying low this morning. Yesterday Gus found himself in the presence of 'chemistry'. Some reaction took place, a crackling and a fizzing, as Ally and Ray faced each other after half a century.

Forty-seven years, Ally.

He doesn't know the full story there, but Gus is certain that there is one. Ray with his knowing smile and leather jacket and uncannily lustrous hair. And an artist to boot.

These last two years, Gus has been so careful, so conscious of Bill, because he knows Ally still feels that loss. The moment last autumn where he looked inside her wardrobe and saw all of her dead husband's clothes has stayed with him. Are they still there now, those trousers and jackets and shirts? If Gus hadn't seen them, of course he would have accepted Ally's invitation to stay that night: gales were blasting over the headland and The Shell House was a cocoon; Ally had such tenderness in her eyes, and in her touch, as she said *stay*.

It is a moment that Gus has replayed a great many times, giving him by turns hope for the future and the sense that he's already blown it. That with this considerable care for Ally – together with his slight awe of Bill – he's mishandled things.

But what does Ray Finch know of any of this? This sauntering man who – and Gus has done the maths here – predates Ally's husband. Who therefore belongs to a life uncoloured by that loss. Does that make him a less complicated proposition?

It certainly makes Ray *something*. Because Gus saw Ally's reaction with his own eyes.

He puffs out his cheeks and hits Refresh. No new mail.

His eyes stray to the window, where Sea Dream commands the dunes. All plate glass and shining metal; a haughty exterior that's the reflection of its original owner, one Roland Hunter. Since then, Gus has watched a parade of prosperous holidaymakers come and go. He's perfected the art of tuning out their braying voices, turning his eyes from the sun that belts off the metalwork of their

SUVs. *To live in Cornwall year-round is to tolerate the seasonal influx of irritants*, he once wrote in a letter to his long-time old-mate pen pals Rich and Clive, *and I say this with the authority of an emmet turned incomer so please don't come at me with your pots and kettles.*

Gus didn't see Gina Best arrive yesterday, but the bright white BMW he presumes is hers is still in the driveway. Will Gina's next of kin come to claim it, amidst the other sorry business to attend to? Gus noted earlier that Harrison Loveday's car has gone. Perhaps he's quit Porthpella, and who could blame him?

The police, perhaps.

At that unfounded thought, a patrol car rumbles down the track. Gus's eyes widen. Is this what Saffron calls manifesting? If so, he should put his talents to better use.

He refreshes his inbox. *Nope.*

An officer Gus doesn't recognise climbs out and looks up at Sea Dream. He crunches up the gravel driveway to ring the bell. As he waits, he does a slow 360-degree turn, taking in All Swell too. Gus can hear the crackle of his police radio. The officer tries the bell again; then, with another look towards Sea Dream, crosses the track.

Gus jumps to his feet, runs a hand over his bald head. He gets to the door just as the officer's hand is poised to knock.

'Good morning there,' Gus says.

'Morning, sir. Have you seen your neighbour here at Sea Dream this morning?'

'The artist Harrison Loveday?'

'That's it.'

'Only at the party last night. And I gave a statement. I was there, you see . . . when the poor lady . . .'

'But you haven't seen Mr Loveday this morning?'

Gus shakes his head. 'Not this morning. I presumed he's left.'

And Gus catches the look on the officer's face, as if Harrison Loveday leaving Porthpella is not on at all.

'Did you see Gina Best here at Sea Dream yesterday?' the officer asks.

'Afraid not. Just at the party.'

And the complier in Gus, the person who wants to do his duty, is aware he's being less than useless. He's racking his brain for something helpful, but the officer is already turning away with a 'Thank you, sir'.

Gus closes the door. The statement he gave Tim Mullins last night wasn't his finest hour. The truth is he was still jittery, and his words were perfunctory at best. *I was waiting for drinks. I heard a cry. Then she was on the ground.* Perhaps because Mullins and his notebook had a whole queue of people to get through – people who occupied the full spectrum from genuinely horrified to gruesomely curious – the constable didn't push it.

Gus drops down on to the settee, a rickety wicker affair that creaks with his weight.

Is there anything he can add, now that Harrison appears to have skipped town? He searches his mind, and his palms sweat as he relives that awful moment. The whole world seemed to stop turning as Gus saw Gideon try to resuscitate her – then resumed its sickly spinning when she was declared dead.

Four words come back to Gus. They thud into his head with untold, if tardy, clarity.

You're being extraordinarily selfish.

Gina Best to Harrison Loveday. A hissed delivery, as lively as a cornered cat. Harrison ignoring her. She was angry. Harrison didn't care. Then, moments later, she died.

Does this mean something? Or nothing?

Gus rushes to the door, throws it open. But the police car has gone.

He snatches his coat from the peg. He'll tell Ally instead. See, that's one thing he's got: Ray and Ally might have ancient history, but Gus has seen Ally blossom into a detective before his very eyes. He has been there for every case, and he's sure she'll find this nugget of information interesting.

The purpose that now propels Gus down the path and over the dunes feels like sweet relief.

20

When Lara Swann walks into Pamela Trescoe's studio, Pamela almost doesn't recognise her. Her long hair is pulled into a bun as tight as a ballerina's. Her lips are picked out in vivid scarlet. *War paint*: that's Pamela's first thought. Not that Lara looks like a woman headed into battle; she's a timid sort, with her sloping shoulders and nervous gestures, and almost total absence of eye contact. Rumour has it she was rejected by the Arts Trail though, which means she showed a certain boldness turning up at last night's invite-only party. Gideon did his best to welcome her, but Pamela could tell he was ruffled by Lara's presence. Though petty gripes soon paled into insignificance, didn't they?

If Pamela's own work was rejected . . . Well, here's where her imagination runs out. She is a stalwart; every Easter holiday for the last fifteen years she's thrown open the door to Seathrift Studio to showcase her ceramics. The committee might have wanted to shake things up this year, luring in the big I am, Harrison Loveday, and involving that boy Milo Nash in a perfunctory way, but the fact is Pamela Trescoe is part of the Arts Trail furniture. And she does quite well from it too, usually making enough to go a little wild with her Waitrose order in the weeks that follow. A new set of linens for the summer. Once, a cottage holiday in the Lakes, where she skinny-dipped in a cairn – solo, of course – making her wishes to the moon. If Pamela does well this year, she likes to think she'll be able to persuade Donald to throw caution to the wind and join her on a post-trail jaunt. Or perhaps just a splendid dinner somewhere faintly ridiculous, like the Sandcastle Hotel. Her aspirations are modest, really.

But perhaps thoughts of 'doing well' are inappropriate. Pamela was fully prepared for Gideon to pull the plug on the whole thing after last night. But he's a focused sort. Ambitious too, though he disguises it with his foppish hair and languid gestures. No, Gina Best's death hasn't stood in the way of the Arts Trail.

Gina Best. Such a perky name, so carefree. And what a disconnect: that unfortunate woman, lying on the terrace with her red hair splayed out like its own pool of blood. Pamela remembers feeling a roaring in her ears at the sight of her: it was as loud as the tide, heat rushing to every extremity of her body. Pamela realised then that the shock of death is a full-body experience. The statement she gave the police was cartoonish, peppered with 'but how?' and 'but why?' While, beside her, Donald appeared preternaturally calm, as untroubled as a standing stone. But Pamela knows Donald feels more than he shows. Perhaps that's true of most people, because despite tossing and turning all night, images of the evening strobing behind her eyes, this morning Pamela pulled on a voluminous dress, tied her clay-streaked apron over it, and is turning up with her best smile.

The show must go on.

What about Lara Swann? Is she feeling more than she shows too?

Pamela greets her as she would greet anyone. 'Hello there. Welcome.'

'Hi,' says Lara quietly, her eyes fixed a metre to Pamela's left.

Pamela considers herself good at reading the room; that's what all these years of the Arts Trail have given her. She happily engages visitors in conversation but she's not in the business of cracking

98

the hard nuts and would rather lose a sale than grovel for one. Fortunately for Pamela, neither her ego nor her livelihood depend on the sale of her pottery. Her ex-husband came from money, and when he left her – the best part of two decades ago – Pamela gained substantially more than she lost. And these days, she lives small. The things that Pamela wants are not costly by standard metrics, but thus far love – or at least intimacy, companionship – has proved beyond her means.

Pamela watches as Lara dutifully shuttles from piece to piece. Why exactly is she here? Perhaps because, as the crow flies, Pamela's home is closest to Westerly Manor, the granite pile that Lara's mother, Billie Swann – *darling of the London art scene in the eighties, yes, yes, we all know* – purchased some years ago. Billie was both aloof and elusive as a neighbour. When she deigned to occupy that second home of hers, she all but raised the drawbridge, though Pamela did flatter her into giving her a studio tour on one memorable occasion. Rumour has it that Billie is now withering away in a high-end nursing home somewhere in the Home Counties. Lara moved in full-time six months ago. With her eagerness to be part of the trail, Lara was presumably keen to engage with the community, but aside from the ill-fated application Lara hasn't made an effort in Porthpella. Early on, Pamela flagged her down as she passed in her little red car and, in an attempt to be neighbourly, invited her in for a cup of tea. But Lara never accepted, despite her reiterations. *I'm just along the way, see. Sure you won't? There's cake!* And a reciprocal invitation has never once been floated.

'Is it true?' says Lara. 'What I've heard?'

Ah, that's why Lara is here. Crisis bringing cohesion. Plus, Pamela is approachable: in the know, but a little apart from the committee that alienated Lara. *Well, fine.*

'Were you not there, dear? I thought I saw you.'

Lara studies her shoes. 'I was. Briefly. But I realised it was a mistake to come, so I left.'

'Before that poor woman . . .'

'Yes.'

'Haven't the police been in touch? They were fastidious about taking all of our statements.'

Lara shakes her head. 'I haven't been at home this morning. But I heard it on the news . . . and I wondered what people were saying. People who were actually there.'

Pamela rocks on her Crocs. 'You know how people are. There's gossip. Speculation. But mostly there's shock that this should happen within our community. Not just Porthpella, but the creative community specifically. We have our ups and down, our little fallings-out' – and here she pointedly eyes Lara, despite knowing she's unlikely to return her gaze – 'but us artists . . . we have to stick together. And to think . . . Well, it looks a heck of a lot like sabotage to me.'

Incredibly, Lara's eyes meet Pamela's, dead on. Her pupils are tiny, no more than pinpricks in a watery blue.

'Sabotage?'

'Only someone who wanted the Arts Trail to fail would kill someone at the launch party. And you must have heard about those ominous messages written left, right and centre? There's one at White Wave, emblazoned across the trail map, of all things. I saw it this morning when I went for the paper. Another by the beach too, by all accounts. "Who's next?" Well, that sounds like a threat if you ask me.'

Pamela keeps her voice even, but actually she's more rattled than she'd like to admit. Those two words – *who's next?* – have been buzzing around her head like a couple of trapped flies. Lara's cheeks flare, until they're almost as bright as her lipstick.

'A threat? What, to other artists?'

'I'll be bolting my door tonight, put it that way. I'll be sleeping with the light on.'

'But the woman who died had nothing to do with the Arts Trail. She was a gallery owner in London. Wasn't she?'

And Lara sounds as innocent as a little girl.

'Lara, she represented Harrison Loveday, and Harrison is the star of the show. If I were the police, I'd absolutely be looking at sabotage as a motive. It's clear as day to me.'

Pamela has to believe that the police are already considering this angle. And if they aren't, perhaps she should be the one to suggest it. Thus distracted, she only notices that Lara is on the move when the woman's already at the door.

'Oh, goodbye then,' she calls out pointedly, and makes to follow her.

But as Pamela steps forward, her right ankle suddenly goes from beneath her, folding like a letter in an envelope. It does this from time to time, an ongoing weakness of hers, though you wouldn't know it; from the outside her fetlocks look as sturdy as a bullock's.

'Blast!'

The pain is sharp, electric. Sometimes Pamela gets away with it, the pain passing as quickly as it comes. Other times her ankle balloons to comedic proportions, and then it's frozen peas and hospital waiting rooms for hours on end.

Lara stops in the doorway. She turns around.

Surely her neighbour will ask after her? Pamela is doubled over and hopping. She knows she appears ridiculous – and clearly in need.

Lara looks at her, lips moving but no words coming out. And then the callous creature is gone.

21

Jayden sits in the window at Hang Ten, going over the notes he made as he talked to Saffron and Broady. It's quiet in here, with just one other guy sitting at his laptop with his headphones on. Jayden settles back against the cushions. For a second, he lets himself close his eyes, Saffron's electro beats carrying him away.

He'll always connect Hang Ten with becoming a detective. Him and Ally at the corner table, surrounded by surf posters and wall-mounted skate decks. How shell-shocked Ally was after seeing the body at the foot of the cliffs. And how, as she talked about Lewis Pascoe, Jayden felt an unexpected feeling rising. He wanted to get involved.

Jayden's old mates and colleagues back in Leeds thought him and Ally teaming up was a one-off. That it wouldn't last, just like Jayden in Porthpella – a city boy through and through. But the more sensitive among them knew that after Kieran died, Jayden's partner and fellow PC, anything that might help him find his way back was all good.

As Jayden hears a bleat from Benji, he snaps his eyes open. His son is awake and currently being bounced around by Saffron.

'Oh my God, Jayden, he's so cute. I can keep him, right? We've got a deal?'

And he feels a swell of pure fatherly pride. Benji hasn't even learnt to smile yet and he's already Porthpella's most charming resident; though he'd need to keep that under wraps from Jazzy, who's rocking the Terrible Twos as if she invented the concept. How Jayden's rooting for that first smile; he's giving his boy pep talks at every turn. He really, really wants Cat to see it happen. And for her own face to light up in return.

Saffron drops into the chair opposite Jayden. She holds Benji high against her shoulder; her pink hair tickles his head.

'So . . . what are you thinking? What's the next move?'

'That's what I'm trying to work out. There's not a lot to go on.'

'Yeah, I'm sorry Milo didn't wait around to talk to you.'

As they stood in front of the wall earlier – and those massive letters, WHO'S NEXT? – Saffron explained that the artist wasn't especially bothered; he figured it came with the terrain. But Broady didn't see it that way. And Saffron was straight-up upset. Then Jayden told her about the same words sprayed on the Arts Trail map outside White Wave Stores – and he saw the way Saffron's face changed as she took it in.

'There's no other vandalism round here,' says Jayden now. 'Just the Mahalo wall and the Arts Trail poster in the village. So it's targeted.'

'Milo asked if anyone was against the surf school opening. But we didn't know about the Arts Trail poster then.'

'And what did Broady say to that?'

Jayden looks to the sand, where there's a group of people in Mahalo rash vests lying belly down on their banana-yellow boards. Broady demonstrates a pop-up, as nimble as a big cat. His shaggy blond mane reinforces the look: King of the Jungle, or the beach anyway. But an easy-breezy guy; too laid-back to make enemies.

'He acted like it was a stupid suggestion, but I thought Milo had a point. But now you've said about White Wave too . . . That changes things, right?'

'It does. The surf school building's been open a few weeks now, right? And Broady was running lessons last summer anyway. The timing makes me think it's more about Milo's piece itself, but now if we factor in the Arts Trail poster . . .'

Jayden glances at the other customer, but the man's still focused on his laptop, headphones firmly on.

'Like you said, it changes things,' he finishes.

'But it's just kids messing about, right?' she says, cradling Benji close.

'Maybe.' Then, 'What's Milo Nash like?'

Jayden holds up his phone, where there's a picture of Nash in a full face mask, brandishing two spray cans at the camera as if they're weapons.

'He's not scary, if that's what you're thinking,' says Saffron. 'He's cool. A free spirit. I only met him through the commission but . . . we get on well.' She tucks a strand of hair behind her ear. 'So, Jayden . . . you'll take the case? Broady says he doesn't want to pay out anything, he's already lost the art, but I will. I'm not out for a freebie.'

Jayden waves his hand dismissively. He's not going to pull out the rate card for Saffron, who's one of the biggest-hearted people he knows. 'Ah, we'll figure that out.'

'I didn't know if you'd be too busy, if you guys are getting involved in the murder or not.'

'I've been tapping Mullins for info, but he's holding out on me.'

'He likes to play hard to get. You know he'll need your help eventually.'

Jayden gives a wry smile. 'It does seem to go that way, right?'

Benji starts to make snuffling noises, pushing his tiny fists towards his face. He whimpers.

'Hey, mister,' murmurs Saffron. 'Do you want your daddy?'

'What he wants,' says Jayden, rooting in the bag, 'is milk.'

Benji's whimpering notches up. Nought to sixty in less than seven seconds: that's his boy. Saffron passes him back as Jayden pulls out the bottle. He settles his son in the crook of his arm and Benji quits his full-throttle scream to fasten his lips round the rubber teat. Peace resumes.

'How's Cat doing? I haven't seen her in ages.'

'Tired.' Jayden looks down at his son. Eyes closed as he drinks, his lashes are almost unfeasibly long; his cheeks round as a ball. 'But she's okay,' he adds. 'So, apart from this walking tour thing, has Milo got any other connection to the Arts Trail?'

'Not that I know of.' Saffron tips her head. 'You look like you're thinking.'

'I'm always thinking.'

Benji splutters, and Jayden takes the bottle from him for a second. His son opens his perfect little lips and milk jets out. Jayden swipes the cloth from his shoulder and gets busy wiping them both down as Benji, totally unbothered, lolls like a drunkard in his arms.

'That you done already, mate?' says Jayden. Then he looks back to Saffron. 'What I'm thinking is that it's only day one of the Arts Trail, and we've already got a murder and two lots of vandalism. Vandalism that connects to art in both cases but could also be directly referencing Gina Best's death.'

'Not Gina Best's death, but whoever's next.' Saffron holds her hand to her mouth. 'God, did I just say that?'

'I think it's what someone out there wants us to think.'

'But who? The killer?'

'That'll be the Arts Trail Killer.'

The voice comes from behind them.

Jayden swivels and sees the guy at his laptop, sitting back now in his chair with his arms folded. His headphones are slung around his neck. His grin is sly.

'You willing to go on record with that, guys?' he says.

22

'Bingo,' says Skinner. 'Cyanide.'

And okay, Skinner called it, but Mullins doesn't love how happy his boss looks. Like cyanide poisoning is good news.

'Fast work,' says one of the Newquay lot.

'Lab rats pulling their finger out,' says Skinner. 'Stranger things have happened. So, cyanide . . . fast-acting and highly toxic. Symptoms begin a few seconds after exposure. Death usually occurs within minutes. In the case of Gina Best, it was almost instantaneous. We'll be issuing a statement to the media, because there's reporters already sniffing around. Not helped by that graffiti nonsense. Right. To business.'

Mullins sits straighter in his chair.

'When Gina Best collapsed and fell, a number of glasses were broken,' Skinner goes on. 'Forensics have confirmed that traces of cyanide are on some of the shards, confirming the method of poisoning. On other shards there are fingerprints and saliva from both Gina Best and Harrison Loveday. Plus, an as-yet-unidentified individual, possibly the bartender, possibly the killer. They're currently working on piecing together the glasses. It's a safe assumption that Gina Best's fingerprints and saliva will be present on the one that contained cyanide. If Harrison Loveday's fingerprints are also present, did Loveday give her the glass? And, if so, did he do it knowingly?'

Mullins has already passed on the news that Harrison Loveday is out and about, manning his exhibition at the Bluebird as if nothing has happened. *Cool as a cucumber, apparently, Sarge.* A uniform has been dispatched to confirm it.

'Is it enough to haul him in?' asks Mullins.

'Not yet,' says Skinner.

'I can't see this Loveday bloke choosing to poison her at a party, when the two are shacked up together in a beach house. Easiest thing in the world to stick poison in her coffee cup.'

One of the Newquay lot, piping up from the back.

'If Gina Best died at Sea Dream, Harrison Loveday would be the prime suspect,' says Skinner. 'The only suspect. But do it at a gathering, where any number of people are present . . . See where I'm going?'

'Five people,' someone says. 'You said five people knew her. And we're looking at each of them.'

'So a party where five times as many people, at least, are under suspicion,' says Skinner. 'Well, I know which I'd go for.'

Mullins chews his pen thoughtfully. They've got sixty-one statements in the system. How many are reliable? Memory is as slippery as a fish – and everyone notices different things. According to the statements – most of which were just long-distance first impressions – Gina Best was both charming and moody, memorable and forgettable, happy and sad, north and south, apples and pears. Most of it's nonsense, isn't it? It's a shame that Ally Bright was so far from the action. Before Ally turned detective, Mullins used to see her sometimes, wandering the shore; a beady-eyed beachcomber, plucking treasure – well, her kind of treasure – from tangles of weed and hunks of old driftwood. And that's Ally all over: she sees things that other people don't.

Mullins tries to imagine Gina Best and Harrison Loveday at the bar as the cocktails were being mixed. Did Harrison pick up both drinks and hand one to Gina? How could anyone be sure who drank which? And there were waitresses doing the rounds with glasses of champagne and canapés too.

'Sarge, in Harrison Loveday's statement, did he say what he and Gina were drinking?' he asks.

'Mai Tais.'

'Both of them?'

'That's what he said. But Harrison admitted he was half-drunk already. Once Forensics have pieced together the glasses, then we'll know conclusively.'

Mullins writes *Mai Tais* on his notepad.

'If the cocktails were fresh, it's got to be the barman, hasn't it?' he says.

'Lee Coleman,' says one of the Newquay lot. 'Works with the catering company. Twenty-seven years old, lives with his girlfriend in Hayle. He didn't know the hosts. No connection to any of the guests either. But we'll keep looking at him and obviously check his prints.'

'Now, listen up,' says Skinner. 'We've got a time of death, and we've got a cause of death. Mullins, I want you to cross-reference all of the witness statements to place people at the party. I want to plot out who was in sight, and earshot, of Gina Best when she died. Meanwhile, we need to get our ducks in a row for the press. No loose talk.'

'You know who one of the closest people was,' says Mullins. 'Gus Munro.'

As he says it, Mullins looks down at his phone, buzzing on his desk. And whose name should be flashing? *Gus Munro.*

'Talk of the devil,' he says. 'Alright if I take it, Sarge?'

Skinner nods, and talk in the room moves on to the graffiti: should they be taking 'who's next?' seriously or not? Mullins has a pretty good idea of where Skinner has landed on that one.

As Mullins walks from the room, his phone clamped to his ear, he feels like a hot shot. *Get me, Mullins! Only Mullins will do!*

'Oh hullo, Tim,' says Gus. 'I might have remembered something potentially useful. At least, Ally thinks it could be, and she's usually right about these things, isn't she?'

23

As Ally passes the Bluebird, she sees the sign is now flipped to 'Closed' and the Arts Trail easel is gone from the pavement. She looks through the window, surprised by all the white space. Harrison's paintings, of which there are only a handful, are on the small side. But she can understand why Sunita felt pressured to give the gallery exclusively to Harrison Loveday.

It's bothering her, though – why Harrison said yes in the first place. Ally knows he's being paid a fee to be here; Sunita told her as much, although she doesn't know the sum. Gideon and Connor are funding it privately, convinced that it's in the Arts Trail's best interests to have a VIP guest aboard: more publicity, more visitors, more money coming into the community. Only, now the publicity is for the wrong reasons. How many people asked Ally today if she knew anything about the death at Island View? And what about if it was connected to the graffiti on the Arts Trail poster and at the surf school? Her reputation as a detective has grown in the last year, and one man, an elderly chap with a quivering moustache, asked if she'd be getting her magnifying glass out – his condescension made her grit her teeth. A death isn't entertainment. And not that Ally has ideas above her station, but she and Jayden take what they do seriously. Every bit as seriously as if they carried badges.

She hurries on to The Wreckers. It's not like Ally to be late, but it took her a while to get ready after she closed the doors to her studio. She sold a piece too – which is remarkable, as she knows she wasn't the most attentive today. It wasn't just that it felt strange to have so many people moving through her private space; her head was taken up by a swirl of thoughts. Most of them to do with Gina Best's death and the vandalism – but not all.

As she walks in, she scans the bar, with its familiar low beams, the ships in bottles over the fireplace, the seafaring oils in gilt frames. There's a young family settling in for their dinner and she can't help thinking of Bill and Evie. Whenever the three of them came here, Evie chose sausage and chips. And Bill? Steak. *I'm in it for the onion rings, Al,* he'd say, every time. When you're the one left behind in a place, the people you miss are everywhere and nowhere.

Ally checks her watch: it's ten past seven and Ray isn't here yet. She pulls out her phone but there are no messages. A trio of three young women sitting by the door spin their heads to look at her, then turn back to each other.

'It's freaky,' one says. 'It's basically saying "which one of this lot is going to get it next?" I've told Sarah to tell Liam's dad that he has to quit the Arts Trail.'

'Could be too late already.' Her friend's eyes are wide as windows. 'What if they're all marked?'

'She wasn't an artist,' says the third. 'She ran a gallery. And she wasn't even from round here, was she?'

There's a cluster of people at the bar and Ally hears the words *who's next?* rising from the tide of conversation like flotsam. She slips past unnoticed, reluctant to be drawn into the throng, and takes a table in the corner. Of course it's the talk of the village, that spray-painted question being repeated over and over. It's not as if Porthpella is a stranger to suspicious deaths, but the graffiti in two such prominent spaces has caught people's imagination.

Ally checks her watch again and decides she'll give it ten minutes, then send Ray a message. She settles back and realises she's watching the door. Suddenly it swings wide and Ray surges into the pub. It's a determined entrance, like someone cannonballing into a pool. His shoulders are square in his leather jacket, and he pushes his hand through his hair as he scans the room. He sees her and he grins; she feels herself smiling back. For a split second, Ally is in Falmouth. She's nineteen, and his attention is a lighthouse beam.

'Sorry I'm late,' he says, leaning in to kiss her on the cheek. He's hot, as if he hurried to get here. But his aftershave is as fresh as a wicked south-westerly.

◆ ◆ ◆

Two hours later, and the conversation has not run dry. Ray wants to know everything: about her cases with Jayden, her art over the years, her life with Bill and Evie. And in turn he's told her about his rose-pink cottage between Aldeburgh and Southwold – crumbling, by all accounts, but a labour of love, with its vegetable garden and attic studio and a rakish tomcat called Alf. Two wives, two grown-up children. *I flatter myself that I'm easy to live with, but the evidence seems to suggest otherwise*, he said with a grin. *But then you know a little about that.*

It was Ally's second week of art school, when she met him. They were in the same life-drawing class, his easel next to hers. She was so thoroughly focused on the task that she hardly noticed him. But when the session was over, she looked across at his work and saw that it was as lacklustre as her own. He grinned. *Can I get away with calling it abstract?* To which she replied, *Only if I can.* And they both agreed they preferred landscapes. A few days later she bumped into him with his sketchbook on the banks of the River Fal, in the exact spot at which she'd planned to sit and draw. Afterwards, they went for a cheap pub dinner. Spanish wine. And when Ally left him on the steps of her lodgings, a tiny fisherman's cottage, there was a kiss too. It was the first of many.

Ray glances at his watch. 'I did mention to Harrison that I was meeting you. That he should drop by if he wanted company. I hope you don't mind.'

'Not at all,' says Ally.

She's surprised, in truth, that he's only mentioning it now, because Harrison was a topic of conversation earlier: his arrogance at Falmouth; Ray's admiration for his paintings. *One of those people I always kept an eye on afterwards. He's the only one from that time who's really made it, isn't he? In one sense, anyway. Profile. Success.*

Ally narrowed her eyes at that. *Depends how you define success,* she said.

To which Ray grinned and held up his glass. *Cheers to that. My last radish crop was a resounding success, thank you very much.*

But Ally's relieved too, because if she knew, she'd have expected the man to arrive any second. While the detective in her would welcome a conversation with Harrison Loveday, what she's had this evening – this meander down memory lane; the landscapes of their separate lives – has been an unexpected pleasure.

'Though selfishly, I'm rather glad he hasn't turned up yet,' says Ray, with a sideways smile. 'Another drink?'

She hesitates. 'I think . . . it's home time, for me. It's been a long day. And yesterday, well, it was a long night.'

Ray shrugs; smiles. 'Still a hellraiser then. Let me walk you back, at least?'

But he's staying in a cottage around the corner from The Wreckers, so Ally won't hear of it.

◆ ◆ ◆

Ally welcomes the quiet on the walk home. Her feet shushing through the dunes, the sea caressing the shore. It's a mild night, and the tide is all the way out. A crescent moon tints the landscape silver. Ally rarely thinks about her art school days, and if she does, they're full of Bill. The little flat they moved into together. How she stayed up late painting when he was on the night shift, and how they'd go to bed together in the dawn light. Ray Finch? He came and went. A fly-by-night, by some people's estimation. He left after the first term. He never wrote.

That's why it's so very strange that all those years should fall away. How, over the course of one evening with Ray, Ally's realised she remembers everything about him.

And the Ray of today? Every life is extraordinary, but Ray told her nothing to make her jaw drop. She can square it all with the Ray she knew back then. The years teaching art in a rural comprehensive; his rather distant relationship with the grown-up children from his first marriage. His wry acknowledgement that his commitment to his art is matched these days by a commitment to his vegetable patch and his barstool at the local pub. The look on his face though, as she talked about the detective work in detail. All that she and Jayden have done together. Yes, Ally knows she made his jaw drop.

She can't remember the last time she enjoyed the surprise on someone's face quite so much. It made her feel like someone new. Or was it that she was telling it to someone new? *Old, but new.*

She sees a light on at Gus's and wonders what he's doing now that he's finished his novel. Gus knew she was meeting Ray. She had thought about inviting him but told herself he'd find their nostalgic talk dull. But perhaps there was a little more to it.

As she moves on, she looks across to Sea Dream. It lies in darkness, as if empty, but there are two cars by the entrance. The one Gina Best arrived in, and Harrison's. Ally's drawn towards the house, and as she steps a little closer the security lights click on. The sudden illumination makes her feel like a trespasser and she's set to go on her way when she stops. Does a double take.

The front door is open. Not wide, but ajar. And like a phone ringing in the middle of the night, an open front door unsettles. It's resoundingly out of the ordinary. Especially at ten o'clock at night, when the cars are in the driveway and the house is in darkness.

There are numerous explanations, of course. Absent-mindedness, for one; Harrison must be preoccupied, for all the cool exterior he presented when he thought Jayden was a customer with a wallet. Unfamiliar locks on a rental property, for another.

But as a sudden breeze picks up over the dunes, Ally shivers.

She moves towards the door. Presses her hand to the wood and pushes the door wider. Beyond, the hallway is dark. She could just pull it closed, avert the security risk and call it her Good Samaritan part done. But she's not just a Good Samaritan, is she? She's a detective. She's been talking all night about being a detective.

And Detective Ally would investigate.

'Hello?' she calls.

No answer.

She steps inside, and her hand finds the light switch. At a flick, spotlights illuminate the entranceway. It opens up into a vast open-plan area, with a shimmering granite-surfaced kitchen and sleek sofas. On the glass-topped dining table there's a coffee pot and a laptop. On the kitchen counter there's two empty bottles of wine and two glasses. A tangerine-coloured scarf is draped over the back of the sofa, and a straw hat hangs on the back of a chair.

Gina Best left this house – is that her glass; her scarf? – and went to the party. And she never came back.

Ally steps cautiously into the space, her heart thrumming. She eyes the stairs.

'Hello?' she calls up. 'Is anybody there?'

Silence booms back.

Jayden would go up. But Jayden is a trained response officer. She puts one foot on the bottom stair.

Isn't it dangerous? Ray said to her at dinner. *The work?*

Occasionally, she replied. *Not always.*

But you're not afraid?

Of course. But you can't let that stop you, can you?

As she said it, she felt the pleasure of subverting his expectations.

'I'm coming up,' she calls now.

And, with each stair, she can hear her blood pumping harder.

As Ally reaches the landing, she doesn't call out again. Perhaps because the feeble sound of her own voice scares her. Perhaps because she no longer expects anyone to answer.

Ally doesn't know why she goes into the first bedroom. Later, Jayden will suggest it was on instinct; that she simply sensed that something was wrong, and she wouldn't stop until she found out what.

As she pushes open the door, light from the hallway pools in the room and she sees the shape of a man in bed. For a moment it looks like he's sleeping, but then she realises the bedspread isn't patterned – it's soaked in blood. And Harrison Loveday's eyes are wide open.

24

Gus is woken by a banging at his door. He didn't mean to nod off, but the television was chuntering away with an *Inspector Morse* episode he's seen a hundred times, and he had a blanket pulled over him which simultaneously made him feel very old and very infantile – but, most of all, very cosy. It's a jolt, this hammering, and in response his heart beats a raucous tattoo in his chest.

Not much good comes of a late-night knock, in Gus's opinion. Which perhaps goes to show that he hasn't quite lived his life to the fullest.

But it's Ally. Ally with a pale drawn face and wide eyes. Ally clutching his arm. Ally scaring him, actually.

'Gus, I need to call the police.'

And his mind thunders like a runaway horse. Ally being burgled, Ally being chased, anything at all happening to Ally.

'But are you alright?' he says, ushering her inside, shutting the door fast behind them. And it's a foolish question, because she's clearly not.

'It's . . . Sea Dream. Harrison Loveday.'

She takes her phone from her bag and, with a trembling hand, dials 999. But Gus? Gus is awash with relief. *Harrison Loveday. Not Ally.*

'Gus, Harrison is dead.'

And he immediately feels very bad indeed.

'Police, please,' she says into the phone. 'Porthpella Towans. Sea Dream . . . Yes. A man is dead. He's been murdered . . . Yes. I found the body . . . Yes, that's right. Ally Bright.'

Gus feels his blood run cold. Which is a sensation he's written about – indeed, as he did a final check of his manuscript, he realised he'd used the expression three times, which is at least twice too many – but never actually experienced. Not even when he saw Gina Best lying on the terrace.

Another murder? And Ally found the body?

Those spray-painted words that everyone is talking about in the village drop into his mind.

Who's next? Harrison Loveday.

Gus realises his mouth is dropped wide. Which doesn't make him look terribly in control. And yes, his blood is still cold.

He squeezes Ally's shoulder, but she turns slightly away from him. She's trying to focus on the call; to offer the right information. He gives her space and moves to the window, his head buzzing with questions. Pulling up the blind, he looks towards Sea Dream, his hulking, upmarket neighbour. *Not so fancy now.* But he sees nothing except for his own reflection, and the dim shapes of the room behind. Suddenly fearful of that old chestnut, the Face at the Window, he drops the blind and turns back to Ally.

'Thank you,' she's saying. 'I will.'

Her voice is more composed now. He can't quite trust his own yet, so he goes to put the kettle on. A cup of hot, sweet tea, that's the thing for shock. Or else he's got a bottle of brandy that hasn't seen the light of day since an ill-fated foray into Brandy Snaps last Christmas. A gift for Ally, but they turned out less 'snap' and more 'couldn't break with an axe'. As he's caught between the indecision of getting out mugs or glasses, he realises Ally is off the phone.

She's standing very still, her shoulders hunched. One hand is pressed to her mouth. It takes a moment for him to understand that she's crying.

'Oh, Ally,' he says, going to her. 'It's okay. You're okay.' Then, tentatively, daringly, 'I'm here.'

And he holds her in his arms. They stay that way until the sound of sirens fills the dunes.

25

Cat's awake feeding Benji, and Jayden's awake for moral support. Earlier, she told him how lonely she feels when she sits up with their boy in the middle of the night. Cat has never said she feels lonely; let alone when she's not actually by herself.

It wasn't like this with Jazz. I don't know why. I just feel like I'm the only person awake in the whole world, she said.

Apart from Benji. Then, realising that wasn't very helpful, he added, *And me. I'll be awake too, if it helps.*

No way. Divide and conquer.

But when Benji woke crying, Jayden pushed himself up on his pillows too.

Want me to sing? he said. *I could sing. Or read? For you, not Benji.*

Just you being here, Jay. And her hand found his, while the other settled the squalling Benji against her chest.

There's a fourth in the bed too. Jazzy, who crept in sometime around midnight. She's sandwiched between them, arms thrown out like she's sunbathing.

Jayden's phone buzzes. In the quiet of the bedroom, it's startling.

He quickly reaches for it, says, 'Sorry, I thought that was off.'

'God, who's texting at this time?'

Ally is texting at this time. Jayden sucks in a breath as he reads.

I know you won't see this until the morning, but Harrison
Loveday has been murdered. Killed in his bed.

Two words bolt into Jayden's mind: *who's next?*

He looks across to his wife; her already furrowed brow and
bitten lip.

'Cat,' he says gently, 'there's been another death.'

'What? No. There can't have been.' Then, 'Who?'

'Harrison Loveday. An artist.'

Jayden feels a grim kind of validation, already imagining the
headlines. The guy who threw out the name 'Arts Trail Killer'
in Hang Ten told Jayden he was a local journalist, here for the
weekend with his family. He'd heard about the suspicious death
at Island View House, then was one of White Wave Store's first
customers in the wake of the 'who's next?' discovery. Wenna, of
course, had been happy to share her theories – and then Jayden
unwittingly did the same. While he refused to go on record, there'll
be the line 'a source close to the investigation' in the article – or, if
he's really unlucky, 'a private investigator working the case'. Because
the journalist recognised him – *love your work, by the way, Jayden,*
he said, going for charm but hitting smarm. That guy's going to be
rubbing his hands at this one.

Jayden quickly taps out a reply. Because, apart from anything,
how does Ally know that Harrison Loveday was stabbed in his bed?
There's no way the news has broken yet.

I found him. I was walking past Sea Dream and saw the
door open. I went to investigate.

He shakes his head. 'Jeez, it was Ally who found him.'

'Does she want you to go down there?'

'She thought I wouldn't see the message until the morning.'

'But do you want to go down there?'

Jayden hesitates.

'Jay,' says Cat, 'Ally just found a dead body. I think you should probably go down there.'

'But . . . what about you guys?'

Between them, their daughter laughs in her sleep. Do all kids do that, or is it a Jazzy thing?

'Jay, we're good. Seriously. Go. This is important.'

This is two deaths in two days. This is who's next.

Jayden kisses all three of them, then he jets out the door.

'Are you sure you want to do this now, Al?'

She nods. 'I've already gone over it with the police. I want to do it with you too, in case I remember anything else.'

It's one o'clock in the morning. They're in The Shell House, and Jayden's making coffee. As he drove past Sea Dream he saw the tape, the lights, the uniforms. Part of him wanted to stop, but the other part needed to see Ally, to make sure she was okay. And to note down every detail, before it slipped away.

It's cosy with the lamps lit, but the atmosphere crackles with strange energy. Fox, sensing it, won't settle. His paws tap-tap the wooden boards as he turns laps. Ally sits on the edge of the sofa. She jumps as the coffee pot hisses and bubbles.

'Gus didn't stay?' asks Jayden, as he brings the mugs through. And he's careful, the way he says it. Last summer, he thought Ally and Gus would get together, but since then Gus has said that he's had an indirect but clear message that Ally's not in the market for a relationship. Friendship, all day long, but not a relationship.

When Jayden tried to press him – *indirect?* – because from where he was standing Ally seemed all in, Gus said, *She's still married to Bill, Jayden. Perhaps she always will be.*

'Gus offered, of course. But I'm fine. And it's not as if I imagine the killer is stalking the dunes. I've never been afraid at home.'

Those words: *who's next?*

Jayden doesn't want to say that, after tonight, maybe Ally should be wary. Maybe they all should.

'Perhaps Gus was afraid,' he says lightly.

Ally obliges with a low laugh. 'Now that's unfair. He was wonderful, actually.' She takes a deep breath, trying to steady herself, then says, 'As are you. Jayden, thank you for coming. It's above and beyond.'

'Cat said I had to. Plus, you're a witness, and for once we've got direct access.' He grins. 'That's worth getting out of bed for.'

'I want something to come of this. Of me finding Harrison, I mean. I want . . . to be useful.'

'You're going to be useful. *We're* going to be useful.'

'I don't think I gave the police anything very helpful.'

'If you hadn't investigated the open door, who knows when Harrison would have been found? It would have made the window for the murder a hell of a lot bigger. That's already helpful.' He looks at her carefully. 'Skinner didn't make you feel like you were interfering, did he, Al?'

Because Jayden wouldn't put it past the guy. Their relationship with Skinner seems to ebb and flow, case by case.

'He was nice,' says Ally.

'Good. Okay . . . If you're ready, do you want to talk me through it?'

So Ally begins to tell him, starting with leaving The Wreckers.

'You didn't see anyone on the walk over the dunes?'

'Not once I was clear of the village.'

'What about in the village? Any cars driving faster than usual? Anyone who struck you as behaving in a way that was out of the ordinary?'

She shakes her head. 'No. In truth . . . I was preoccupied. Probably not as observant as I might usually be.'

And Jayden doesn't have to be a detective to suspect that this is something to do with dinner with Ray.

'But you did notice that Sea Dream's front door was open.'

'And I immediately thought it was strange. The house was dark. I don't know, I just had a feeling, Jayden.'

Instinct. And he mentally applauds Ally. But it was reckless of her to go in. Unaccompanied; as defenceless as the next person, despite her smarts as a detective.

'Tell me what you did next.'

'I called out. I think I said "Hello?" I didn't just want to close the door and carry on past. It was possible Harrison was outside, and if he was without a key I didn't want to lock him out.'

'So you called out, and got no reply.'

'That's right. And I felt I should check inside. I suppose I thought the house could have been burgled. And Jayden, I just thought of Gina Best. Of her being killed and . . . now this anomaly at the place that she was staying. A minor anomaly, maybe, but to me it put a different light on things.'

Jayden nods. Ally was already making connections. Legitimate alarm bells ringing.

'So, I called out again, but I think I already knew no one was there. There was this heaviness to the silence. I went upstairs.'

'That was a bold move, Al.'

'But what else could I do? It would have felt alarmist to call the police at that point.'

'You could have called me.'

'At ten o'clock at night, just because a neighbour's left a door open? Cat wouldn't thank me for that.'

'You can always call me.'

'I . . . Oh, I don't know, Jayden. I was halfway up the stairs. I just kept moving. It didn't even feel like a choice at that point.'

Instinct.

'The first door was ajar. I pushed it open, and I saw him right away. The light from the hallway was enough. Harrison Loveday. Lying in bed, on his back. This look of . . . sheer horror frozen on his face.' She knots her fingers. 'Instantly I knew he was dead. And the blood, there was blood all over the bedspread. And it smelt. I've never smelt blood before, not like that. It was . . . horrific.'

A dark house. Ally all alone. A murder victim, the blood still fresh. It *was* horrific. Trained police officers would struggle with a scenario like that.

Jayden has struggled with a scenario like that.

'I froze. For two, three seconds, I was completely paralysed. And then . . . I checked his pulse.'

'You checked his pulse?'

'Even though I knew he was dead, I had to at least see. I was worried about contaminating the scene, but . . . I just approached very carefully, and . . . well, there was no pulse. After that I more or less ran. I went straight to Gus's and called 999.'

'You did great, Al,' says Jayden. 'Really good.'

She just shakes her head.

'What about the scene in the bedroom?' he asks. 'What can you remember about it? Did anything strike you as unusual, beyond the obvious?'

'He was naked on his top half. That was all I could see. There was an alarm clock lying on the floor, as if it'd been knocked. His clothes were draped over a chair.'

When Skinner took Ally's statement, he wouldn't have asked her about Harrison Loveday's wounds. He wouldn't have had to, because he had a CSI team on the case. And he'd seen the body himself.

'I think he was stabbed, Jayden,' she says, as if reading his mind. Her eyes offer wordless recognition. She knows all about what happened back in Leeds.

Him and Kieran, responding to a call on a summer's night. Hot pavements, air thick with noise. The brawl outside a pub; the speed of escalation. Kieran falling. Jayden hurtling through the crowd, catching him. Blood everywhere. *Everywhere.* Now, three years on, Jayden accepts that there was nothing he could have done. He accepts it, but he hates it.

'All that blood,' she says, so softly he can hardly hear her. 'And . . . gashes. There were gashes. On his chest.'

What happened to Kieran was Jayden's last job in uniform. It was logged as a stabbing in the city centre. Reported, in the papers, as an officer killed in the line of duty. To Jayden, it was the end of so much. And a line drawn between his time in the force and everything that lay after.

'I'm so sorry,' says Ally. 'I hope this isn't . . . bad memories.'

'No,' he says, bringing himself back to the here and now. 'It's different, Al. Do you think Harrison was attacked while he was asleep?'

'He could have been.'

If Harrison was lying in bed when Ally found him, the attack would have been relatively contained; restrained. The assailant could have delivered that first strike without meeting much resistance. And from the moment the knife went in, any fight that Harrison had in him would have been diminished.

'This was a deliberate, calculated attack,' he says.

'Like the poisoning. And Jayden, I overheard Mullins talking to Skinner. Gina Best's killer used cyanide.'

'Cyanide? Jeez. They meant business. Nice work, Al. Did you hear anything else?'

'Just that.' After a moment she says quietly, 'The vandalism, the "who's next?" message, how do you think it connects, Jayden?'

So he tells her about the journalist, and how he gave them the name 'Arts Trail Killer' in Hang Ten. Just a guy looking for a story. But now Harrison Loveday is the answer to that 'who's next?' question.

And the journalist has his headline.

They sit quietly, each lost in thought. Jayden looks to the dark window and the garden beyond, where Ally's studio lies. For the next week, it's open to all comers, just like all the other venues in and around Porthpella. Two days ago, this was a good thought: a trusting community throwing wide its doors. Now, it feels like an invitation for trouble.

Or something much worse.

26

'A serial killer?' Saffron's hands cover her mouth. 'You're not serious?'

'I didn't say "serial killer",' says Mullins, looking over his shoulder. Because in a place as small as Porthpella, you never know who's listening. According to Saffron, she and Jayden found that out yesterday. Well, that's Shell House for you, isn't it? Amateur through and through.

'It's a double murder. A serial killer is a whole other thing, Saff,' he says with more authority than he feels. 'You need at least three bodies. With time between them too, because it's not about the heat of the moment, it's a compulsion.'

'But what if they're just getting going?' says Saffron. 'What then? Look outside, Mullins, the writing's on the wall. And at White Wave too. Who's next?'

And to be fair, it's the exact question Mullins asked Skinner earlier – only without the soundtrack of a milk frother in the background.

After the night of action, and the early-morning briefing, Mullins has been sent home to grab a couple of hours' sleep, then as much overtime as he wants awaits. He's bone-tired, but he's up for it. That's why he's going for a hot chocolate and not a coffee; something to send him off to snoozeland, not buzz him up. And the reason he's cut into his sleep time by diverting via Hang Ten?

He could use a smile from Saffron, after seeing the state of Harrison Loveday. Hard on the heels of Gina Best, it was nasty stuff. Only, Saffron's not really smiling this morning.

'It's alright, Saff,' he says. 'We're going to catch them.'

'You'd better.'

'Be vigilant though, yeah?'

Her mouth makes a small 'o'. 'In what way?'

'In all the ways.' He doesn't want to freak her out. 'You should be anyway, hey? Everyone should be. Standard stuff, isn't it?'

Don't talk to strangers. Which isn't exactly an option, working in a coffee shop.

Her forehead crinkles with worry. She's still got her Hawaii tan, her strings of necklaces, cowrie shells and tiny blue beads, bright against her skin. Her hair is pink as a flamingo. *There's no one like her*, he thinks. *No one at all.*

'Milo's piece. At first I just thought it was someone wrecking his art.'

'Probably just kids, Saff. Getting lucky with this second death.'

And even Mullins knows that's not exactly the way to say it.

'Anyway,' says Saffron, 'Ally and Jayden are on the case too.'

'Course they are. See, us professionals are looking at the full picture, but unless we can establish a tangible connection . . . well, it's priorities, isn't it? Especially now, with this second murder . . .'

'But it's the second murder that should make you take the vandalism seriously.'

'I'll keep my ear to the ground, Saff.'

'I know you will,' she says, then holds up his cup. 'Cream and marshmallows?'

And he wants to say yes, but how would that look? A ruthless killer on the loose and Mullins is headed home for beddy-byes via a party-time hot chocolate.

'Maybe just a bit of cream,' he says. 'And sprinkles. Have you got any sprinkles?'

◆ ◆ ◆

Three hours later, Mullins is back at the station, rubbing his eyes as he puts his best foot forward. DCI Robinson has pulled everyone into the briefing room, which means Skinner's been toppled from the top spot. The DCI draws himself up to his full height and addresses the room. Mullins likes DCI Robinson. Even if he's a golfer.

'We're working on the basis that these two murders are linked,' says Robinson. 'Which makes them headline news. You'll have seen that stories are already breaking, so prepare for an onslaught. My personal least-favourite headline? "Arts Trail Killer: who's next?" Now, in the case of the beach house murder, we're appealing to the public for information, which means we'll be flooded with both well-meaning citizens and fanciful time-wasters. As you know, we need to take every piece of information seriously. We're drafting in extra help for the phone lines. It goes without saying that no one should speak to the press, though a Porthpella shopkeeper and another unnamed source "close to the investigation" already have. We don't need rumours and sensationalism whipping up panic. Those hacks are looking for a story, and the nastier the better. So don't give it to them. What we'll give them instead is a solved murder come tomorrow morning.' Robinson looks at his watch. 'Or Tuesday. Wednesday at the latest. Okay, troops? I'll let the detective sergeant take it from here.'

Skinner shuffles into the hot seat with a tweak of his tie. He passes his marker pen from hand to hand as he begins to speak.

'Harrison Loveday. Sixty-eight years of age. Celebrated portrait artist and star attraction of the Porthpella Arts Trail, stabbed

131

to death. There were no signs of a struggle, so it's our working assumption that the first blow was inflicted while the victim was asleep. Or possibly drugged, given the poisoning of Gina Best. We're waiting on toxicology. Should the deaths be linked, we have a chemist on our hands. The pathologist has estimated that death occurred between six and ten o'clock yesterday evening. The first timing is based on the last known communication with Harrison Loveday. Sunita Singh, owner of the Bluebird gallery, said she messaged Harrison to confirm he'd sold a piece. He replied with one word: "Good." This brevity is, according to Sunita, consistent with their previous dealings. He left the Bluebird at lunchtime, having complained of a headache. He intended to return to Sea Dream and sleep it off. It's possible he stayed at the beach house until his death. A public appeal for information might fill in some blanks. Just before ten o'clock, resident of the dunes Ally Bright—'

'Shell House Detective?' pipes someone.

'*Amateur* detective,' says Skinner. 'She was walking past and saw the front door was open. She went inside and found the body. The 999 call was made at 10.01 p.m. She estimated a two- or three-minute gap between discovering the victim and making the call. She left the property and phoned from a neighbour's house, that of Gus Munro.'

A four-hour window in which somebody stabbed Harrison Loveday to death.

'He was naked, wasn't he?' says Mullins suddenly.

'Save for his boxers.'

'So, he'd gone to bed? I mean, he wasn't still sleeping off his headache. Because if he was just having an afternoon lie-down, he'd have had his clothes on, wouldn't he?'

'Probably,' says Skinner. 'Where are you going with this, Mullins?'

'Trying to close that four-hour window, Sarge. Isn't it more likely that he went to bed later than earlier?'

'He was bereaved. The most important person in his professional life, and possibly his personal life too, was murdered not twenty-four hours before. All bets are off for acceptable bedtimes, wouldn't you say?'

And Mullins hears a snigger from behind. He feels the tips of his ears turn pink.

'No signs of forced entry?' calls out one of the Newquay lot.

Skinner shakes his head. 'Nope. Given how Loveday was found, we can assume that he opened the door to them, or they had a key, or the door was unlocked. And that on exiting the property in haste, the door was left open.'

That's a lot of different things to assume.

'If he was basically naked,' says one of the Newquay lot – sharp suit, big watch, oil-slick hair – 'could the killer have been in the bedroom with him by invitation? Maybe the headache was an excuse to ditch the exhibition and get back to his beach house. Just as things are getting interesting, the killer strikes.'

'It's a decent line of enquiry,' says Skinner. 'But a very different modus operandi compared to Gina Best's death. And, as said, there are no signs of a scuffle.'

'A versatile killer,' says DCI Robinson. 'Two victims, two MOs.'

'Or two different killers,' says someone else.

Or one killer, one intended victim.

The idea divebombs into Mullins's brain like a seagull after a chip.

'What if it was the same killer, but they bodged it the first time?' he says. 'What if the drink with the cyanide in it was meant for Harrison Loveday? And when the wrong person drank it, they had to try again.'

Mullins waits for a round of applause. Or at least a pat on the back.

'That's the obvious assumption,' says someone at the rear.

And just like that, he's a punctured balloon.

'I think we'd all prefer to have an inept brand of murderer on our patch than a serial killer,' says Skinner, 'because it significantly reduces the chance of them striking again, if they only meant to strike once in the first place. Which brings me to the elephant in the room. The graffiti incidents. Naturally, the media are loving it. Means they've got a picture to go with their headlines. We'll fingerprint both sites, check CCTV, but it feels unlikely that it's our perpetrator running around with a spray can out there.'

'Agreed,' says the DCI. 'The first MO was sly, the second rampant, but both were focused. The graffiti is clumsy, and frankly sensationalist. A vandal who thinks they're being funny.'

'But they did call the second death,' says Mullins. 'Didn't they?'

He feels his ears go pink again. He shouldn't have interrupted.

'It's my belief that that was a coincidence,' says Robinson, with a press-conference-style grin.

Mullins decides not to point out that the police aren't supposed to like coincidences.

27

At Island View House, Connor Rafferty is enjoying a rare brunch for one. Gideon sometimes reminds him of the border collies he grew up with on the farm: whip-smart, loyal, energetic, but so ceaselessly attentive that, sometimes, Connor wants to say, *Sit. Stay.* And then make a run for it.

He's joking, of course. But as he takes a forkful of avocado, breaks off a triangle of sourdough and dunks it in his egg, the silence around him is like the most beautiful symphony. Too beautiful, actually. Because taking much pleasure in anything feels wrong, given the circumstances.

After the party, Connor was disturbed, almost profoundly so. Not least because of the piercing memory of Harrison Loveday being present the night another woman died, all those years back in Chelsea. But together he and Gideon have picked apart their memories of that event – Meghan's death was ruled accidental. *There has to have been someone else here who knew Gina Best,* Gideon urged, *someone we can't possibly imagine.* Speculation has been buzzing through their house like a cloud of mayflies. Disputes, vendettas, spurned lovers, professional enemies; anything Gideon has floated feels as if it's from a soap opera, and wholly implausible for their corner of Cornwall. Connor has kept telling him the police will solve it, to let it lie, that rehashing it over and over helps no one. But when he thinks back to his own response – the immediate return to the ancient party in the Chelsea studio – he feels guilty. If Gideon is theorising at a gallop, it is Connor who first cracked the whip.

Then there is the question of 'who's next?' The words daubed across the Arts Trail poster, and crudely wrecking that beautiful piece of art at the surf school. It's an act that's divided the community, and divided their own household too. For Connor's part, he thinks it's no more than a stupid prankster. Gideon, however, believes in a more sinister explanation. *Even if it's not the voice of the killer, what kind of person seeks to amplify our fear like that? It's dangerous, Connor. And it's cruel.* And then he triple-checked all the locks on the doors before bed.

Yesterday they laid low, supervising the stream of police tramping through their home and garden, all bulky bodywear and buzzing radios and 'oh go on then' when they proffered tea. Today though, Sunday, Gideon's restless energy has turned to something useful. He's out on the trail, showing his face and reassuring the artists that the show is right to go on. Gideon even tried out the line 'It's what Gina would have wanted' yesterday, but Connor made a face. Because what Gina Best probably would have wanted was to never have come to Porthpella in the first place.

It was perhaps mean of Connor to decline to accompany Gideon this morning; his show of community and solidarity is genuine. But Connor also knows that Gideon's theorising will gather pace as he finds new audiences. There will be bucketloads of gossip. And Connor isn't into bucketloads of gossip. He's not even into teacups of the stuff. The only drawback in staying behind is that Gideon will want to do an extensive debrief when he returns.

With that thought in mind, Connor reaches into his pocket for his phone. How much time does he have left before the wanderer returns? But it's not there, so he takes a last bite of toast and goes to look for it. It's on his bedside table.

Fourteen missed calls.

Thirteen from Gideon, and one from Sunita. Plus, three voicemails.

He feels a pang of concern, sharp as a bee sting. There's nothing good about fourteen missed calls and three voicemails.

He's just about to listen to the voicemails when he hears a door bang, and fast footsteps. His own name shouted, with such a note of urgency that Connor's heart drops.

Gideon.

'I'm here!' he says, going out into the hall. 'Gid, what is it?'

As soon as he sees him, Gideon slams on the brakes.

'My God. My God, you're okay.'

'Of course I'm okay.'

'You weren't picking up, so I thought . . . something terrible had . . .'

Connor places his hands on Gideon's shaking shoulders. His eyes are hectic as he tells Connor that last night Harrison Loveday was stabbed to death in his rented house in the dunes. That there are police and reporters everywhere in the village because there's a killer on the loose in Porthpella. And everybody's saying they're targeting the Arts Trail.

'Who's everybody?' says Connor.

'Everybody,' repeats Gideon. 'We can't just stand by. Not on our watch.'

'Gid, I don't see . . .'

Gideon pulls himself up to his full height. Says, 'You know what we have to do, don't you? Ally Bright and Jayden Weston. We have to hire them.'

28

'I'm still wrapping my head around it,' says Ray. 'I'm sorry, just . . . it doesn't seem real.'

'I know,' says Ally.

But the image of the dead Harrison Loveday is imprinted on her mind with shocking clarity. *It's real.*

They're on the veranda. Ally has stuck a note over the Arts Trail easel that says: *Closed today, sorry.* It's chilly out, despite the spring sunshine. A lively breeze is pushing over the dunes and the blue sky is blotted with clouds of all shapes and sizes, some more threatening than others. The sea is a strange colour: milky, almost green; the horizon a dark blue line. Ray is staring out at it all.

'That lighthouse,' he says. 'Don't suppose anybody mans it?'

Ally looks at him questioningly. 'They're all automated.'

'Course they are.' He gives a short, sharp bark of laughter. 'Sorry. Ridiculous. I don't know what to say. Or think. I suppose you're used to this.'

She feels her brow wrinkling. 'Used to it how? Death?'

'Murder, I mean. The cases. You and Jayden.'

'I don't ever want to be used to it,' she says quietly.

She doesn't add that finding a body is a quite different matter. The feeling she had as she pushed open that door and saw Harrison lying there is, she thinks, indescribable.

'Do you feel safe here, Ally?'

Ray turns his eyes from the lighthouse and looks at her intently.

'Because . . . if you're at all uncertain about being on your own at the moment, there's options. My rental is a two-bed. You'd be very welcome—'

'Ray, I'm absolutely fine.'

'But it's so isolated, out here in the dunes.'

'I'm used to it.' Then she adds, 'I love it here. It's my home.'

'But if this killer really is targeting artists . . . you might feel safer in the heart of the village. Plus . . . did I tell you I know karate?'

'You know karate?'

'I used to know karate. At least, I know how to spell it.'

She laughs. 'Oh, well now I feel very safe.'

'Promise me you'll consider it? If things . . . carry on.'

'You're kind. But I very much hope they won't carry on.'

'Yes, quite.' He rubs at the back of his head. 'Look, how does it work? Hiring you, Ally?'

'Hiring me?'

'Whoever killed Harrison, and Gina Best. I want them caught.'

'And they will be.'

Ray looks down at his hands. There's a cut on the side of his thumb and he runs a finger along it absently.

'What happened to your finger?'

'Grappling with the dodgy lock on my place last night,' he says. 'I stayed on after you left. Had a couple more jars with the locals. Look, Ally. I'm serious. I read about you and Jayden. I told you that, didn't I? The cases you've solved. Cases where the police just haven't got it or didn't want to. Surely you want in on this?'

'A moment ago you were trying to protect me, now you want me on the case?'

'Can't I do both?'

The look in his eyes is so sincere that Ally finds she can't hold it.

'Ally, you know the Arts Trail,' he says. 'You know artists. How many of the police can say that? You have to work on this. And . . . I want a stake in it. I want to officially hire you.'

Ally shakes her head. 'Ray, Jayden and I are already—'

'Look, Harrison was my mate. A long time ago, and not for very long, but still. Some people . . . stick.'

The appeal in his voice is undiluted. Ray flicks a glance at her, then pushes his hand through his hair. It's a precise combination of gestures that she has seen before, countless times. A long time ago, and not for very long.

But still.

'I'd like to pay you and Jayden to investigate. I've got the money. My old man popped his clogs a few years back and it turns out he was hiding his financial light under a bushel. The mean old sod was loaded. Ally, I live a simple life. A quiet life. My little house. My veggies. Alf. I don't spend much on anything. But what's happened here? This hellish thing in this beautiful place? The best people have to be on it. You're modest, you always were, but I've read about every one of your cases. And I want you to solve this, Ally. You and Jayden.'

Ally thinks of Jayden and how the campsite doesn't bring his family any income through the winter. They often bend the rate card on their detective services, or don't accept anything at all. But this time? Ray's money from the father that he didn't even like? She remembers, years back, Ray saying, *The only thing my dad and I have in common is we both like a drink, Ally. But he gets nasty with it. Big pair of fists. So, the comparison stops there, thank God.*

'Plus . . .' He hesitates; sends her another meaningful look. 'It feels like the right thing to do. I don't want to run away this time.'

Ally can hear her phone ringing inside the house, and she jumps up to get it. Rather too fast, probably.

'It could be important,' she says apologetically.

She's expecting Jayden, or perhaps Gus. He messaged earlier checking in, and in the flurry she hasn't replied yet. She must, or he'll worry.

But it's Sunita.

'Ally,' she says, 'I heard the dreadful news. I can't believe it. And I'm so sorry you had to go through that. Finding him.'

Ally murmurs something reassuring.

'Then that awful omen on the map. At Mahalo too. It's sickening. Listen, Gideon and I have just been talking. We, the Arts Trail committee, want to hire you and Jayden. We've got some budget left, and we'll both contribute separately too. These shocking deaths . . . they feel personal. Personal to the Arts Trail, Ally. We have to do something.'

Ally's about to say something about there being possible connections but that it's best not to jump to any conclusions, but Sunita runs on:

'I live alone, Ally. We both do. I don't know about you, but I won't sleep at night until this person is caught. I keep hearing the words "who's next?" in my head. It's terrible.'

After Jayden left earlier, Ally checked the bolt on the door. She settled on the sofa under a blanket, because it felt better than tucking herself away in the bedroom; a sentry, sleeping with one eye open. She told Jayden she never feels afraid at home – but that isn't always true.

'And Gideon's convinced they'll strike again,' says Sunita. 'Two days, two murders. What happens on day three?'

It's no wonder that this is the talk of the village, because in the early hours of this morning, it was the talk of The Shell House too. Meanwhile, certain news outlets are having a field day, with pictures of the spray-painted writing alongside photographs of the victims. It feels, to Ally, gory and sensationalised – as if Porthpella has become a show that anyone can tune in to.

'I know Saffron hired you to investigate who vandalised Milo's art, before she realised what was going on. And of course it's a violation, but . . . the picture has changed. Gideon's convinced it's a campaign against the Arts Trail, and while he's prone to hyperbole . . . honestly, I'm with him. And it terrifies me to say that.'

Ally looks to the veranda, where Ray sits watching the water. She feels a rush of tenderness. Somehow, they're in this together.

'Sunita,' says Ally, 'I need to speak to Jayden, but . . . we'll do it. There's actually someone else who wants to hire us too. Perhaps there can be a pooling of resources. Have you met Ray Finch? He came to see Harrison yesterday, and—'

'Of course. He's charming, Ally, very charming. He said he was an old friend of yours. He wants to hire you? Well, good. That's a show of strength. It's not that we don't trust the police, Ally, but this is a tragedy in our little community. Not just Porthpella, but the artistic community. It's our duty to do all we can.'

Ally agrees to speak to Jayden and call Sunita straight back.

'Then can you both come for a meeting at the Bluebird?' says Sunita. 'With your friend Ray too. We can tell you everything we know. Because that's the other thing I have to tell you. We do have . . . ideas. Motive – that's what they call it, isn't it? We have some ideas on motive. And if Ray cares enough to hire you, perhaps he's got some ideas too.'

29

Jayden is staring hard at a giant seagull. Its massive blade-like beak is stuffed full of chips and its face is pure trouble; a winged gangster who knows he can always get away with it. This Milo Nash piece, on the side of the chip shop – just across the square from White Wave Stores – was painted a couple of years ago and the colours are as vibrant as ever: the orange of the gull's feet; the splatter of ketchup, like blood on the ground. Why hasn't this piece been vandalised? Does the surf school have a part to play after all? Jayden turns on the spot. Cottages ring the square, and there's The Wreckers Arms with its steady flow of Easter holiday customers. Even under the cover of night there'd be a chance of someone being seen here. Unfortunately, CCTV doesn't seem to have come to Porthpella: White Wave Stores has never had it, and nor has The Wreckers or the Bluebird.

Jayden walks back to the community noticeboard and looks at the space where the Arts Trail poster was. It's been taken into evidence by the police now, but it's as if the words are still there in glaring white: *WHO'S NEXT?*

That's the headline the sensation-courting newspapers are loving too. That local journalist started the ball rolling, and now the 'Arts Trail Killer' is everywhere. Even his mum-in-law is at it. Sue turned up at their door earlier, bearing a freshly baked cake and saying, *Go and do what you do, Jayden, because someone needs to catch this Arts Trail Killer. Just be careful. You're a father of two now.*

Like he needs telling.

It feels good to be officially hired though, and with the prospect of a pay cheque. They're not pushing Saffron's request aside, because in looking for the killer, Jayden's confident they'll find the spray-painter too. Maybe they're even one and the same: a publicity-seeking individual, enjoying the attention. *Who's next?* as both signature and threat.

And someone like that? Scary. Really scary.

He sees Ally then, walking across the square, headed for their briefing at the Bluebird. Ray strolls beside her with his hands in his pockets. He looks untroubled; happy, in fact. And then Jayden's wondering why he's making any particular observation of Ray at all.

Because he's clearly someone who was important to Ally once.

Because he knew Harrison Loveday. And, in passing, Gina Best.

Because basically Jayden's looking at everyone, and everything, right now. He's suspicious of everyone and everything.

Jayden can imagine the energy down the station at this moment. People trying to ignore the headlines, but the media attention will feel like a storm lashing against the windows. The pressure to get this solved before the killer strikes again. A thought that's not theatrical, but logical: until they understand why Gina and Harrison were killed, there's every chance someone else will be next.

'Jayden,' says Ally. 'You remember Ray.'

They shake hands. Ray's grip is firm.

'Thanks for doing this,' says Ray. He nods towards the Bluebird. 'And good to know I'm not the only one thinking this way.'

Over Ray's shoulder, Jayden catches a movement. A young woman is hovering on the corner, watching them. Everything about her posture looks wary. If he and Kieran were out on patrol, they'd have noted her; slowed. Jayden makes a mental list: Caucasian female, slight build, mid-thirties, long, light brown hair, cream-coloured coat.

'Are you wondering why this one's intact?' asks Ally, nodding to the seagull piece.

'Yeah, I was. And I've asked Saffron to get Milo more involved. See if anyone he knows recognises the style. It could be a riff on someone's tag.'

But it's a long shot, because there is no style as far as Jayden can see. Just simple block capitals.

'That's good thinking,' she says. 'And we must ask the committee if there was anyone who objected to Milo Nash being included. The trail has been quite traditional in the past. It feels notable that of all the potential canvases, they chose the Arts Trail poster and his new piece.'

Ray looks from one to the other. 'Are you sure you've got time to bother with the graffiti side of things? I mean, I can see why the gutter press are getting excited, but surely it's just . . . No, sorry, ignore me. I'm not teaching Granny to suck eggs.'

'If there's a connection, we'll find it,' says Jayden. Then he lowers his voice. 'Al, when we go into the Bluebird, just take a quick look at that woman across the square. Tell me if you recognise her. Because she's been watching us this whole time.'

'What woman?' says Ray, with a noisy attempt at a whisper. He spins round.

And the woman flips her hair, then disappears down the lane.

◆ ◆ ◆

'Okay,' says Sunita. 'I called this meeting, but I don't actually know how this works. Do you liaise with the police? So, whatever we say here, you say to them too?'

'Not necessarily,' says Jayden. 'We make a call on it.'

They've pulled together a couple of tables from the café area. On the other side of the stone archway the gallery gleams white, Harrison's portraits punctuating the space. As they walked through, Ally looked at each picture carefully. Jayden heard Ray say, *What a shame that these are his last works.*

Gideon clears his throat. 'The fact is, it looks like sabotage. Of a particularly gruesome kind. That's what the vandalism is shouting loud and clear, isn't it? Which means Gina and Harrison are victims in the truest sense: their connection to the Arts Trail got them killed. And if it is about the Arts Trail, then we three, as the committee, are vulnerable too, aren't we? And you as well, Ally.'

'Gid, I really don't think we're vulnerable,' says Connor. 'No more than anyone else.'

'I feel vulnerable,' says Sunita, 'but mostly I feel heartbroken. That this should happen here. Now.'

'We're ruminating on taking the unprecedented decision of closing the trail,' says Gideon. 'We don't want to, but if it's inappropriate or dangerous to continue then we must.'

'I don't think we should,' says Connor. 'Some artists' livelihoods depend on their sales from this week.'

'Yes, but what about their *lives*?' says Gideon.

'What have the police advised?' asks Jayden.

'They haven't yet,' says Sunita.

'Of course they want to play it down,' says Gideon. 'But they've been dusting the noticeboard out there for fingerprints, so they're clearly taking "who's next?" seriously.'

Jayden nods. 'They'll be looking at all angles. And if it's a question of public safety, or any interference with the investigation, they'll advise closure. Have they been to see you all this morning?'

'They came to see me early,' says Sunita. 'I suppose because I'm hosting Harrison's show. And the text message I sent him, saying that he'd sold a piece, was his last known communication with anyone.'

'What time was that text?'

'Six o'clock, Jayden.'

'I saw the red dot just now,' says Ally. 'Who did he sell the fisherman piece to?'

'A couple who have a holiday home along the coast. Carol Markham was the woman's name. Nothing remarkable about them, to be honest.'

'The police came up to see us,' says Gideon. 'God, when was it, Connor? Around lunchtime. Not long after I got home from the village. I suppose because Harrison was a visitor here, they're following up with all known contacts. But, honestly, we had very little to tell them. Except for the fact that it has to be about the Arts Trail.'

'How did they take that?' asks Jayden.

'Wrote it in their notebooks,' says Connor, 'but that's about it. If they were looking at us as suspects . . .'

'Why would they be looking at us as suspects?' asks Gideon.

'Because everyone's a suspect.' Connor shrugs. 'Anyway, they weren't exactly asking probing questions about the trail. Just focusing in on Harrison Loveday.'

'And Gina, of course,' adds Gideon.

'What about you, Ray?' says Sunita. 'You got there first, wanting Ally and Jayden on the case. Do you feel as if the police aren't doing enough?'

'Well, I've always been a little bit anti-establishment,' he says with a grin, 'but I'm sure they're doing the best they can. And yep, they pounded on my door this morning. I guess as I'm one of the few people here who actually knew Harrison, I'm a person of interest. Right, Ally?'

'I expect you are,' she says. 'Just because you knew him.'

'Ray, when did you last see Harrison?' asks Jayden.

'I told the police I saw him yesterday lunchtime, here at the gallery. I tried to tempt him for a pint, thought he'd appreciate the support, but he said he had a headache coming on. We chatted for a few minutes, then I left him to it. He was in decent spirits. As you noted yourself, Jayden.'

'Yes, he left the show around two o'clock,' says Sunita. 'I think he bit off more than he could chew, turning up to man it. What with Gina.'

'How did you spend the afternoon, Ray?' asks Jayden.

'Me?' Ray shrugs. 'I followed the trail. I'd only been planning to stay the weekend, so I wanted to get round the whole thing. We've similar set-ups in Suffolk and I wanted to compare notes. There's a lot of enthusiastic amateurs in our neck of the woods, but some decent talent too. Don't ask me where I fall on that spectrum.'

'Not that I don't consider us a leading light,' says Gideon, 'but it is a long way to come for some research.'

Ray levels a look at him.

'I wanted to take the chance to see Harrison. His exhibitions are few and far between. Seemed like a good way to kill two birds with one stone. Sorry, unfortunate language.'

'Ah yes,' says Gideon. 'You said that in your email to me. I liked the cut of your jib. "I've heard you're hosting a party – may I crash it?"'

'Once upon a time I'd just have gatecrashed,' laughs Ray.

Jayden frowns. 'Ray, I thought you said you went to the party as Harrison's guest?'

'Did Harrison tell you he was taking part in the trail?' asks Sunita.

Their questions overlap, and it's Sunita that Ray turns to. *Deliberate avoidance?*

'No,' he says, passing a hand across his mouth. 'No, I saw that he was the guest artist and then I dropped him a line.'

'Search engine optimisation doing its thing,' says Connor. 'Good to hear.'

'Well, actually . . . Oh hell, I might as well come clean. I was in a maudlin mood, happens to the best of us, and thought I'd wander down memory lane, look up a few old acquaintances and see where life had taken them.' Ray turns to Ally. 'I saw you were based in Cornwall still. And then I started reading about Porthpella. And I couldn't believe that Harrison Loveday was exhibiting here. What were the chances? It was a spontaneous thing, really, this weekend.'

'What terrible luck,' says Gideon. 'That it should end like this, I mean. Don't let it put you off spontaneity.'

Ray grins. 'Oh, I won't.'

'Let's not get off-topic,' says Sunita. 'Look, we think it's time we shared our thoughts. We wanted to tell you about people who have a possible grudge against the Arts Trail. Not to . . . point fingers. It's not a witch hunt.'

'No,' says Gideon, 'it's a hunt for a killer. So, if there are fingers to be pointed, then . . .'

Connor holds his hands up. 'I've got to say, I'm not quite on the same page as these guys with the so-called suspect. Not because I disagree – I just think there's a lot we don't know, and a little knowledge is a dangerous thing . . .'

'Well, Lara Swann is a dangerous individual,' says Gideon. 'And there's no two ways about it.'

30

'I don't get why they haven't told the police about Lara Swann,' says Jayden. 'If they think she's a genuine threat.'

Ally and Jayden are walking back over the dunes, the gathering at the Bluebird having morphed into a committee meeting. Item one on the agenda: should the Arts Trail carry on? Sunita had already put a 'Closed due to unforeseen circumstances' notice on the gallery window.

Harrison Loveday's name hasn't been released to the press because, according to Jayden, they can't have notified his next of kin yet, but everyone around here knows who the second victim is. Meanwhile Ray has returned to his rented cottage. He seemed, Ally thought, at a bit of a loose end.

'I think,' says Ally, 'they're worried about sounding petty. Because if the police turned up at Lara Swann's door in the middle of a murder investigation, talking about the emails she sent to the committee, she'd never forgive Sunita and Gideon and Connor for sending them there. And in a community as small as this, that kind of rift can be very difficult.'

Gideon had printed out the emails, ready for Ally and Jayden to look at. Ray whistled as he read over their shoulders. *I almost admire her vigour*, he said. Connor obliged with a laugh, but Sunita and Gideon seemed affected by Lara's response in a deeper way.

'Okay,' says Jayden, 'I'll buy that. Us turning up, saying we're speaking to everybody, feels like less of an accusation than uniforms or badge-carrying detectives on the doorstep. By the way, it was Lara Swann watching us on the square. Her description matches.'

They pause at the crest of a dune. It's one of those perfect spring days when the sky is an artist's palette, a swirl of blue and white. The air is crisp as an apple. Out on the water, a handful of surfers bob like seals.

'What's your gut instinct?' says Ally.

Jayden rolls his shoulders; stretches. She knows he's tired, but his energy never seems to dim.

'Lara Swann obviously bears a grudge, right? Maybe she's the one behind "who's next?" and wanting to cause a scare, but to kill? I think she'd have to be . . . unwell. Or psychopathic. I wonder if she has a record. I'm going to ask Mullins to run a check.'

'But wouldn't that alert the police to her? The committee won't thank us, if we end up doing the opposite of what they asked for. Which was a discreet investigation.'

Even as she says it, Ally disagrees with herself. Because the image of Harrison Loveday, blood-soaked, eyes glazed, rises up. She stares fixedly at the view, trying to root herself. The island lighthouse. The white-topped waves. The first sea pinks blooming on the clifftop. All that matters is catching the killer.

'Ray doesn't care about community relations,' says Jayden. 'And he's hired us too.'

'He has.'

Jayden looks at her sideways. 'I don't want to discredit him, but . . .'

'But?'

'I reckon he's got an ulterior motive, Al.'

'And what would that be?'

'I think he likes being around you.'

'*Jayden.*'

'I'm not saying he doesn't care about Harrison Loveday. But beyond the shared history at Falmouth, they didn't have that much of a connection, did they? And it's kind of a big thing to put your hand in your pocket and fund a private investigation.'

Ally would be lying if she said that hadn't crossed her mind. Together, they walk on.

'The other possibility is that there's more to it than Ray's said. A more significant connection with Harrison and Gina.'

'Well, I know which I'd prefer,' says Ally, dryly. 'On balance.'

'It's a minor detail but . . . didn't Ray say that he went to the party with Harrison?'

'Did he? I can't remember.'

'At your studio this morning he told us he was Harrison's plus-one. But then Gideon said Ray emailed him to request an invite.'

Ally furrows her brow. 'You sound suspicious.'

'I'm fair-minded, Al, because that suspicion goes for the committee too. Four people have hired us to investigate the murders, right? And as far as we know they're the only four people round here who, at some point, have had contact with either Gina or Harrison. It makes sense that this case feels personal for them. But as far as the police are concerned, they've all got to be suspects too.'

'You don't really think one of them did it, do you?'

Sunita is one of Ally's favourite people in Porthpella. She knows Gideon and Connor less well, but their reputation in the community is one of openness and generosity. They hosted the Arts Trail party out of their own pockets, wanting it to feel like a proper celebration for everyone taking part. And Ray? She doesn't know Ray at all these days. But she did once. Once, she knew him better than almost anyone.

'I think,' says Jayden, 'we rule no one out. Because, being cynical, it could be a tricky little decoy, to hire us, right? To send us off in one direction, in order to cover up another? Wanting updates on the case too, along the way. Maybe even inside info on what the police are doing.'

What happens now? Sunita asked. *Will we get regular updates?* To which Jayden replied that they tend to just get on with it.

Ally lets this thought of Jayden's settle. He's right, of course. They can't rule anyone out. Her head feels very full suddenly. Perhaps she's too close to this. The Arts Trail. The sudden appearance of Ray. Finding Harrison's body.

'Al, I don't want to freak you out. I'm just being . . .'

'You're being a good detective.'

'But for what it's worth, Lara Swann's a solid lead. So, from here, I'm thinking we do some desk research, get the basics, then head out to see her.'

Immediately she feels calmed at the prospect. Ally has always liked the methodical parts of an investigation, and an internet search can be akin to wandering the strandline, looking for a glint of something interesting. She'll snip some garden mint, brew some tea, and then, piece by piece, they'll build a picture of Lara Swann.

31

'Sarge, we've had a breakthrough.'

Not a sentence that Mullins gets to say too often, that. And it tastes as sweet as one of Saffron's oven-fresh brownies.

'Talk to me.'

Mullins passes him a printout. 'Harrison Loveday's phone records. Nothing much to see, except for this . . .' He points. 'Three messages over the last week, sent to someone called Annabel. She reads them but doesn't reply.'

Skinner reads aloud. '"I'm going to be in Cornwall, staying in Porthpella, from this Friday. Would love to see you, darling." Then the next one: "Just arrived here. Say the word and I'll come." And then, "I won't keep pressing you, but I would very much love to see you." He sent that last one yesterday afternoon. Just hours before he died.' Skinner looks up. 'And the tech boys and girls have traced this Annabel, have they?'

'They have.' Mullins puffs his chest out a little bit. 'Annabel Crosby. She lives in Carbis Bay.'

'What do we know about her?'

'Age forty-five. Works in admin for a holiday lettings company.'

'Girlfriend, do you think? Or Loveday wishes she was? There's a caution to his tone, as if he's already thinking he's going to get knocked back. But he's not above a bit of emotional blackmail.'

Skinner offers a cockeyed grin. 'And don't say "Takes one to know one." Alright, you and I are making a house call.'

'What about the Newquay lot?'

'Between hassling the lab for the next set of results, following up on the misinformation from the great British public, and keeping on those known connections of Best's and Loveday's from the statements, they've got their hands full. This one's for us, Mullins. By the way, "breakthrough" might have been overstating it. But it's something, and so far, we've got diddly.'

'But that's not all of it,' says Mullins. 'The name Crosby rang a bell. So, I went back through the statements from the party, and there it was: Donald Crosby. He's one of the exhibiting artists.'

'I know who he is. Bit of a sad sack. What are you telling me?'

'This Annabel? She's only Donald's niece.'

A sunny Sunday afternoon in the Easter holidays, and the road to Carbis Bay is bumper-to-bumper. Most will be shunting on to St Ives, but that doesn't help them.

'Shall we stick the lights on, Sarge?'

'Take this next left, Mullins.'

'What, this one?'

All Mullins can see is a track cutting through a field, but he's already making the turn, bumping over the uneven ground.

'That's it. We'll give the farmer a scare if he sees us, but just follow it on round. We'll pick up the main road just outside of Carbis.'

Mullins puts his foot down, a cloud of dust in the rear-view mirror. A patchwork of fields dips to the left. Off-road, cross-country, Mullins feels like he's off the telly. *This is how serial killers are caught!*

Sorry, double murderers.

As they cut through a yard, they pass a barn crowded with square-headed bullocks. Mullins thinks of Shoreline Vines and the last case with Ally and Jayden. Sinister bunch, bullocks. He's surprised he hasn't heard more from the Shell House lot today. Ally must have taken a knock, finding Harrison Loveday like that. One thing he knows, Jayden will have her back.

Skinner winks at him. 'Nippy enough for you, Mullins?'

'Nippy enough.'

Then they're out and on to a lane, and there's the trundling traffic of the A road again. Two minutes later, they're pulling into the driveway of a small family home, on a quiet cul-de-sac. The kind of place where people wash their cars on Sundays and do back-garden barbecues if the weather turns out nice. Little kids on bikes, mucking about. There's an old Ford Fiesta in the driveway, with a faded 'Baby on Board' sticker.

'They're home,' says Mullins.

'Unless they're a two-car household,' says Skinner. 'Or they're off for a Sunday afternoon walk. Using their legs. Stranger things have happened. Ah, they're home.'

A sturdy-looking woman is standing at the doorway, a pre-schooler pulling at her arm. She wears pink leopard-spotted leggings and a faded sweatshirt that says *Hello Sunshine*. Her face is stormy.

'I know what this is about,' she says as they get out the car. 'I wondered if you'd find me.'

32

There's no answer at Lara Swann's house. Jayden steps back and looks up. Westerly Manor is a large grey-stone farmhouse, not dissimilar to Cliff and Sue's but without any of the genuine farm accoutrements. No randomly strewn tractor tyres or sharp-toothed plough fixings or bags of grain; probably no rats in the barns either. From where they're standing, Jayden can't see any neighbouring properties. The place feels kind of lonely; forgotten.

'It's not as remote as it feels,' says Ally, as if reading his thoughts. 'Just beyond that dip is the potter Pamela Trescoe's house. Venue 15 on the trail.'

'So we'll talk to Pamela on the way back? Suss out how well she knows Lara.'

'Yes, we should.'

Jayden's just raising his hand to knock again when the door opens. And there's Lara. The watchful woman from the square. Her long hair is parted dead centre and hangs like curtains, half-covering her face. She's skinny, swamped in a massive cardigan. The buttons are red apples, a playful touch to an otherwise serious demeanour.

'Yes?' she says.

They've done their research on Lara Swann. She's not on social media but she does have a basic website showcasing her work.

Illustrations, mainly of minimal, angular figures: a woman with a cat on her lap; a man with a saxophone. Jayden's no art critic, but he can see why Lara didn't make it on to the Arts Trail. If he's being really harsh, he can imagine Jazzy knocking up something similar. But Lara Swann's biography, on the 'About Me' page, makes a lot of her artistic heritage. A paragraph is given over to her mother, Billie Swann. *A legendary figure in the London art scene, Billie Swann's work – ranging from photography to printmaking and gouache – is a favourite with collectors. Growing up with this formidable creative presence has made Lara Swann the artist, and the woman, she is today.*

Ally read it with interest. Said, *Is that a good thing, 'formidable'?*

They agreed Ally would lead.

'Hello,' she says. 'Sorry to disturb you. Are you Lara?'

As Lara nods, Ally offers a tidy explanation for their presence here. She says they're concerned about the deaths – she deliberately says 'deaths', not murders – and that they know there are various rumours flying around after the 'who's next?' graffiti. So, they're making house-to-house enquiries. An all-hands-on-deck approach – that only seems right in a community such as theirs. Oh, and they happen to be private detectives.

'So no one sent you?' says Lara, eyes narrowed.

'No. Porthpella's such a small place, and these deaths, they've rocked the whole village, but especially the artistic community.'

And the way she puts it is inclusive. Lara as part of that community; not an outcast, rejected by the committee.

'You must be feeling it,' says Ally. 'Especially up here on your own. I'm down in the dunes, rather a remote spot, which I usually love, but I'd be lying if I didn't say I was a little worried.'

Nice, Al.

'It's those words "who's next?"' says Jayden. 'It's stirring things up.'

He doesn't want to go in too hard with the graffiti, but he's still interested in Lara's reaction to it. But Lara ignores him and focuses on Ally.

'I know your work,' she says. 'You're on the trail. And before that you had pieces at the Bluebird. You're afraid, are you? You think artists should be afraid? Because of the murders or because of the graffiti, or both?'

'I think we should be vigilant,' says Ally. 'And both, I suppose. Because I'm not sure the two can be separated.'

Lara folds her arms across her chest, tight as a belt.

'So what is this, neighbourhood watch?'

Jayden's father-in-law called them that once. Way back, when Cliff thought the first murder they'd solved was a fluke.

'As Ally said,' says Jayden, 'we're private detectives.'

'I know who you are. I've read up on you.'

Interesting.

'There's not much to read.' He grins.

Lara looks down at her feet, scuffs the door sill.

'You solved the vineyard thing. And the Rockpool House case. My mother knew Baz Carson a little. From back in the day in London. That's where I grew up. We actually used to live in Soho. I mean, does anyone live in Soho? Not many kids' doors to knock on round there. No skipping ropes in the street.' She darts a look in their direction, then drops her eyes again. 'Anyway. . . Now you're trying to work out who killed Gina Best and Harrison Loveday, are you?'

'Well—' begins Ally.

'There's no point talking to me,' Lara cuts in. 'I'm not part of this community. And I'm not on the Arts Trail. But then I expect you know that already, if you're any good at your job. Though all you need to do is pick up a programme to see that.'

'Sometimes it's useful to get more of an outside perspective,' Ally says.

Lara flinches. And Jayden wonders if it was the word *outside* that did it.

Lara's kept herself to herself ever since she took over the house from her mother, Gideon told them at the gallery. *The trail would have been a good opportunity to get to know her, but the work just isn't up to snuff. And, turns out, she's barmy.*

For all Lara's shuttered manner, there's a runaway style to her speech that makes Jayden feel like she doesn't say that much, that often, to that many people. They need to keep the conversation going.

'But you were at the launch party, weren't you? At Island View House?' says Ally. 'I think I spotted you.'

They only know Lara was at the launch party because of Gideon and the committee telling them. Jayden watches her response carefully.

'I wasn't invited,' she says, 'but I went anyway. I only stayed five minutes. I didn't like the atmosphere. And before you ask, I didn't see that poor woman get poisoned.'

'What was it about the atmosphere?' asks Ally.

'Cliquey,' she says. 'Exclusive. Bitchy.'

'Did you see Gina Best and Harrison Loveday?' asks Jayden.

'I wouldn't have known who they were. I could have been standing right next to them for all I know.'

But if Lara is bitter that she's not been included in the trail, surely she'd check out the artists who did make the cut? Especially the star attraction, Harrison Loveday. She appears brittle, Lara, but somehow hard-edged. Could she handle a spray can? Move from the square to the beach without anyone catching a glimpse of her? What about being capable of a whole lot more?

'How long have you lived in Porthpella, Lara?' says Jayden. 'This is a great house, by the way.'

'Well, it's my mother's,' she says. 'And if she had her wits about her, I expect she'd have sold it by now. But it's too late for that, so it's mine, I suppose. I moved in before Christmas. I thought, "Why not? It's just sitting there." One of those second homes everyone round here hates. Well, it's my first home now. My only home.'

'It can be hard to move to a place like this, where everyone knows everyone. Especially from the city. I was in Leeds before, so imagine the culture shock.'

The point of connection is genuine. There were times in the beginning when Jayden felt like a fish out of water in Porthpella. He still does, sometimes. And Lara is all on her own. She flicks a look in his direction. He smiles back at her.

'Look, can we come in for a minute? We'd love to pick your brains about some of the people involved with the Arts Trail.'

Lara shakes her head; plucks at one of the apple-shaped buttons on her cardigan. He shouldn't have suggested they come in. He's seen it before: you push that bit too hard, cross a line you didn't know was there, then a sudden shutdown, a fast retreat.

'Just five minutes,' tries Ally. 'I think you could really help us.'

Lara's reaching for the door handle, ready to close it.

'Two people murdered,' she says. 'Why aren't the police going door-to-door? Like you are.'

'They will be,' says Jayden. 'And they're looking at the graffiti angle too. It's not just about the scaremongering – Milo Nash's wave mural at the surf school was destroyed. That's criminal damage.'

'I can't imagine anyone's bothered about that.'

And Lara's hard edge is suddenly even harder. Jayden can't get a read on her dismissiveness, whether it's for Milo's work or the fact that a double murder overshadows vandalism – and then some.

'He's the guy who's been living out of his camper van, isn't he? He was parked up in a lay-by near here for ages. It shouldn't be allowed. I mean, where's he going to the toilet?'

They're getting off track. Jayden wants to tell Lara that he saw her watching them on the square. He wants to ask her why she was so interested. But he's willing to bet if she detects even a single beat of accusation, the door will slam in their faces.

Jayden glances at Ally.

'Look, we've heard the committee have ruffled a few feathers this year,' she says. 'Not everyone appreciates how they've cut back on the venues. It used to be that if you wanted to be part of the Arts Trail and were willing to open up your home, then you could.'

Lara raises her head and looks directly at Ally for the first time.

'So that's your theory too, is it? You think the trail's being targeted?'

'It's what some people are saying,' says Ally.

'Well, Pamela Trescoe said it yesterday. She was very certain. Like some people always are.'

The way Lara talks, there's more than a trace of bitterness. One thing is clear: she doesn't seem to care what people think of her. But, going by her emails to the committee, she *does* care what people think of her work. Select phrases flash into Jayden's head.

A pathetically short-sighted response.

Unfair bias to Cornish-born artists.

There's a reason my mother never agreed to be part of this poxy outfit.

'And what do you think, Lara?' asks Jayden.

'I think . . . I'm locking my door at night. I'm locking it in the day too.'

'Well, thank you for sparing the time—' begins Ally.

'And I'm glad I'm not exhibiting on the stupid trail,' she says as she pulls the door closed. 'I don't want anybody coming into my home, pretending to look at art but wanting to kill me.'

33

'Well, that's his next of kin notified,' says Skinner, settling in the passenger seat. 'Last thing I was expecting, if I'm honest.'

Mullins swings the car out of the cul-de-sac and on to the coast road. It's quieter in this direction and he puts his foot down. Inside his head, it's lumpy as bad custard. What a weird half hour.

They offered Annabel Crosby a lift to the mortuary, but she didn't take it. In fact, she asked if there was anyone else who could do it, because she didn't feel qualified to identify Harrison Loveday's body.

Even if he was her dad.

'So, let me get this straight,' says Skinner, rubbing his hands together as if he's gearing up to catch a cricket ball. 'Five years ago, Loveday gets in touch with Annabel and says he's the dad she never knew. She tells him to get lost. He tries again, and they briefly speak on the phone – him in Tuscany, her in Carbis Bay. But after that she doesn't want to have anything to do with him, thanks very much.'

Annabel Crosby described him as arrogant, haughty and unrepentant. *Not that I needed him to say sorry, but it would have been . . . something. I just felt like I was talking to a total stranger.*

Actually, that's not true, because I'm probably more open to total strangers. I was predisposed to dislike him and guess what? I did.

Harrison Loveday had had a brief relationship with Annabel's mother, Kitty Crosby, and then left before Annabel was born. Kitty was, so the story goes, heartbroken. And then, when Annabel was just a few months old, her mother had died. Drowned. Killed herself, most people said, because she'd never got over being loved and left – and being a single mum at eighteen had been hard. Really hard. Kitty had been sad and lonely and almost certainly had undiagnosed depression, and even though her family had helped out as much as they could, she couldn't cope.

That's how Annabel put it. *My mum couldn't cope. And I'm not going to judge her for that, because I've got kids, and I know how dark my days got at points. And I've a husband who loves me to the moon and back.* So, baby Annabel had been raised by her grandparents, and they couldn't really cope either: missing their daughter like mad; angry as you like. Didn't want to be tending to a screaming newborn, a lairy toddler, a fussy preschooler – they'd already been there, done that, hadn't they? But they raised her as best they could. And she turned out alright, didn't she? That's what she said. *I've turned out alright. And I know my own mind, I'll tell you that much. And I've never had any time for Harrison Loveday.*

'So, she heard about Harrison Loveday's murder from Donald Crosby,' says Mullins.

'Uncle Donald, you mean.'

Uncle Donald was broken back when Mum died, Annabel said. *He went to pieces, and he's never quite put himself back together. We're not really in each other's lives, to be honest, and I think that's fine with both of us.*

'So, Donald phones Annabel up and tells her what people are saying. That the sixty-eight-year-old male found murdered in a beach house in Porthpella is, in fact, her dad.'

'That's it,' says Skinner. 'And instead of getting in touch with us, she sits on it. There's indifference and then there's . . . playing silly beggars.'

But it doesn't seem like Annabel Crosby was playing silly beggars. It's more like she wanted to pretend it wasn't happening. Maybe, for her, it *wasn't* happening. Because Harrison was just some murdered bloke. Blood thicker than water? Not likely.

'I can't help wondering if there's more to this,' says Skinner. 'If the lady doth protest too much, when she says she doesn't care about her dad.'

'You think she killed him?'

'Her only alibi is watching telly with her husband, kids asleep upstairs. Speaking of, that lad of hers had a set of lungs on him. Imagine that, twenty-four seven.'

'I believed her,' says Mullins. 'Everything she said, really.'

'She was cold though, Mullins. And detached. Capable of murder?'

'I think she was cold and detached when it came to Harrison Loveday. Not in general.'

And he can't help thinking of Saffron and Wilson Rowe, and how their connection was more or less instant. Mostly because of Saffron's whopping great big heart, and Wilson getting all sentimental in his old age. And then him and his own dad. Different kettle of fish, that. If he suddenly showed up out the blue? Mullins honestly doesn't know. Maybe he'd be all Annabel Crosby about it too.

'That's a bit close to an intelligent observation, that. Well, the boys will fingerprint her anyway. Just to eliminate her from our enquiries, as we're fond of saying.' Skinner rubs at his moustache. 'Now, I don't know about you, but the one name that I'm hearing loud and clear is Uncle Donald. There's a good chance he blames Loveday for his sister's death. That's the family line, according to Annabel.'

'Why now though?' says Mullins.

'Because Loveday's in Cornwall and he's bothering Annabel. Sending her messages.'

'Not a lot to the messages really though, Sarge.'

'Maybe it doesn't take much, once Uncle Donald's fuse is lit. Suffice to say, we're going to have a little chat with him, Mullins. If Donald Crosby hasn't got an alibi for Loveday's murder, we're pulling him in.'

'But what about Gina Best?'

Skinner beats a tattoo on the dashboard. 'One thing at a time, Mullins. For now, I call this progress. And good thing too, with the world and his wife breathing down our necks. Not to mention the tabloids.'

'The Arts Trail Killer,' says Mullins. 'It's because of the graffiti, isn't it? All that "who's next?" rubbish.' He shoots Skinner a sideways glance. 'If it is rubbish, anyway . . .'

'All I know is that the minute you stick a moniker on a murderer . . . well, it gets the public in a frenzy. And that's a dangerous business, in and of itself, Mullins.'

Skinner's phone goes then. Meanwhile, the word *dangerous* ricochets around Mullins's head like a pinball.

'So, no mention of "who's next?" then?' Skinner barks into the handset. 'No, well, in that case I don't think an email is anything to get worked up about, is it? Tell her not to delete it and if she receives another, get in touch. Oh, and tell her to stop reading the newspapers!'

As Skinner hangs up, he curses.

Mullins shoots him a look.

'Sarge?'

'Some potter called Pamela Trescoe making something out of nothing.'

And is it Mullins's imagination, or does Skinner sound less than certain?

34

Saffron watches Broady help two kids carry their surfboards after a lesson. He's trudging with his head down and has none of his usual bounce. She's waiting to wave, but he doesn't look up. They disappear from view, headed for the board store, and Saffron carries on with the job at hand: wiping down a table in smooth figure-of-eights. She follows the beat of the music, trying to lose herself as unwanted thoughts push in.

It's as if a giant, threatening cloud has moved in over Porthpella. And there's no sign of a break in the weather. First, a woman poisoned at a party. Then, a man stabbed in his beach house. And between the two incidents, those haunting words, *who's next?* Saffron thought Milo's work being destroyed was bad enough. Then the significance of the graffiti burnt through.

Harrison Loveday was the second person to die, but what if the attack on Milo's work means he's the next target?

The door clangs over the music and Saffron jumps. Apart from the inevitable rubberneckers, and the remnants of today's Arts Trail crowd, it's been slow this afternoon.

'Hey.'

Milo. In a hoodie and baggy cords that sit above his ankles. A tattered pair of trainers. He looks effortlessly cool, in a kind of skate-rat-meets-circus-acrobat kind of way.

What does it mean, if you're thinking about someone and then they suddenly appear?

He runs his hand over his razor-short blond hair and says, 'I thought I'd see if there's been any more action.'

Despite everything, she returns his smile. 'Like what?'

'Porthpella's suddenly hitting all the headlines. I heard about the guy in the beach house. The big swank one, right?'

'Sea Dream.'

'You don't live here, no?'

'What, at Hang Ten?' She laughs. 'No, there's nowhere to sleep. I wish there was.'

'So where are you then?'

'Sun Street.'

'You're making that up.'

'Sun Street? It's off Trebilcock Terrace. At the top of the village.'

'Saffron lives on Sun Street. The sunny side of the street?'

She throws him a glittering grin. 'Hey, that's me.'

'Well, okay. Cool. Top of the village. Away from the drama then. Good. I thought you and the boyfriend were . . . in the mix.'

'What about you? You don't live in Porthpella, do you?'

His smile is suddenly a bit secretive. 'I move around.'

'Because you're so underground, right?'

'Underground, under the radar, under the wave . . . I'm in my camper, mostly.'

'Hashtag Van Life?'

'Yeah, you're not going to find me on Instagram though.'

It feels like he's kind of hovering. But then she remembers that's what people do in a coffee shop when they haven't ordered yet. *Look sharp, Saffron.*

'Coffee?' she says.

'Yeah, go on. But first . . .' He reaches into his backpack and hands over a brown envelope. 'You seemed sad it was trashed, so . . . kind of low-impact, but here's a souvenir.'

Saffron draws out an A4 printed photograph of Milo's wave mural. It's a beautiful-quality print, almost creamy textured. The colours are fire. Stupidly, she feels her eyes filling.

'Oh! Oh wow.'

'Maybe your boyfriend wants it, to put up in the surf school or something.'

'Oh sure. Yeah. Yeah, definitely. Well, he'll love it.'

Milo rubs at the back of his head. 'Or you could have it in here,' he says.

She can feel herself blushing. 'I really loved watching you work. Seeing it come together. It was amazing.'

'It was a pretty tame set-up. You should see how I do it sometimes.'

He holds her eye – and she holds his right back.

'By the way,' she says, 'I know you didn't want to stick around to talk to my mate Jayden, but I've got him and Ally on the case. They're going to find who wrecked it.'

'I'm with the police on this one, and I don't think I've ever said that in my life. Priorities, right? There's a lunatic out there.'

'Jayden thinks it could be the same lunatic.'

'Bit of a leap. Some idiot enjoying the noise, maybe.'

'But what if it isn't just that? Look, I know you're not bothered . . .'

He pulls a face. 'Yeah, so I've been thinking there. It's, like, a personal attack. Trashing the map was different, there's a whole bunch of artists listed there. This is . . . total erasure. Of just one person.'

Saffron bites her lip. He's saying what she's been thinking.

'I don't like being erased.'

'Nobody would.'

'You could read it as a warning. A warning signal.' His face suddenly looks a lot younger. Then he shrugs; goes for a laugh. 'I don't know. I'm being paranoid. Check me out, from zero bothered to losing it. It's the murders. They'll do that.'

'Maybe you should go away for a bit. Seeing as your house is on wheels, it's easy, right?'

'What, run? Because someone thinks they're handy with a spray can? That lettering is trash, by the way. They don't know what they're doing.'

She smiles inside. Milo looks down at the coffee she's just handed him. The teardrop heart in the micro-foam is one of her best. She does it for everyone she likes.

'Sweet,' he says. 'Good froth work. So . . . have they got anywhere with it? Your mates?'

And Saffron tells him that when she hears, he'll hear.

'In fact,' she says, 'I should probably have your number. So I can update you.'

'Tell me yours and I'll call you.'

She rattles off her digits, and two seconds later she hears a buzz.

'Okay, so you've got my number. And I've got yours.' He raises his coffee cup. 'How much for the . . . ?'

She shakes a head. 'A thank you for the print. It's really kind of you. I know you're not into the whole "permanent" thing, but . . . I love it. Broady will too. And just . . . take care, okay?'

'Back atcha. I'm glad you're not sleeping at the beach. Take it easy on Sun Street, Saffron. And hey, if I decide to do anything, to strike back, maybe I'll tell you.'

'What do you mean, "strike back"?'

'Like maybe the best reaction is to make more art. Where they're least expecting it.'

Saffron grins. 'Like where?'

'I've got your number,' he says with a wink.

35

'I did wonder when someone was going to come and speak to me,' says Pamela Trescoe, 'and I'm rather glad it's you two. It's quite an accolade to be interviewed by the Shell House Detectives. All hands to the pump with a case like this, is it? Well, I'm glad to hear it.'

Pamela, Ally notes, is of the Wenna school: she answers her own questions. But so long as she answers theirs too, that's fine.

'That hoity-toity sergeant tried to tell me there was nothing in it, but I knew his gut was saying otherwise. Anyone can see there's something distinctly unsettling about an email like that. And of course, it's horribly intimate, the way it lands in one's inbox. Rather like a brick tossed through a windowpane. It's an assault, of sorts.'

Ally glances to Jayden and he raises his eyebrows in reply.

'You've received an email?' says Ally.

'You mean you don't know?' Pamela gasps in frustration. 'Well, typical. I thought the police had sent you. But you're here now anyway. Come in, come in, I'll tell you all about it.'

Inside, Pamela settles into her armchair and leans her crutches against the wall. She nods to her foot. 'Damn nuisance, this. Not that I have to move about much in trail week. It's peaceful, usually. Tiring, in its way, but peaceful.'

'What have you done?' asks Ally, because Pamela's looking at her like it's expected – meanwhile other questions are firing through Ally's mind. *What email? Who from?*

They're in the open-plan lounge of Pamela's barn conversion, and from here they can see her garden studio. Pamela's venue is open today – as are most of the others, aside from Ally's, Island View House and the Bluebird. Light pools into the large space, drawing out the honey colours of the wooden beams; the white walls shimmer. It feels every inch an artist's home.

Pamela's a potter, the maker of curvaceous vases and deep bowls; glazes that evoke ocean sunsets. They're quite beautiful. And serene too, unlike their creator, who has something of a busy, almost chaotic energy. She wears a pair of glasses on a string around her neck, and another pair pushed up into the curls of her silver hair. Colourful earrings fight for attention with a chunky beaded necklace and two armfuls of bangles.

'Oh, I turned my ankle. I broke it playing hockey decades ago and there's been a weakness ever since. Now and then it just goes. Damned inconvenient. Especially as it meant four hours in a blasted A&E waiting room yesterday. Honestly, the NHS is broken beyond repair. But don't let me up on my soapbox, I'll never get off it. Now, you came from Lara Swann's, did you say? Yes, she was here when I turned it, actually. Not a lot of sympathy in my direction. But then she's a strange one, so I don't know what I expected.'

Ally glances at Jayden. There's something accusing in Pamela's tone, as if Lara's response to her injury is indicative of a deeper flaw.

'Lara never came when her mother, Billie Swann, had Westerly as a holiday home, but now she appears to have moved in. Which, by the way, I'm all in favour of. There's enough places around here standing empty for most of the year. I just wish she was a better neighbour. Her mother was famous in art circles and as such valued her privacy, but she and I had a cup of tea once. I think Billie wanted to show off a little, and she gave me a tour of her studio. Very sweet of her. But Lara isn't open at all. Who have we got, all the way out here, except for one another? And by that, I mean Porthpella. Our little community. And God knows it's been rocked.'

'What you said before,' says Jayden. 'The email. Can you tell us about that?'

'Tell you? I'll show you.'

And Pamela reaches for her phone on the coffee table. She brings it close to her face and squints hard at it as she taps once, twice, three times.

'There you are,' she says, holding it up, 'tell me what you make of that. The police affected to dismiss it, but I know it will have set a cat amongst the pigeons in the incident room or whatever one calls it.'

> Dear Pamela. I was horrified, and so sorry, to read about the disturbing events in your beautiful village of Porthpella. As a talented artist you must be feeling particularly vulnerable at this present time. I urge you to remain vigilant 24/7. Lock every door, every window. Be careful after dark, Pamela. We must not allow tragedy to strike again in this special community of creative people. Best regards, J.S.

It's from a sender called John Smith.

'Presumably you don't know a John Smith?'

'No, I do not,' says Pamela. 'It's sinister, that's what it is. It's . . . well, it's revelling in the situation, isn't it? I obviously haven't replied.'

Be careful after dark, Pamela. To Ally, it's more than just revelling; it's almost a threat.

'Is your email address readily available?' asks Jayden.

'Well, it's on my website. My rather poor excuse for a website but . . . still.'

'And you've never had an email from a John Smith before?' asks Ally.

'Not once.'

'When a case is in the news,' says Jayden, 'the public can get emotionally invested. And there's always some people who want to feel involved. That's probably all this is. I think you did the right thing reporting it though.'

Ally watches as Jayden taps the email, looks closely, then screenshots it.

'Pamela, can you ping this screenshot through to me? I'll give you my number.'

Ally waits, then asks, 'Do you know if anyone else has received an email like this?'

'I wouldn't know. I should do a ring round, probably. I suppose it would be a comfort, to know if it wasn't just me. "Who's next?" That's the trouble. That's what I can't stop thinking about. Those damn words. And, of course, I was at the party when that poor woman died. I saw her convulsions.'

'Have the police come to see you since the party?' asks Ally.

'No, and I call that an oversight. They took my statement up at Island View House, but after Harrison Loveday . . . well, I'd have thought they'd be back to see us all.' She looks up sharply. 'The horrifying acts of vandalism in the village, now an email like this . . . well, everything points to it being an attack on the Arts Trail, doesn't it? And that's not a thought I want to entertain . . . particularly as I can't exactly make a quick getaway.'

Pamela laughs noisily, but nevertheless there's an anxious look in her eyes. She glances to the garden gate, where a couple holding Arts Trail programmes are studying the pages. They peer at the studio, then push the gate open.

'They've decided to risk it,' says Pamela archly. 'People often skip the pots. It's as if they think you have to *need* a vase or bowl or whatever, rather than simply wanting to own something beautiful. Still, sorts the wheat from the chaff. And those two? They look like chaff. They can browse unattended.'

'We spoke to Lara Swann earlier. She told us about you feeling strongly that the murders are an attack on the Arts Trail,' says Jayden.

Pamela tugs at a string of beads and the necklace makes a clacking sound, like the tide pulling over pebbles on a beach.

'Lara said that, did she? Shows she listened, I suppose. You simply can't tell with her.'

'We were talking about the feeling within the community,' says Ally. 'In general.'

'I shouldn't have thought Lara would be a spokeswoman for that. But it has to be about the trail, doesn't it? Otherwise, why spray "who's next?" on the map showing all the venues? Why go to that trouble? And the mural at the beach. That boy's work is Arts Trail fringe, if not the trail itself.'

'But Gina and Harrison are more connected to one another than they are to the Arts Trail,' says Ally.

'Listen, I don't like the idea of it any more than you do, Ally, but . . . what else could it be? And now I'm getting strange emails.'

'But who would have a reason to be against the Arts Trail?' asks Jayden innocently.

'Oh what, because you think it's all happy-clappy creative stuff? You'd be surprised. There's a lot of delicate egos among artists. Jealousy. Affairs. All sorts.'

'Affairs?' says Ally.

'Oh, there's always affairs.' Pamela looks at them both; heaves a sigh. 'I sound like I'm making light of it. I'm really not. I left my lamp on all night long. Jumped at the slightest sound. I almost summoned my friend Donald to keep me company like an old watchdog, but I do have some pride.'

She shakes her head.

'Look, of course I'd rather think it was a personal vendetta. Wouldn't you? Because, if it's against the Arts Trail in general, then who's to say they won't strike again?'

36

Wenna always keeps White Wave Stores open until lunchtime on a Sunday, just so people can get their newspapers and essentials: eggs, bacon, milk, bread. Where would you be on a Sunday without a lie-in and a fry-up? Not that Wenna's ever been one for lie-ins, personally. Nor Gerren. Soon as their eyes click open, their engines are revving – and a good thing too, with a shop to run. Though whether it's nature or nurture she can't say; they've been behind the counter at White Wave for thirty years.

Wenna moves to the door, and she twitches the 'Open' sign. By rights she should have closed up hours ago – they're well into the afternoon now – but she takes their role in the community seriously. People come to White Wave for the things they need, and today she's not just been selling the news – she *is* the news.

When that journalist – local bloke, so he said, but he had more than a whiff of upcountry about him – came in asking her what she thought about those words scrawled on the Arts Trail poster right outside the shop, what was Wenna supposed to say? That it was pure coincidence; just some joker getting handy with a spray can on the very night that a gallery owner from London died at a Porthpella art party? Or . . . that the killer struck and was letting everybody round here know that they weren't nearly done? And, speaking as a pillar of the community – *on the record* – Wenna felt more than a little destabilised by that.

It wasn't gossip. That's what she said to Gerren later: *It wasn't gossip, Gerr.* Then, *Was it?*

The headline appeared online first – *Arts Trail Killer: who's next?* – but then it was in print this morning too, a big stack of newspapers here on the counter and a weird feeling building in Wenna's chest as she flicked through them. Then news came up from the beach, blowing through the marram grass, moving over the village like foul weather – and stopping. Porthpella under the darkest cloud.

A man stabbed in his beach house. The artist Harrison Loveday.
That is who was next.

Wenna turns the 'Open' sign to 'Closed'. Suddenly, she feels very tired. She's had enough chit-chat for today; locals and Easter holidaymakers coming in for the basics and then staying for the latest. *Have the police got any leads? What should we be saying to our children? Will the beach be closed? And what about the Arts Trail, surely that's not going on?*

What she really wants to do is get Gerren, get in the car and get the hell out of here. Pelt up the A30 and keep on going. And it's not often you'll hear Wenna say that, except for once a year when she's got a plane ticket to Lanzarote burning a hole in her pocket. She loves Porthpella – it's everything she is and everything she has. The last things she wants to hear before she clocks out of this life are the push and pull of the tide and the shrieking song of the gulls: these are the sounds she was raised on. But she's not ready to clock out yet – not even close. She'll take another thirty years, God willing (if she believed in the fella).

When Wenna was a little girl, Great-Granny Belle lived in the cottage with them. She was so old her cheeks were hollow as buckets; her voice sounded like a bird stuck at the bottom of a well.

And Great-Granny Belle chilled little Wenna to the bone, because Wenna could see that death was creeping for her, that death had her in its clutches, even: Great-Granny Belle could be whisked away at any moment.

But Wenna knows now that she had it all wrong. You make it to ninety-eight, you're a living legend. You've beaten all the odds. Great-Granny Belle was walking towards the light with her eyes wide open.

What's scary – Wenna wants to tell her six-year-old self – is when death doesn't creep slowly, but cuts like a blade when you're lying sleeping. Sets off a medley of toxic fireworks when you sip at a drink. Sprays warnings on walls under the cover of night. It's when death dresses like everyday people, and drops into the shop. Buys a newspaper. Smiles a smile, teeth bared and gleaming white, and Wenna says: *Morning, love.*

As she turns the key in the door and slides the bolt across, a movement catches Wenna's eye. A police car. Not idly patrolling but moving with purpose and conviction across the square.

No sirens; no lights. Is that a good sign?

Or a really bad sign. That it's already too late.

37

Donald hunches over his palette, mixing grey. Currently it's the collar and cuffs of an old school shirt. He squirts in some yellow, to bring it into an old man's tobacco-tinged moustache territory. That's closer. What he wants is the almost-neon tint when a storm is about to break. *There.* He drags the paint across the canvas and its swathe of grim estuary water.

The effect? Trouble brewing.

Pamela once described Donald's paintings as 'wilfully miserable'. There's a discussion in there somewhere, if he could be bothered to hunt it out: to what extent is art instinctive, a true expression of our inner selves, versus an intentional manipulation? Does Donald paint gloomy pictures because he is of a gloomy disposition? Surely it cannot be vice versa, because when he's working, it's the closest he comes to happy.

Alright, not happy. That's a nonsense sort of word: greetings cards and rampaging toddlers and dogs chasing their own tails. But content? Yes, perhaps. When Donald is at his easel, he experiences whole minutes, even hours, of contentment.

Not today though.

He glances up at the sound of entry, then darts his eyes back to his canvas. There's been a steady stream of visitors to his studio all morning. The usual sort of crowd, including a few familiar faces with whom he's swapped a greeting, but he's been able to keep his head down. Firstly, he's behind an easel. *The Artist at Work: do not disturb.* Secondly, he has a pervading aura of unapproachability. Pamela calls it 'wilfully distant'. Pamela is fond of using the word *wilfully* in connection to Donald, as if his manner is cultivated as opposed to just . . . him being helplessly him.

For a long time, Donald has believed himself incapable of change. His feelings and actions hardwired; fixed as rock strata. But now Harrison Loveday is dead. Not a gentle meeting with his maker but a violent and explosive journey to the pearly gates.

And how does Donald feel?

In his muted palette of emotions, he is firmly in the greys. But when he thinks about it, he suspects that when all this is over, when he's closed his studio door and is left alone again, he may be devastated. Furious.

Ashamed? That too.

Pamela, of course, was on the phone to him the moment she heard the news. He let it go to voicemail and when he called her back, he was monosyllabic. *It's a lot to take in,* he offered eventually. A point Pamela did concur with – only, said in a voice that was so robust, so full of vigour and vim, that Donald could tell she wanted to throw a party; that she couldn't understand, really, why he wasn't delighted too.

But who's next?

'Donald Crosby?'

He peers past his easel to see a man in a grey suit and a young police officer. He thinks he recognises them from the other night at Island View House. But then they all look the same to him, these suits and uniforms.

'Detective Sergeant Skinner and Police Constable Mullins. We wondered if we might have a word.'

'What, here?'

He sees Skinner glance at the handful of people moving through the studio: an elderly man, two women who look like sisters.

'Perhaps some privacy,' says Skinner. 'In the house? Mullins here can man the stall, as it were.'

And how would that appear? The constable is a clumsy-looking youth, it seems to Donald. He shakes his head. 'I'll simply shut up shop for a few moments . . .'

Giving themselves away as eavesdroppers, the trio of art lovers cast curious and frankly rather peeved looks in Donald's direction, then trail out.

'We should get you on duty for kickout at closing time,' says Skinner. 'Nicely done.'

And Donald has the impression that this is a strategy. *Soft-soap the fellow!* He moves to the door and turns the key, then pulls down the blind for good measure. He treads back across the uneven concrete floor, aware of every step.

'How can I help?'

'Harrison Loveday,' says Skinner, 'was the father of your niece.'

Donald blinks. He knew they'd get there. And that when they did, they'd be at his door. But it's still a shock to hear it so baldly put. Such familial terms employed.

'Only biologically speaking.'

'We've talked to Annabel. We understand that there's been very little contact between her and Harrison Loveday over the years.'

'That's right.'

'Can you tell us about him. About him and her.'

'Annabel and Harrison Loveday?'

'And Harrison and Kitty. Your sister.'

As if he doesn't know who Kitty is. As if he doesn't think of her every single day, even though she's been dead now for more than twice as long as she was ever alive.

'Ah now,' says Donald.

And for all that he was anticipating this moment, he feels the energy drain from him, as abruptly as a pulled plug. He wants to sit down. *Needs* to sit down. He sees the two officers swap a look at one another. It's an affirmation: *we've got him bang to rights.*

'Is there anything you'd like to tell us?' says the detective.

'Not really.'

But he has no choice.

Kitty, eighteen and green as a blade of grass – and just as easily crushed. His lovely sister, who for some reason fell under the spell of a big-headed, loud-mouthed man like Harrison Loveday. She was a waitress at a Falmouth tearoom. He was about to graduate art school. Harrison took advantage of her, then skated off into the night. She was devastated afterwards. *I know it's silly, Donny, but I loved him. I did.* Then the pregnancy. The months of sickness, and turmoil.

'Our parents weren't so much God-fearing as village-gossip-fearing, which can be just as damning, Officers,' says Donald.

He tells them how Kitty ghost-walked through that time, heavy-footed, glassy-eyed, her ever-growing stomach like a ball and chain. All the time hoping and wishing for a word from Harrison Loveday.

Then, the baby.

'Well, you've met Annabel. Strapping girl. And she was like that as a baby too.'

It seemed extraordinary to the young Donald that this sturdy creature – as loud-mouthed as her father, if he's being honest – could have come from his wisp-like sister. The baby was relentlessly hungry. Ceaselessly furious. No more than the size of a Bible, but as vast and unknowable as a sea monster. Exhausted little Kitty hardly stood a chance, did she?

'My sister was like the living dead. And then just . . . the dead. She left the baby in her crib and went to where the river meets the sea. Obvious place to do it, I suppose, what with the currents. She was desperately unhappy. She couldn't cope.' He looks up sharply. 'Annabel told you that, didn't she?'

'She did,' says Skinner. 'And she says you took it hard.'

'Took it hard? My sister dying? Having seen her suffer, near enough every day since she met that man? Yes, I suppose I did take it *hard*.'

And there's an energy to his voice that shocks him. A sudden sparking. In this moment, Donald feels as if he could grab hold of the lapels of this detective's cheap suit and shake him to bits.

'Did you blame Harrison Loveday?'

'I did.' The fire quells as quickly as it came. He pushes his glasses back up his nose with the heel of his hand. 'Very much so.'

'Donald,' says Skinner, 'where were you yesterday evening, between the hours of 6 p.m. and 10 p.m.?'

'What's that?'

The pudgy young constable – as empty a vessel as one of Pamela's new-formed pots – repeats the detective's question.

'You mean, do I have an alibi?' asks Donald.

And for a moment he imagines the ensuing process like the unstoppable descent of a rollercoaster. Nothing to do but submit. Perhaps scream. Hide your head in your coat.

'No,' he says. 'I don't.'

Then the tears are upon him. Because Harrison Loveday is dead. And there's nothing that Donald can do about it.

185

38

Jayden and Ally are crunching down the gravel path from Pamela's when their phones both beep at the same time. They swap a look and reach for them. Jayden gets there first.

It's Sunita. His eyes widen as he reads.

I just saw Donald Crosby in the back of a police car.

'Okay, Al,' he says. 'Development.'

She looks up. 'Donald. Pamela's friend. She mentioned him, didn't she?'

Jayden turns back to the house, where Pamela is standing in the doorway, leaning on her crutches. She waggles one in farewell. But after a nod from Ally, Jayden is already turning, heading back up the path.

'Sorry, Pamela,' he says. 'Have you got another five minutes?'

'Are you about to tell me they've arrested someone called John Smith for murder?'

Jayden can't figure out if she's joking. He tells her about Donald Crosby and Pamela's face immediately falls.

'Oh God. Well . . . I suppose you'd better come in then.'

They crowd back into the hallway, with its toffee-coloured boards and framed paintings, an elaborate coat stand and a shoe rack. Once again, Ally removes her shoes carefully and places them on the rack. Jayden kicks off his trainers and speeds after Pamela.

This time, Pamela offers them wine instead of coffee, and while Jayden declines, Ally accepts a small glass. And that's when Jayden knows there will be a story: not just because of her reaction but because of the reinforcements in the beverage department. As Ally follows Pamela into the kitchen, Jayden settles in the lounge. A cat, as round and orange as a basketball, slinks into the room and eyes him with suspicion; Jayden makes like Jazzy and sticks his tongue out. There's a copy of the Arts Trail programme on the coffee table and he flicks through it, reading Donald Crosby's entry. His paintings are murky views of land and water. Jayden looks up and sees one on Pamela's wall. He goes to examine it.

'Yes,' says Pamela, crutching her way back in. 'That's one of Donald's. Stunning, isn't it?'

'Does Donald make a living from his work?' asks Jayden.

He can't imagine too many people wanting a painting like this. It's kind of depressing. If Donald struggles to sell his work, is professional jealousy a factor? But Jayden's getting ahead of himself. Pamela still hasn't said what connects Donald Crosby to Harrison Loveday. Only that she had, in her words, *a horrible feeling this would happen.*

'He jolly well should,' says Pamela.

Behind her, Ally sets down a tray with two glasses of wine, a can of Coke and a bowl of cashew nuts in a shimmery blue bowl.

'Oh, thank you, dear,' says Pamela. As she takes the bowl from the tray, she says, 'It's a duff – see, the glaze is blistered. I usually smash them, but I rather like this one. Nut?'

Jayden takes a handful then cracks the ice-cold can of Coke, dipping his head to catch the bubbles. It all feels like a slightly bizarre prelude to something.

But what?

Ten minutes later, Pamela has told them the tragic story of Donald Crosby's sister Kitty dying – and the Harrison Loveday connection. She narrates it quietly, respectfully, without drama; her bouncy demeanour all but gone. In fact, the transformation is so abrupt that Jayden wonders which Pamela is the real one. Maybe both? *We contain multitudes, et cetera.*

Jayden can feel Ally looking at him. He can see she's moved by the story. He suspects, too, that she's thinking of Cat.

'Look, I know what you're thinking,' says Pamela, taking a sip of her wine. 'I didn't know whether to mention Donald to you. But you have to believe me, I wasn't withholding. But it just . . . confuses things. You see, Donald is the gentlest man in the world. He's incapable of harming another individual. So whether he has a problem with Harrison Loveday or not is insignificant.'

'Is it widely known?' asks Ally. 'In the village, I mean?'

'I shouldn't think so.'

'What about the committee? Surely they wouldn't have invited Harrison if they knew about the complexity for Donald. He's been active on the trail for years.'

'As have I, but us humble souls hardly have a casting vote, Ally. Or indeed any vote. Were you asked who you'd like to see as guest artist? Indeed, whether you thought a guest artist was needed at all?'

'But wouldn't Donald have spoken up?' says Jayden. 'Sunita, Gideon, Connor, they're a friendly bunch. I'm sure they'd have listened.'

'Good God, no. Because that would have required Donald confronting the issue. I love him dearly, but he's head-in-the-sand. Always has been.' Pamela holds her hand to her mouth. 'The thought of him . . . under interrogation. It's hell. The last thing he would have wanted.'

'There's been two murders,' Jayden says. 'Like it or not, interrogation is the name of the game.'

'Well, so long as someone's interrogating my email,' she snaps back. 'It's obvious John Smith isn't a real name. Anyone can see that.' Then she looks down, her chest heaving. 'What, so you think it makes sense that Donald's been pulled in now? Arrested?'

'It's very possible he went voluntarily,' says Ally. 'To offer a statement.'

'Yeah, definitely. Pamela, how long have you known about Donald's connection to Harrison Loveday?'

Pamela stares past them through the window. 'Oh, I don't know. There was some . . . blockage. He's a lovely man, you see. A kind man. But he's sad, so sad, and . . . well, he told me everything one day. How the loss of his sister shaped his life, more or less. A few years ago? It blurs, at our age. Anyway, we'd become close, by then. Of course, as artists, he thought I'd have heard of Harrison Loveday. I hadn't, as it happens. I don't keep up with painters. But I can see why he's a big noise. Very talented and all that.' She bites her lip. 'Was. Gosh. *Was* very talented. I should think those pieces of his at the Bluebird will double in value now. Sorry . . . Crass.'

'So once the committee announced him as the guest artist . . .' begins Ally.

'Yes, exactly,' says Pamela. 'I knew the emotional significance of it. We spoke about it. I thought it an opportunity to bury the hatchet, but Donald wasn't having any of it. He couldn't bring himself to confront the man.'

Confront. It's a particular choice of word.

'What about the two of them just crossing paths naturally?' says Jayden. 'Like two nights ago at the party. Did they speak then?'

Pamela laughs humourlessly. 'You think someone like Harrison would pay attention to Donald? He wasn't interested in meeting any of us old guard. It was just him and his gallerist with their heads together. If you're asking if Harrison knew who Donald was, then no, I don't think he did. Why would he? Harrison is, by all accounts, extraordinarily self-absorbed. *Was.* Sorry. Even Sunita intimated as much. Kitty Crosby meant nothing to Harrison, so her big brother would hardly be on his radar.'

'And Donald didn't speak to him?'

Again, the bitter laugh. 'Not one word. I would have but . . . not my place. I can be tactful sometimes, believe it or not. Besides' – she looks down at her hands – 'we all want the trail to be a success. It's part of our calendar. Isn't it, Ally? A falling-out with the guest of honour would have been very much frowned upon.'

'With that logic,' says Ally, 'you don't think the killer is an artist?'

'I think the killer could be just about anyone,' says Pamela. 'I'm talking about an artist having the decorum not to raise a difficult topic, not about a lunatic resisting the impulse for murder. One thing I do know is that they're clever. Because the police are nowhere near catching them, are they? Not if they're messing around with Donald.'

'They won't hold him unless they have cause to,' says Ally.

Pamela runs on, as if she hasn't heard.

'And the graffiti, "who's next?" That's clearly against the Arts Trail, not an individual. And that's not Donald running around with a spray can, for goodness' sake.' Pamela's voice has almost a pleading note. 'We have to trust in the system, don't we, Ally? Jayden? I mean, they won't pin this on Donald?'

'Everything you've said about his sister, it's circumstantial,' says Jayden. 'A case like this, forensics will be everything.'

'He'll be finding this devastating, being forced to go into it all. Utterly devastating. I'll tell you now though, no matter how the police press, they'll find Donald unimpeachable. I'd bet my life on that.'

Pamela is convincing in her delivery, but this story of bitter resentment and old hurts makes Donald a person of interest.

Perhaps even the prime suspect. Maybe the police have had the lab report back and are working with something more. Circumstantial *plus* hard evidence?

'So, Donald didn't declare his connection to Loveday in his statement?' asks Jayden. 'The one at the party?'

'Why on earth would he? It was Gina Best who'd died. The police were only interested in people who knew her. Which, on the face of things, was practically nobody. But people lie, don't they? People lie all the time.'

Ally looks to Jayden, and he knows what she's thinking.

Apart from Harrison, practically nobody knew Gina Best. Except for Connor Rafferty. Gideon Lee. Sunita Singh. And Ray Finch.

'Pamela, what happened to Donald's sister's daughter? Harrison's child?' asks Ally.

'Annabel? She's in Carbis Bay. She and Donald aren't close at all.'

Jayden's eyes are wide. 'What about her and Harrison?'

39

Ray takes the path to the beach. He's already explored the Arts Trail from top to bottom. He's swapped small talk with painters, potters, printmakers. He's trained his ear to the gossip too, the scaremongering. As an outsider, he hasn't been drawn into any confidences, though the committee – Gideon, Connor and Sunita – have included him in a specially created WhatsApp group, which has been pinging intermittently with a combination of speculation and handwringing. *No, that's unkind.* After the meeting at the Bluebird, there was no suggestion that he stay on in their company. And Ally? Well, she and Jayden have work to do. As such, Ray feels like a bit of a spare part.

He's in an idyllic holiday spot – if you close your eyes to the 'who's next?' scrawls, that is. Arguably he should be able to enjoy the charms of Porthpella like anyone else, but he's too distracted. It'll do that, the murder of an old mate.

'Old mate' is about the size of it, because in the brief window in which Ray knew Harrison, they weren't close. Ray suspects Harrison wasn't genuinely close to anyone. He always seemed too big for a place like Falmouth. Yes, even with its famously deep harbour. Ray pictures Harrison as a giant cruise ship surging into the docks and far beyond; stopping for nothing. And, sometimes, Ray was along for the ride. The two of them the last men standing in those smoke-filled waterside inns, the backstreet pubs. It didn't take much to become a face. Legends were easily made.

Harrison was in his final year of art school when Ray met him. He was already lauded as a talented painter, the recognition giving him an undisputed glow. He wore a uniform of black t-shirt and blue jeans and was as lithe and muscular as a fly-half. He drank like a sailor on shore leave.

Did Ray ever really like him? Not a question he pondered at the time. His brief stint at art school was awash with casual acquaintances. He found Harrison entertaining: a firework that might go off at any moment. At that point in his life, Ray enjoyed drama.

But then there was Ally.

Ray stops at the crest of a dune, stands with his hands on his hips. His feet sink into the soft sand; marram grass brushes his waist. Despite the scudding clouds, and the rain forecast for later, the sea is a breathtaking blue. It's hard to imagine anything terrible in the world, staring into a blue like this. And Ally Bright lives not just at the edge of it, but more or less *in* it. And that makes sense too, because there's something serene about her, like she knows all the secrets of living. Maybe that's the Porthpella effect. Or maybe she's always had it, because he felt the same in Falmouth.

Ally was different from any girl he'd fallen for before. A glass of cool water, after all the too-sweet cocktails and bitter pints. She seemed to see something in him that Ray wasn't even sure was there – not back then – but he was all too happy to believe it might be real. Now, four and a half decades later, he thinks he might actually be worthy of her. Given half a chance.

Ray walks until he can see the bright purple and yellow of the beach café, where he's been told he'll find the best coffee in Cornwall. Beyond that is Sea Dream, Harrison and Gina's rented place. His mind turns to the next guests. Prosperous holidaymakers, rolling up for a luxury break. How does a place like that recover? A good bleaching, then some of those aromatic sticks in pots that his last ex-wife used to be mad for? Ah, the old joke reflex. But it doesn't mean he doesn't feel something underneath.

Ray was surprised by his strength of feeling yesterday, when Harrison laughed at him at the Bluebird. He'd stopped by to see how the guy was holding up after Gina's death, but Harrison was jibing, antagonistic. First, he rubbished the idea that the graffiti had anything to do with anything (oh, the grim irony in that). Then the conversation turned to Ally Bright.

I saw you two together at the party. Finally forgiven you, has she?

His grin wide, teeth gleaming, as if the thought of someone else's drama – however ancient – was a comfort. A delight, even.

You really messed that one up, my friend.

And a gale of laughter. The kind that slams you in the face.

Ray doesn't blame Harrison Loveday for what happened between him and Ally all those years ago. But any other man might have said, *Hey, sorry it turned out that way.* Mellowed, rueful, acknowledging their part.

But not Harrison.

This isn't how Ray wants to remember him – a source of irritation; hurt, even – but no one gets to choose their last moments, do they? Just ask Gina Best. Just ask Harrison.

Ray slows as he approaches the coffee shop. He sees the surfboard-shaped sign with its wave logo. Another man is coming from the other direction. Bald-headed. Flannel shirt. Corduroys. Classic geography-teacher chic. And seeing as Ray was a teacher himself for thirty years, he feels qualified in this appraisal. It was always a consolation to him, that the kids thought he was kind of cool. There were even a few schoolgirl crushes along the way – which he ignored, of course. Not that he looks especially cool now.

But there's rain forecast for later, so he's swapped his leather jacket for his old green anorak; it's stood up to many a North Sea storm.

He sees then it's Ally's mate Gus. The guy who scuttled off to get drinks at the ill-fated party. There was no horn-locking; instead Gus beat a beetle-like retreat, casting anxious looks in their direction. Ray called it then: this Gus is in love with Ally.

He stops himself. He's being cruel. Playground stuff. Late-night-jostling-in-the-bar stuff. *Are you starting?* But lately Ray's been doing a lot of thinking on the road not taken. Too much, probably, on those long Suffolk nights when it's just him and a mid-range Merlot. At the bottom of his wine glass, he's found sediments of regret. Traces of what-if. And how can he help it if his mind keeps turning in a particular direction? The siren song of nostalgia.

'Hello, sir,' he calls out. Jaunty as you like. Too jaunty, given recent incidents.

Gus looks up. 'Oh, hullo.'

Then his face changes. He seems to be looking at Ray's coat. Staring at it, in fact. With a frankly weird expression.

Like Gus has just seen a ghost in a mackintosh.

40

'I kept my mother's name when I married,' says Annabel. 'It felt like it was the least I could do, really.'

As Ally and Jayden sit in Annabel's compact lounge, it almost feels like an act of time travel. Just an hour ago, they were at Pamela's – learning, out of the blue, that Harrison Loveday had a daughter who lives locally. A quick internet search turned up an Annabel Crosby working for Sandpiper Holiday Lettings in Carbis Bay. And here they are. A small housing estate: crescent driveways, tidy lawns, the sea looking further away than it really is.

It was easy to find Annabel, so it's no surprise to hear the police have been here too. Twice in one day. Once to inform her, as next of kin, of Harrison's death. Then to confirm that Donald is helping them with their enquiries, and did she have anything to say about that? Annabel delivered this last in a flat, detached voice, as if it was a perfectly ordinary turn of events.

Meanwhile, a red-cheeked pre-schooler is ramming his giant plastic truck into Jayden's leg, and Jayden is doing his best to pretend he doesn't mind.

'So, you don't have much to do with Donald?' he asks. Then, to the child, 'Hey, easy there, mate. Not so hard.'

'Hardly at all,' says Annabel, dragging her hair back into a ponytail as she speaks. 'Christmas cards, you know. That's about it. He's always done his own thing. Art. Boats. Et cetera. And Luca, you stop that.'

'Are you surprised that the police are talking to Donald?' asks Ally carefully. She doesn't use the word *arrest*, because perhaps he hasn't been arrested at all.

'It's no more surprising than them talking to me. I suppose they're interested in anyone who had any connection with Harrison Loveday, aren't they? Not that I think Donald ever did. But my mum is the common factor, so obviously they reckon there's something there.'

'Were your mum and Donald close as siblings?' asks Ally.

'Very. Or so the story goes. But he was never much use to her when she was struggling, from what I hear. I feel like Donald is one of those people who gets knocked about by life and then blames it on certain things. Instead of taking responsibility and just . . . getting on with it. When I was a teenager, I remember he was still making a huge deal out of my mum's death, and, you know, that wasn't helpful for me, actually. Who wants to walk through life feeling like there's this big tragedy overshadowing them? Not me. Sorry if that sounds blunt, but it's how I am.'

'Did Donald ever meet Harrison?' asks Jayden. 'Like, in later years.'

Annabel shrugs. 'I don't think so. I've never even had anything to do with Harrison. Not until he got in touch out of the blue five years ago. And even then, it was mostly me batting him away. He sent me the odd text message. Phoned me once too. Okay, yes, he slept with my mother, but that doesn't make him my dad, does it? Not in any of the ways that matter. Luca, stop that!'

'He's fine,' says Jayden.

'Give him an inch and he'll take a mile.' Annabel sighs. 'Look, I can see why you've come to speak to me, but I'll tell you what I told the police. Harrison Loveday has got nothing to do with our family, and we've got nothing to do with him. Luca, *last warning*.'

The little boy flings his truck at the table leg and plops down on the floor. Arms folded; lips pursed.

'Do you think Donald would say the same?' says Jayden.

Annabel yawns; pats a hand to her mouth.

'God, sorry. I'm done in. What, Donald? Yes, I think he would. Not that we've ever talked about it. Look, if you think my uncle has something to do with that man's death, then I've got to laugh out loud. He might say he hates Harrison Loveday because of how he hurt my mum once upon a time, but a man like Donald would never have the balls to do anything about it. He wouldn't *say* anything to Harrison, let alone swing a punch. Let alone anything more.'

'And you don't bear any animosity yourself?' asks Ally, gently.

'Me?' Annabel sighs again. 'What would be the good of that? I decided, years back, that I was going to have nothing to do with Harrison. And that was a cool-headed choice, not an emotional one. I learnt a long time ago that there are some things in life you choose, and some things you don't. The one thing you've got control of is how you feel – and your own actions.'

'I think that's probably a good attitude,' says Jayden.

'Well, it's working so far. And, look, I'm not as unfeeling as you think.'

Annabel reaches down, scoops up her little son.

'Shall we show them Granny's seashell?' she says.

She takes the boy's hand and they walk out of the room together, returning moments later with a small tin. She unscrews the lid and there, resting on a bed of tissue, is a perfect little cowrie shell. Tawny-coloured, with a milk-white interior; an immaculate lacy edge.

'When they were looking for my mum, they found her shoes at the beach. That's why they thought suicide. That and her mental state, obviously. This little shell was inside one of them.'

Ally looks at it carefully. It's beautiful, just like all cowries are.

'And you have it,' says Ally simply.

'I'm not a sentimental person, but my nan gave it to me when I was eight years old, and I kept it. Nan said she carried it in her purse until she thought I was old enough to appreciate it. Nan was so sad about my mum, and so cross with herself, and with Mum too – and I understand that, because grief's the strangest thing – but she saw this little shell as . . . I don't know. An emblem of something.'

Ally nods. She would see it that way too.

'I think Nan viewed it as a message. You know, the way some people see white feathers? But I prefer to think that no matter how desperate Mum was feeling, maybe she found this shell and it gave her a small moment of joy. Even though she still did what she did.'

She looks down at her little son; pulls him close to her in a hug.

'I mean, in reality,' says Annabel, 'it probably just got stuck in her shoe in the way that sand and pebbles always do when you're at the beach. But hey, we believe what we want to believe, don't we?'

'And what about Harrison?' asks Jayden. 'How do you feel about his death?'

'Just like if anyone died,' she says. 'It's never good, is it? But I'm not sad, if that's what you mean.'

41

'Donald Crosby's guilty, Sarge. I know he is. You saw the way he started blubbing.'

Mullins peers through the small window into the interview room. Donald is sitting as if he's in a doctor's waiting room, hands folded in his lap, eyes staring into the middle distance. He looks, Mullins thinks, resigned to his fate. And resigned to his lack of an alibi too. Because once he got himself together Donald had nothing to offer in that department. He couldn't even confirm what he'd been watching on television. *I don't know, it's all the same on the box these days.* So, they arrested him. He's being held under caution for twenty-four hours. And he's refused a lawyer. Can Mullins picture Donald Crosby playing games with a spray can, on top? Not so much.

Skinner squints at his phone. 'Hold on. It's the lab. Wait two minutes.'

And he swings off down the corridor. Mullins turns from the window and observes his boss; tries to read his body language as he takes the call.

'Thanks for telling me,' Mullins hears. Skinner's voice is as gruff as always. But the way he walks back up the corridor? Like a footballer heading out the tunnel and into the match of their life.

'Mullins, Crosby's prints were at Sea Dream. Front door and the bedroom.'

'So we've got him?'

Skinner rubs his hands together. 'He was there, Mullins. He was there.'

'What about on the body – any DNA?'

'Looks like he got his act together and put some gloves on once he got to the business end,' says Skinner, his face grim. 'I've said it before and I'll say it again, most criminals are stupid.'

But Donald Crosby has no criminal record. Not so much as a speeding violation. Is it a case of an ordinary bloke snapping, when faced with extraordinary circumstances? The way Donald told the story about his sister – all that quiet fury – would have been enough for a kangaroo court.

'To really wrap this up, we need that murder weapon to surface,' says Skinner. 'Best guess it went in the sea, but it's too vast an area for the dive teams to do anything.'

'And what about Gina Best, Sarge? Are you liking him for both?'

'No Crosby paw prints at that crime scene, unfortunately. But the lab has reassembled the glass, and the vessel that contained the cyanide bears the prints of both Harrison Loveday *and* Gina Best. So it's plausible that Harrison took the cocktail as the killer intended, but for some reason didn't drink it, and passed it to Gina who knocked it back and paid the price. That's a workable theory, that is. Harrison Loveday as the intended victim all along. Gina Best killed in error. So Crosby goes back the next night to finish the job.'

Mullins nods. It's basically what he said yesterday, when he was told off for being obvious. With Crosby in custody, he knows the DCI will favour this theory. But the press, with their shouty headlines? 'Who's next?' and all that? They want an Arts Trail Killer.

'I can't see him peddling that "who's next?" message, Sarge, can you?'

'I've said all along that's a prankster, and there are no workable prints on either canvas, as it were. Scratch it, Mullins. Now, come on, let's see what he's got to say for himself. See if we can't wrap this one up.'

As they push into the room, Donald barely stirs. He doesn't look like someone who's been arrested on suspicion of murder. Or maybe it's more that he doesn't look like someone who's going to fight it.

'Tell us again about your evening,' says Skinner. 'Walk us through it, step by step. From the hours of six o'clock to ten o'clock.'

'I was at home watching television.'

'For four hours?'

Donald nods.

'But you can't remember what?'

He shakes his head – looking, Mullins thinks, like a wooden puppet he had as a kid. Its head fell off in the end.

'No dinner in that period?'

'I suppose I ate something. A bit of bread and cheese.'

Skinner sits back in his chair, hooks one leg over the other. *Oh, here we go*, thinks Mullins, *a bit of theatre.*

'How well do you know Sea Dream?' Skinner asks.

'The holiday house? Well enough. It sticks out.'

Just like its original owner, Roland Hunter, wanted it to. The fanciest place in the dunes, and now it's a murder house.

'Have you ever been inside?'

Donald shakes his head. 'It's a holiday house,' he says again.

'And when you knew Harrison Loveday was staying there, you didn't call in on him the day he arrived?'

'No.'

'Or the morning after the party? I know you two weren't on good terms, but . . .'

'We weren't on any terms. He barely knew I existed.'

'And that must have hurt, considering his impact on your family.'

Donald says nothing. But his jaw moves like he's chewing a tough steak.

'What about yesterday afternoon? Did you go to Sea Dream then?'

'No.'

'Yesterday evening?'

'No.'

'The trouble is, Donald, we have hard evidence that places you at Sea Dream. Incontrovertible evidence.'

Donald draws in a quick breath. As if he's reached out and burnt his fingers.

'So that lawyer you said no to, perhaps you want to reconsider.'

'But I can't afford—'

'Duty solicitor,' says Skinner. 'Nice bloke. Terry March. Get him, shall I?'

Mullins takes his cue and gets to his feet. At the door he turns and looks again at Donald. He's no longer sitting like someone in a doctor's waiting room; instead he looks like a boxer between bouts. Slumped in a corner of the ring. No obvious signs of impact, but a devastating internal injury? Probably. And by the expression on his face, dreading the next round.

Is this their killer? Despite all logic, Mullins feels a pang of sympathy. Then he rubs at his chest, as if it's indigestion, and hustles out to summon the solicitor.

42

'Sunita called us the moment she saw Donald being carted off in the police car,' says Gideon.

'"Carted off" is a bit of artistic licence, Gid,' says Connor. 'Like these guys say, he might just have been making a statement.'

'But either way, he's got something to say. That in itself is surprising,' says Gideon. 'I don't know if I feel relieved or . . . confused.'

Ally stands at the vast kitchen window of Island View House, looking out over the scene of the first crime. The immaculate garden appears to sweep all the way down to the cliff edge, the island itself just a few deft strokes across the bay. The lighthouse, neat as a chess piece, looks close enough to touch. Of course, it's an illusion. There's the cliff path between, then a vertiginous drop to a straggle of beach, and to actually get to the island requires a boat or watercraft – or a very bold swim. But standing here, it all seems within such easy reach.

Unlike the case.

Harrison Loveday's daughter in Carbis Bay felt so important: a true glint on the strandline. But Annabel seemed so straightforward, and her interpretation of Donald matched Pamela's.

'I'll go with confused,' says Connor. 'Because I can't see Donald being involved. He's such a mild-mannered guy.'

'Don't they say "It's always the quiet ones"?' says Gideon. Then he turns to Ally. 'Sorry, I'm being flippant. It's a protective mechanism. Deep down I'm . . . deeply anxious. And I still think Lara Swann has something to answer for. I really do.'

When Ally and Jayden knocked at the door of Island View, Gideon's first words were: *Well? What did Lara Swann have to say?* Followed by a nervous laugh. Now he wrings his hands; he looks tired, drawn.

'We're hoping to get some info on why Donald was taken in,' says Jayden.

Jayden tried calling Mullins earlier, and then Skinner, but they've had no response. With Gideon and Connor, they both agreed not to relay any of Donald's history with Harrison. To an outsider, it'd look, Jayden said, like a slam dunk.

'How did you come to select Harrison Loveday as the guest artist in the first place?' asks Ally.

Gideon and Connor look to one another.

'Do you know,' says Gideon, 'it was just one of those things that happened very quickly. I had the idea that we should bring in a big name—'

'And, being realistic,' cuts in Connor, 'to get a big name to come and join in with the trail is a bit of an ask . . .'

'So, we went to our little black books. As did Sunita. We thought about who has a Cornwall connection, and who hasn't exhibited out west in a while. The second part was important because we wanted the show itself to be story-worthy. PR mileage and all that. Anyway, we struck gold with Harrison. Born and raised here, studied here too. Then more or less left the Duchy, never to return. No links left.'

Ally quietly notes this: they clearly know nothing of Harrison's daughter.

'It took a while for him to reply to the invitation, but then he came through, didn't he, Conn? Even suggested bringing new work, which we'd hoped for, of course, but didn't expect.' Gideon briefly closes his eyes. 'My God, talking like this now, the responsibility . . . We brought him here. Him and Gina both. If it wasn't for us . . .'

'Can't think like that, Gid,' says Connor, with a shake of his head. Then, 'Why are you guys asking all this now?'

'So you knew Harrison from the London art scene?' asks Jayden, swerving the question.

'Not in a meaningful way, but our paths had crossed enough that I knew he wouldn't ignore an email from us.' Gideon gives a sharp bark of laughter. 'Actually, that's not true. He could have ignored us. But I was always very open in my admiration of his work, and naturally that pleased him. Harrison liked to be admired. As do we all, I suppose.'

'Did you admire his work too, Connor?' asks Ally.

'Technically, yes. He's very skilled.'

Ally waits for more, but Connor doesn't offer it. Instead, he gets up and starts making more coffee. An elaborate machine clanks and hisses into action.

'How much did you know about his life in Cornwall, Gideon?' asks Jayden.

'Well, only what his bio tells anyone. Born in Saltash. Studied in Falmouth,' says Gideon. 'I remember shortly after we decided to move here, I saw Harrison at a friend's show on Cork Street. I talked to him about Porthpella, but he didn't know it. Said he wasn't a surfer or a hobo – those were his words – so he had no interest in heading west. That was seven or eight years ago.' He strokes his chin, sends a questioning look in their direction. 'Why the Cornwall talk, anyway? Are you thinking it's relevant to

Harrison's death? Because Gina Best had nothing to do with this place. Nothing at all.'

'But they were both killed here,' says Connor. 'Course it's relevant, Gid.'

'Connor, you met Gina separately, didn't you?' asks Jayden.

Connor carries a tray to the table; his movements are slow and deliberate as he sets out mugs, a bowl of sugar.

'You're talking about the Dorset retreat?' he says eventually.

Jayden nods. And Ally knows he's thinking of the blog. The documented falling-out. Even if it didn't amount to much more than a few frosty words over a communal dinner.

'Yeah, that was some time ago. And Gina was there for just one night.'

'What was your impression of her?' he asks.

Connor stands with his hands planted on his hips. 'A saleswoman. Very good at what she does.'

'What about on a personal level?' asks Ally.

'Oh, come on, Conn, they're detectives. They've obviously read that gossipy little blog.' Gideon turns to them. 'They didn't see eye to eye, okay? Gina *was* a saleswoman. And lord knows we need them in this business. You've seen the artists on this trail. Most of them are useless at it: standing by their work, quietly dying inside. But . . . Gina was all business. That's probably what Harrison liked about her. She was hard-nosed. Ruthless. And she presented the young artists on the retreat with a rather depressing picture, by all accounts. Either get a good gallery on side – or fail. And Connor thought that was discouraging. Didn't you, Conn?'

'We'd spent all week building up people's confidence, this fantastic creative atmosphere, then she steamed in with a shedload of reality. Warped reality too, because not everyone's out to be a rock star. It's possible to feel creatively fulfilled without being the talk of the damn town.'

'Says the man who's been known to command six figures for his pieces,' says Gideon, nudging him. 'The truth is, you and Gina were chalk and cheese, Conn. And you told her as much.'

'So is that why you went straight to Harrison instead of via Gina?' asks Jayden. 'Because if Gina knew Connor was part of the committee, are you saying she might not have gone for it?'

'Best will in the world,' laughs Gideon, 'I don't think Gina cared very much what Connor thinks. Or anyone. It's like I said, she'd have thought we were small fry, not worth Harrison's time. And any new pieces? Well, obviously she'd want them for the Dashwood Gallery, not Porthpella.'

Ally looks to the terrace. As everyone milled about two nights ago, drinks in hand, Gina Best ingested cyanide. Ally's done her homework, and the smallest dose is lethal. But ensuring that it went to Gina, and no one else, would have taken intricate work. A cool head. And immaculate timing.

'Can you walk us through the night of the party? Who was standing where, and when?'

'My God, it was a movable feast, Ally.'

'Just in the moment when Gina died. As best as you can remember it.'

'Sure, follow me,' says Connor. 'Hey, Jayden, a word in your ear first?'

Ally watches as Connor and Jayden take the lead, heading from the kitchen, through the sitting room and out into the garden. She's intrigued as to what Connor has to say to Jayden specifically. Judging by his puzzled look, Gideon feels the same. As they follow, Ally slows her step and affects to take in the living room.

'What a truly beautiful space this is,' she says. And Gideon is too courteous to race on.

'We like it,' he says, with one more glance towards the garden doors. Then he turns his attention to Ally. 'The light,' he murmurs. 'The light is everything.'

And it is full of sunlight: beaming off the high ceilings, the toffee-coloured wooden boards, the oriental rugs and patchwork quilts. The walls are chock-a-block with framed pictures and Ally moves slowly, Gideon matching her step. Her eye settles on a photograph. It's an old-style portrait; deep, rich, with a distinctive silvery hue. Victorian-era in execution, but the subject is startlingly modern, a lithe musician holding his guitar above his head; silvered dreadlocks flying.

'Caught your eye, has it?' says Gideon, at her shoulder.

'It's remarkable,' says Ally, leaning closer.

'It's Billie Swann. Behind the camera, I mean. Obviously.'

'Lara's mother?'

'She shot it down here, apparently. This piece was a gift from a friend. I wouldn't have chosen it, if I'm honest. I don't like these old-style prints; they always feel faintly creepy to me. But the pal that gave it to me was supposed to be coming down for the trail, so I dug it out and hung it on the wall. You know, in that way we must when great-aunts visit? Dig out the dreadful vases, ghosts of Christmas past? Shall we go on out to the garden, Ally?'

Ally nods, then pulls her phone from her pocket.

'Do you mind if I take a snap? I've a friend who'd love it.'

'Be my guest. So, Ally, you really didn't get much from Lara? I don't want you to think we're overreacting there. When it comes to obvious animosity for the trail . . . well, Ms Swann takes the top spot.'

Ally checks she's captured the image, then slides her phone back into her pocket.

'She seemed to me to be as concerned about the murders as anyone,' she says.

'Perhaps she's a damn good actor.'

And, as of one minute ago, Ally is inclined to agree.

43

Gus watches Ray carefully. Ray has shaken off his green anorak and looks irritatingly natty in a denim shirt, the sleeves pushed halfway up his forearms. Meanwhile he's laughing with Saffron about the reign of the flat white, and just when it was that cappuccinos stepped aside to make room for the cool guy.

'A flat white gives you everything,' says Saffron. 'It's strong *and* smooth.'

Gus turns his attention to Ray's anorak, draped over the back of a chair.

He's seen this coat before, and he knows where. Going past his window yesterday evening. Which is the equivalent of going past Sea Dream yesterday evening. And Ray, of course, was wearing it.

Gus didn't realise it at the time. He mistook that green-coated man for the dad of a family holidaying in one of the beach houses further along. *Nice holiday they're having: murder in their back garden.* He certainly didn't look at that swamping old anorak and think of the suave guy who'd stood on the lawn at Island View in his leather jacket, busy charming Ally.

Gus gave a statement to the police after Harrison was found, and of course he mentioned the man in the green coat. But he also presumed that they'd traced him. Has Ray accounted for himself?

'Gus,' says Ray, 'you look troubled.' He drops into the seat at the next table and sends Gus an easy grin. 'You okay?'

'I think troubled is rather the default when there's been a double murder on one's doorstep.'

'Sorry, clumsy of me.' Ray runs a hand through his absurdly lustrous hair. 'False sense of security, see. I've hired Ally and Jayden. A few of us have, actually. Clubbed together, sort of thing.'

Gus blinks. 'Since when?'

Of course he knew that Ally and Jayden were on the case, but Ray hiring them? What does that mean – more meetings and briefings and cosy dinners at The Wreckers? Though Gus supposes it makes some sense, considering Ray knew Harrison Loveday. Does it cast a different light on this anorak issue?

'Since when?' says Ray. 'Since Ally found Harrison Loveday stabbed to death.'

I know, thinks Gus. *I was there.*

'I've more or less spent the morning with her, actually,' Ray goes on. 'She's shaken but . . . focused. I've got nothing but admiration for the woman.'

Suddenly Gus thinks of a tennis match; each pushing the other to the corners of the court. He was never much good at tennis.

'She came to me after she found the body,' says Gus. 'It was . . . very intense. I'm just glad I could be there for her.'

Ray rolls on, as if Gus's shot was nothing.

'The Arts Trail committee and I, we feel strongly that we need an artist on the case. And this feels personal to us all. Us artists, I mean. That's something Ally understands.'

But what can be more personal than being just steps away when a woman is poisoned? And when your closest neighbour is murdered in cold blood, and your best friend – your best person, all round – is the one to find him?

'We all feel that way,' says Gus. 'All of us locals.'

Because Gus can do unnecessary too. When it's necessary.

Ray grins. 'Exactly. And no better person for the job.'

'Ally and Jayden. I agree. No better people.' He takes a sip of his coffee. 'I actually think the police are being very thorough this time.'

'Can't afford not to be. Two deaths in as many days, just as you're going into holiday season. It's not a good message, is it?'

'They've been doing house-to-house, of course. Lots of questions. "Did you see anything unusual?" That sort of thing.'

'Fantastic coffee,' Ray calls out to Saffron. 'First-class.'

Saffron grins and pops a thumbs up, then goes back to her phone. Perhaps she's glued to the latest press reports. *Arts Trail Killer on the loose.* Gus refocuses, even if Ray is changing the subject.

Deliberately changing the subject? Because suddenly Gus feels rather bloody-minded about making this point.

'I expect they wanted to talk to you too, did they?' he says to Ray.

'Oh yes. I gave my statement. Two of them.'

'That's the trouble, when you've been in the vicinity of a crime. You immediately have to account for your actions.'

'Well, there were a lot of us, weren't there?' says Ray with a shrug. 'A whole house and garden full.'

'Oh, I don't mean the party. I'm talking about yesterday evening.'

'Ah, now, yesterday evening was somewhat more intimate.' A pause. 'I was with Ally.'

And Gus knows this. Ally had dinner with Ray. She told him, and Gus was fine, absolutely fine with it. If one of his old gang popped back up, well, wouldn't he do the same?

But it's the way Ray says it. The inflection. The calculated pause after the word *intimate*. What does this blustering man care for treading carefully? The trouble is, Gus has been so mindful of not pushing Ally that he's stepped too far back.

What if he's fallen completely out of the picture?

'But you were down here too, weren't you?' says Gus, no longer trying for casual. 'In the dunes. Early in the evening.'

Ray gives a brief shake of his head.

'You walked past my window, Ray.'

And the look on Ray's face says Gus has him bang to rights.

'Curtain twitcher, eh?' he says, then follows it with a laugh. A laugh, if you ask Gus, that's as hollow as a coffee cup. 'Well, it's no bad thing to be keeping an eye out, mate. Must feel a bit hairy, down in the dunes on your own. At least Ally promised me she'd decamp to the village if need be.'

'Ally's decamping to the village?'

'I offered up my place,' says Ray.

'Your place?' Gus is faintly aware of sounding like a hopeless sort of echo.

'Look, I've known her since she was nineteen. Can't blame the protective instincts kicking in. Old habits die hard and all that.' And he pushes his hand through that infernal hair. 'For both of us, I guess.'

44

Jayden and Ally are in the thinking room. Ally sits in Bill's old chair, her eyes glued to her laptop. The light's flat, the giant palm fronds cramming the window, but she appears to give off a glow. The glow that comes from making headway? Maybe that's wishful thinking but, on the way back from Island View House, Ally said, *I need to check something. I'm not at all sure, but I've got an idea . . .*

But first, Jayden has news.

'So, Connor got an email too,' he says. 'Sent from John Smith, same kind of tone as Pamela's.'

She looks up. 'Gosh. So that's what he wanted to talk to you about.'

'Connor got a bad vibe off it, so he didn't tell Gideon. Said he's twitchy enough as it is.'

He shows her a screenshot, and Ally frowns as she reads it.

'Jayden, this line, "I expect you're feeling afraid. Jumping at shadows." It didn't get that specific in Pamela's email, though the rather ominous warning was there.'

'No. I'd say the tone wants to be "concerned citizen" but is closer to . . . I don't know, someone getting a kick out of the drama. It's not threatening, exactly . . .'

'Actually, I think both emails *are* threatening,' says Ally. 'I know I wouldn't like to receive something like that. It's unsettling. Especially for someone living on their own, like Pamela.'

Like Ally too.

Jayden nods. He knows he's playing it down, because the fact is two people are dead and what if it doesn't stop there? What if the graffiti and the emails are all part of the killer's game, stirring up fear, loving the column inches? Jayden isn't into serial killer documentaries, but he knows the folklore around certain cases: the spotlight of attention; the public fearful – and gripped. Is that what's happening in Porthpella?

'I think we should find out if there's a pattern,' he says. 'See if more people are getting emails like this.'

'People connected to the Arts Trail?' says Ally.

'Anyone. The Arts Trail might be the link.'

He sees Ally take an unsteady breath, and his instinct is to reassure her.

'Look, it's what I said to Pamela. As soon as something's in the news, people can get weird. And the emails aren't connecting to the "who's next?" line, are they? There's no tangible link in the text. Anyway, I've got enough to find the IP addresses and see what we can trace from there. I'll see if Fatima can help.'

Fatima is gold. His old training buddy, who works for the Met and is always on the other end of the phone when Jayden needs a little extra background info.

'Now, your turn. Come on, Al, you've got something, haven't you? Spill.'

'Okay,' she says, glancing towards her laptop. 'Jayden, I think . . .' She pauses. 'Hold on, was that a knock at the door?'

Jayden rocks back. 'Al, you're killing me here.'

'Let me just see who's at the door.'

And she gets up, closing her laptop as she does so. Well, he's not going to steal her thunder by sneaking a peek. If she's got anything then he's happy waiting, because right now? This case is headway-light.

Jayden studies the whiteboard. He's written the names of the deceased and the names of the suspects – the suspects that have presented themselves, in any case. Donald Crosby is underlined because the guy's got motive, and the police have nicked him. They could have already charged him too, for all Jayden knows, but something tells him that's not the case. Not least because Jayden believed both Pamela and Annabel when they said Donald would never hurt anyone.

Jayden adds Pamela's name to the board, because she knew about Donald's complicated relationship with Harrison and it's clear she cares for the guy. Plus, they could really do with a few more names up there, because at the moment most of them are their friends – and the people paying their bills. Then he stands back, as if that's going to cast some new light, and goes through people one by one.

Annabel Crosby and Donald Crosby. Well, the police are understandably interested in them. But Annabel didn't present like someone who has something to hide. As for Donald, he's out of their reach now. All they have are the things that other people have said about him.

Lara Swann. She was twitchy, nervous. Jayden got the definite feeling she was hiding something, and Ally agreed. Plus, her grievance towards the Arts Trail committee was clear. Gut feel, though? Not a killer.

Gideon? Everything about Gideon adds up to concerned, and professional. He's got no obvious motive, either. While it was Gideon's idea to invite Harrison to Porthpella – and by default

Gina, perhaps, if the two came as a package – his explanation for choosing Harrison as the guest artist rings true.

Connor? Okay, he had a minor falling-out with Gina a few years ago, but unless there's a bigger story there, that's not the kind of thing to shapeshift into murderous intent. Not when Connor seems so easy-going and reasonable.

Sunita? Maybe they need to talk more to Sunita. But other than being involved in the decision to bring Harrison to Porthpella, and swapping a couple of emails with Gina because of it, she has no motive. Plus, she's Sunita. She is, as Gus described her once, 'a good egg'. Alright, she's hosting Harrison's show at the Bluebird, and maybe there will be more people coming through her door now as a result of his death, but higher footfall? Column inches for the gallery? Jayden shakes his head. *Not Sunita.*

Ray?

Ray.

Really, what do they know about Ray? He is a stranger in town – even if he's Ally's old friend. He's made a long trip for this Arts Trail, and why would he lie about being Harrison's plus-one for the party? Does he want to hire them just to keep close to the investigation? Cynically, that is possible. The same goes for the committee members, but Ray's the unknown quantity. As soon as Ally's finished up with whoever's at the door – and then told Jayden whatever thought she's ruminating on – he wants to dig into Ray Finch. However awkward it might be.

Next, he writes *Emails* then adds Pamela and Connor's names. Then: *Who's next? graffiti* and lists the Arts Trail poster by White Wave and the mural at Mahalo.

He pricks his ears, the boom of a voice cutting through.

Is that Skinner?

Jayden heads out into the hallway, marker pen in hand. He can see Skinner and Mullins sitting on the edge of Ally's white wicker sofa. Tension comes off them in waves.

For a moment, Jayden thinks there's been another murder. Not Ray? Because why have they come to Ally's?

'I'm sorry,' she's saying, 'but beyond the obvious, I didn't see a sign of anyone else having been there. Other than the open door. If someone wanted to delay discovery of their crime, then they'd have shut the door fast, wouldn't they? But someone chancing upon the scene by accident . . . the shock of it . . . Well, yes. I can imagine in those circumstances a person might flee and leave the door open.'

'Hullo Jayden,' says Mullins.

'Jayden,' nods Skinner.

'The officers,' says Ally carefully, 'are asking if I noticed any sign of someone else having been in the house before me. At Sea Dream.'

Interesting.

'After the killer, presumably,' says Jayden.

'Smart cookie, you are,' says Skinner. And there's a bit of bite in it, which, these days, Jayden knows to shrug off. But then Skinner heaves a sigh, pulls at his tie, and says, 'Look, you two, we're under pressure on this one. We've got a suspect with motive. His prints are all over the front door of Sea Dream. The bedroom door too. But he claims he didn't kill Harrison Loveday. Or Gina Best. Reckons he dropped by for a heart-to-heart with Loveday and came face-to-face with him dead. But unlike Mrs Bright here, he didn't call the police. Instead, he says he ran off and thought no one would ever be the wiser. Didn't reckon on basic forensics. Beggars belief, really.'

Jayden looks at Ally. Skinner has never volunteered case information so easily. He must be really feeling that pressure. Mullins, on the other hand, is grinning goofily, looking around as if they're one big happy family.

Jayden cuts right to it. 'You're talking about Donald Crosby.'

'Ah, you Shell House Detectives,' says Skinner, 'always one step behind.'

'Yep,' says Mullins. 'Donald Crosby.'

'We know his family's history with Harrison,' says Jayden.

'No need to beat about the bush then. He hated the guy's guts, didn't he?' says Skinner.

'Fingerprints on the two doors, but nothing physical to tie him to the victim?' asks Jayden.

'Not yet.'

'What do you make of Donald's explanation for his presence there?' asks Ally.

'What, wanting to talk to Loveday?' says Mullins. 'Crosby admitted he's been building up to it for years, then the prime opportunity comes along. Harrison Loveday's actually in Porthpella. But he bottled it at the party, and then after Gina Best was killed he didn't know if he still should. But then he went to Sea Dream anyway and . . . well, he was too late. That's his story.'

Donald must have kept his intentions to himself, because Pamela thought he was totally non-confrontational. At least that's what she told them earlier.

'And his story's consistent with the evidence?' asks Jayden.

Skinner juts his jaw. 'For now it is. We need that murder weapon.'

'And there's nothing to link Donald to Gina Best?' says Ally.

'Other than he could have bungled it,' says Mullins. 'Tried to poison Harrison Loveday and instead got Gina Best. That's our theory.'

'And it was definitely poison?' asks Jayden innocently. Like Ally didn't overhear it last night.

'Cyanide,' chirps Mullins.

Skinner shoots Mullins a look, then says, 'You can have that for free, but it'll be in the press soon enough anyway. Seeing as they're all over this case like a rash. And yes, before you get on your high horse, Jayden, we're aware they're two very different MOs. Look, we know you two have been hired by the committee or whatever they call themselves, but this is the kind of case that's going to live or die by forensic evidence.'

'And motive,' says Jayden. 'Surely?'

'If we've got hard evidence, we don't need motive.'

'Sergeant, did you believe Donald?' asks Ally.

'I don't want to,' he says.

But that's not the same as *No, I don't*.

'Pamela Trescoe told us she reported an email,' says Jayden.

'And clearly Pamela Trescoe thinks we've got nothing better to do,' snaps Skinner.

'Connor Rafferty received one too,' says Ally. 'The writer said "I expect you're feeling afraid" in it.'

Skinner rolls his eyes. 'The general public,' he says, 'or certain factions of it, are drama-loving pests. Catch up, Shell House.'

But Mullins is furrowing his brow. 'And is Connor Rafferty afraid?' he asks.

45

Ally watches Skinner and Mullins clump down the path and push through the gate. The clutch of sun-bleached buoys swing vigorously in their wake.

'I've never known the DS to be so forthcoming,' says Ally.

'Tell me about it. But we're in different territory now, Al. We're proven. He trusts us.'

Ally turns. 'He was rather dismissive about the committee hiring us.'

'The committee plus Ray.' He darts a look at Ally, but she doesn't react. 'It sounds like they're putting all their eggs in the Donald Crosby basket. Like he's their only lead right now.'

'Agreed. I know we haven't spoken to Donald, but his story sounds plausible on the face of it. If he was seeking to confront Harrison and then came face-to-face with his dead body, well, I can understand why he would run. He must have known he'd be a suspect as soon as his link to Harrison was unearthed. I expect he felt pure panic.'

'Skinner didn't give any timings, but it closes the window for the murder, doesn't it? If you went in at ten o'clock, Donald had been and gone before you.'

'He could have only just gone.'

'True. But you didn't see him on the way, did you? Or notice a car? He'd have got out of there *fast*. And if you were coming from the village, he'd have passed you.'

Ally thinks back. It was one of those cloudless nights of silvery light, a crescent moon worthy of a Christmas card. She was preoccupied, but she's certain she would have noticed if Donald Crosby were in the vicinity.

'Pamela will be stunned,' says Ally. 'Jayden, do they have enough evidence to charge Donald?'

He shakes his head. 'No, Skinner needs more. Way more. If he could link Donald to the body, with one stray hair, one fibre . . . he'd be made up. So, they can't have anything. Which means the killer was meticulous.'

'As meticulous as spiking a drink in the middle of a party?'

'Yeah, I'm not sure I buy that Gina Best was killed by accident. It feels too convenient. Like . . . an easier story for the public to swallow. Look, I know the police will be investigating this crime in all its complexity, but when you've got a room full of journalists chasing Arts Trail Killer headlines, it's a pacifier to say actually no, this is a personal vendetta. This is only about Harrison Loveday.'

'Because now that he's dead, it's over,' says Ally.

'Exactly. The threat's gone. I just don't know if it is. That line about forensics. Skinner doesn't think you and I are getting anywhere. *Are* we getting anywhere, Al? Please tell me you're sitting on something good.'

'Let's go back to the thinking room. There's something I want to show you.'

And there's a spring in Jayden's step as he walks ahead down the hall, which Ally hopes her research merits.

'Alright,' she says, opening her laptop. 'Photography lesson.'

Jayden drops into the chair, says, 'I'm here for a photography lesson.'

'At Island View earlier, I noticed a picture on the wall. A striking, old-fashioned-style portrait shot. It was by Billie Swann.'

'Lara's mum.'

'Lara's mum.'

She pulls out her phone and shows Jayden the snap. He zooms in on the details of it: the silvery hues, the dark shadows, the otherworldliness.

'Cool pic,' he says.

'I suppose I've been thinking about my art school days lately, and . . . well, a lesson came to mind. You see, in the beginning we had a go at everything. Printmaking, illustration, photography. And we learnt about the evolution of photographic processes. Seeing this picture, I felt sure it was wet-plate photography, the technique they used in Victorian days. You know those huge cameras where the photographer is under a hood? It's both camera and darkroom. You develop the pictures on the spot.'

Jayden nods. 'Okay.'

'I wanted to check two things. One, whether I was right, and Billie Swann did work with this method. And two, the exact process for wet-plate collodion photography.'

'Al,' says Jayden, 'I'm loving being down this rabbit hole with you, but I have zero idea where it's going.'

'Where it's going is to the poisoning of Gina Best. Because, traditionally, this photographic process uses cyanide.'

Jayden spins in his chair. 'You're not serious?'

'It's one of the chemicals used to expose the image. These days, for people wanting to achieve a similar effect, there are less toxic alternatives, but it seems the purists swear by potassium cyanide, because it brings out the warmer tones.'

'So a lethal poison is used as an art material?'

Ally nods. 'Look, Billie Swann had a mixed-media exhibition twelve years ago, and she displayed a number of these photographs.

It was one of her last shows. The photos didn't garner much attention in terms of art world press – the focus was more on some huge oil paintings of naked figures – but one of Gideon's friends bought him one. It was pure chance that I saw it on the wall, Jayden.'

'And Gideon doesn't know anything about the cyanide part of the process?'

'He'd have mentioned it if he did. He and Connor have suspected Lara from the beginning.'

Jayden steeples his fingers.

'Okay,' he says. 'So, Billie Swann had access to cyanide, but she's in a nursing home hundreds of miles away. So obviously we're talking Lara.'

'It's possible Lara knew about it. Gideon said Billie shot the image here in Cornwall. If Lara ever stayed at Westerly Manor while her mum was there, she'd probably have warned her that she kept lethal chemicals in her studio.'

'So, let me get this right,' says Jayden. 'Lara Swann has a personal grudge against the Arts Trail because she didn't make the cut. The first murder was poisoning by cyanide. And Lara Swann has, potentially, direct access to the stuff.'

Ally nods. 'It's possible.'

'Al, this is brilliant work. And we know Lara was at the party. She turned up, uninvited, and then left. Before Gina Best died – or so she says. If the motive is a grudge against the Arts Trail, then anyone could have been the target on Friday night, right? All she'd need to do is put cyanide in one of the glasses, the busy bartender would slosh in the cocktails, no one would notice. Everyone's looking at that individual, asking, "Why Gina Best?" It's possible Gina Best just got very unlucky.'

'And then Harrison was killed because he's the big star?'

'Exactly. Hit the trail where it hurts.' Jayden shakes his head. 'It works, Al.'

'My only problem is it's such a disproportionate reaction . . .'

'And murderers are known for being reasonable people, right? Look, it only needs to make sense to Lara. People rationalise their reactions in all kinds of crazy ways. So her work's rejected? The Arts Trail needs to pay.'

Ally thinks of Lara Swann all alone in the big house at the top of the hill. Her apparent timidity, then her runaway tongue when she talked of the loneliness of her childhood, her bitterness towards the cliques of the art world. Perhaps the committee rejecting her work had been one rejection too many; the straw that broke her back.

'Can you bring up a picture of Billie Swann?' asks Jayden.

Ally taps the name into the search engine, and dozens of images fill the screen. She clicks on one dated 2005, so Billie would have been in her fifties. She looks like a rock star: skinny jeans, an oversized t-shirt with a rough red outline of a shattered heart on it, black lace-up boots. Berry-red lipstick and bleached, spiked hair. She's snarling at the camera; holding up two fingers.

'She's a character,' says Ally. 'On Lara's website she describes her mother as formidable. I wonder what it was like growing up with such a celebrated artist for a mother. One that probably split opinion too. The traditional art world can be rather snobbish . . .'

'You mean they prefer the likes of Harrison Loveday? What a surprise.'

'From what we've seen of Lara, she seems so mild. I wonder if that's a reaction, to be so different to her mother. Growing up in her shadow . . .'

'Remember the emails, Al. Not mild. Plus, think about everything Lara was saying this morning. Sure, she's quietly spoken, but she's opinionated – and resentful.'

'She was dismissive about Milo Nash's work being destroyed too.'

'Add it to the list, Al. She probably did it.'

Lara Swann's campaign against the Arts Trail. It makes sense. And the picture of Lara as a more complicated individual than she appeared at first glance is starting to make sense too.

'Right,' says Jayden. 'We've got two options.'

'Tell the police our thinking?'

'Yeah, that's one. The other is that we follow it up some more first. We check out Lara again, see if we can take a look at her mum's studio.'

'Well, I think I'd feel more confident in taking this theory to DS Skinner if we found all of the equipment for wet-plate photography first,' says Ally wryly.

'Yeah, that would be good. Including a neat little half-empty bottle of cyanide, right?' He gives a low laugh. Then goes to the board and circles Lara's name. 'Al, I think it's worth the conversation with Skinner now. Especially given the angry emails Lara sent the committee after being rejected. It's time to tell the police about them too.'

But despite his words, Jayden looks, to Ally, divided.

'Because the thing is, this isn't like our other cases, is it? If we're right about Lara, she's killed twice. There's nothing to say she won't kill again. If the clock's ticking, do we want to waste time going in quiet and subtle, when the police could just march in with a warrant?'

And for the first time in a while, Jayden sounds like he'd prefer to be the one with the badge; the ability to make an arrest.

'But . . .' he goes on, 'I think we've got Lara's trust. A little bit, anyway. Definitely more than the police would.' His face looks hopeful suddenly. 'We can go in on the Donald Crosby ticket. That's not confidential – Sunita saw him and told us. We can take the reassurance line, say that progress is being made. Lure her into a false sense of security.'

'I could pretend to be a fan of her mother's work,' says Ally. 'Ask to see her studio, while we're there.'

'And if we see, hear or think of anything to corroborate this theory, we're straight on the phone to Skinner and Mullins. Deal?'

'Deal,' says Ally.

Jayden checks his watch. 'It's coming up on six o'clock.'

'Are you alright for time?'

'Sue's pulling a long shift. Cat's given me a pass for this one. But I think we need to get up to Lara's now if we're going. If we call too late, it's not going to look casual.'

Ally gets to her feet. She feels a flicker of excitement in her chest.

'And Al, if we're not going to stuff this one up, we really need to make it look casual.'

46

Lara holds a piece of kitten in her hand. Probably an ear. Though it could be a nose. She turns it around, then tosses it back in the pile. This jigsaw is harder than it seems. The saccharine image – two kittens in a wicker basket, with peeping tongues and fluffy tails – makes it look like they're going to hand it to you on a plate. But no. And today, Lara's not feeling it. She wouldn't call herself a jigsaw fanatic, that would make her sound a little mad, a little sad, and that's her mother talking – *Really, a jigsaw? You've nothing better to do?* – but she is undoubtedly keen on them.

The world makes sense in jigsaw form. Broken things can be reassembled. Hopeless situations fixed. When Lara's hard at a jigsaw, everything else falls away. It's just her and some laser-cut cardboard.

She decides to turn her attention to a different part of the puzzle. Forget the kittens, what about the pink ball? Focus on the pink ball. That fade from fuchsia to candyfloss. Those nice curves.

As she moves a piece into position, her ears prick. It's the sound of a car engine.

Lara's fingers tremble, and she stuffs them in her mouth, bites down hard against her nails. It could just be someone turning round in the driveway, couldn't it?

But then there's a knock at the door. She steals to the window, fully expecting to see a police car. But it's a battered old Land Rover, and those two people from this morning. The private detectives, with their CV of missing women, dead chefs, drowned rock stars, and bullock attacks. So much for them pretending to be concerned neighbours doing the rounds. If there's a murder case, then Ally Bright and Jayden Weston are right in the middle of it.

They can't fool her.

They knock again.

For a moment Lara thinks about not opening the door. She could be anywhere, couldn't she? She could have upped and left. But something inside Lara – something stubborn, hard as a stone – makes her stand her ground. And polish her armour.

Where's your confidence? Her mother again. *How did I end up with such a shrinking violet?*

Like a violet is a nasty thing, not something sweet and rare.

Yes, how did you, Mother?

Lara sucks in a deep breath and smooths her hands over her skirt as she walks to the door. Bites the inside of her mouth until she can taste coins. She pulls back the bolts, turns the key, and opens up.

'Sorry, it's a little late to call,' says Ally.

You're not sorry at all, thinks Lara. It's not that she hates these two, but when they came here this morning, she knew they'd been sent. *Lara Swann, the weirdo on the hill. The girl who thinks she can draw. Would you believe she's Billie Swann's daughter?* Then peals of laughter, probably.

'We wanted to check in with you,' says Jayden. 'There's been some developments.'

Then they say something about a suspect in custody, and what a relief it is that progress is being made. Lara wonders if they can hear the swear words reverberating in her skull. It gives her a dangerous pleasure, to fix a smile and yet be cursing inwardly: a tirade of violence and disgust. She used to do it with her mother. Outside: *Yes, of course, Mother.* While inside?

You can't imagine.

But the way they're looking at her, she almost wonders if she's grown sloppy, her inner thoughts leaching outward. Lara feels horribly visible suddenly. She squirms under their scrutiny, like a sample on a Petri dish.

'Well, I'm glad,' she says stiffly. 'Of course I am. Because it's frightening knowing this is going on under our noses. And me up here, all on my own.'

And the fear is real, isn't it? They must have heard those bolts she dragged back just now.

'Plus, I got a strange email,' she says.

The two of them swap a look. *Now who's holding the cards?*

'Some nutcase telling me he was sorry about what was happening in Porthpella, and he hoped I wasn't feeling afraid.'

'Was it sent from a John Smith?' asks Ally.

'Yes,' says Lara. Her heart quickens. 'Why? What do you know about it? It's not . . . it's not connected, is it? I thought it was just some creep.'

'You didn't reply, did you?'

'I'm not stupid.'

And Jayden's asking if he can see the email, and he's taking Lara's phone, clicking into the message and screenshotting it.

'Can you text it to me?' he says, giving her his number. 'A couple of other people have had them too.'

'Who?'

'Pamela Trescoe and Connor Rafferty.'

Lara bites her lip. 'Artists,' she says. Her hair falls in front of her face and she swipes it with her hand. She watches Ally. 'But you haven't had one?'

230

Ally shakes her head. Then says something about having an ulterior motive in coming here. A confession to make. But she's sort of smiling. And Lara wonders where this is going, and why Ally thinks it's okay to move on from the emails so quickly. Then, of course, it goes where it always goes – to Lara's mother.

Ally Bright is a fan of Billie Swann.

Lara wouldn't have imagined it of her, but then didn't the whole world worship at the altar of Billie Swann?

'Did she have a studio here?' asks Ally.

Lara isn't very good at reading people; she thinks they're laughing at her most of the time. *Thinks? Knows.* Once that's your lens, it's hard to see anything different. But it seems a straightforward question.

'Yes, she did.'

'I'd love to see it, Lara. Just a quick look inside. I don't know if you're like this, but other artists' studios are always so fascinating to me. Do you work out of the same space?'

'Me?'

The question takes her by surprise. How pathetic she is that, for a split second, she glows at that word, *work*.

'I can do my stuff anywhere,' she says, dipping her head. 'They're just little drawings. Silly, simple things.'

'I think the simplest things are the hardest to pull off,' says Ally. 'That's what I've always found, anyway.'

And for a second, Lara imagines standing talking to this woman about art. Forgetting everything else. That wouldn't be so bad. But then guilt and anger curdle in the pit of her stomach. She suddenly wants to get rid of these two people. Get rid of them so they never come back.

'Her studio's one of the outbuildings. The red door. But don't expect a guided tour. My mother never let me go in there and old habits die hard. See yourselves out after, okay?'

She watches them as they cross the yard and push open the blood-red door. She doesn't care if they root around in there, admiring her mother's doodles in sketchbooks, her splayed brushes and congealed paint pots. They won't find anything. Because Lara's already hidden the one thing that matters.

47

'Wet-plate what now?'

Mullins eyes Skinner. The DS has his phone clamped to his ear; the other hand pressed to his forehead. It's been a long day for him, which means it's been a long day for them all. DCI Robinson has mostly been holed up in his office, with one or other of the Newquay lot scurrying in and out.

For a feeble sort of bloke, Donald Crosby's proving immovable, sticking to that story of his. He had a bone to pick with Harrison Loveday, he went to talk to him at Sea Dream, he found him dead – then he bolted. End of.

The DCI thinks Crosby's lying, and if he has his way, they'll keep him beyond the twenty-four hours. Skinner *wants* to think he's lying. What's easier? Proving a lie is a lie, or unearthing a whole new truth? But then it's never about what's easy, is it? Back in the old days, Mullins would take Easy Street all day long. If you asked him what his favourite parts of the job were, it was the low-brain stuff. Holding the speed gun in his hands, going after the boy racers and the cashed-up flash pants. He didn't mind breaking up a scuffle from time to time: *You've had one too many, mate. We've all been there.* Truth is, he liked what the uniform did for him. He didn't always stop to think what he did for the uniform.

Then Ally and Jayden came along.

In the beginning, Mullins wished he'd known Bill Bright, because he might have had a better start in the job if he had. But now he's just grateful that he knows Ally. As for Jayden – *whisper it* – he'd be a better response officer than anyone they've got down here. A better detective too. The thing is, Skinner knows it. And the fact that Jayden prefers 'playing detective at the beach' – which is how Skinner still likes to put it – is basically an insult to the force. It's like someone preferring to kick a ball about barefoot in the street instead of signing with Man City.

And now Mullins is pretty sure that's Ally or Jayden ringing in, because Skinner has a special tone of voice that he saves just for them. And 'wet-plate what now' sounds suspiciously like a bit of Shell House blue-sky thinking.

Or, best will in the world, Shell House nonsense.

'So hold on,' says Skinner, 'you found the camera gear but no chemicals. So what exactly are you telling me?'

Mullins gets up out of his chair and goes over. He can hear Ally's light voice on the other end of the line.

'Yes, we do know about Lara Swann's emails to the committee. She told us as much herself. She said she didn't want them held against her.'

In response, Ally says something Mullins can't catch.

'I'm with you there,' says Skinner. 'Well, it was worth the thought.'

And that's that. Shell House over and out.

Skinner puffs out his cheeks. 'Artists,' he says. 'They always want to make it about the art. Ally Bright dredging up some theory about ancient photographic processes and toxic chemicals.'

'That's good thinking, isn't it?' says Mullins. 'I mean, it being the Arts Trail Killer and all that.'

Skinner shoots him a look. 'The minute we start reading the headlines, we're toast, Mullins.'

'And cyanide is used in this process, is it?'

'It can be.'

'And Lara Swann does this sort of photography, does she?'

'Not Lara, her mother. But all the gear's up at the house. No cyanide though. Ally and Jayden went in with the sniffer dogs and came up with diddly squat.'

Mullins can't imagine Ally using her precious Fox to sniff out cyanide.

'Don't look so confused, Mullins. I'm talking figuratively. They had the sense to say they trod carefully, because they know this is a big-scale investigation and we're all over it. No, look, I'll hand it to them, it's a decent idea. But cyanide is not the sole preserve of people with an interest in Victorian photography. Jewellery makers use it too. And I'm not going to bang down the door of every amateur jeweller in these parts, am I?'

'Why not?' says Mullins.

Skinner raises his eyebrows.

'Well, what if Donald Crosby is telling the truth? What if he didn't kill Harrison Loveday, and what if Gina Best dying wasn't a mistake? What if it is all about the Arts Trail?'

'Lara Swann,' says Skinner quietly to himself. 'One of the Newquay boys took her statement.' He turns back to his keyboard, performs a few quick taps. 'She applied to be on the Arts Trail but didn't make the cut. Bit of a kick in the teeth. Must have thought she was a shoo-in with her famous mother. And yes, she was at the party. Left before Gina Best died. Sounds suspicious on the face of it, but she says she felt unwelcome. Turned up as a bit of a provocation, then realised she was just shooting herself in the foot. She was upfront about it. Unlike Donald Crosby.'

'Let's have a look at her,' says Mullins.

He peers at her photograph. Her pale face and delicate features. Her hair, long and straight as a curtain. Hair he's seen before; swishing, swinging.

'Sarge,' he says, 'I saw her running.'

'Running?'

'The night of the party. We were headed up to Island View and she was running down the coast road. I thought she was a jogger.'

'A jogger in party gear?'

'She wasn't in party gear. She was just . . . ordinary.'

Skinner gives him a hard look. 'Mullins, if we're on our way to the scene of a suspicious death, and you clock someone running – and they're not head to toe in Lycra – you investigate that.'

'I only half saw her,' he says.

'And yet you're now certain of her identity?'

Mullins folds his arms. *When you put it like that . . .*

He wants to say, *But you were in the car too, Sarge.* He wants to say, *One of the Newquay lot, the actual Major Crimes team, took her statement and didn't blink an eye.* He wants to say, *Ally and Jayden just handed you an actual link between someone in the community with an axe to grind and cyanide and you don't want to hear it.*

But, instead, he says, 'Sorry, Sarge.' Then, 'So what are we going to do now?'

At that moment someone comes to the door and says, 'A report's just come in of antisocial behaviour and damage to public property in Porthpella – currently in progress. At the bridge near Prospect Lane.'

'That's what you're going to do now, Mullins,' says Skinner. 'I'll get one of the Newquay DCs to help me here.'

And as Mullins gets to his feet, he knows it's a punishment.

48

'Hi-vis and a hard hat? Who's that going to fool?' says Saffron with a grin.

'You're the one who's going to give me away. Not too many maintenance workers have glamorous assistants.'

'Oh, I'm assisting, am I?'

Saffron was closing up Hang Ten when Milo called. Said he was planning a mission and did she want to come along. *See how I really do it, out in the wild.* And of course she wanted to go, but it felt weird explaining that to Broady. It shouldn't, because, really, why is it any different to going to any of the Arts Trail shows and watching an artist at work?

But it does feel different.

Broady made it easy, at first. He said a friend of his wanted to get some photographs and they were doing a sunset session out at Gwenver. But then he asked if she wanted to come. So she was totally upfront. *It's like, Arts Trail fringe or something. Why should the trad lot get all the attention?* To which Broady replied that Milo Nash wasn't exactly short of attention but, hey, if that's how she wanted to spend her evening then he wasn't going to stop her. *But, Saff,* he added, *it's not a great time to be hanging out with new people.*

At first, she didn't know what he meant, but then he mentioned the Arts Trail Killer and she actually laughed. Not that any of it is funny. Not even close. But Milo Nash? So she kissed him quickly on the cheek and said she'd have Mullins on speed dial.

So here she is, looking up at Milo, who's halfway up a ladder with his spray cans. Life is about to get a lot more colourful for this bridge – this boring, grey concrete bridge that Saffron must have cycled or driven under a thousand times, and never once pictured as a canvas for an artist.

'Are you coming up?' he calls down.

'There's no room.'

'Sure there is.'

Saffron gasps as Milo steps from the ladder and presses himself against the stone of the bridge; his feet finding an invisible ledge. He grins at her, looking like a kid at the top of a climbing frame: *Hey, look at me, no hands!*

'What if you fall?'

'Not my first rodeo. Come up.'

His spray cans are lined up on the top of the ladder: all colours of the rainbow. The work's already underway, though she doesn't know what it is yet. Saffron glances back down the lane. It's quiet this evening. Only two cars have passed, and both times Milo's tweaked his stance to look like he's cleaning graffiti from the wall instead of spraying it on. He explained to her that he's had a couple of police cautions. That while most of the time his work's appreciated, it depends on the location. And this? It's not like a ramp down the skate park.

Saffron puts a hand to her hard hat, adjusts her hi-vis vest. Then starts to climb.

From up here, everything looks further away than it really is. The rooftops of Porthpella; that lone tractor tracking over the hillside; the sea.

Well, this is new.

238

She's suddenly aware of how close Milo is, his body just millimetres away. He's practically dangling, like an acrobat on a rope, the muscles in his arm taut. He throws her an easy grin. And it's a buzz. The whole thing. She feels herself grinning back.

'Alright,' he says, reaching into his pocket, pulling out a piece of paper and holding it up. 'Now you're an insider.'

It's a sketch of the bridge, with *Here Be Monsters* written across it in massive, old-style lettering. There's the edge of the land and the span of the sea, but unlike on ancient maps it's the land that's teeming with unknowable things. A double-headed octopus, wielding weapons with every tentacle. A skeleton in a captain's hat, dancing on somebody's grave. Out on the water there's an upturned boat; a snapped surfboard. It's frenzied and frightening, nothing like the happy scene he did for Mahalo. But . . . it's also kind of cool. She looks again at the shape of the coastline, and it dawns on her: it's Porthpella.

And suddenly she doesn't know if she likes it the same.

'So, look, I've started laying the foundations with the blue here, the outline of the land. I've got to work fast. It's not a high-profile spot, but there are cars passing.' He hesitates, seeing her face. 'What is it? You don't like heights?'

And he reaches out to hold her arm.

'You're all good up here, Saffron. A natural.'

'No, it's just . . . this is Porthpella. And you're talking about the murders, aren't you?'

'Here be monsters.'

'Yeah, so . . . I just don't think it's very . . . respectful. Is that the word? Just . . . What about the families?'

'There's no disrespect.'

'No, I know. Not intentionally. But it's like you're making entertainment out of it.'

'It's a statement,' he says.

'Is it?'

'A moment in time.'

'The skeleton dancing on the grave . . .'

'A moment in time that's going to be lost if we don't get a move on . . .'

'I think it's clever, and cool, but . . . real people live here, Milo. And those people are worried. People are scared.'

Saffron is aware that her hard hat has tilted, and she feels kind of ridiculous looking up at him from beneath its rim.

Milo's brows knit together. She notices the sprinkle of freckles on his cheekbones. His eyes are brown as conkers.

'I want a reaction,' he says. 'Everyone's wrapped themselves up in cotton wool. Headlines in newspapers are throwaway. Who really cares? People just get on with their ordinary little lives. Porthpella's in the grip of something, and I don't know what it is, but two people got killed and my work was trashed. I'm going to make a noise about that. The only way I know how.'

Saffron tightens her grip on the ladder. For a second, she forgot that she's fifteen feet up, balanced on a single rung. And Milo's holding on to basically nothing.

'Okay, I get it,' she says. Then, 'So why not go bigger? This spot, it's quiet. We've been here, what, twenty minutes, and only two cars have gone by. Don't you want more people to see it? When you did your thing on the chippie there was uproar. Because it was right on the square.'

'Hold on, a minute ago you thought it was too much and now it's not enough?'

Saffron laughs. But it dies at her lips, because in the distance, she sees the colours of a patrol car on the approach. And lights: not flashing, no sirens, but heading this way.

'Right, let's move.'

'Who called the police?' cries Saffron.

'There's a killer on the loose, but oh no, get the artist. Let's move, Saffron.'

'I am, I am.'

She goes as quickly as she can, but her palms feel hot and slippery. She's into the lower section of the ladder: six, seven rungs left.

'Take it steady,' Milo says from above.

And just like that, she loses her footing. It feels as if she's in freefall, but she hits the ground almost instantly. She's fallen off enough skateboards to know how to do it: tuck and roll. But she doesn't do that here. Not even close. Her wrist, the one she hurt in Hawaii, takes all of her weight. It buckles. She screams.

Milo's instantly beside her, landing like a cat on all fours.

'Your arm?'

She feels his hand on her shoulder, sees the concern on his face as he bends over her.

'Can you get up?'

He looks back at the sound of the approaching car.

'Go,' she says. 'Don't get caught.'

Because mostly she wants to stay curled on the ground, clutching her wrist. The thought of jumping up and running brings on a whack of nausea.

'Saffron, I'm not going to leave—'

'Milo, seriously, I'm good. You go . . .'

And he's taking the ladder, contracting it, eyes already on his van further up the road. He holds out his hand.

'Come on,' he says.

The engine in the lane is loud. It's his last chance, and they both know it. There's a quick bleat of a siren as the car draws up.

'Go!' she says.

So he does. And then another face is bending over her. A familiar face. A friendly face, in its way.

A confused face.

'Saff?'

And she starts to cry, because it really hurts. Plus . . . Mullins.

49

'I guess if I'd used poison to kill someone, I wouldn't just put the bottle back where it came from either,' says Jayden.

As they bump along the track through the dunes, Jayden drums his fingers on the wheel. They struck gold in Billie Swann's studio. All the gear for wet-plate collodion photography was there – Ally had her tick list – just no fixing chemical. In other words, no cyanide. It was the only thing from the list that was missing. But crucially, there was no non-toxic alternative either. As soon as they were clear of the house, Ally phoned Skinner. Jayden and Ally were buzzing. The DS's response? Not buzzing. He said the police had taken a statement from Lara Swann, and she wasn't a person of interest. Is Skinner now going to percolate the information and be clearer-eyed?

Maybe even change his mind?

'I suppose it was strange that Lara let us go in the studio on our own,' says Ally, uncertainly. 'She didn't seem bothered by us looking there. What do you think that means?'

'No, I think she was bothered,' says Jayden, 'but she was trying to hide it. A double bluff.'

Most people Jayden meets, he gets a handle on, but he can't quite figure out Lara Swann. Is she capable of these killings? Taken on its own, the Harrison Loveday murder could have escalated from a confrontation. Though given that there's no decent forensic evidence, that's unlikely. And put together with the Gina Best poisoning? No, these murders were premeditated. There was considerable planning in the timing and the execution.

'Lara's intelligent,' he says, thinking out loud. 'And she's got time on her hands. No one's aware of her having a job. She lives an isolated life. Pamela said she tried to befriend her, but Lara wasn't interested.'

'Plenty of people like their privacy. A small community isn't to everyone's tastes.'

'Maybe not, but she's sitting up there in that big house, nursing a grudge against the Arts Trail. A grudge that could get out of proportion, because there's no one talking her down from it.'

Jayden feels like he's trying to persuade Ally. Has Skinner's response given her doubts?

'If Lara is guilty, then the fact that she received one of the emails makes this "John Smith" seem a bit less sinister, at least,' says Ally. 'Pamela and Connor will be reassured by that.'

'I've been thinking on that. When Lara was telling us about it, she said that John Smith wrote that he was sorry to hear about what was going on in Porthpella. Am I remembering that right?'

'Something like that, yes.'

'It's the "something like" that's bugging me. Because the email Lara showed me just said that he'd heard about what was happening in Porthpella, that it was a tragedy, and he hoped she wasn't afraid. John Smith didn't use the word "sorry" anywhere. Unless she's been swapping notes with Pamela, whose email did say "I'm sorry", I bet Lara's behind the emails.'

'What, and she sent one to herself to cover her tracks?'

'Exactly,' says Jayden, triumph jumping into his voice. 'She's playing games.'

'What if she's responsible for the emails but not the murders?'

'No, the cyanide connection is strong, Al. I think we should talk to more of the partygoers. Try and track Lara Swann's movements for the window when she was there.'

'Gideon said he spoke to her very briefly,' says Ally. 'And Sunita certainly noticed her.'

'And if our theory's right, Lara killed Harrison too. Which means there's a second murder weapon out there somewhere.'

Though she's probably disposed of that as well.

Then an inconvenient thought lands.

'Al, why would Lara get rid of the cyanide but then leave all the old-fashioned photography gear? Because it's the only tangible thing that links her to the poison, isn't it?'

Ally hesitates. 'The equipment wasn't immediately obvious though. We had to know what we were looking for.'

Billie Swann was an eclectic artist, and it looked like she'd kept a bit of everything in her studio. The giant old camera was at the very back, in a cupboard, along with assorted boxes holding gloves, trays, chemicals. To get there, they'd had to clamber past canvases, pottery wheels and easels. Not an easy path. But if you were turning the place over – or had a search warrant – you'd find it, no problem.

'Maybe Lara wasn't counting on anyone making the connection but . . . this place is full of artists. And tracing the source of the cyanide will be right up there on the police's to-do list. If it were me, I'd have got rid of all the photography stuff. Unless it's a test. More games. She wants to see how clever we are.'

Ally turns to look at him. 'Do you think that's her style?'

'I don't know,' says Jayden. And the thought nags at him. 'If she's behind the emails, and the graffiti too, then she's a game-player for sure. So maybe it is her style. But when it comes to the murders, she's executed her plan meticulously – there's obviously nothing tying her to the crime scenes. So why stop short of crossing those t's and dotting the i's, you know?'

They're just pulling up to The Shell House, and the thinking room is calling for a late shift. Jayden checked in with Cat earlier and her voice wasn't just frazzled, it was cinders. He hesitated – fully torn – then told her they were getting close to solving this; he just needed this night. *We're okay here, Jay*, she told him, and, these days, 'okay' is a win. So, he leant into the positive and said all good things down the phone. Plus, Sue's next door. It's not like he's leaving Cat all on her own, is it?

'Oh, there's Gus,' says Ally.

And sure enough, Gus steps out from the veranda. As they climb out of the car, he holds up a hand in greeting, but his smile is slow to join it. In fact, Jayden can see the worry lines in his forehead from miles away.

'Something's up with Gus,' he says.

And their friend proves this theory immediately by saying, 'Oh dear, I'm sorry, but I had to come.' And while he darts an anxious look at Jayden, it's Ally he's talking to.

Five minutes later, Gus has got what he needed to off his chest. And Jayden understands those worry lines.

'But Ray was with me at The Wreckers,' says Ally. 'We met just after seven o'clock.'

'And it was probably around six-thirty that I saw him in the dunes,' says Gus.

Jayden looks from one to the other. 'Maybe he was taking a pre-dinner walk,' he offers.

But hasn't he considered Ray too? Lara and the cyanide just loomed larger.

'But he's staying in the village,' says Ally, 'just around the corner from the pub. He didn't say he'd been for a walk. Gus, are you sure it was him that you saw?'

Gus rubs the back of his head. 'Well, it's true that I wouldn't bet my life on it.'

'Because at the time you didn't recognise him?' says Jayden.

'That's right. But then I saw him in a different coat, and I realised that it was him after all.'

Gus explains about the green anorak, and how it was such a different style to the 'trendy leather jacket' that he'd come to associate with Ray that he didn't put two and two together.

'But Gus, he was wearing a leather jacket when he met me at the pub. It must have been somebody else.'

Gus shakes his head. 'Well, I did ask him. I saw him at Hang Ten earlier. And he rather brushed the whole thing away, actually. He didn't deny it, put it like that. In fact, he got rather defensive, Ally.'

Ally looks to Jayden, her face questioning.

'Look, I know you might be a little biased, Ally, so . . .'

'Biased, Gus?'

'Well, I know you and he have a certain history, and that probably makes it harder to appraise someone objectively, I mean . . .'

Beside him, Jayden can feel Ally bristle.

'I've just observed,' says Gus, digging himself even deeper, 'that . . . connection, and I know he's been making a big show of trying to protect you and perhaps that's what you want, but . . .'

'He's done no such thing. And I don't need *protecting*—'

'Hey, look,' says Jayden, cutting in, 'it's a good observation, Gus. And it's not like we haven't considered him. Because out of everyone, Ray has the closest relationship with Harrison Loveday. Ally?'

Ally's distracted; her arms folded defensively.

'Ray and Harrison weren't particularly close,' she says. 'And that was years ago, anyway.'

'Maybe, but Ray travelled the width of the country to see his show,' says Jayden. *And to see you, Ally.* He's not going to say that last part; Gus looks troubled enough. 'And I do think it's weird that Ray told us he was Harrison's plus-one for the party at first, when he actually got in touch with Gideon asking for an invite. That could be nothing. But . . . it's still an anomaly.'

Ally looks from one to the other. And in that moment Jayden realises something that Ally might not have acknowledged to herself yet: she really cares about Ray Finch.

'Look, Ally, I don't want you to think I'm stirring,' says Gus. 'The last thing I want to do—'

'He's hired us, Gus,' says Ally. 'Ray and the committee together. He's desperate that the killer be found.'

'Just . . . we don't always see people clearly, do we? Not when we're close to them. And I'm rather certain it was Ray I saw. I had to tell you first, Ally.' His face crumples with apology. 'Before, you know . . .'

'Before what?' says Ally.

'Before telling the police.'

50

Ally watches from the window as Gus tracks his way back over the dunes. Rain is falling and his head glints like a wet pebble. Her heart clenches. She has come to care for Gus a great deal. She trusts him implicitly. But this line he's taking, suspecting Ray of murder? She feels rather like she's standing on the shoreline, the tide pulling out, the sand shifting beneath her feet. And she needs to throw out her arms for balance.

Rationally, Ally knows Gus is simply reporting what he saw. In a murder enquiry, every detail is potentially important. If Gus had come to them saying he'd seen someone who looked like Lara Swann in the dunes early that evening – or indeed just about anyone else – she'd have jumped at the relevance.

She hates that she can see through herself. *And he must see it too.*

Gus disappears from view, and the rain comes down harder, as if somebody's tossing handfuls of shale at the pane. It feels like a bombardment.

If Ray really did go walking in the dunes that evening before she met up with him at The Wreckers, and didn't tell her and Jayden that as part of their investigation, then why on earth not? The thought that Ray might be somehow untrustworthy is unsettling. But any more than that? *Unthinkable.*

But what also rankles is Gus's presumption. This talk of 'history' with Ray, of him wanting to protect her. Ally has never been one to wear her heart on her sleeve. How can Gus think it's so obvious?

'Al, you okay?'

She turns. 'The rain's really coming down now. Gus will be soaking.'

Jayden gives her a small smile. *He's good at this*, thinks Ally. Knowing when to talk – or not.

'Of course he has to tell the police,' she says. 'It's important that he does.'

Jayden nods.

'And I know he felt awkward telling me.'

That's part of it too: Gus's awkwardness. As if he has a better grip on Ally's feelings than she does herself. She holds a hand to her forehead. *These tangles.* With Bill, it was simple: their marriage was as consistent and reliable as the tide. She doesn't want to be subjected to the push and pull of other people's feelings. Ray swooping in with his memory lane talk. Gus watching, faintly wounded, as if sidelined.

What she wants, what she really wants, is Bill. To turn around and have him be there, sitting in his chair. A crossword book balanced on his knee; not cryptic, but quick. A test of vocabulary, really. Calling out: *Al, unguis, four letters?* That smile of his.

'Why don't I put a coffee on, and you tell me about him,' says Jayden.

'Ray?'

'Ray.'

As Jayden moves to the kitchen, Ally sighs. Too many different emotions are pulling at her. She takes up her phone and clicks into her email. She has a new message.

A grim feeling of inevitability descends, like rain spitting from a dark sky. Of course it's an email from John Smith. She's been waiting for it, one way or another. Pamela, Connor, Lara: why not her?

She opens it.

> Dear Ally Bright. I should imagine your detective brain is in overdrive with the terrible goings on among the artistic community in Porthpella. We need you now more than ever. But it's a lonely spot, your Shell House. Do be careful, won't you? Best regards, J.S.

'Jayden,' she says.

He hears the note in her voice and looks up sharply. He's by her side in a second.

'Right. I'm getting Fatima on this. See what else we can get from the IP address.'

'It's a threat,' she says. 'Isn't it? More so than any of the others.'

'Yeah, the concerned-citizen act has slipped.' Jayden passes his hand across his mouth. She can see his brain working. 'Want me to stay here with you tonight, Al?'

She shakes her head. 'Absolutely not.'

'I can.'

'Really, I'm fine. Besides, you can't leave Cat and the children.'

'Then what about Gus?'

'Ray's already offered, actually.'

And she's surprised by the note of defiance in her voice.

'Is that what Gus meant when he said Ray wants to protect you?'

'I don't know. Gus can't have known. And I didn't say yes, anyway.' She resets. 'Do you still think the emails are Lara?'

'We show up at her place and then you get an email? Yeah, I do.'

251

Somehow, it feels less disturbing to see John Smith as Lara. But two people are dead. Any reassurances are empty. For half a moment, Ally imagines packing a bag and knocking on the door of Ray's rented cottage.

'Jayden, let me finish the coffee while you speak to Fatima. Honestly, I feel fine. I'm not going to be scared away from The Shell House.'

'Okay. And then, if you feel like it, you'll tell me about Ray?'

Ally takes a breath. Yes, she'll tell him about Ray. But first she moves to the window and closes the shutters. There are all sorts of noises out there. Rain against the pane. The music of the sea, lifting and dropping. Despite herself, she listens for others: the rumble of an engine; the creak of the veranda underfoot.

Jumping at shadows. That was the phrase in Connor's email.

But seeing the name of her home like that, her sanctuary, pitched as a threat. Despite what she told Jayden, it's done something to her.

Ally starts as something bumps against her legs. It's Fox. Of course it's Fox. She bends and scoops him into her arms. Presses her nose to his fur. She can feel his heartbeat beneath her hand.

Then she goes through to the kitchen and gets on with the coffee.

'Alright, Al?'

'Alright.'

Ally settles on the sofa, Fox at her feet, and Jayden takes the armchair. Mugs and biscuits. For the moment the outside world is closed off – and she goes back to Falmouth. It feels very far away at first. And then it doesn't.

'He was my first boyfriend,' she says quietly. 'He wasn't like anybody I'd met before. I remember the feeling of him having noticed me, and liking it, but thinking, "Oh no, Ray's too much."

He was one of those people that everyone knew. I was shy, you see. Liked my own company. But . . . I really did like him a great deal.'

I loved him.

'Anyway, somehow, we started dating. We sketched together. We went for long walks. Sometimes I felt like he was two people. When it was just me and him, I had his full attention. He was kind, very funny. And . . . ardent, I suppose is the word. I actually think that was just his way. That he'd have been like that no matter what girl he was with.'

And some part of her knew that, even then. But he was her first boyfriend, and she was head over heels because that's what she thought love was.

'That first term at art college, I was away from home for the first time, falling in love for the first time too. But it ended before the Christmas holidays.'

'How did it end?' asks Jayden.

'Ray always liked a drink. A late night.' Ally darts a look at Jayden. 'He had that in common with Harrison. I remember sometimes, if we went out somewhere, and saw Harrison propping up the bar, I'd think, *oh no*. There was competitiveness between them. In everything.'

'Alpha males?'

'Alpha males. I knew if Harrison was in the pub, then Ray wouldn't leave first. They used to sing sea shanties, try to get the whole bar going. I cringe to think of it now. Those two . . . emmets.' Ally smiles; shakes her head.

'I thought Harrison was born in Cornwall?'

'He was, but he liked to think he had more in common with the metropolitan students. Ray was from London. A city boy. A wealthy family. Not that he was spoilt . . . He hated his father, actually. But . . . I'm digressing.'

'You were saying how it ended with Ray.'

'Ah yes.'

Ally reaches down to pat Fox. She hasn't talked about this time – has barely thought about this time – for forty-seven years.

Until two days ago.

'Well, it ended rather quickly. We were supposed to meet for supper. It was the last week of term, and we talked about having our own Christmas celebration, just the two of us. Ray had heard about an atmospheric old pub along the coast. We'd ordered a taxi, an extravagance. But then . . . he didn't turn up. And I never heard from him again.'

Jayden's sitting forward in his chair. 'What, never?'

'I pieced together what happened. It was the talk of the art school, so it wasn't hard. He went out drinking with Harrison Loveday and he ended up being arrested for being drunk and disorderly and spent the night in a cell. Then his father drove down to Cornwall, all the way through the night, and hauled him back to London. His father never wanted him to go to art school in the first place, that was what Ray always said. And seeing as he was bankrolling him . . . that was it. The end of Ray's Cornish chapter.'

'He never got in touch?'

Ally hesitates. 'One letter. A short one.'

I was never good enough for you anyway. Call it a lucky escape, Ally! But I really am sorry.

'As first break-ups go, that was a tough one, Al.'

'What was hardest was the rumour mill. A story like that – an arrest in the town centre, thrown out of art school – everyone was talking about it.'

'I'm kind of amazed Ray rocked up in Porthpella without getting in touch first. That's confidence. I mean, you break someone's heart . . .'

And Ally knows he's trying to figure out Ray's character. Does confidence equal callousness? How close does unreliability run to dishonesty – the capacity to outright lie? But everyone makes mistakes. And most people have regretful stories from their youth.

Jayden looks at her. 'Did he? Break your heart?'

'Oh goodness, water under the bridge, Jayden. And . . . well, the story doesn't quite end there.'

'No?'

'In a way, I have Ray to thank for everything that came afterwards.'

She glances to the fireplace. The framed photograph; that sturdy grin. Outside, the sea ups its tenor.

'You see, the officer who made the arrest that night was PC Bill Bright.'

51

Milo can't see Saffron at first. The A&E waiting room is crowded, like they always are. An archipelago of discomfort, islands of pain; everyone alone in the wait, the ache. And then he spots her pink-streaked hair. She's sitting on her own, at the back of the room, cradling her wrist with her other hand.

Milo nods to the guy on the triage desk as he walks past. Clocks the sign: average waiting time three hours. Saffron must have been here an hour already. Milo messaged her after it happened, pulling his camper into a track further down the road. And by the time she replied, she was already at the hospital in Truro. Turns out she knew the cop, and he drove her in. She told Milo no need to come, but he's here anyway.

He feels weirdly nervous walking towards her.

'Hey,' she says, looking up. 'What are you doing here?'

He drops down beside her and crosses his ankles. What *is* he doing here? He could have been miles away by now, but instead he's sticking around. He'll park his van back in its old spot on the wooded lane outside of Porthpella. And just see.

'Waiting,' he says, 'with you. For . . . probably another two hours, according to the sign over there.'

An old man opposite says, 'And the rest. I've been here four hours.'

It's not obvious what's wrong with the old guy. Perhaps everything. Perhaps nothing. His cheeks are as sunken as pockets; his fingers are like talons. He's holding a newspaper. Headline: *Arts Trail Killer: who's next?*

Milo offers him a grin. Says, 'We'll die of boredom first, hey?' and the man tips his head back and laughs like it's the best joke ever.

Milo lightly touches Saffron's arm. 'Scale of one to ten, how much does it hurt?'

'What's ten?'

'Ten's, like, screaming agony.'

She wrinkles her nose. It's a pretty nose, he thinks. Bit of a ski jump. And her big wide eyes are green as a cat's.

'And what's zero?'

'Blissed out.'

'I'm looking at a six. But I'm pretty good with pain, so I don't know. It's relative, right?'

'Want me to distract you?'

She nods. And he's reaching into the pocket of his jacket, pulling out a pen. Because he always carries pens.

'Shall I get to work on the other one, then?'

'Get to work how?'

It's hot in the waiting room, recycled air hanging heavy, thick with other people's angst. Saffron's wearing a yellow t-shirt, her tanned arms bare. There's a tangle of bracelets at her good wrist, cowrie shells and plaits and turquoise leather. He touches them with his finger, clearing his canvas.

'*Saffron,*' he says. 'I looked the word up. It's from the crocus.'

'Full marks.'

'A three-pronged stigma. Most expensive spice in the world.'

'That's me.'

'Is your mum into cooking or something? Or flowers?'

'She was into cooking and flowers.'

And he notes the 'was'.

'Nice name, anyway,' he says. 'So . . . can I?'

And he scribbles his pen in the air, just above her skin. Saffron nods. And he starts drawing intricate six-petalled flowers, one after another. It looks like a sky full of stars – or an arm full of flowers.

'So, where's Broady?'

He almost said *the boyfriend*, but it's too dismissive. He's on the back foot with her already, because he left her lying on the ground as the cops swooped in. It doesn't matter that she told him to go; that Saffron knows her own mind – and is clearly capable of sweet-talking an officer of the law when she needs to.

'He's surfing.'

'And he can't find the shore?'

'He can't hear his phone.' She gives a brief shake of her head. 'I told you. Tim dropped me here.'

'First-name terms with the cops?'

Why am I being so chippy?

'Mullins is a mate. And luckily, he wasn't too interested in you. The murder case is hotting up.'

'So why bother us?'

'He was just answering a call. But then he had to rush off again. They're making an arrest.'

Milo's pen hovers. 'They've got them?' Then, 'Look, Saffron. I should have stayed and faced the music. With you.'

'No way. It's fine. Look, I hurt my wrist out in Hawaii a couple of months ago, and falling on it again just now . . . I don't think it healed properly.'

'I bet Broady didn't leave you then.'

He sees her hesitate. 'Actually . . . different situation.' She nods to her arm. 'Hey, that's looking amazing. I'll obviously never wash it.'

'And it's working, right? Distracting from the pain?'

'What pain? Oh. Hey!'

Milo's pen hovers in the air. Saffron's boyfriend is sauntering through the waiting room, and in this house of pain he looks grotesquely fit. A shimmering surf star. Milo suddenly feels every inch the street rat: puny, sallow. So what if he's got a name for himself. So what if, as street artists go, he's right up there.

He pulls his hood up, like he's done something wrong. *Muscle memory.*

'Babe,' says Broady, and he bends to kiss her. He doesn't even give Milo a first glance, let alone a second one. 'I was late seeing your messages. How bad is it?'

'Not that bad. I think it's fractured. Same place.'

'Damn. I'm sorry.'

'Everyone's being great,' she says.

Broady turns to Milo. His face is hard. 'You brought her in? Thanks, man.'

'Her cop mate did. Muggins.'

'Mullins,' says Saffron with a laugh.

'Why did Mullins bring you in?'

And Saffron explains. Headlines only: the bridge, the art, the police car.

'And you left her?' says Broady to Milo.

'I told him to,' says Saffron.

'She told me to.'

And Milo realises how pathetic it sounds.

'Yeah, so . . . I'm going to go,' says Milo. 'Saffron, you okay?'

'Ah yeah, she's great. Broken wrist. And . . .' Broady stares at her arm. 'And you're drawing on her?'

'He was distracting me,' says Saffron. 'And it worked. Broady, it's all good, Milo's been great.'

Milo gets to his feet and looks down at her half-finished arm. There's one saffron flower with just three petals but he's pretty sure he'd need A&E treatment himself if he tried to carry on with it now. Sometimes he feels like all he can do is draw, and a lot of the time it's enough. And then sometimes it's not.

'Saffron, I'm really sorry about what happened.'

He says it like Broady isn't watching, because it's really important that this girl knows he means it. And maybe she does, because the smile she gives him in reply? Heart-melting.

As Milo turns away, he catches the old man opposite's eye. He pops a thumbs up with one of those taloned hands of his, then sends Milo a comradely grin.

'Be lucky,' the guy says.

But Milo walks away feeling anything but. And the sensation follows him as he climbs into his camper and drives back through the dark lanes to Porthpella.

52

Jayden checks his phone. He's had a missed call from Cat, but she hasn't left a message. He drops her a quick text, asking if all's okay. Then he pulls himself back into the room.

After Ally shared her story about Ray, she seemed a little altered. Though maybe that's to do with the John Smith email too. Fatima didn't give Jayden much hope on that front; tracing emails to owners is a complicated process. The IP address is Truro, but that doesn't mean the sender is based there.

Knowing Ally lives at The Shell House? Well, that's common knowledge round here; and further afield too, since their detective work has given them a profile. Jayden doesn't like the tone of that email. *A lonely spot.* Three out of four of the email recipients – Pamela, Lara and Ally – are women living on their own. Though Jayden is still going with the Lara Swann theory, which shifts that pattern.

But what about Ray Finch?

The thought returns: that the vandal and the killer are two different people.

'Okay, Al,' he says, 'let's recap where we're at – and focus on the things that we can control. We've made a link between Lara Swann and the poison that killed Gina Best. Meanwhile Donald Crosby is in custody, because his prints were at the Harrison Loveday crime scene. And there's been a possible sighting of Ray in the Sea Dream area at the time of Harrison's murder.'

'And Gus is telling the police about Ray,' says Ally.

'Yep, so Ray will likely be taken in for questioning.' Jayden watches Ally as he says it, but she's level.

'Jayden, I know I haven't seen the man in decades but . . . I just don't think he's guilty. He's not acting guiltily.'

'Do you know him well enough to spot the difference?'

'I suppose that's the same thing as asking whether people change, fundamentally. And I don't think they do.'

But Jayden's not with her on that one. There are a hundred ways that life can reshape a person. Sharpen their edges, deepen their resentments, drive them to behaviours that they couldn't have imagined before. Perhaps Ray's life hasn't turned out the way he wanted it. Maybe there was something more going on between him and Harrison Loveday. Ray could have any number of motives.

'And this is a double murder,' says Ally. 'So while Harrison figures in Ray's history, Gina Best doesn't.'

'But Gina's connected to Harrison. Hurt her and it hurts him too.'

Ally shakes her head. 'At the party, he was so casual. When he walked over to see me, he was . . . well, he was just like he used to be. Charming. Fun. I don't think there's any way on earth that he'd just set up a poisoning. Gina Best dropped dead while we were talking, Jayden.'

'So perhaps we need to consider the possibility that these two murders were committed by two different people. Two different motives.'

Two murderers and a vandal. Anyone else?

'Isn't that incredibly unlikely?'

In a place like Porthpella, where there's no span of a city between the two attacks, just a handful of stone cottages and a run of dunes . . . *Yeah, it is.*

'Okay,' says Jayden, 'let's look at where it's all been happening.'

He takes the Arts Trail programme and opens it to the middle, bends back the staples and pulls out the map. Then he sticks it up on the wall of the thinking room. Every venue is plotted; the markers look ominous now, like little daggers. He takes a red pen and circles Island View House. Sea Dream doesn't feature, but The Shell House does. He runs his finger an inch along the map and circles a spot in the dunes. Writes *Sea Dream*. Then he carries on along the beach and circles Mahalo.

'I don't like the feeling this is giving me,' says Ally.

And he knows what she means. Is it only a matter of time before there's another circle on this map?

It's a lonely spot, your Shell House.

'I keep thinking about Lara,' says Jayden. 'How she let us look in the studio so easily. And that she didn't get rid of the rest of the photography gear.'

'But she's the only one with a motive that fits with both murders,' says Ally.

And he notes that, since their focus on Ray, Ally's confidence in Lara as prime suspect is renewed. Is that unconscious?

'Jayden, she's against the trail, rather than an individual. And if you're right about her misstep with the wording in the email, she's responsible for those, and possibly the graffiti too.'

'Okay, what if that's all she's responsible for? She's bitter about being overlooked for the trail, so she retaliates by scaring people with the emails and the graffiti. And there's still a chance that Gina was killed accidentally. That Harrison was the real target. That's Skinner's theory for Donald Crosby.'

Ally takes a deep breath. 'I need to talk to Ray, don't I? Ask him straight out.'

'If he killed Harrison Loveday?'

'No, Jayden. Though that might well come up in the natural flow of conversation.' She gives a little shake of her head. 'I need to ask him if he went walking in the dunes before he met me at The Wreckers.'

They hear a ringing, and then Jayden's reaching for his phone, his mind suddenly on Cat. But it's Ally's phone. She holds it up: Ray.

Talk of the devil.

'What should I . . . Should I say anything?' Her face is tight with worry.

'See how the conversation runs,' says Jayden. 'Put him on speaker, if you want.'

Ally's already reaching for the speaker button. So no matter how personal a conversation Ray has in mind, she wants Jayden to hear it.

'Ally,' says Ray. 'Sorry to call you late.'

'Oh, it's not so late.'

Her voice is self-conscious. Maybe the speaker thing is a bad idea.

'Look, something's happening in Porthpella. I'm in The Wreckers, and it's like a bloody ringside seat. The police went shooting up the lane, then ten minutes later there was an ambulance and another police car. Are you and Jayden in on this?'

Jayden hears his phone ringing; he signals to Ally that he's going to get it.

'No,' she says. 'No, we've no idea. But Jayden's just taking a call now . . .'

'Something major has happened,' says Ray. 'Thought I'd do the eyes-on-the-ground thing . . .'

Jayden sees Gideon's name on his phone screen. He walks into the other room to take it.

'Jayden . . .'

The man's voice cracks.

'Gideon, are you okay?'

'There's been a hit-and-run. We were driving and . . .'

Jayden hears the crackle of background noise. A gust of wind.

'Are you at the scene?'

'We're with the police. Jayden, we were driving home. We'd had dinner with some friends. We saw the . . . body. It was lying in the lane. We thought he was dead.'

Jayden feels a bolt of adrenalin. *Another body.*

'Where are you?'

'On Beggar's Lane. It was so dark, we almost missed it altogether. But then the headlights just picked it up and . . . Connor swerved. My God, it was close. We really thought he was dead.'

Beggar's Lane. Jayden heads back to the thinking room. Ally's finished her call – and is on her feet.

'But he's not dead?' asks Jayden.

'Unconscious. Broken bones. Someone hurt him and left him there. I don't know, I . . . It's another attack. Isn't it? It has to be. You don't just get bodies lying around Porthpella. We don't . . .'

Jayden looks to the Arts Trail map on the wall. Beggar's Lane is a narrow, winding road leading out of the north-east side of the village. Two venues are marked: Pamela Trescoe's pottery studio and a printmaker called Caroline Ross. Jayden taps a finger on the map. Further up Beggar's Lane is Lara Swann's house.

'And the police are still there with you?'

'Yes. Yes, we called them. The ambulance . . . It's taken him. It's . . .'

'Gideon, we're on our way. One last question: did you recognise the victim?'

He hears the man haul a breath, try to steady himself.

'Milo. That poor young Milo Nash.'

53

It's all happening here tonight. Mullins passes his hand across his brow, wiping the rain away. He's set up a roadblock and the CSIs are hard at it. The ambulance has been and gone. Skinner and his Major Crime dogsbody have been and gone too, but the sergeant's bad mood lingers like a foul smell.

'A body on the roadside' was the call that came in. But in reality, the body was right in the road – and its heart was still beating. But with the dark having closed in and the rain coming down? It could have been curtains.

Lucky that Connor Rafferty wasn't driving too fast. Lucky that Gideon Lee saw it – *I thought it was a deer!* – and yelled to stop. Lucky that they phoned it in, that there was no delay getting the ambulance out, that the guy was still breathing when the paramedics got here. Unconscious, limbs at all sorts of unnatural angles, but breathing.

Milo Nash. *Saffron's bad influence.* Stupid fella. Unworthy fella. But, tonight, in the grand scheme of things, a lucky fella.

It was a hit-and-run, that's the assessment, judging by Milo's injuries and the position of the body. No tyre marks though; not from the initial vehicle, only from Connor and Gideon's Volvo, which came along later. Connor was able to say just where he was when he hit the brakes. Which means no sign of that initial driver even trying to stop.

Bad news on any day. But given events around here lately, *very* bad.

Right now, the CSIs are combing the area for minute shards of metalwork. They'll be examining every fibre of Milo's clothing too. And okay, Mullins is no crash investigation expert, but he's attended enough collisions to know that ruddy great cars can't cover their tracks.

'Reckon you blokes saved his life,' says Mullins, clapping Connor on the shoulder, offering Gideon a cheering grin. 'If you hadn't seen him, it'd have been a different story. That was some good driving.'

Now that Skinner has left the building – left the lane – Mullins can be himself a bit more. The sergeant and one of the Newquay lads had been up at Lara Swann's, wanting to slap cuffs on her. But there was no answer to their knock at the door, and without a warrant they couldn't go steaming in, looking under the beds. Seeing as Lara's car was in the driveway, they'd checked the bumpers. No obvious signs of damage, but that'll be the next stop for the CSIs.

After all that, Skinner came swooping down here. He was hot under the collar about another body – even if this one still had breath left in it. *We need to find Lara Swann*, were the sergeant's parting words. Knife-sharp, they were too. As if it was Mullins whose fingertips she'd slipped through. Just because he didn't log the woman running away from the party.

'Will he make it?' asks Gideon. His voice shakes like something's come loose inside him.

Milo was still unconscious when they took him away. The paramedics reckoned on head injuries, at least one broken leg, one broken arm. Possible spinal damage. But he was breathing.

'I'm no doctor, but . . . yeah. I reckon so.'

Based on what, Mullins?

He can hear a vehicle on the approach. It'll soon be turning back around, the driver probably effing and jeffing that their route is closed, no clue that a bloke's in the hospital. Mullins looks back to Connor and Gideon. They're standing close together, heads bent. He's taken their statements. There's no reason why they can't go home now.

'I called Jayden,' says Gideon. 'He and Ally are coming up.'

So that's why they're hanging about.

'Last thing we need – more people tramping the scene,' says Mullins.

But he wouldn't mind seeing Ally and Jayden. Because Lara Swann is now Porthpella's Most Wanted, and it was Ally and her photography tip-off that kickstarted that.

Mullins looks down the lane and clocks the bobbing light of a torch beam. It's a narrow one, this, the hedgerows as tall as bungalows and meeting in the middle. Light rain's still falling and it's making a kind of music on the canopies above. Every so often a cool drop tickles Mullins's collar.

His hand goes to the phone in his pocket. He should tell Saffron. He wants to see how she is anyway. He went off-piste running her to Truro A&E – Skinner would maul him for it if he knew – but Mullins still felt bad leaving her at the hospital all on her own. Where was that so-called boyfriend of hers? And what was Saffron doing hanging out with Milo Nash anyway? Apart from anything else, she might have a handle on who Nash's people are – because the guy is in bad shape.

If the artists hadn't been able to swerve and miss him, they'd have finished him off. And how would that have felt? They'd have been in bits.

Milo Nash would definitely have been in bits.

'Mullins.'

It's Jayden. And Ally. Raincoats and squeaky shoes; concerned faces. He realises how glad he is to see them. Because this was almost death number three.

'It's connected, right?' says Jayden.

Punchy opener.

'Milo Nash got himself hit by a car. And the car didn't stop.'

'Part of a pattern though, isn't it?'

Mullins turns suddenly. He thought he heard a movement in the hedgerow.

'Mullins?'

'Maybe,' he says.

And despite himself, he feels a prickle at his spine. Mullins turns again, peering towards the source of the noise, but now all he can hear is the tap-tap of raindrops. It was probably a bird. Or a rabbit. Or something bigger, like a deer.

Jayden's looking past him, eyes on the narrow verge where the CSIs are working.

'Much to go on?'

'There'll be something.' Mullins rubs his nose. 'Milo Nash's camper van is just further up the lane in a lay-by, like it was stopping for the night. I'd say he was going for a pee. Or trying to get some phone reception. It's patchy up here.'

'Lara Swann said he's been parked up here lately,' says Ally. 'Didn't she, Jayden?'

Mullins raises his eyebrows. 'You were talking about Milo Nash with Lara Swann, were you? Anyway, you might want to know we tried to nick her just now, but there was no one home.'

He sees Jayden and Ally swap a look. They want a knuckle bump, probably. Even though down at the station they've fielded hundreds of calls from the public, combed through hours and hours of CCTV, meticulously examined the forensics, cross-compared the witness statements, Ally Bright just puts on her artist hat, looks at a photo and says, *That's done with cyanide, that.*

'Did you find the cyanide?' asks Ally, quick as a fish.

'Don't know.' *No.* 'But there'll be a full search.'

'Skinner came round to the idea though, did he?' says Jayden.

'If you want to know, a witness saw Lara Swann fleeing the party after Gina Best was killed.'

An unreliable witness, as it happens.

Mullins gives a little cough. 'So, as you can imagine, we've got a fair few questions for Lara Swann once she shows herself.'

'Lara told us she left the party before Gina Best died,' says Ally.

'Well, she would say that, wouldn't she?'

'How hard are you looking for her?' asks Jayden.

'Hard enough, thanks, Jayden. And before you ask, there's no sign of damage on her car, so it's not her that's been rampaging down this lane.'

'Unless she was driving a different vehicle,' says Jayden.

'We're checking it all out. There's the entire Major Crimes team on this one, guys.'

'Have you any idea on the timing here?' asks Ally. 'With Milo Nash?'

Mullins shakes his head. 'No witnesses to the incident itself.' He nods towards Gideon and Connor. 'These blokes called it in, and they would have been the first to go up this lane since it happened. No telling how much time between. I'd say not much. The blood was wet, put it that way.'

'This is Lara Swann's route home, if she was driving from Porthpella. Likewise, if she was heading further out of town . . .'

'I know you want to join the dots here, Jayden, but—'

'And Donald Crosby's still in custody, right?'

Mullins nods.

271

'But we've got a third victim,' says Jayden. 'So if Lara has an alibi . . .'

'Every chance it was a random idiot,' says Mullins, wanting to dampen the flame a bit, even though he knows this same talk will be raging down the station. 'Taking the lanes too fast. One drink too many.'

Gideon and Connor are over here too now, swapping Shell House hugs and handshakes.

'The shock,' says Connor.

'Missed him by inches,' says Gideon.

Mullins's voice is getting drowned out, so he says it again.

'A random idiot. Let's not rule that out. Now, we've got work to do here – and no offence, but you lot are getting in the way, so . . .'

But Gideon's got his hand on Jayden's shoulder, is saying, 'Connor told me about the email. Better late than never, I suppose. You said they've been going around. That Pamela Trescoe had one as well.'

'Ally too,' says Jayden.

Gideon's eyes widen.

'Look, what if we doubled the money? Would that help? Conn, we could double it, couldn't we? Because this is getting out of hand. This killer needs to be caught before . . . Well, I don't even want to say it.'

And Mullins tries not to care that Gideon's looking at Jayden and Ally as he talks about catching the killer. He turns away, just to show how not bothered he is. And then he hears that noise again. A shifting in the undergrowth. The snap of a twig. And Mullins knows this time, deep in his bones, that it's not a bird, or a rabbit, or a deer.

He moves towards the source. Fast, determined.

'Oi,' he calls out. 'Police! Stop!'

He's aware of Jayden clicking into action behind him as if he's on a pull cord. But Mullins wants to get there first. This is his collar. So he runs right through the hedge as if he's a ram-raider. And while it puts up a fight – sharp sticks; a net of brambles – it's no match for this man on a mission.

Mullins breaks out the other side just in time to see a figure flying up and over the bank.

54

Jayden goes through the hedge with ease; Mullins made a sizeable hole. He follows the constable up the bank and through the tangle of trees, his trainers skidding on the wet ground. His phone torch isn't bad, but he can see Mullins's much stronger beam playing off the undergrowth. In a few long strides, Jayden catches up to him.

'This way,' he says, swinging his torch. 'He went this way.'

'You got a look at him?'

'He went this way,' Mullins says again.

They plunge on. Ahead of them, a wood pigeon rises up with a panicked clap of wings. They're barrelling through the dripping foliage. Not careful trackers, pausing to examine snapped twigs or prints in the mud, but two men on a foot chase. Jayden really hopes Mullins has got the direction right.

The ground rises, and they're clambering now. Hands slipping on loose stones. Feet scrabbling.

Jayden knows this wood, but only from afar. If you stand at Cat's favourite spot on the farm – the Lookout, as she used to call it as a kid – it's a dark triangle in the distance, surrounded by fields running to the sea. Now they're in it, it feels bigger. Deeper.

Jayden and Mullins reach the top of the steep section at the same time. Jayden catches a glimpse of a figure, Mullins's torch beam briefly illuminating them just before they disappear between the trees.

A woman. Long, straight hair, blowing behind her like a cape.

'It's Lara,' he says.

'On it,' says Mullins, breaking like a greyhound from a starting box.

Then, suddenly, he's gone.

Vanished.

For a second, it seems like a magic trick. Was it an incredible turn of speed? Not even a puff of smoke in his wake. Then Jayden hears a shout. It's as if it's coming from deep underground.

'Mullins!' he calls out.

Another sound now, like a wounded animal.

Jayden moves forward, his torch picking out a hole in the undergrowth, less than a metre across. He gets on to his knees, shines his light down.

'Mullins?'

He hears swearing. Then a clear shout. 'Jayden, don't stop! Go get her.'

His beam just about finds Mullins's pale face. It's contorted with pain. 'Don't stop!' he yells again.

And Jayden knows how to take an order from a fellow police officer. He tells him he'll send for help, then he's sprinting again. He dials Ally as he runs, hitting speaker to keep the torch beam.

'Al, call 999. Mullins is in a hole. A mineshaft, I think. About two or three hundred metres from the lane, more or less straight up into the woods. I don't know his injuries. And, Al? I'm pursuing Lara Swann.'

Then he's charging on. Wary, too, of more drops. How much time did he lose with Mullins? Twenty seconds? Thirty? Enough for Lara to gain a lead. She could have gone in any direction, but instinct takes Jayden in a straight line. He follows a natural kind of path. One made by a deer? Maybe. Cliff's always moaning about deer. When they first moved here, Jayden used to hear them barking at night, thinking they were dogs.

As he runs, thoughts of Mullins push in. That sound he made, like a wounded beast. He could have broken his back, his neck, a fall like that. Mullins was coherent, as he told Jayden not to stop, but he doesn't like leaving a man down.

Even if it means catching a killer.

Then Jayden suddenly sees her. She's slowed. Limping. She leans against a tree trunk and turns and looks in his direction. His torch picks out her white face. She's as small and scared as a hunted fox.

He holds his hands up, as if he's the wanted one.

'Lara, it's me. Jayden.'

He moves closer, lowering his torch so it doesn't blind her. He sees her hand reach inside her coat, and he stops.

Is this the woman who poisoned Gina Best? Stabbed Harrison Loveday? Hit Milo Nash and left him for dead?

He makes a quick calculation, keeping his eyes on her hand.

'Lara,' he says, in his steadiest voice, 'it's okay.'

55

'Should I have gone too?' asks Gideon.

Connor and one of the CSIs are in the woods, helping locate Mullins. Ally wills the sound of sirens to carry on the air. The fire service. Paramedics. Police. People who know what they're doing.

The night Ally found Jayden clinging to the cliff edge, two winters ago now, is high in her memory. The crash of waves against the rock; the stinging rain. That time, the murderer had already done their worst. Is Mullins safe now? Ally doesn't want to think about collapsing rocks. She doesn't want to think about Jayden pursuing a suspect with no backup.

Lara Swann. Gideon's first assessment, 'a dangerous individual', felt like hyperbole at the time. But not anymore.

'No, but I should go,' says Ally.

'But I thought you said—'

'Jayden's got no backup, Gideon.'

'He's a trained officer, and you . . . you're . . .' His eyes soften. 'A brilliant detective, obviously, but you can't go charging off up there, Ally. You're . . .'

What? Sixty-six years old? A woman? With no training whatsoever?

But then suddenly everyone is here, arriving in a roar of engines and bright lights. Paramedics surging into the copse. Black-jacketed firefighters. And Skinner, shouldering his way through.

'Jayden with Mullins, is he?'

'Jayden carried on pursuing the suspect,' says Ally.

And she feels faintly silly using police language. But Skinner nods, sets a hand on her shoulder.

'Alright,' he says. Then, with a look that shows he knows exactly what she's thinking, he adds, 'But you stay here.'

Ally draws a deep breath. Petrichor: earthy, rich, damp. It fills her throat. This dark lane feels a very long way from the sea.

'That told you,' says Gideon.

'In his defence, we've got form.' She wants to switch her focus. 'Gideon, how are you doing?'

'How am I doing?'

'Finding Milo like that. It must have been such a shock.'

'Not as bad as finding Harrison Loveday,' he says. 'His pulse, it was strong, Ally. He's a tough young man.'

'He is.'

'He'll make it,' says Gideon. Then he repeats it, as if convincing himself. 'I keep thinking of what-ifs . . . If Conn hadn't stepped on the brakes . . .'

'But he did. He was brilliant.'

'He was, wasn't he? Brilliant.' Gideon's voice breaks and he dips his head. 'I wasn't flashing the cash, you know, this talk of doubling your fee. But I mean it. What's happening here, with the Arts Trail . . . with Lara Swann. So the police already tried to arrest her, did they?'

'And she wasn't at home.'

'She was here then, wasn't she? Spying. Listening in. What if she was waiting to finish the job? And she *ran*, Ally. She's guilty.' He draws a quick breath. 'The rumours flying around about Donald too. Could they have been working together?'

'Donald maintains he had nothing to do with any of it.'

'But what do you think?'

278

Ally can hear voices carrying on the breeze; sees the occasional bobbing light of a torch. While there's a skeleton crew around the emergency vehicles, nearly everyone is up in the woods.

'Ally?'

She's not going to pass on confidential information, even if theories are gusting through Porthpella like an onshore wind. Even if, on a night like this, it feels like all bets are off.

'Given what the police have,' she says, 'I think Donald is probably telling the truth.'

Gideon rubs his face with both hands. 'We should have taken those emails of Lara's to the police immediately. We could have saved lives, Ally.'

'The emails Lara sent to the committee, you mean? Apparently, she already told the police about those. They ruled her out, Gideon.'

The relief on his face is palpable.

'How well do you know Milo Nash?' she asks.

'Hardly at all. I approached him about being part of the trail and he said it wasn't his thing, but he didn't object to us featuring the walking tour. He's a huge talent, Ally.'

Ally knows the spot where Milo's camper van is parked: a narrow lay-by just up from here. A quiet, out-of-the-way place. Or that's what he would have thought.

'After the surf school piece was destroyed, I was sure he'd leave,' says Gideon. 'With that van of his he can go with the wind, you see.'

She thinks of how Saffron had wanted them to investigate the vandalism, without yet realising the significance of those words – *who's next?* On the drive over, Jayden indicated that Saffron was close to Milo; that they were friends. Ally looks down at her phone. There's nothing more from Jayden. Nothing from Ray either, since that first call.

When she thinks about Ray – and the fleeing Lara – she can't help a feeling of relief washing over her.

'Can I ask,' she says carefully, 'have you heard much from Ray today?'

'A little. We have a WhatsApp group, Team Shell House. Sunita's idea. Just the four of us are on it, but Connor's awful at WhatsApp so, really, it's the three of us.'

'Team Shell House? What do you talk about?'

'The case. Sharing information. I mean, that was the idea, but we haven't actually got any new information to share, and . . . well, Connor was sitting on that sinister email, too afraid of upsetting me, so . . . it's not the most reliable of sources.'

'It was Ray who told us about the ambulance and police cars shooting through Porthpella,' says Ally. 'He phoned me.'

'Yes. He put it on the WhatsApp group too. Though of course he didn't know Connor and I were plum in the middle of it. Speaking of . . .' He checks his watch. 'Dear Sunita's on her way up to our place with some soup. I need to put the brakes on that. She thought we'd want some fortitude. I did try to say we'd just been for dinner . . . She invited Ray too, not to leave him out, but he said he's staying put for the night. One too many pints in The Wreckers, apparently. He's really a lovely man, Ally. Fantastic charisma. No wonder you're delighted to see him after all these years.'

And it feels like such a strange collision of worlds.

'Let me call Sunita,' he says.

'Wait, Gideon, did Ray say anything about having to talk to the police again?'

Gideon's eyebrows jump. 'Why would they want to talk to Ray?'

Ally is saved from having to answer by a sound in the lane. The tap-tap of crutches. Huffing breath. It's Pamela Trescoe in a voluminous raincoat, her face crumpled with worry.

'My God, my God,' she trills, by way of greeting. 'Will someone tell me what's going on here?'

'Pamela,' says Gideon smoothly. He goes to her, offers his arm, the head of the Arts Trail taking care of one of his flock. 'You shouldn't have come, dear. Not with that ankle.'

'How could I stay cooped up? I heard the kerfuffle from my sitting room. Has something terrible happened? Again?'

Pamela places a hand on her chest; her breath coming fast.

'Milo Nash was hit by a car,' says Ally, trying to take all possible drama out of her voice.

Pamela's eyes widen to the size of saucers. 'The young graffiti artist?'

'He's going to be okay,' says Gideon. 'We got to him just in time.'

Pamela looks as if she's lost for words. Then, in a low, tremulous voice, she says, 'It's number three, isn't it?'

'The Arts Trail Killer,' murmurs Gideon. 'For once the press aren't exaggerating. But you'll be glad to hear the suspect is being apprehended as we speak.'

'Apprehended? Who?'

'And PC Mullins is injured. Fallen down a mineshaft. Half a dozen firefighters just went to rescue him,' Gideon runs on.

Pamela looks as if she needs to sit down. Ally offers her arm, but the woman bats it away.

'But who?' she says. 'Who do they have?'

'Lara Swann,' says Gideon.

'But she's my neighbour.'

'She's everyone's neighbour,' says Gideon gravely.

'And I haven't heard a peep from poor Donald,' says Pamela, revving back up. 'I can't believe they're keeping him there . . . Surely now they'll have to let him go?'

'He'll be released after twenty-four hours unless there's a case to hold him.'

'Of course there's no case to hold him, Ally! With all of this drama, this circus, how can any of it be to do with Donald?'

And perhaps it's beside the point, but Pamela doesn't know Donald as well as she thinks. Pamela was so sure that he'd never confront Harrison Loveday, but Donald had every intention of doing so the night he went to Sea Dream.

'Ally,' says Gideon. 'Look.'

Lara Swann. She emerges from the undergrowth, flanked by two uniformed officers. And she's in handcuffs.

56

When Mullins is winched back into open air, the person he focuses on is Jayden. Not the gaggle of firefighters doing the job. Because Mullins should be the fixer, not the problem. He thinks of how that 999 call might have gone: *PC Tim Mullins has only gone and fallen down a ruddy great hole.* There's a lot of points on his body that hurt, but his pride is right up there too.

'Mate,' says Jayden, laying a hand on his arm. 'I'm glad to see you.'

And Mullins squeezes his eyes shut. He's got a horrible feeling he's going to blub.

'You got her?'

'I got her,' says Jayden. 'But—'

'Alright, Tim, we're moving now. Steady as we can.'

It's the paramedic. The lady who came down on a rope: a guardian angel not just descending to earth but fifteen feet below it. Suspected fractured coccyx is her verdict. Otherwise known as your tailbone.

Yes, PC Mullins has busted his bottom.

'Is Skinner here?' he asks.

Jayden's walking by the side of the stretcher and, looking up at him, Mullins feels like a kiddie in a pram.

'He went with Lara.'

'Happy, was he?'

'Yeah,' says Jayden, 'but . . .'

'But what?'

'You sure you want to talk about the case? You've got to be in a hell of a lot of pain right now, mate.'

'I want to.'

'Alright.' Jayden lowers his voice. 'Lara told me she's responsible for all the "who's next?" stuff, and the emails, but that's it.'

'That's it, is it?'

'She said she destroyed Milo Nash's piece at Mahalo because she didn't think it was real art, and because she hated the way the committee were all over him. And then she sprayed the same message on the map outside White Wave.'

'Now why would she do that, Jayden?'

'Because she's got a grudge against the Arts Trail, and she saw it as an opportunity to stir things up. She admitted sending the emails too.'

'What emails? The one Pamela Trescoe got?'

'And Connor and Ally too. Same reason. Lara was getting a kick out of it, and once she started, she found it hard to stop. She was buzzing on the press coverage. All the Arts Trail Killer stuff.'

The stretcher tilts and his coccyx twangs; Mullins quickly inhales.

'Wind them up and watch them go?' he says, teeth gritted. 'Yeah, well, Lara would say that, wouldn't she. Admitting to the lesser crimes – that's the oldest trick in the book, that is. Gullible, you are, Jay.'

He's never called him Jay before.

'She ran away from us because she was frightened. It's an impulse, isn't it? Someone chases you, you run. And she knew she'd crossed a line with the emails and graffiti.'

'When it's the police, you're supposed to stop. End of story. Anyway, she was already on the run.'

'Lara said she genuinely wasn't home when the police called. She went for a walk, and then saw all the drama.'

'Saw Nash get hit, did she?'

'No, just you guys arriving on the scene. Then Ally and me.'

'Alright, Tim,' says the paramedic, turning with a smile. 'Here we are. We'll get you checked over, go in for x-rays. But beyond your tailbone, I think we're mostly looking at bumps and bruises.'

Somehow, they're back out on the lane. A lane that's chocka with emergency services. All for Tim Mullins, who fell in a hole and broke his bum. The patrol car's gone, taking Lara Swann along with it. The Arts Trail Killer under lock and key. Only, Jayden won't let them have the win. Which doesn't make sense because it was a Shell House theory in the first place.

'She admits her grudge with the committee,' says Jayden, 'and she admits taking revenge by scaring people. But that's it, Mullins.'

'What about the cyanide? The photography gear that only she knew was there?'

'We didn't get into that.'

So Jayden didn't conduct a full-scale interrogation in the forest then? Shell House Detectives have their limits after all. Or maybe he was trying to when Skinner waltzed in and took over.

As he's transferred into the ambulance, Ally Bright's at his side too, her face a picture of concern.

'Hullo, Ally. I'm alright.' Then he closes his eyes. Says, 'Can someone call my mum?'

57

Jayden glances in the rear-view mirror as they leave the scene. The ambulance and fire crews have long departed. The CSIs are wrapping up and a sole uniformed officer remains in the lane. Right now, Skinner will be questioning Lara Swann.

Lara, who was so afraid in the woods. Whose confession poured out of her, along with her tears. She was adamant that she'd hurt no one; neither by accident nor on purpose. She just couldn't resist taking advantage of the situation and causing some Arts Trail drama. But then Skinner and his Major Crimes team took over, so she'll be saying it all again for the record.

And they may or may not believe her.

For all the forensics work, their best hope of identifying the driver will be when Milo Nash regains consciousness. Mullins said, from the angle of his limbs, his body was thrown with force, but they haven't confirmed the direction he was walking in yet, nor where the vehicle came from.

As Jayden grips the wheel, he thinks of his own brush with high-speed metalwork two winters ago. The way his eye sockets hurt with the burning headlights, the roar of the engine inside his skull. There's no match at all, in man versus car. But that time, Jayden could take in the details of the car – and the identity of the driver.

When Milo wakes – if Milo wakes – he could have all the answers they need. Or, in the split-second shock of the moment, none at all.

Is it possible that Milo was specifically targeted? An escalation of the vandalism on his Mahalo piece? Even before they saw Lara Swann in the woods, Gideon had been sure it was another attack on the Arts Trail. Meanwhile Mullins was flying the flag for a random accident. Given what Lara had to say, any of these ideas is possible.

'Thank you so much for the lift, dear. This is me just up here.'

They're running Pamela home. Thankfully the multiple incidents didn't draw any more onlookers, but Jayden knows Porthpella. Phone lines will be buzzing. Neighbours knocking on doors. The Wreckers will be rammed. And the narrative? Milo Nash has dodged death and the Arts Trail Killer has been caught.

But neither of these things is certain.

Jayden can't wait to get rid of Pamela – *no offence, Pamela* – and put his head together with Ally.

He pulls into the driveway, swivels in his seat.

'Want a hand getting out?'

She's holding her crutches but shows no sign of moving.

'You're quite the hero, Jayden. The foot chase. That poor young man though . . .'

'Hopefully there'll be news on Milo soon.'

'And PC Mullins.' She gives a deep sigh. 'Goodness, what a night. And now they'll release Donald, won't they? They have to. All this, he won't be coping at all well . . .' Her voice breaks.

Ally leans forward, says in a kind voice, 'Try not to worry about Donald.'

'Oh, now that's easier said than done!' Pamela gives a small, hiccupping laugh. 'Sometimes I feel as if it's become my life's work, worrying about that man.'

She settles back in the seat and sighs again. Despite the running engine, Pamela's still showing no sign of moving. Jayden glances at the house. All the lights are on inside. By her studio, the Arts Trail easel is still in place. Maybe she's lonely. Afraid too. But he feels like there's something else.

'Do you want to tell us something, Pamela?' he asks gently.

'This will have brought up a lot for Donald. That's all. Being cross-examined on the most private of subjects. I just want him to put it all behind him.'

'He will,' says Jayden.

If he's innocent.

'He's a good man,' she says quietly. 'He deserves to be happy. As long as I've known him, he never has been. Happy, I mean.'

The light is low in the car, but Jayden watches Pamela's face carefully. Emotion moves across her features, like light on water. A thought starts to dawn.

'You're good friends, aren't you,' he says. 'You and Donald.'

'We are.'

'So you know him better than anyone around here.'

'Oh yes. We're very close, Donald and I.'

Jayden nods. 'And you're certain he's innocent?'

'I'd bet my life on it.'

And at that she finally opens the car door, thanks them both, and clambers out.

'Pamela,' says Jayden, leaning over the passenger seat, 'if we get any news about Donald's release, we'll let you know. We'll keep you posted, okay?'

'I would appreciate that.'

Jayden watches her crutch her way up the driveway.

Ally swaps seats, and as she belts herself in, she raises her eyebrows.

'That line of questioning,' she says. 'You don't think Lara Swann did it, do you.'

Jayden shakes his head.

'And you think it's Donald?'

'No,' says Jayden.

He puts the car in gear and swings back out into the lane. It feels too soon to say it, but it's Ally, so he does anyway.

'I'm thinking Pamela.'

58

In the thinking room, Jayden stands in front of the board. He points to Lara Swann's name. A name that's now circled in red.

'Okay. Lara was spying in the lane, and she ran when Mullins spotted her. And she kept running. But, Al, she was terrified. I believed what she said to me about wanting to wreck Milo's piece and stir up trouble around the Arts Trail. She's incredibly bitter, but she was freaked out by us thinking she's the killer. Like, it wasn't even on her radar that she'd be suspected for that. All she was worried about was being caught for destroying the art, and fanning flames around the murders.'

'And you believe her? Because those emails she was sending, they had an agenda, Jayden. Lara might not have started off wanting to pose as the killer, but I think that changed.'

'Okay, fair point. She got carried away.'

Ally's face is grim. 'She was focused on hurting the Arts Trail. And anyone who's part of it could suffer too.'

'In the forest, all of Lara's barriers were down, Al. What I keep coming back to is that she didn't stop us from going into her mum's studio. And she didn't hide the photography gear. We both said it, right? That's weird.'

'Presuming that she was thinking straight.'

'Well, yeah. I bet all she was thinking about was the spray can. She said she'd got rid of it; her version of hiding the weapon.'

After Jayden dropped his Pamela bombshell in the car, he and Ally agreed no more talk until they got back to The Shell House. Jayden wanted to order his thoughts. Sometimes it helps to chat an idea through; sometimes he wants to strength-test it in his own mind first.

And there's still Ray.

'So basically, despite Lara having motive, means and opportunity for both murders, I don't think she's guilty.'

'Remember, Mullins said she was seen running away from the party,' says Ally.

'Maybe that's her modus operandi. She bolts when things get too much. She goes to the party to try and make a point but then loses her nerve, then Gina Best dies so she panics.'

'Or wants to get started on the graffiti.'

'Exactly.'

He rubs his hands together. Lara's with the police now – and Jayden wants to talk about Pamela Trescoe.

'Al, I think Pamela is in love with Donald Crosby.'

He watches Ally's face.

'I can see why you'd think that.'

'And what do you think?'

'Well, I agree that she seems to care very much for him.'

'And maybe she cares so much for him that she'd murder Harrison Loveday on his behalf.' It feels good to say it out loud. 'Al, look. Pamela keeps talking about how unhappy Donald is, and how he blames Harrison for what happened to his sister. How he's never got over it. What if Pamela thought that the way to make Donald happy was to kill Harrison?'

A simple equation. *Too simple?*

'Pamela's the only person round here who knew Donald's history with Harrison,' he goes on. 'And she's obviously distressed that he's under arrest. Well, she would be, wouldn't she, if she's killed Harrison to fix a problem and only ended up making it worse.'

'Because now Donald is having to face difficult questions,' says Ally thoughtfully. 'I do agree that she's putting a lot of focus on Donald being held.'

'Her focus is way off, Al. Milo Nash is fighting for his life, a police officer was put in an ambulance, the potential culprit has been arrested. All on one night, literally on Pamela's doorstep, and she's still talking about Donald being wrongfully held.'

Jayden's pacing now, his theory gaining momentum.

'But that's also quite a natural reaction,' says Ally. 'I don't think any of us would imagine that our closest friends are capable of murder, would we?'

Jayden sees Ally pause, and he knows she's thinking of Ray.

One of the reasons that he wanted this extra thinking time on the drive is because Jayden needs to be 100 per cent sure of his own motives. If they're pursuing a line of enquiry, of course he'd rather it was focused on Pamela Trescoe than Ray Finch. But if Pamela has motive, then Ray has opportunity. Pamela loves Donald, and Ray was seen in the dunes.

'Ray is the elephant in the room, isn't he?' says Ally, as if reading his thoughts.

'We don't do elephants, Al.'

'No. I've decided I'm going to go and see him.'

Jayden checks his watch. 'Tonight? It's late.'

'Tomorrow morning, first thing.'

'We could go together?'

'I think it's best I go alone.' She closes her eyes for a second, then snaps them open again. 'Jayden, back on Pamela, she has an alibi, remember? When Harrison was killed, she was at A&E in Truro.'

'We can easily check that. But even so, there's a possibility they were working together, right?'

'Donald and Pamela?'

'It could explain why Donald's prints are in some places but not others.'

'But not if Pamela was at the hospital.'

Jayden pulls his phone from his pocket. 'Okay, no point in speculating. The hospital won't give out patient information, but they might confirm if she was there. If I get my tone right.'

He dials, then waits as he goes through various switchboard options. Ally passes him a piece of paper with Pamela's address and date of birth scribbled on it. A tidy bit of internet research – in case they need particulars.

'Pamela told us she has ongoing problems with her ankle, Al. Those crutches could belong to her and not be newly issued at all.'

But three minutes later, hope dies. An amenable receptionist confirms that, yes, Pamela Trescoe was at the hospital yesterday evening and was signed in before the time of Harrison Loveday's death.

'When did she leave?' asks Jayden, trying his luck, because maybe this receptionist is new on the job. 'Can you tell me that?'

'She didn't see a doctor until nine o'clock.'

Jayden hangs up, deflated. 'It doesn't work, Al. Truro's half an hour away. It's unlikely that Pamela would see a doctor then go pelting back to Porthpella to commit a murder, right? Damn.'

'It was a good thought,' says Ally. 'Especially . . .'

'What?'

'Well, Pamela did say she'd been to Lara's house when Billie was staying there. A few years ago. Do you remember? She said she got the tour.'

'*Damn*. Pamela could have seen the photography gear then. And know that the wet-plate process uses cyanide.'

Despite Pamela's alibi, this theory has legs.

'Billie Swann's studio wasn't locked, was it? We just walked right in. Which means anyone could walk in. If Pamela knew cyanide was kept in the studio, she could easily have taken it, without Lara being any the wiser.'

Ally's on her feet now. 'So, the next question is, does Pamela have an alibi for the night of the party? Well, the simple answer is that she was a guest there. So . . . lots of alibis.'

'But also lots of opportunity. Okay. So . . . Pamela sets out to poison Harrison Loveday but accidentally kills Gina Best. That works, right?'

'That works.'

'Then the next night . . . someone else kills Harrison. And Donald's looking like the favourite, surely? So, we're back to them working together. Like . . . the Bonnie and Clyde of the art world or something.'

Ally turns a pen between her fingers. 'But if we're saying anyone could have broken into Billie Swann's studio, then arguably anyone could have taken the cyanide. It might not have been Pamela at all.'

'But Pamela has motive. Because Donald has motive. Who else could have motive?'

And, again, the name pushes in: *Ray?*

'But what about Milo Nash? Are we saying that incident isn't connected after all? That it was a random hit-and-run?' Ally's voice is full of doubt.

Jayden turns back to the board. The Milo Nash vandalism is up there already, but now he writes: *Hit-and-run. Connected?*

Because it feels like it has to be.

59

It's coming up on dawn and Gus is out walking. It's a new sensation, waking in Porthpella and feeling . . . flat. Flat Gus belongs to Oxford and his decades-long war of attrition with Mona. To aimless trudges across Port Meadow. To hiding in his hut in the garden, impotently watching the slugs ravage his delphiniums. Even in the early days of his time in Cornwall, before he met Ally, before he felt anywhere near at home, he'd wake feeling stirred. In fact, Gus would challenge anyone to sleep within earshot of the bellow of the Atlantic and not be invigorated. And what about last summer? When he came home from hospital. Despite being troubled by headaches and dizzy spells, his baseline mood was of gratitude; and a happiness that, at times, bordered on pure joy.

Today though? Flat. And a little sleep-deprived. But given what else is happening in their corner of the world, perhaps flat and sleep-deprived aren't bad going.

Gus tramps with his head down, shoes sinking into the sand. The sunrise isn't much to look at anyway, thwarted by cloud as it is. The sea pushes sulkily at the shore, devoid of all conviction. Gus sneezes – *that's right, you'll get a cold next* – and reaches for his hanky. As he looks up, he sees the hunched shape of a person on the rocks.

Oh God, what now? Who *now*? But the fact they're sitting and not lying is a good thing. Corpses are apt to topple, are they not? Unless it's the killer, taking time out from their spree to watch the not-quite-sunrise. Gus can feel his heart quicken at the thought. Silly old ticker. He never could control the thing. First sign of trouble and it flutters like a butterfly caught in a net.

He's debating whether it would be cowardly to turn on his heel when the figure swings their hooded head towards him and says, 'Morning, Gus.'

'Saffron!'

And, quite honestly, there's no one he's happier to see. Since the awkwardness of their conversation about Ray, Ally is a complicated proposition. Even before he accused her old flame of being a murderer – *well, didn't you? Essentially so* – Gus has felt unsettled. It was the way Ray Finch walked across the lawn at the party. The presumption in his stride. And how, as Ally coloured and smiled, Gus saw that Ray was, after all, right to presume.

Chemistry. Gus doesn't know much about the stuff, except he thought he had it with Ally Bright. And then this Ray Finch flew in and atoms were, undoubtedly, rearranged.

Now Gus has hammered a nail in his own coffin by phoning the police information line. Obviously, Ally will thank Gus in the long term if he helps put the killer behind bars. But there's probably a way of doing these things. And he can't help feeling he's bungled it.

'Good lord, Saffron. Is that a plaster cast?'

'Yeah.'

Gus, so selfishly caught up in his own thoughts, now takes in her demeanour. Looks like he's not the only one having a flat day.

'Alright if I join you?' he says.

She shifts up on the rock and Gus plops down beside her.

'What happened? You didn't come off that skateboard of yours, did you?'

'Fell off a ladder. It's my coffee-making hand too. And the season's just kicking in. Bad times, Gus.'

'Is it the same one that you hurt in Hawaii?'

She nods. 'It's nothing though, nothing compared to . . . Did you hear what happened last night?'

Yes, Gus heard. *A man in his twenties severely injured in a hit-and-run.*

He saw the news in the early hours of the morning, during one of his sleepless spells, when the light from his phone kept drawing him in. And like a moth he fizzed and burnt.

'It was my friend who was hurt,' says Saffron, her voice splintering. 'My friend Milo.'

'The artist? Oh, Saffron.'

Fat tears roll down her cheeks, as if they were just waiting behind her lashes. Gus puts his arm around her, and she leans into him. He feels almost like a granddad, and it gives him a fleeting moment of contentment. Then the impact of this new crisis hits.

'You weren't there too, were you? Your wrist?'

'No, no. But we were together earlier. And Milo came to see me in A&E. And now he's in Intensive Care. That's what Mullins said. Mullins messaged me. Mullins was there too. Not in the ICU but in A&E. Getting x-rays.'

Gus feels like his head is about to pop.

'Mullins is hurt too?'

'Everyone,' says Saffron. 'Everyone's getting hurt. Who would do that? Who would crash into someone and just leave them? I can't

297

stop thinking about it. I can't . . . I was only just getting to know him, and . . . what if he dies?'

A third death. That's what. And if it's connected – *another artist? Surely it's connected* – then isn't that serial killer territory? He should message Ally. Or Jayden. Perhaps Jayden would be better, given everything.

Gus tightens his arm around Saffron. He says, 'There, there. He won't die, of course he won't die. He's in the absolute best place. He's being looked after.'

And now Gus is worrying about Mullins too. He's worrying about everyone, in fact. And where does Ray Finch sit in all of this? Is he anywhere at all? What of Broady? Saffron hasn't mentioned him.

'What can I do to make things better?' he says.

'There's nothing. It's all a nightmare.'

And he's never seen her like this. Not even when everything was happening with her dad, two Christmases ago.

'Things aren't great with Broady either,' she says quietly.

'I'm sorry to hear that.'

'To be honest, they weren't great in Hawaii.'

She gnaws at the end of her thumb. The sleeve of her hoodie drops and on her good arm he sees a pale but intricate drawing of flowers. Did she get a tattoo, when they weren't looking? He's about to remark on it when she says: 'It wasn't like anything went wrong between us, but we were both just . . . not getting what we wanted from each other. You know? I was super unlucky, slipped on the walk to the beach on, like, the third day. I trashed my wrist. Then that was it for me. I couldn't surf. Broady knew I was gutted, but . . . I don't know what I wanted him to do. Not mope about on dry land but . . . I don't know. It was a lose–lose situation. Of course he still went surfing. It was why he was there.'

Gus nods. 'Hard though, to have to watch from the sidelines. It was why you were there too, wasn't it?'

'Yeah . . . Then suddenly he gets word of this small business grant. And his friend tells him about a job falling through with these builders and how they'd offer mates' rates on the surf school build if they started, like, that second. It was an amazing opportunity. Pure serendipity. Suddenly we were packing our bags to zoom back to Porthpella.'

'I remember,' says Gus. 'You were excited.'

'I was. I know it's illogical, but I was also kind of upset that he'd ditch Hawaii for the surf school, but he wouldn't even cut back on time in the water for like, one minute when I got hurt.' She waves her good hand. 'I'm rambling. It doesn't make sense when I say it out loud. Not even to me. I sound like a really annoying girlfriend.'

Gus looks to the sea. It's still grey, still sullen. A mizzle's blowing in, the air thick with salt. Gus wants to offer something wise, encouraging. But in his experience, once you start to feel disappointed, by God it builds. Until it's a landslide.

'He disappointed you,' he says quietly.

'And now I'm disappointing him.'

Saffron doesn't say why, or how, but Gus suspects it might be something to do with the young chap in Intensive Care. He leaves a space for her to elaborate if she wants, but she doesn't.

'What about you?' she says instead. 'You looked like you were walking with the weight of the world on your shoulders. Plus . . . it's way too early for you to be out.'

'Ah now.' He hesitates a beat, then says, 'Oh, I'm just fretting. I sent my manuscript off to agents and I don't know what to do with myself now.'

A kernel of truth.

'Wow, Gus. Nice one.' She puts her head to one side. 'But that's not all, is it? Come on – misery loves company, or haven't you heard?'

Gus Munro: never much of a poker face.

'Oh, nothing much, just . . . I more or less accused Ally's old friend and obvious, um, admirer of being a murderer.'

'Wow, Gus,' she says again. 'And I thought I had relationship troubles.'

60

Dawn breaks without fanfare. Nevertheless, Ally's on the veranda for it, wrapped in her coat. She cradles her mug of coffee, and watches drifts of mizzle move across the bay. Fox, meanwhile, is still sleeping easy in his basket.

It's a relief, knowing Lara was John Smith. Ally loves this so-called lonely spot; she doesn't want to ever doubt it.

Doubt. There's enough of that already. Last night, when Jayden left, they felt like they were getting somewhere, but now, in the cold light of morning, Ally's wondering what they actually have. Pamela could be in love with Donald. She could have worked with him to plan and kill Harrison Loveday. Gina Best could have been killed in error. Perhaps Pamela panicked after that mistake, and Donald saw the job through. But these are all suppositions. And Milo Nash? That incident doesn't fit. Unless there's a connection they can't see yet.

Ally's bedtime lullaby was internet research. She absorbed all that she could about Pamela Trescoe and her simple, beautiful ceramics – which wasn't much. There was a three-line mention in the newsletter of a small private girls' school announcing her retirement, describing her as 'devoted'. Ally looked for more on Donald Crosby and his melancholy estuary oils, but beyond his own one-page website there was little to be found of Donald in the infinite acres of the internet either. And then Milo Nash. His bold and playful work was much more documented. An interview in a skateboarding magazine. Several write-ups on graffiti-focused blogs. Born in Bristol, where he made his name in the street art scene, heading west three years ago. *Artists bang on about the light in Cornwall*, he said in one piece, *but there's a whole lot of dark here too.*

And then she looked up Ray.

When Ally finally went to sleep, her dreams were filled with narrow, twisting lanes, a chase through the woods. She woke pushing brambles from her face. And the first person she thought of when she opened her eyes? *Ray.*

Ally checks her watch. The sky is as bright as it'll get now. She's already decided not to contact Ray in advance. She'll just turn up. *The element of surprise* is the phrase that jumps into her mind, but in her heart of hearts, she knows he can't be involved. Instinct: as invisible as music, as undeniable as sound. But perhaps too intangible to be trusted entirely.

She leaves Fox at home, and by quarter past eight is standing outside Ray's rented cottage. It has olive-green windowsills and a whale-shaped knocker. And it's just steps from the square. She thinks of him turning up to meet her at The Wreckers, hot and bothered and running late. She hasn't shared this detail with Jayden. Because Ray was only a little late: five, seven minutes? And perhaps he wasn't so hot and bothered. Just that, as he bent to kiss her on the cheek, she noticed his warmth – and perhaps that is a different thing altogether.

She glances back down the street, then she knocks.

He answers in his pyjamas: a white t-shirt, and baggy blue cotton trousers. His thick hair is ruffled from sleep.

'Ally.'

His smile is as wide as the bay. As if there have been no murders, no attacks, nothing wrong in the world at all. Then he's proffering coffee, flipping the shutters to let the light in, his bare feet padding over the flagstone floor.

'I've heard the news,' he says. 'Lara Swann is in custody.'

The Arts Trail committee WhatsApp group. Gideon and Connor saw the arrest, and despite Jayden speaking up for Lara, perhaps they still believe she's the killer.

'We don't think she's guilty,' she says. 'Of the vandalism, yes, but not of the murders.'

Ray's face changes. 'Come on, Ally, take the win. Jayden collared her, I hear . . .'

'You were walking in the dunes on the evening that Harrison was killed.'

She doesn't even frame it as a question.

Ray shakes his head. Not a denial, just . . . an expression of confusion. Or perhaps disbelief at her manner. No coffee. No swapped news. Just the flinging of this statement.

Inside her chest, her heart is going like a drum.

'Ah, so this is Ally the detective at my door,' he says.

And for a flicker of a moment, she wishes Jayden were here too. Then it's back to her, and Ray, and her next question feels easier.

'Why didn't you say anything?'

'I did. I told the police.'

'Yesterday?'

'Yesterday. A witness – and if we're talking suspicion then I'd lay it on your pal Gus – came forward. Reported a dodgy bloke in a green anorak loitering outside Harrison's beach house. So I cleared things up.'

He turns and goes into the kitchen. Sets the stovetop coffee pot going. Carefully selects two mugs. Artisan ceramics; Pamela's style. His movements are smooth and unbothered – but deliberately so. Even after all this time, she can read him like a book.

'Was this before we met at The Wreckers?'

'It was.' Ray picks up a mug and inspects it. He takes a tea towel and gives it a quick wipe. 'Just before.'

So, he's decided to make this difficult for her, and she feels a ripple of frustration. But then, isn't she making it difficult for him too?

'Look, Al,' he says.

And the short form feels wrong, on his lips. Jayden calls her Al. Bill called her Al.

'It's embarrassing. I was embarrassed.'

'It's a murder enquiry,' she says stiffly. 'There's no room for feelings like . . . embarrassment. Nothing matters but solving this.'

'And why do you think I hired you?' The coffee pot starts to hiss. 'I didn't bother telling you because it was insignificant.'

'Nothing's insignificant in a case like this.'

'Trust me, this is.' Behind him the coffee pot is spitting. 'Yes, I was in the dunes. I had a plan to come and knock at your door. Call on you, like a boy going to a high school prom. I even picked flowers. But then I got all the way down there and decided it was ridiculous. We were meeting at The Wreckers, it was too pushy, picking you up. I was still . . . gauging things with you.'

The coffee pot's bubbling now. Liquid sizzling as it trickles down the sides.

'So, I did an about-turn. Retraced my steps. Got back to the square and ducked back here to swap coats because I was being vain. It looked like rain, then it didn't, and I wanted to meet you looking sharper.' He pushes his hand through his hair in that so-familiar gesture. 'Overthinking everything, which, believe me, is not my style at all.'

'So you *were* in the dunes,' she says, pointlessly.

He makes a noise of exasperation. 'I wasn't going to volunteer it, because the escapade made me look . . . unconfident. A bit lame, frankly. If I thought it was going to raise questions about the case,

304

I'd have told you. Course I would. So, there you have it. That's the full story. Nothing to see here, Detective.'

And he holds up his hands.

'But what about the party at Island View House? You told us you were Harrison's plus-one, but then Gideon said you emailed him asking for an invitation.'

'Now you're worrying about that?'

'It's an anomaly. Jayden thought—'

'Well, you can tell Jayden that when he asked if I was Harrison's plus-one, I went along with it. I wasn't thinking, but if I was, I suppose I thought it gave me an extra bit of cachet. And yes, I know that sounds pathetic.'

He turns to rescue the coffee that's now filling the cottage with a bitter smell. The set of his shoulders is obstinate. His mouth a hard line.

'Ray . . .' she begins.

He swivels back, the pot in his hand. Burning liquid spurts from the top and hits his hand. He sets it down with a smash.

'Here, run the tap,' says Ally. 'Is it burnt?'

She holds his hand under the jet of water. He looks at her from beneath his lashes.

'You didn't honestly think me capable of . . . *that*?'

'Keep it under there,' she says. Then, 'No. But, rule nothing out. Rule no one out. That's what I've learnt, and . . . you came all this way . . .'

'I did come all this way.'

For a moment there's just the sound of the running tap; the splash as the water hits his hand then the sink.

'I know you're only asking the questions you have to,' he says quietly.

'I don't want to be asking them,' she says back. 'Not of you.'

'Ally, look. About a year ago I went through a bad time. Felt like life had passed me by. I wasn't the artist I wanted to be. Sure, I'd been married, but I wasn't great at it. And my kids . . . I don't think I ever won any dad awards. I started to wonder what I'd actually achieved in life, and decided it wasn't much. So I saw a counsellor. Friend-of-a-friend-of-a-friend sort of thing. And he got me talking . . . I realised I was probably happiest of all at Falmouth.'

'But Ray, you were hardly at Falmouth. Just one term.'

'Tell me about it. But quality not quantity, ever heard that one? So my Proustian mission to Porthpella was to recapture the past. And maybe carve out a new present.'

He doesn't take his eyes from her. Then he smiles at her, and it's a trick of time. Falmouth, again. She looks away first.

'But then Harrison died. And . . . I didn't want to go anywhere.'

Ally realises she's still holding his hand beneath the tap.

'I'd love for you to see my place in Suffolk. Walk with our sketchbooks, like we used to. You'd feel at home there, I think.'

She gives a brief shake of her head. As she slips her fingers from his, Ray sighs.

'So . . . you and this Gus guy, you're together?'

How does Ally explain Gus? How does she draw lines in the sand?

'We're close,' she says.

'I've been a bit of a prat there. He's a nice guy, Ally. Bit soft, but a nice guy.'

'Gus isn't soft.'

'I know who you married, by the way. The Falmouth grapevine didn't stretch back to Putney but . . . years later, I heard it. From Harrison, of all people. He thought it highly amusing. My darkest hour becoming your brightest dawn and all that.'

'It wasn't like that,' says Ally. 'I had no idea Bill had arrested you. And it was later . . .'

'Al, I'm teasing. Look . . . here's the thing. A lifetime ago, I was crazy about you. But I was too young and stupid to know what to do about it. Coming here now, there's still something there. Tell me you don't feel it too. Even just a little?'

She's nineteen and head over heels; body tingling. She hasn't felt like this in the longest time.

'All I can think about is the case,' she says.

But by the look on his face, he can see right through her.

61

'One tea, two toast and a kiss.'

Jayden delivers Cat's breakfast. Downstairs the TV blares with cartoons, Jazzy's laughter rising through the floorboards, but upstairs Benji Weston is fast asleep, curled like a hedgehog on his mum's chest.

'Shall I take him?' he says.

'What, and wake him? No way.'

It was a bad night. One of the worst. Jazz was in full sleep-talking, duvet-stealing, epic-wriggling mode, her presence in their bed as disruptive as a hand grenade. And Benji? Well, he seemed to hardly sleep at all. When Jayden got in, after eleven o'clock, he found Cat pacing and crying. Benji purple-faced and screaming. Jazz splayed in the middle of the bed like a starfish.

As they met eyes, the look on his wife's face was one that he didn't recognise. Not on her. But he'd seen it often enough in his line of work.

Desperation.

Let me take him, he said. And he lifted Benji from her arms – his little son's body stiff with fury and anguish – and held him close. Bounced and swayed. Murmured songs. He was almost embarrassed by how quickly Benji settled. But it didn't last. And through it all,

Jayden kept thinking of the case; the sharp and shifting pieces, not like a puzzle but something animate and dangerous.

Now, he watches Cat chew her toast. A crumb drops on Benji's head. She closes her eyes.

Last night, she didn't want to hear about what had happened in the lane. She said she'd never sleep. But then she hardly sleeps anyway, these days.

'So today,' he says tentatively, 'I need to catch up with Ally. I think we're on the brink of a breakthrough.'

Cat takes another bite of toast. 'And what about the police?'

'They've arrested the wrong person.' He tries a laugh. 'In my humble opinion.'

'I looked it up,' she says. 'I wasn't going to, because I knew I wouldn't be able to get it out of my head. Three deaths. Well, two plus the hit-and-run. It could be three, by now. If he doesn't make it.'

'He'll make it,' says Jayden.

'This isn't like your other cases, Jay.'

'I know.' He tries for lightness again. 'We're actually being paid. Gideon doubled the money last night.'

Cat holds his gaze. The lights are off in her electric-blue eyes.

'But what's it worth? If anything happens to you, I . . .'

'Nothing's going to happen to me.'

'I won't be able to cope.'

He slides in beside her, wraps his arm around her stiff shoulders. Benji shifts and parts his lips, his tiny fingers flutter. He is, Jayden thinks, painfully beautiful.

'I'm barely coping now . . .'

She says it so quietly.

'Babe.' He presses a kiss to her temple. 'You're doing amazing. Right now, we're in the hardest bit. It'll get easier.'

He's aware of how parroted his words sound. A cop-out response.

'What if it doesn't?'

'Then we'll ask for our money back.' He nudges her, going for a smile, because this is the route he's chosen now. And he's tired too. Then, 'Your mum's coming over again today, right? She'll help take the strain?'

She nods.

'Want me to take Jazz out with me though?'

'Chasing a serial killer? Yeah, right. That'd be great. Five-star daddy day care.'

'Cat . . .'

'You've got to do what you've got to do.'

And it feels like there's a bigger conversation looming. Not one to be had after a sleepless night. Maybe his face is doing something because Cat says, 'I'm not being snarky. I know this case is important.'

He kisses her again. 'Call me. If you need anything at all. And I'll check in, alright? As for you, little man . . .'

He touches a finger to Benji's round cheek and it's like Jayden's pressed the on switch. His son screws up his face and starts crying.

The sound is like a car alarm.

'Oh, great. Thanks, Jay.'

Guilt follows him down the stairs and out into the rain-splattered morning. Guilt and – worst of all, as he gains distance – relief.

◆ ◆ ◆

First stop: Ocean Drive. Jayden wants to check in on Mullins. As a mate, but with a few questions too. Like, has Pamela's name come up in the case? What about her witness statement from the party?

Are there any holes in Donald's story? He knows Mullins won't like being sidelined from the case, but it could have ended a lot worse.

As Jayden walks, he dips his chin inside his jacket. It's wet and blustery; one of those spring days that Cornwall seems to specialise in. He checks his phone for a message from Saffron. He had a brief exchange with her earlier about Milo Nash – and she's taking it hard. Mullins had already informed her of the accident but at least Jayden was able to tell her that they knew who wrecked Milo's art. One mystery solved.

Maybe he should drop by hers too.

Meanwhile, Ally is out seeing Ray. She messaged him on her way over, and said she'd call afterwards. No word yet.

Should he worry?

There seem, suddenly, to be a lot of people to worry about. It's always like that – the base note to policing, being with people at their worst moments – but these are his friends.

His *wife*.

He sends Cat a message: I love you. And I love our family.

He wonders about giving his mum-in-law a buzz. Let her know that it was an especially rough night, and Cat barely slept. And now she's thinking about the murders too.

But then Ally phones.

'Ray was in the dunes,' she says, 'but he's got nothing to do with it.'

'Okay.' Then, 'So you're happy with his story?'

'Yes. He's given a statement to the police too. Trust me, there's nothing to connect him, Jayden. Nothing at all.'

He can hear the relief in her voice, but something else too. Ally sounds all churned up.

'Okay,' he says. 'Al, I'm glad.'

Jayden reaches the house where Mullins lives with his mum. It's a tidy bungalow with crazy paving out front and a blue gate.

A garden gnome stands grinning by the door. He sees the curtain twitch, as someone inside spots him.

'Sunita wants a catch-up at the Bluebird,' says Ally. 'She says Gideon and Connor will come down too. And Ray. They think Lara's arrest is final. That the killer's caught.'

'I'd prefer a one-on-one with you. I'm about to see Mullins. I'm still really liking Pamela, Al . . .'

'Pamela in combination with Donald?'

'Has to be.'

'Shall I put Sunita off then?'

'Tell her we'll drop in at the gallery, but no need for the whole gang because it isn't case closed. I want to talk it all out with you first, Al.'

Mullins's mum is on the doorstep. Other than the fact that she's in a pleated skirt and a pink cardigan, she's the spit of her son.

'Al, I'll see you soon,' he says. Then, 'Morning, Mrs Mullins.'

She smiles. 'It's Jenny. Tim said he had a friend coming. He's like a bear with a sore head this morning. Well, bear with a sore bum, actually.'

Jayden follows her in, already liking Jenny Mullins. It's light and bright inside, the wide windows trying to let in the best of the day. He looks around, taking in the framed photographs: Mullins sitting on Santa's knee in a tinselly grotto, wearing blue dungarees and a look of outright fear on his face; Mullins in school uniform, round-faced, leery, a gap between his teeth; Mullins in his police uniform, squinting into the camera with a smile Jayden hasn't seen before. Hopeful: that's what it is.

'Here he is,' says his mum, 'in 3D.'

Mullins is settled on a sofa, a crocheted blanket up to his waist. It's hard to look tough in that set-up, but Mullins is giving it a go.

'What have you brought me then, mate?'

'A bunch of dumb questions. Couple of half-baked theories.'

'Classic Shell House. No box of chocolates then? Bottle of Lucozade?'

Jayden pulls up a chair and accepts Jenny Mullins's offer of a cup of tea.

'How it's feeling?'

'Pain in the arse.'

Jayden laughs.

'Seriously. I'm sitting here on one of those rubber rings the kids bob about on.'

'Any news on Milo Nash?'

'He's regained consciousness. But he's too out of it to be interviewed. The docs won't let anyone near him yet. Multiple breaks. He's drugged up to his eyeballs.'

'But he's going to make it?'

As Mullins nods, Jayden feels a rush of relief.

'What about you, mate? What was the verdict at the hospital?'

'Three hours in the waiting room, and they told me the same thing the paramedic said at the scene. Fractured coccyx. And nothing you can do for it either, except wait and let it heal. So that was a waste of my night. I tell you, sitting in that waiting room was worse than being down that hole. Three hours, Jayden. I could have had six pints and come back again. Might have helped the pain.'

A thought comes out of nowhere. Jayden catches it, like an outfielder. Feels the immediate rush.

'You could have done,' he says.

'No chance. I could barely walk.'

'I mean . . . technically. Once you'd signed in, gone through triage, all you do is wait, right? Nothing to stop you leaving for an hour or two.'

'Apart from missing your slot and having to wait another ten hours. But sure, I respect your commitment to fitting a pint in, Jayden.'

'When you first get there, they estimate the waiting time, don't they? So, it's possible to get signed in, disappear for two hours, then go back and sit in the same chair. No one would be any the wiser.'

Mullins narrows his eyes. 'Where are you going with this?'

'Pamela Trescoe,' Jayden says. 'That's where I'm going.'

He stops talking as Jenny Mullins brings them their tea in two Garfield mugs, plus a plate of custard creams.

'We all need this killer caught,' she says, helping herself to a biscuit from the plate. 'And I think you two are just the ones to do it.'

Mullins rolls his eyes at Jayden, but he's taking the pat on the head all the way. As his mum heads back to the kitchen, Mullins shifts on the sofa.

'Pamela flaming Trescoe then, is it? Talk me through this one, Jayden.'

So he does. Mullins listens carefully. Halfway through, he loses his custard cream to his tea – a dunk gone wrong – and there's some low-grade cursing, then a failed attempt to extract it.

'Alright, it's not the stupidest thing I've heard,' he says.

'You sound like Skinner.'

'No, Skinner would say it *is* the stupidest thing he's heard, because he's already got two suspects in custody, thanks very much. Though, speaking of . . . Crosby's twenty-four hours must be up in a tick.'

'So maybe there's a case for extending that.'

'So . . . what, you're saying Pamela's ankle injury is a fake? And the whole A&E thing was just to get an alibi? Because otherwise it's a big ask, to go and murder someone when you've got a sprained ankle. While, by the way, leaving no trace evidence. Nothing we can match to her, anyway.'

'I think the ankle injury's genuine, but not as bad as she's making out.'

That's guesswork, but Jayden saw the way Pamela moved on her crutches. It wasn't like they were the only thing in the world holding her up.

'What about footprints?' he asks suddenly. 'Any footprints at the scene? Because if Pamela was on crutches, she'd have been favouring her left foot. There could be distinctive marks.'

Mullins risks another dunk. He chews thoughtfully.

'The CSI lot did turn up some footprints, as it happens. But before you get excited, Jayden, they were matched to Gina Best.'

'Where were they found?'

'By one of the downstairs windows.'

'Why would Gina Best be looking in a downstairs window? Ally and I saw her arrive. She walked straight in with Harrison Loveday.'

'I doubt you kept her under surveillance though, did you, Jayden? She could have spent the afternoon looking in all the windows she wanted.'

'Gina was wearing high heels when she turned up at Sea Dream. So the prints were of high heels, were they?'

'Trainers. Running shoes.'

'Okay.'

'Size six. Nike Air Pegasus. Gina's shoes. Her spare shoes, if you want to be accurate.'

Jayden nods. 'Okay, what about crutch marks? Any note about that?'

'No nice little circles of blood tracking back down the hall, if that's what you're thinking.' Mullins drains the last of his tea and sets the mug down with a clunk. 'Let me get this straight. You think Pamela Trescoe is so in love with Donald Crosby that she'd kill Harrison Loveday just to make him happy. She has a crack at the Arts Trail party but bodges it and gets the wrong person. The next night she plans to make it right and her sprained ankle gives her just the alibi she needs. No one's going to question A&E waiting time, are they? Broken Britain and all that. This time she gets it done. Stabs Loveday to death. Then shoots back to Truro to smack back down in the waiting room, before meekly seeing the doc.'

Jayden rubs the back of his head. 'That's it, yeah.'

'And Milo Nash? Because he's got nothing to do with Crosby's grudge, has he?'

'Like you said, could be random.'

Mullins folds his arms across his chest; he looks as obstinate as a toddler.

'You want me to take this to Skinner, do you?'

'I'd have loved it if there'd been footprints at Sea Dream, left foot only.'

'And those little crutch marks too.'

'And those. But one look at the A&E waiting room CCTV will confirm it. If Pamela leaves, we've got her.'

Mullins purses his lips.

'Skinner's liking Lara Swann for it, Jayden. I expect the DCI is too. There's more evidence to connect Lara than Pamela Trescoe.'

'At the moment.'

'There you go, then,' he says. 'You just answered your own question.'

Jayden isn't sure he asked one.

'If you want me to take this to Skinner, you need to find some actual evidence.'

'I could take it to Skinner now, because that CCTV would provide the evidence.'

'Sure. Go for it. Good luck. Three crime scenes, Jayden. And alright, we don't have everything from the third yet, but we took the prints of everyone at that party, including Pamela Trescoe. If she's the mastermind here, she's one slick operator. Decent debut, for someone with no criminal record. Because yes, we ran those checks too.' Mullins winces suddenly. 'It's time for my painkillers. Couldn't grab them for me, mate? Just on the table there.'

Jayden stands up. 'Yeah, sure.'

Painkillers and hard evidence? Coming right up.

'This is your problem, Jayden. I'm not being funny, but you and Ally only ever work with a little bit of the picture. I don't know how you put up with it, personally. Shouldn't have been so quick to ditch your badge . . .'

And there are a lot of things he could say to this, but in the end, Jayden chooses just one.

'We've done alright so far though, hey, Mullins?'

62

'So, are you saying you don't think Lara Swann did it?' says Sunita.

Her face is troubled. Sunita said last night she slept easy, knowing that Lara was in custody. Now it's as if Ally has ruined everything.

'Gideon and Connor didn't say it was all over, they weren't that . . . absolute. But they were optimistic,' Sunita goes on. 'And they said it was Jayden who caught Lara in the woods. So you *have* cracked the case. We knew you would. You always do. Only now you're saying you haven't . . .'

'Sunita, Lara's guilty of the graffiti. And she sent various unsettling emails to artists on the trail, me included. She admitted that. But she says she's got nothing to do with the murders. And Jayden believes her.'

Sunita drops down into a chair. 'But anyone can say anything. They can pull the wool over anyone's eyes. Meanwhile that poor boy Milo is lying there . . .'

'The police have twenty-four hours to question her. They'll leave no stone unturned.' Ally changes tack. 'Sunita, did you ever meet Billie Swann?'

'Once or twice. She was very private.'

'Was anyone around here close to her?'

'A few of us made attempts, when she first bought the place. We're talking more than a decade ago though, Ally. And her daughter . . .'

'So you don't know if she welcomed people into her studio?'

'I think one or two people went. Yes, I seem to remember there being some . . . not boasting, as such, just . . . talk of it. Now, who was it . . .'

Sunita's forehead wrinkles as she tries to remember.

'Pamela lives closest,' says Ally, casually.

'Yes, I suppose it could have been Pamela. Though I don't think she has anything to do with Lara. None of us do, Ally. Why are you asking?'

Because if there was cyanide in the studio, someone else could have known about it.

Ally checks her watch. Jayden said he was on his way.

'Ally,' says Sunita again, 'why are you interested in Billie if you don't think Lara did it? Are you back at the beginning?'

'Not quite.'

Sunita sighs. 'Your friend Ray was very complimentary on the WhatsApp group. I think he's amazed by what you've become, Ally.'

But she doesn't want to think about Ray. Not now. She casts around for a subject change – and sees red.

'All those red dots,' she says.

'We've sold every piece. I've no idea where the money will be going yet. I'm waiting on a call from Gina's gallery. Presumably they'll have more insight into Harrison's estate.'

Perhaps Harrison's next of kin, Annabel Crosby in Carbis Bay.

'Look,' says Sunita, 'I trust you to solve this. We all do. And we also know that you and Jayden know far more than you're telling us. Of course you do. About Lara, about Donald. About everyone.

Just tell me one thing . . . Should we still be afraid? Or do you think this killer's work is done?'

But that's a question that Ally can't answer.

◆　◆　◆

'Venue change,' says Ally. 'I've already caught up with Sunita.'

As they drive back to the dunes, Jayden tells her that Milo Nash has regained consciousness. That he's in no shape to be interviewed, but he's going to make it. She breathes a sigh of relief.

Suddenly Ally wants the quiet of the thinking room. Those four protective walls. Or, better still, the beach; the tide pushing at the shore. But then she might bump into Gus. And she doesn't want to bump into Gus. She's never felt that way about Gus before.

The way Ray looked at me. The way he held my hand.

'Mind elsewhere, huh?' says Jayden.

'Not anymore. Only on the case. Jayden, the committee have a WhatsApp group. Ray's in it too. Gideon set it up, so they could swap notes.'

'Swap notes on the Arts Trail?'

'No, swap notes on the case. It's just the four of them. Because they hired us.'

Jayden pulls a face. 'So long as it is just them. Social media can totally disrupt an investigation. It's misinformation central.'

'That's not Sunita and Gideon, it's . . .' She runs out of steam. 'This case. I'm beginning to think we shouldn't have taken it. The four of them. Paying us. The expectation. The obligation. I just . . .'

'Al,' says Jayden, 'we wanted in on this. We'd have investigated anyway. You know we would.' She can feel him looking at her. 'Is this about Ray?'

'He's in the clear, Jayden.'

'I mean, is it about him hiring us?'

Ally knows she can tell Jayden anything. That perhaps the mysteries of the heart are not so different from the other kind.

Many years ago, I loved Ray. And it's not that that love's been reawakened but . . . these last few days I've felt something. And it's surprised me. And confused me.

But, instead, she says, 'Ray made it clear that coming to Porthpella . . . He wanted to see me after all these years. It's complicated.'

'Too complicated?'

They're outside The Shell House. And it feels so reassuring to be home. To retreat back to the familiar.

Maybe Jayden senses her hesitation because he says, 'Well, look. Let me make one thing uncomplicated. We're back on with Pamela.'

She catches his arm. 'Tell me.'

'Her alibi for Saturday night might not be so rock-solid after all. Let's get in the thinking room.'

But Jayden can't wait, and neither can Ally, and as they head up the steps, he tells her his A&E waiting room theory.

'So, Al, one look at the CCTV, and if Pamela leaves, we've got her. The hospital will be full of cameras. I bet they can track her all the way from the waiting room to the car park and back again. The request has to come from the police though. They'll never give it to you and me.'

'And Mullins can't help?'

'He thinks Skinner will want more from us, because they're fixed on Lara Swann. He's feeling the heat from the DCI and the Major Crimes team.'

Ally draws in a long breath. She looks at the board. It's as if Pamela Trescoe's name has grown a metre high. Ally thinks of her exuberance and self-assurance. Her obvious feelings for Donald.

'It's a very clever alibi,' she says. 'Everyone knows waiting times are horrendous at A&E.'

'It's clever and it's confident.'

'If Pamela drove from Truro, and was on the clock, she'd park somewhere near the dunes. Even if her ankle wasn't too bad, she'd have wanted to avoid taking unnecessary time.'

'Exactly. So her car could be caught on camera on the route to the beach.'

'Wouldn't the police have gone through all that footage?'

Jayden rubs his chin. 'Well, yeah. But Pamela knows these roads. She knows where the cameras are. And, wild guess, I think that ankle injury isn't as bad as she's making out. So maybe she did go a decent way on foot. Speaking of, there's no unaccounted-for footprints at Sea Dream. I'd have loved it if there were.'

'Is that what Mullins said?'

'It is. And he also said it's a hell of a debut for a first-time law breaker. Which is true. Let's go back to the first murder. Poisoning someone at a party . . . that's logistically very hard to pull off. A lot harder than stabbing someone while they're sleeping.'

'Which perhaps explains why she didn't pull it off,' says Ally. 'She got the wrong person. If we're right, anyway . . .'

'If we're right. But she got close. Gina instead of Harrison. It wasn't a random hit. So she must have calculated it. Intercepted the drinks from the barman, because he was freshly mixing cocktails.'

Ally closes her eyes, brings up Island View in her mind's eye. The fairy lights, the lawn, the crowded terrace. When she and Gus first arrived, she pointed out everyone, and Pamela was among them, talking to Donald, nowhere near the bar. But that was a good twenty minutes before the murder. They'd all have changed positions multiple times.

A sudden intake of breath. 'Jayden! Pamela was wearing black and white.'

He sends her a questioning look.

'A linen tunic. Black culottes.'

'Okay.'

'The waiting staff were in black and white too. Classic garb.'

Jayden's face lights up. 'And you're thinking it was deliberate.'

'Well, mightn't it have been? If Pamela's plan required her to be near the bar, possibly intercepting drinks, then it'd help if she blended in, wouldn't it?'

'Because a busy barman isn't going to give her a second look if she's dressed like a waiter.'

'But not so like a waiter that she could be confused for one by the other guests. She still looked very much like Pamela. Arty, you know, bold. But . . . in black and white.'

'I like it, Al. But it's not the hard evidence that we're looking for.' Jayden's on his feet, energised. 'There's got to be something. Two crime scenes. If not three. She must have left some trace.'

'If she had, the police would have already connected it, wouldn't they?'

'They fingerprinted everyone, but they'll only take DNA from suspects. Like Lara Swann and Donald Crosby. One ran from the police, one left fingerprints at the scene. But if there was a random hair, say, the police would have been on that. Mullins just said about the footprints. Which turned out to be Gina Best's trainers. Nike Air Pegasus, for the record.' He sighs. 'I still think those crutches would have left marks . . .'

Ally's closing her eyes. She's envisaging Pamela's hallway. The toffee-coloured wooden boards, the elegant artwork, the soft lamplight. The coat stand, and neat shoe rack.

'Jayden, did you say Nike trainers? Pamela has Nike trainers.'

He stops. 'Pamela has Nikes?'

'I saw them in her shoe rack. When we were at her house.'

'Pamela has Nikes?' he says again. 'Al, this could be it. This could be the detail we need. If she's the same shoe size as Gina Best, then they could have been her prints, not Gina's.' He grins. 'This is it.'

'So, do we call Skinner?'

'No. First, we go to Pamela's. And we take a look at those trainers. If they're size six, then we're in business.'

63

Should they go to the police? Probably. But Mullins's comments earlier hit home. Jayden knows he and Ally are a long shot, but maybe it's because they only have part of the picture – as Mullins put it – that they work so hard to see the rest of it.

And maybe it's about Cat and the kids too. Because after the night they had, Jayden needs a damn good reason for why he's left them again today.

Even though it's my job, I need a damn good reason.

Ally drives, and Jayden drums his hands on his knees. As they approach the section of the lane where Milo was hit, he talks about Saffron's fractured wrist. How half of Porthpella has been in A&E lately.

'Let's not add to it,' says Ally, glancing sideways at him.

'Al, we're going to look at a shoe. No one's getting hurt today.'

Jayden already teed up a possible reason to give Pamela for their return. As they dropped her off last night, when the idea was only just dawning in his mind, he said they'd keep her updated with any news about Donald. A tactical move, so she would open the door to them without suspicion. And now he knows from Mullins that Donald is going to be released soon – that's their ticket in.

Unless Skinner decides to apply to extend. But without the Pamela angle, what reason would he have?

Beside him, Ally's looking in the rear-view mirror.

'Alright, Al?'

'I'm just thinking about how dreadful it would have been if Connor and Gideon hit Milo when he was lying in the road.'

'I know. He was left for dead. And I still think it's got to be connected.'

'Because he's an artist?'

'Because it's an act of violence. But yeah . . . because he's an artist too.'

'But the Arts Trail angle, that was a flame fanned by Lara. And the media. The Arts Trail was never Pamela's target.'

'But it suited her, didn't it, everything that Lara was doing? Because as far as Pamela was concerned, it moved suspicion away from the motive being personal when it came to Harrison and Gina.'

'Until Donald's fingerprints were found at Sea Dream, anyway,' says Ally.

The lanes are tight here, the hedges bulky and overreaching. It's a green tunnel. Ally drives carefully, as Jayden's thoughts buzz like mad.

'What if that was the catalyst?' he says suddenly. 'The suspicion is squarely on Donald, so Pamela's getting desperate. She loves him, remember? So she pulls focus from him by launching an attack on Milo Nash. Another victim for the Arts Trail Killer.'

Ally draws a quick breath. 'So Milo's nothing but . . . a decoy?'

'Exactly. I mean, it'd take some planning. Maybe Pamela lay in wait and followed him, saw him leave his camper van and took her chance. This is her neck of the woods, isn't it? Look, we're basically here . . .'

Pamela's house comes into view and Jayden feels a thrum of anticipation.

'It's not as clean as the other methods, but maybe she was getting desperate. Sloppy. She rocked up at the scene playing the concerned neighbour card, didn't she? But maybe she just wanted to see what was going down.'

'My God. Jayden, I think you're right. Should we try and look at her car too? See if there's any sign of damage?'

'Definitely.'

He and Ally have already talked about how they're going to do it. Good cop/good cop is the vibe. News of Donald will get them through the door; Ally will keep the artist-to-artist chat going; Jayden will escape to check the shoes and get a photograph.

First, they need to be a size six. And if the police are satisfied that they have a match with Gina's Nike Air Pegasus, then Pamela's Nikes need to have the same outsole, to ensure the same prints. Jayden gets out his phone and brings up the picture he showed Ally earlier: the tread on a pair of Pegasus, but one that's used across a bunch of Nike's running shoes – a distinctive arrangement of small waffle-like polygons. Harrison was killed two nights ago, so any mud would have dried. Sand caught in the tread? Well, that'd be nice. But also easily explained away. Live in Porthpella, you're going to have sand in your shoes.

Nike, size six, waffle tread: that's what they need to take to Skinner. And now a vehicle check too. Any signs of damage and he's getting his camera out. If the shoe doesn't fit? If the car looks pristine? It doesn't mean Pamela's not an option, but their sell to Skinner will be harder.

'Ready, Al?' he says.

'Ready.'

Knuckle bumps.

Jayden's just opening the car door when his phone starts ringing. He frowns.

'It's Sue,' he says. 'Why's Sue calling?'

He closes the door.

'Sue, hey.'

'Jayden . . . Is Cat with you?'

His heart drops. It's not her words, but her voice.

'No, she's not with me. Sue, you're with them all, right? At home? You were coming over.'

There's a beat of silence on the end of the line. Then, in the background, Jayden hears Benji's cry.

'Sue?'

'I went upstairs to see Benji, and when I came back down, she was gone.'

'Gone? She won't be gone. She'll just have . . . Where's Jazz? You're with Jazz, right?'

'She was watching television. When I came back down Jasmine was still watching her cartoons, and Cat . . . She's not here, Jayden.'

The urgency in her voice is palpable. And Sue doesn't do drama.

'How long's she been gone, Sue?'

'At least fifteen minutes. Perhaps twenty. She's not in the farmhouse, Cliff checked. I don't want to make a fuss, but . . . she left her mobile. She always has that thing glued to her. She left it, Jayden.'

'Are you sure she didn't say anything about going out? Sudden nappy emergency or something?'

'Her car's here. You've got a whole cupboard full of nappies. I'd only just got here. Cat was making us both a cup of tea, she even put the cups out . . .'

Jayden looks to Ally, and she's already restarting the engine. Reversing back down Pamela's drive. His heart's beating double-time.

'I'm coming. I'll be home in five.'

'Jayden, where is she?'

'I'm on my way. Don't worry. There'll be an explanation. Jazz and Benji, they're okay, right?'

'They're fine. Oblivious, of course.'

'See you soon, okay?'

He hangs up. Looks to Ally.

'I need . . .' he begins.

Then finds he can't actually speak.

A response officer. That was his job, twenty-four seven. Calls came in and off they'd go. First responders. Any and all emergencies. Lights on. Capable. Confident. Calm.

He draws in a breath and feels Ally's hand on his arm. She's already got them rocketing down the lanes, as if the blues and twos are going. As if they're heading for a crisis. There to help but, also, deep in it.

Deep in it.

Why would Cat leave without telling Sue? Where would she go? Leaving her phone, leaving her car, leaving Jazz on her own. Okay, Sue was upstairs, Sue was with Benji, but just going out? Leaving them?

Jayden can't think of a good reason why she would do that.

Which only leaves bad reasons.

And he knows this moment. He saw it so many times as an officer. People not wanting to make a fuss, who think there's a reasonable explanation, sure that their loved one will turn up any moment but . . . there's a feeling.

A feeling.

As they head up the drive at the farm, Jayden sees Cliff in his pickup. He pulls on to the verge and buzzes the window down.

'Sue's going spare. But Cat could be having a pint in The Wreckers, all we know.' Cliff tries for a smile but it's more of a grimace. 'I'll cover the village.'

'I'll do the beach,' says Jayden.

His father-in-law gives him a hard look, then shoots the window back up and that's it. He's out of there.

'He thinks it's on me.'

'He's worried, Jayden,' says Ally. 'And it's not. How could it be?'

But the feeling that it is is a stone in his gut. This morning Cat told him she was struggling, and he left anyway. The stone becomes a rock.

As Jayden parks and heads to the cottage, his daughter throws herself at his legs and hangs on like a wrestler looking to take him down. Her giggle is almost hysterical. Sue gives him a brisk hug.

'Benji's dropped off. Jayden, this isn't like Cat. This isn't like her at all.'

So he tells Sue that Cat's been finding things tough. That what is like Cat, and what isn't, is perhaps not so fixed right now.

'What are you saying?' says Sue.

'I'm saying . . . she's exhausted and stressed and maybe not thinking right. Sue, when did you last see her? She was here when you first arrived, right?'

'She was making tea. I went upstairs, and when I came back down . . . she was gone.'

'How long were you up there for?'

'Four or five minutes? I was just with Benji. Jasmine was watching television. I came back down, and she was nowhere to be seen. I gave it ten minutes, then I checked our house, the garden. I called for her, Jayden. But then I saw she'd left her phone. That's when I rang you.'

Jayden's looking around his own house – the scattered toys, the TV paused on a cartoon – like it's a place he doesn't recognise. As if, without Cat, it makes no sense.

'Did you ask Jasmine if her mummy said anything to her?' asks Ally.

Sue nods. 'Nothing. Should we . . . call 999? Just, with everything that's happening around here . . . the Arts Trail K—'

Jayden glances at Ally.

'There's one place I want to look. If she's not there, I'll make the call.'

◆   ◆   ◆

Outside in the yard, Jayden turns to Ally. 'You go to Pamela's, Al. Do what we talked about. If it's too much to check the car and the shoe, just focus on what's accessible.'

'But you need me here.'

'I've got this.' He's bouncing on his heels, ready to run. 'Sue's got her mate Jan coming. Cliff's out driving. If Cat's not at the Lookout, I'll call 999. But she will be. I know she will be. She'll have wanted a breather. She'll have thought *Mum's with the kids, it's all good*. And just . . . not thinking straight. Honestly, please go see Pamela. That's the most helpful thing.'

And he means it. He really means it.

Ally gives him a quick hug. 'Radio contact?'

'Radio contact.'

Ally jumps in the car, and Jayden starts running. Across the yard and into the empty camping field. He pelts across the grass like an athlete. Then over a gate – a clean vault – and up into one of Cliff's cauliflower fields; the next crop ready to be sown. Jayden knows the rhythms of the farm now; maybe they're even becoming his rhythms too. But not like Cat. She was born here. She toddled these fields, just like Jazzy does now and Benji will before long. And the Lookout? The Lookout has always been Cat's favourite spot. A bench at the highest point of the farm. Huge, wild views across the bay. The place she'd go to as a child, spinning stories of pirates, and as a teenager, figuring out her place in this minuscule corner of the wide world. The first time Jayden came up here, they'd been dating just a few months; they drank cans of Red Stripe and kissed on that bench, as the sun went down in carnival colours. *Nice place for a weekend*, he thought then, never imagining they'd live here; raise children here.

The Lookout has always been Cat's place.

He powers up the hill and reaches the crest. Looking over to the next field, he sees the outline of the bench. Nothing but sea rising beyond it; one of those tricks of perspective you get at the coast.

She's not there.

He can see from here that she's not. But he runs towards it anyway. And he's taking his phone out of his pocket.

He's calling 999.

Because if she's not there, it's like she's not anywhere.

64

Ally pulls up at Pamela's with a sense of déjà vu – accompanied by the feeling that she shouldn't be here. She should be helping Jayden look for Cat.

She checks her phone: no messages.

Jayden thinks he knows where Cat will be, and of course he knows her better than anyone, but Ally can't help but think of Gina, of Harrison, of Milo. Of harm befalling people in such different situations and in such different ways. The thought is too much. But Jayden has given Ally a job. She has to do it. For the case, but also for him.

She looks at the image of the Pegasus trainer tread one more time, committing the pattern to memory. Then she takes a breath and gets out of the car.

Ally hears the sound immediately. A crashing, smashing din, coming from the studio.

She turns cold.

Crash. Smash. Fast, relentless blows.

If Jayden were here, they'd swap a look, a word; they'd adjust their approach. But Ally's all alone. What if someone is hurting Pamela? Or wrecking her work, just as Milo's piece was destroyed?

She hurries to the studio, calls out 'Pamela?'

Smash. Crash.

Ally pushes open the door, afraid of what she might find.

Pamela is standing in the middle of the space. She's holding a huge hammer and swinging it. With a wild cry she lets it drop into what looks like a large bin.

Smash. Crash.

Then there's a moment of absolute silence. Ally's frozen; Pamela hasn't heard her come in. Has she got this all wrong? Should she have tiptoed past the studio, tried the door of the house, sought out the shoe covertly? Or snuck into the garage and looked at the car? But she's here now. And Pamela is holding an enormous hammer. And she's smashing things.

Ally resets.

'Pamela!' she calls, with all the appearance of calm. 'I heard the noise and was worried, are you alright?'

Pamela spins round. For a second her face is pure confusion, then she smiles widely.

'Ally!'

Her cheeks are bright red, and she puffs a fallen strand of hair from her face. As Ally steps closer she sees Pamela's brow is glistening with sweat. Her eyes are sparkling.

'You've caught me in the act.'

Ally gives a brief shake of her head. She notes that Pamela's crutches are leaning against a worktop. Standing here, her ankle looks fine. Perhaps a slight favouring of the left foot.

'My absolute favourite thing. Have you any idea how therapeutic it is?'

'What . . . are you doing?'

'Smashing pots! The seconds, the misshapes, the godawful attempts. Can't sell them. And God knows I've enough about the place as it is. Nothing to do but send them to smithereens. And it feels sensational, Ally.' She holds out the hammer. 'Try it! Let it all out.'

Ally takes the hammer. The handle is slick; she wipes her hands on her jeans.

'Go on,' says Pamela. 'Take a good swing. Hold on, let me feed the fire.'

Pamela reaches over to the workbench and tosses in two more pots. A large vase. A bowl. Ally looks down into the bin. A mass of ceramics.

'Just take a jolly good swing. Do your worst.'

And Pamela's right. It's satisfying. Ally feels her throat burn, all manner of feelings rushing in. She blinks quickly and strikes again with the hammer. The smash of pottery rings in her ears.

'Ah, you've got it now,' says Pamela, laughing. 'Should be available on the NHS, shouldn't it? Now Ally, I presume you didn't come here to smash my pots. Do you have news?'

Ally works to compose her features, while inside, her mind is thrumming. Is Pamela Trescoe really capable of a double murder and a brutal hit-and-run? All because she loves Donald and hates Harrison? Two years ago, Ally would have said absolutely not. For all that she learned from Bill – that, in extreme circumstances, even the law-abiding can cross lines – Ally would never have suspected that this exuberant, artistic woman was capable of cold-blooded, ruthlessly executed killing. But in her time as a detective, she's come face-to-face, stood toe-to-toe, with at least four murderers. And in every case, she'd once have said, *Oh gosh, not him, not her, surely?*

Not anymore.

If Pamela is the killer, then she's here in the studio with Ally, and nowhere near Jayden's wife. That, at least, is something.

'Yes, I do have news,' she says, forcing a suitable smile. 'I thought you'd want to know. Donald will be released shortly. He could already be out now, Pamela.'

'Oh, thank God for that. Well, I should think so too. I've a good mind to launch a complaint, I . . .'

She leans heavily against the worktop as her indignation ebbs.

Ally realises she's still holding the hammer. For inexact reasons, she doesn't want to hand it back to Pamela, so instead she stands it against the bin.

'And what about the young man? The graffiti artist?'

'I've heard that he'll make a recovery,' says Ally carefully.

'What a relief that is. I walk these lanes all the time, and we could do without dangerous drivers on top of everything else.'

'Quite.'

'And Lara Swann? In the shock of it all, I realised I hardly gave her arrest last night a thought. But it's a huge relief. Though she's such a little scrap of a girl. Extraordinary, really. Well, Ally, thank you. I appreciate you coming all this way to tell me about Donald. I really do.'

'Pamela, sorry to ask, but could I use your loo?'

'Of course. There's one just off the hall. I'll come into the house with you. Cup of tea?'

With Pamela in the studio, Ally was hoping for a clear run at the shoe rack. How can she keep her out here?

'No, no. Thank you. I've been drinking tea all morning, hence the bathroom request.' She gives a little laugh; hopes it rings true. 'You keep smashing your pots, Pamela. You're right, it was a thrill. Oh, what do you do with the fragments? I'm just thinking of my collages. Some of these shards would be wonderful to incorporate. And they're such beautiful pieces, it'd be a shame for them to go to waste entirely.'

'Ah now,' says Pamela, peering into the bin, 'there's a mosaic artist over in St Just that I generally supply. But I could give you a bagful, Ally. Of course I could. But don't you solely use beach finds? I thought that was your thing.'

'I'm always open to experimentation. And your glazes are just so gorgeous,' she adds. 'There's something oceanic about them.'

Pamela smiles, pink-cheeked.

'You use the bathroom, and I'll make you up a bag.' She takes a pair of gloves from the workbench. 'They're sharp though, some of these pieces. Could cut your hand off, so be careful when you're working with them.'

Ally's looking at the gloves – they're tough, gardening-style. Not cocktail-party wear, but for creeping into a house at nightfall? Before Ally's face betrays her, she says, 'Back in a moment,' and hurries up the gravel path.

The driveway is empty, and the garage is closed. Shoe or car? Jayden said to prioritise the most accessible. And she has no good excuse if Pamela finds her trying to get into the garage.

As she opens the door to the house, Ally glances back at the studio. Impossible to tell if Pamela is watching her. She closes it carefully behind her.

The scents of the house greet her. Coffee; the lingering traces of fried bacon. Warm, comforting smells. But she feels queasy. Ally walks a few steps down the hall and kneels at the shoe rack. She has moments, at best. Pamela could come in at any second, persisting with her offer of tea.

She sees the Nike swoosh immediately.

Ally takes out a shoe. She checks the label on the inside of the tongue and sees an eight. Pamela's an eight, not a six.

It's a dead end.

But this shoe doesn't look like an eight. Eight is large for a woman's shoe size. Ally pulls the tongue out further. They're old trainers, and the printing is worn. She peers closer.

Size eight. Then, in brackets, the letters, faded: *US*.

She breathes out. Can she hear movement outside?

Size six UK.

It's written below in smaller type; only just legible.

337

Ally grabs her phone and photographs the label. Then she turns over the shoe and looks at the outsole.

Waffle print.

Are those footsteps? The crunch of gravel? Ally takes a photograph, her hand shaking. She steadies herself, manages a clearer shot. She's about to replace the shoe when something catches her eye. She squints. There's a tiny stone caught in the tread; wedged between two polygons. It's honey-coloured. Smooth. Looks like flint.

She takes another photograph.

Then she puts the shoe back in the rack, neatens it, and gets to her feet. Her back creaks as she moves, the squatting position awkward. She walks stiffly to the bathroom, and as she closes the door and slides the bolt across, she hears the opening of another door.

Pamela's footsteps down the hall. The tap-tap of crutches.

Ally waits until the sound is closer, then she pulls the chain to flush. *Her alibi.*

65

Jayden hangs up the phone. He's handled plenty of missing person call-outs, so the questions were familiar. He answered them straightforwardly; non-emotionally.

Is Cat high-risk?

She didn't leave Jazz and Benji on their own; she knew Sue was in the house. But it was still 100 per cent out of character for her to just walk out.

Jayden knows she's been struggling, but he told himself it was just exhaustion; the relentlessness of life with a newborn and a toddler; the aftermath of a tough birth. It felt like a betrayal admitting to the police that he's worried about her mental health, when he and Cat haven't spoken about it themselves. Like he's been too spineless to broach the topic with her. It's stupid, because he's been there – and she's been right in it with him. When Kieran died, Jayden's head was all over the place. And Cat was brilliant.

Tears fill his eyes at the thought that he's let her down.

And then the other worry. The thing Sue almost voiced, that maybe Ally is thinking too. That this is nothing to do with Cat's head at all.

The Arts Trail Killer.

No. More likely she popped out for five minutes. Slipped and fell and twisted something, and without her phone, she wouldn't be able to ring for help.

But wouldn't she shout?

Maybe she hit her head. Maybe she's unconscious.

But what was she doing to hurt herself so badly that she's unconscious?

Jayden ups his jogging pace. He did as he said he would – when Cat wasn't at the Lookout, he rang 999 – and now he's heading for the beach. He'll take the path the campers use, the one that joins the coast path and comes out at the beach. He phones Sue as he goes, tells her the police are on their way. That they'll come to the cottage, and he'll be back to meet them. He's just checking one more place.

But Jayden knows he won't want to leave it there. Because if Cat's not at the beach, he'll need to go back to the coast path. Eye every rock drop; every ledge.

There must be a simple explanation.

How can there be a simple explanation?

He's up on the cliff path now and the sea is an unending expanse to his right. It's been drizzling all morning, and his trainers slip as he runs. It wouldn't take much. Sheer drops are everywhere. People think inner cities are dangerous places, but so-called beauty spots like this? Cliff faces don't care if you keep your footing; the ocean will swallow you in a second.

Jayden knows that when the officers come to the cottage, they'll ask again how concerned he is for his wife's mental health. And the subtext? He knows the subtext. But that's not where Cat is. That's not where her head's at. Because he'd know. He would never let it get that far.

Then, another question: *Jayden, how widely known is it that you're investigating the Arts Trail Killer?*

Though they wouldn't use the name the newspapers have come up with. They'd say, *involved in the investigation*. Or, *involved in recent events in Porthpella*. But however they phrase it, the implication will be the same.

Jayden stops. The bay opens up before him. He holds his hand to his eyes and scans the sand. In the far distance there's a couple of dog walkers; a kid with a kite.

Then he sees someone in the water.

And he sprints like he's never sprinted before.

66

'Gus, are you at home? Can I ask a favour of you?'

Ally has closed her mind to everything but her one objective – and Gus responds to the urgency in her voice.

'Anything, Ally,' he says.

'Can you go to Sea Dream and send me a close-up photograph of the gravel on the drive?'

'The gravel on the drive? I can do that. Any particular part or . . .'

'Any part of it. A close-up of the stones. Thank you, Gus. Quick as you can. Thank you so much.'

Then she's hanging up, and she's staring at her phone, already waiting. She pictures him heading down the path, through the gate, and out on to the track. Thirty seconds and he'll be at Sea Dream. But because it's Gus, he'll be thorough. Not just one photograph, but several; all angles. Ally resists phoning him again to hurry him along. She knows he'll be moving as quickly as he can.

Sure enough, her phone pings, and one, two, three photos drop in. Four, five, six. Gus has taken his assignment seriously.

Moonstone flint at a guess. It's wet so it's darker than usual. When it's dry it's more amber.

Probably too much detail.

Need more pics?

Ally is zooming in, nodding. She taps out a fast reply:

Perfect. Thank you. Will explain later.

She wants to phone Jayden, but she can't phone Jayden. Not now. Instead, she sends him a quick message.

The shoe ticks all the boxes. I couldn't see the car. I'm calling Skinner.

Her finger hovers . . . What else can she say? That she hopes Cat is found? Ask if she can do anything to help? But Jayden already knows these things; Ally is his partner.

Jayden, I'm here for whatever you need x

And then she's phoning DS Skinner. Ally tells herself that if he doesn't answer then she'll call Mullins. Or 999. But he does answer. He sounds like he's on the move, and there's a gentleness to his voice that surprises her.

She starts from the beginning: Pamela possibly seeing Billie Swann's photography equipment in her studio – and the cyanide – when she had her tour. Pamela wearing black and white to the party, blending in with the waiting staff. Pamela possibly faking an alibi at the hospital. The hit-and-run as possibly a desperate attempt to push the Arts Trail angle. Pamela's trainers matching the footprint that was found outside Sea Dream after the murder. And the single stone caught in the tread of the trainer that matches the gravel on the beach house driveway.

'Moonstone flint, I'm reliably told.'

Ally listens to the sound of silence. She's all too aware of how many times she used the word *possibly*.

'Ally, your pal Mullins already paved the way,' says Skinner. 'Except for the hit-and-run theory. That's a new addition. Listen, we're waiting on the CCTV footage from the hospital. It lives or dies on that. But with the match on the footprint, we've grounds for arrest. And we'll be examining every millimetre of that car of hers too. Good work.'

'Shall I send you the photographs?'

'Yes, do that. And Ally . . . we've sent a car out to Upper Hendra.'

So Cat wasn't at the Lookout.

'Given the situation, we're putting more people on it. Because, between you and me, Lara Swann's not budging. Which potentially means the killer's still out there.'

'Jayden believed Lara when she said she had no part in this,' says Ally. 'The vandalism, the emails, but nothing else.'

'Anyone going missing right now, anyone at all, that's high-risk. But the spouse of someone involved in the investigation . . . we've got to consider that.'

'But if it's Pamela, we were with her when Cat went missing. Or almost, anyway.'

'Ally, I'm not saying that your thinking isn't interesting, but so far we're chasing our tails. Pamela could be one more tail.'

Ally knows by now that Skinner has to get there in his own time.

'So what can I be doing?' she says.

'Don't give Pamela Trescoe even a hint of a suspicion that we're interested in her. You haven't already put the wind up her, have you?'

'The opposite. She offered me tea and gave me some mosaic pieces.'

Skinner snorts. 'Shell House operational tactics, eh? Well, steer clear now and leave this next bit to us. And make sure Jayden doesn't do anything stupid in the meantime. The lad's emotions will be running high.'

As Ally hangs up, she messages Gus again. She tells him that Cat is missing; to keep his eyes open at the beach. Then she sends the same message to Saffron.

She thinks of Ray. He doesn't even know who Cat is, there's no point in messaging him, but he's risen up in her mind. She tries to dispatch him, but he goes nowhere.

Ally sits behind the wheel, unsure of her next move. Unsure, in fact, of everything. The adrenalin of being at Pamela's, of matching the shoe, of finding that tiny piece of moonstone flint, ebbs. In its place, an anxious feeling comes rushing in. And it's as fast, as uncompromising, as a spring tide.

67

Donald doesn't know what to do now. Part of him wants a shower, to send the last twenty-four hours swirling down the plughole. Part of him wants to sink a bottle of whisky, drink until his vision blurs and the ground tips. Part of him wants to go raging over the clifftops, screaming down at the surging water. And part of him wants to just carry on sitting here, his hands on his knees, staring into the middle distance.

Doing precisely nothing.

Because this is Donald: a man of inaction.

Or, more accurately, a man who acts too late. Who whimpered and tiptoed his way to a conversation, a confrontation, that was already dead in the water.

And he is tired; so tired. All those questions. His worst feelings wrenched from him, fingered and probed. The death of darling Kitty no more than an ink-stamped motivation; her devastating loss a basis for interrogation. But worse than the inquisition, worse than the fear of the last twenty-four hours, is the fact that Harrison Loveday is dead.

The man is dead.

Which means Donald will never be able to look him in the eye and say the things he needs to say. It took everything for him to go to Sea Dream two nights ago. Gathering all of his sorrow and animosity; balling it into a shape that he could carry.

What that took.

When Donald knocked, there was no answer, but when he tried the door, it opened. He called Harrison's name, and when there was still no answer, he climbed the stairs. It was as if he was being pulled along by something inexplicable, a grim light drawing him in, ready to dash him on the rocks. Because when he saw the bedroom door wide open and Harrison Loveday lying there, only one thought pushed into his brain.

I'm too late.

And the pain was surely as much as any dagger to the chest.

Now, Donald jumps clean out of his skin. Twenty-four hours away from home and he's forgotten the sound of his own doorbell.

It'll be the police. With a new tack, some grim new detail with which to pummel him, when all the time the real killer walks free. And do you know what he'd like to tell that killer? That two people died that night. Harrison Loveday and Donald Crosby.

The doorbell goes again. A squalling bleat of impatience. Donald grinds his teeth. He considers not moving at all, but then he hears the lifting of the letterbox, a voice calling his name.

'Donald!'

He hauls himself up, and trudges down the hallway. His limbs are lead-heavy.

I was too late.

He opens the door to Pamela, and she drags him into her arms. He feels like a pilchard caught in a net. Her hot breath near his ear, whispering, 'Dear Donald, it's all over now.'

68

Jayden walks towards her. He's reaching for his phone, knowing he should call it in, but he just needs this time alone with her first. Just him and Cat.

Her trainers are on the beach. Her socks neatly balled, as if she was thinking perfectly straight.

He says her name. She doesn't move.

'Cat,' he says again. And he's in the water now, stepping through the incoming tide. No careful removal of his shoes; no balling of socks. He sets a hand on her shoulder. 'Cat?'

The breeze whips her hair and drags it across her face. For a moment, he can't see her eyes. He reaches to smooth her hair.

'Jay,' she says.

And then she collapses into his shoulder. She shakes as she cries, and he holds her tight. He feels her emotion pass through him like electricity, until he's shaking too. The relief of having found her. He pushes down all his questions and tries to focus on that.

'Your mum was really worried. I was really worried. Jazz was—'

'Don't do that. Don't say that.'

And it's not fair of him. Because Jazz was watching TV; Jazz didn't notice.

You left them without saying where you were going. But he knows better than to say it.

'I had to get out. Just for a bit. Those four walls . . . I couldn't breathe. I was going to come right back but . . . I wanted to see the sea. Then I wanted to feel it. I just wanted to feel the water.'

Jayden's mind spins to the police arriving at the farm. To Sue, answering their questions. To Cliff, combing the village.

'Cat, I just need to make a couple of calls.'

'Shell House calls?'

There's a sting in her words.

'No, your mum. And the police.'

Her face crumples. 'What, why?'

Jayden takes a breath. 'Because you didn't tell your mum where you were going. She didn't know where you were.'

Cat stares at him. Her cheeks are dotted with tiny goosebumps.

'I told her. Jay, I called up. I said I was taking a walk.'

'She didn't know.' Then, more diplomatically, 'She didn't hear you, babe.'

'So . . . she just thought I went? And left the kids?'

Cat looks down at the water. It swills at her calves.

She loves the ocean, Cat. It's part of her. *I grew up by the sea*, that's what she said to him the first time they met, *in a place called Porthpella*; like it was important that Jayden know these things about her. Perhaps she was warning him – all those years ago, at that barbecue in Chapeltown – that one day she would want to come back here. That one day she would walk out of her house and into the sea, because she needed to be in salt water: the clarity of that fixed horizon.

'I would never do that,' she says quietly.

Jayden's holding her hand, gently leading her back to the beach. 'I know. I know you wouldn't.'

Out of the water, his jeans stick to his lower legs. His feet squelch in his trainers.

'But . . . it felt so good. For just five minutes. To be on my own. To have no one . . . needing me. I wanted it to be ten minutes. Longer. So, I just . . . kept walking.' She darts a look at him. 'I was about to come back. Just now, I was coming back.'

But Cat was statue-still in the water; so still, she scared him.

'And I thought I told Mum where I was.'

'I'm just making two quick calls,' says Jayden. 'Then, there's no rush, okay? We can take all the time we want. We can stay here, talk. Work out how to make things easier. Better.'

He looks deep into her eyes, and feels the press of her fingers in his palm. Then she takes her hand away.

'I'm not a case, Jay,' she says, her voice a whisper. 'What if you can't solve this?'

69

'But isn't it a tremendous relief? To know he's gone?'

Donald is sunk in a chair. He looks diminished; half the man he could still be. Pamela understands why he's bruised, but she didn't expect him to be so determined to keep licking his wounds. She pulled out a bottle of cava from the fridge before she left and now it sits unopened on the sideboard. Unacknowledged by Donald.

'But he's *gone*, Donald. Finally, you can move on.'

Donald pushes his face into his hands.

'No more worrying about what you should say to him, or how you can ever make it right. No more—'

'I went to the beach house, Pamela.' He looks up from his palms. His hair is wild, his eyes wilder. 'To say my piece. I finally plucked up the . . . courage.'

'Donald, it's over,' she says. 'It's over.'

And she croons as if to a restless baby. *There, there.*

'Don't you see? I finally got myself in a position to say the words that have been in my head, that I've been lugging around, for forty-five years. I was ready. And . . . I was denied.'

The fact that Donald actually made it to Sea Dream is astonishing. For a fraction of a second, Pamela thinks about what would have happened if Donald had told her his plan. Would she have altered her own?

'It wouldn't have done any good,' she says. 'You wouldn't have felt any better.'

And this much she believes. Because Donald would have lost his voice or been shouted down. His words ridden over roughshod by the forceful personality of Harrison Loveday. He'd have found no solace. No justice. He would, she thinks, have ended up feeling worse than before.

No, she was right to do what she did. She was 100 per cent right.

'I will never get over it,' he says.

'Oh, darling Donald, no one expects you to. Your dear Kitty was—'

'Harrison,' he cuts in. 'I will never get over being denied my chance to speak to Harrison.'

Pamela's lips purse. She feels a flicker of irritation. Forty-five years of private seething, of doing absolutely nothing except letting all that bitterness, that sorrow, gnaw away at him, and suddenly he thinks a few words on a Saturday night in Porthpella would have been a silver bullet?

And he never told her. Donald had never said he planned to confront Harrison.

'It wouldn't have got you anywhere, Donald. Even if you delivered the most perfectly worded speech, do you really think it would have made a difference?'

'To me, yes. Perhaps not to him. But to me.'

He speaks so quietly, so sadly, that Pamela feels a surge of emotion. She kneels beside him, puts her hand over his knee.

'You don't need to think about it anymore,' she says.

'I will never stop thinking about it.'

'You've had a torrid time. Seeing him like that, then the police . . . I never would have dreamt they'd haul you in, Donald. I felt so terrible about that part . . .'

'I will never stop thinking about it,' he says again. Louder this time. Then, 'I'm sorry, Pamela. But I'd like to be on my own.'

'I'm not leaving you. Not like this.'

'I know you mean well, but I really do need you to go.'

Pamela sucks in a gusty breath. *Mean well? If only he knew.*

They lock eyes and Donald's are bloodshot, as sad as a basset hound's. But she loves him. She loves every inch of him. And she thought she was giving him the greatest gift. She thought she was freeing him, lifting this infernal cloud. Making him believe, again, in the balance of the universe. In just desserts. In consequences. In good things happening to good people and bad things happening to bad people and . . . Pamela falters. She knows that equation has never held.

Donald's face looks like a tired old punchbag. Sunken and socked. She cups her hands around his cheeks.

'Donald,' she says.

Pamela moves to kiss him, but he recoils from her. As if their lips have never met before. As if they haven't fallen into each other's beds on seven, almost eight, occasions over the last twenty years. As if he doesn't even *like* her, let alone love her.

'Sorry,' he mutters. 'Just . . . I don't want that.'

She decides then that Donald needs to know. He needs to understand her love. Her devotion. Her sacrifice.

'Donald,' she says. 'I wanted to lift this weight from your shoulders. I wanted you to be freed of this miserable obsession.'

And, as he looks at her uncomprehendingly, she tells him everything. She begins with Harrison, then she circles back to the error that was Gina Best. How that misstep – plus all that graffiti and email nonsense playing straight into her hand – gave Pamela the idea for Milo Nash. Because with Donald in custody – *dear you, under fire* – she couldn't let it look like the motivation was a personal grievance. The net had to be cast much wider: a grudge against the Arts Trail. The killer attacking at random, then likely fleeing the county. Gone, clean gone.

Donald stares at her. He carefully removes his glasses and wipes them with the hem of his crumpled shirt. His movements are glacial.

Say something, you hopeless man.

'It's in poor taste, Pamela,' he says eventually. 'Please don't.'

'I won't mention it again. We'll forget it. Put it behind us. But you needed to understand the depth of my . . . What, Donald? Why are you looking at me like that?'

He's frozen, halfway to putting his glasses back on. 'You're joking though. Aren't you? It's a joke.'

'I've never been more serious about anything in my life. Deathly serious!'

This time she gives him his joke. Just a little one. But it doesn't land.

The ticking of Donald's old grandfather clock suddenly sounds chronically loud. She watches his face, expressions moving across it like weather blowing in fast. She waits. *Always an overthinker, dear Donald.* She is ready with her open arms.

'It's alright,' she says, 'I've trodden awfully quietly. I've left no trace. I've surprised myself, Donald. I mean, I'm hardly a master criminal, am I? But it just goes to show that when you're fuelled by the right motivation, anything is possible.'

Donald's mouth moves.

'But Milo Nash didn't die,' he says.

And his voice is so quiet, barely a whisper.

'No.'

'Did he see you? Did he see it was you?'

Pamela waves a hand. 'No. No! Of course not. It was dark. He doesn't know me from Adam. It all happened so quickly. Besides, I shouldn't think he's the sharpest tool in the box . . .'

The lines in Donald's forehead are deep as trenches. He doubles over, retches violently.

'There's really nothing to worry about,' she says, her conviction faltering for the first time. And now this nagging feeling, this stone in her shoe. What if Milo Nash did see her?

70

'You sure you didn't put the wind up Pamela Trescoe?' says Skinner.

His voice is a good deal curter than before.

'She's not at home, Ally,' he says. 'I'll tell you who is though: Cat Weston. So at least I get my officers back.'

Ally grits her teeth. It reminds her of the first time she spoke to the detective sergeant, two years ago now. When he's frustrated, it doesn't take much for Skinner to revert to form.

But Cat is at home.

The relief is immense. And Skinner's dismissive tone is, at least, promising. She won't ask any questions of him, not about Cat. Ally, too, will go home now; she's been out driving, looking for Jayden's wife in the lanes and on the coast road, because she didn't know what else to do. She feels her phone buzz and hopes it's a message from Jayden.

'What about Donald Crosby's house?' she asks.

'Crosby admitted she called in earlier briefly. Wanting to welcome him home.'

'What sort of a feeling did you get from Donald?'

'Same feeling he gave off in his interviews. Quietly obstinate. Thoroughly miserable.' Skinner grunts. 'I'll eat my hat if he knows anything.'

'I can assure you,' says Ally, 'I gave no reason for Pamela to suspect that we're on to her. And she behaved as if she had nothing to hide.'

'Then let's hope her confidence will be her downfall. I've got her house under surveillance. Crosby's too.'

At that he hangs up, and Ally is left staring at her phone. It rings again immediately. *Jayden.*

'Cat's home.'

'Oh Jayden, thank God. How is she?'

'Okay. Can we talk about the case?'

His voice has a tremor to it.

'Of course. You got my message?'

'Nailed it, Al. Moonstone flint. That was a hell of a connection to make.'

'That's thanks to Gus and some nifty photography work at Sea Dream,' she says with a smile.

'So where are we now?'

'Skinner's got Pamela's house under surveillance. Donald's too.'

'She's done a runner?'

'No, I don't think so. I think Pamela believes she's beyond suspicion.'

'But if the cops have gone looking for her at Donald's, then he'll know she's a suspect.'

Ally didn't even think of that. Presumably it's a risk the police are willing to take.

'Donald told the police she was there earlier, but she didn't stay long. She wanted to welcome him home, Skinner thinks.'

'And she didn't stay long? She's supposed to be in love with him.'

'I expect he's exhausted after twenty-four hours in custody.'

'Plus no one said that love's reciprocated, right? But that's weird to me, Al, the fact she didn't stay long.'

Ally nods. It's Jayden's thinking voice. She lets the quiet hold.

357

'So, I'm Pamela,' he says, 'and the person I've killed for has just been released from custody. That's not a quick drop-in situation, is it?'

'She was genuinely very upset to think of him suffering in custody. You're right, she'd want to stay and make sure he's okay. Even if he's resistant.'

'Okay, so why would she leave quickly? What would she have to do that's so important?'

'Skinner accused me of putting the wind up her,' she says. 'But I assured him that's not the case. She was untroubled this morning, Jayden. Startlingly so.'

'So has something happened to make her think twice? Maybe she did tell Donald. Maybe he freaked out – and then she left.'

'Skinner thinks Donald doesn't know anything.'

'I guess Skinner's got a read on him, after that time in custody.'

Ally makes a noise of agreement.

'What if she's tying up loose ends? Al, what if she's heard that Milo is going to make it? That he's been transferred out of Intensive Care? Pamela was counting on Milo dying, so he's a potential liability. He could be talking. He could remember the accident. If she's as ruthless as we think she is, she'd do anything to cover her tracks, right?'

'My God.' Ally can suddenly see it. 'Jayden, do you think she's gone to Truro?'

'Yeah. Yeah, I do.'

'But wouldn't Skinner have said if Milo had told them anything useful?'

'Either way, Pamela doesn't know, does she?'

'But she was calm this morning. She didn't look like someone who was afraid they were about to be caught.'

'She can't have heard about Milo at that point. She must have thought he was still critical.'

And perhaps she thought she was on a roll. That it would go her way.

'No, she asked me, Jayden. I said I heard he was going to make a recovery. And . . . my God. What if it was me?'

At the thought, Ally goes cold from head to toe.

Jayden hesitates, then he says, 'You've done nothing, Al. Except for good. Pamela could have called the hospital and heard via them.'

And even when he's stressed, he's kind. She takes a breath.

'Are you about to say you want to go to Truro, Jayden?'

He hesitates. 'No, I . . . I can't. I'm needed here. But can you make that call? Tell Skinner. He needs an officer watching Milo's ward. Like, now.'

So, Ally calls Skinner. She tells him where Jayden thinks Pamela is. And Skinner doesn't say they're crazy. He hangs up. The urgency is understood.

Ally drops her head into her hands. Her breathing is fast; shallow. She wishes she could feel Bill's hand on her shoulder. That so-strong touch, just one more time.

71

The Royal Cornwall Hospital, two days in a row. Saffron's plaster cast hangs heavy by her side. Her chest buzzes with nerves. She watches as the receptionist taps at a computer keyboard. *They won't let me in*, she thinks, *they'll send me away.*

'He's up on the general wards now,' the woman says. 'And he's popular. He's already got one visitor.'

'Is it okay to still go in?'

'Of course, love.'

Saffron listens to the directions, all the time wondering who the visitor is. She doesn't want to intrude. Is it one of Milo's parents? A sibling? She knows so little about him, really.

Which makes her wonder, not for the first time, if she should even be here.

Saffron told Broady she was coming. He wrinkled his brow as if she'd just set him a puzzle. Eventually he said, *I think the guy needs space right now, Saff.* But Saffron thinks space is overrated. Space sounds considerate, but it's also a good excuse. Better to show her face for five minutes and let him know that she cares enough to come. Isn't it?

I care more than enough to come.

As Saffron follows the signs to the ward, she tries not to dwell on her motivation. Being here is as instinctive as going to someone who's fallen in the street, or helping mop up a spilt coffee, or bending to pat a dog. *Okay, bad examples.* But it's just what you do. And maybe her and Milo don't go back very far, maybe she hardly knows him at all, but she was with him the same night that he was hurt. And before he was hit by that car, he was right here, with Saffron, in her own hour of need. Until he felt like he had to leave.

He probably did have to leave.

There was a weird energy crackling between Broady and Milo last night – and before too. She tries to work out when it started. When Milo went his own way with the mural? When Saffron inadvertently took Milo's side?

She sees the ward number. Milo is apparently in a private room close by. She peers in a window and there's an elderly woman, thin as a stick, sitting on the edge of a bed and staring into space. Saffron realises she's chewing at her lip and stops herself. Hospitals have always made her feel weird. Well, after her mum, anyway. She moves to the next room, and there he is. Her chest contracts.

Milo looks as if he's sleeping. One side of his face is swollen with a livid bruise. Plaster casts on one leg, one arm. There's a pair of crutches leaning against the chair and Saffron marvels at this: he can't be up and walking yet, surely?

She wonders whether to go in and just sit in the chair beside the bed and wait until he wakes. Or get a coffee – *a no doubt terrible coffee* – and then come back in a bit. She doesn't want to disturb him. She has her hand on the door handle, still staring through the small pane, racked with indecision. There's no sign of his visitor.

Then a woman steps up to the bed.

She seems faintly familiar. Milo didn't mention his mum living round here, but maybe she does. Perhaps Saffron's even served her a latte. She looks arty, so it fits. She's holding a pillow in her hand, as if she wants to bolster him, and this maternal gesture pulls at Saffron's heart. She wants, suddenly, to meet this woman. But her son's just been in a near-fatal wreck. Maybe she doesn't want to make small talk – or big talk – with anyone. Saffron hesitates.

Go or stay?

Saffron looks again, hoping to catch the woman's eye, for her to wave and beckon her in. She's still standing with the pillow, as if uncertain how to position it. And Saffron's starting to think it's a bit weird, actually, because Milo's asleep – why fiddle with the pillows now? Why disturb him?

Oh my God.

She can't believe what she's seeing.

The woman is holding the pillow over Milo's face.

Saffron bursts through the door. She's yelling, running to the bed, pulling the woman's arm away. Time slows. The woman turns with a look of confusion. For a moment Saffron thinks she's made a terrible mistake – that this *is* Milo's mum, and she wasn't doing anything wrong at all, she was just trying to make him comfortable.

But then Milo's coughing. Gasping. And the woman yells out, her face split with fury. She wrestles her way out of Saffron's grip and with a pig-like grunt she pushes the pillow down hard on Milo's face again.

Saffron hurls herself against her, amazed at how strong her adversary is. The attacker's wide fingers are splayed against the fabric of the pillow; her body holds firm as a brick wall. But Saffron can fight the ocean; pop up on her board with a ton of water chasing her. She can drop a twelve-foot vertical on her skateboard and come out flying. Whatever wild energy is driving this woman, Saffron's not losing this.

No way.

Even if she's only got one arm that works.

As Saffron wrests the pillow from Milo's attacker, she yells with the effort.

Milo gasps again. He's free.

362

Saffron lunges for the green help button on the wall by the bed. Leans on it, and though there's no intercom, she shouts as loud as she can.

'Help! Someone help!'

The attacker spins round, her large hands going straight for Milo. No pillow this time. She plants them over his face and Milo, helpless, squirms beneath her grip.

Saffron dives forward in desperation. Her plaster cast is cumbersome, useless, and she pivots so she can grab one of the crutches with her good hand. She takes a swing and it's like she's back on the rounders pitch at school; she always had a wicked strike. Trouble is, she's doing it left-handed; there's not enough in it. The crutch connects with the attacker's head. She sways – but holds firm.

Saffron hits her again and this time the woman loses her hold on Milo, falling forward on to the bed. Saffron hears the rush of footsteps, and feels rough hands on her shoulders. 'Drop your weapon.'

Saffron is shaking. She can't let go of the crutch; her fingers are locked on.

A police officer is standing over her. He says it again. *Drop your weapon.*

And they've got it wrong, but Saffron's breath burns in her throat; she has no words. Meanwhile Milo's attacker is cradling her head in her hands, and whimpering, panting, 'Oh, thank God you came, Officers. Oh, thank God.'

Then a man Saffron recognises comes into the room. DS Skinner in his grey suit. Saffron's fingers uncurl and the crutch falls with a clatter. Behind her, Milo is coughing weakly. A nurse rushes in.

'Constable,' says Skinner, 'step back from this young woman.' Then, 'Pamela Trescoe, I'm arresting you on suspicion of murder.'

Handcuffs clink and Skinner's even, steady voice keeps up. Pamela starts keening – a high, wild moan.

Saffron turns and looks at Milo. The whole room, all of its madness, falls away. It's as if it's just the two of them. Milo's eyes shine back at her. Saying nothing; saying everything.

72

'I'll wait in the car for you, shall I, love?'

Mullins can't remember the last time his mum drove him anywhere. But he heard about the search for Cat – and that she's been found. And he heard about Pamela's Trescoe's arrest; the attack on Milo Nash in his hospital bed, and how Saffron saved him. And Ally's call to Skinner. And Jayden's idea that of all the places in all the world, there was a damn good chance Pamela Trescoe would be at the Royal Cornwall Hospital.

Mullins figures Jayden could use a knuckle bump right now, and he'd like to be the bloke to give it to him.

He climbs out of the car and it's a painful process, his tailbone protesting every millimetre's shift.

'Go easy, Tim love,' says his mum.

'No sweat, Mum.'

Police Constable Tim Mullins. *Rock hard.*

He calls at the farmhouse first, but then Cat's mum says they're in the cottage. Mullins hasn't actually been round to Jayden's before. He feels sort of weird on the doorstep, but then Jayden opens the door, and Mullins breaks into a grin.

'Hello, mate,' he says.

And Jayden hugs him. Not one of those chest-bump hugs that get dished out on match days when the final whistle blows, but a proper one. For a skinny guy, he brings a lot to a hug, does Jayden.

'You alright, Jay?'

'We're alright.' Then, 'Skinner called Ally. Ally called me.'

'Porthpella jungle drums, eh?'

'I prefer to think of it as the finely honed communication channels between you and us.'

'Team effort this time, wasn't it? See, you thought I was going to sit on that A&E alibi idea, didn't you? But I buzzed it through to Skinner anyway.'

'Appreciate it.'

'By the time Ally got on the phone to the sarge, I'd done the groundwork, see.'

Jayden grins. 'You were instrumental, mate.'

Mullins glances past Jayden, down the hallway. He wonders if he's going to get invited in. But then he hears a crying baby and thinks maybe the doorstep is better anyway.

'You heard about Saffron?'

'Saved the day,' says Jayden. He gives a shake of his head. 'I should check in with her, she . . .'

'What do you think she was doing there? Saffron, I mean.' Mullins looks down at his trainers. 'Guy's been in a smash, bit soon for visitors, isn't it? If you're not family. Or the girlfriend or whatever.'

What about falling down a hole? No visit for that?

'It was lucky that she was.'

'Hippy-Dippy saves the day,' says Mullins. 'Classic.'

'Is Lara Swann out of custody?' asks Jayden.

'Yep. She'll get a caution and a fine for the vandalism. But that's it.'

'And Donald Crosby knew nothing about Pamela's plans?'

'He says he didn't. Not until this morning, anyway, so we'll get him for obstruction. If he hadn't lied to us then, if he'd relayed the conversation that Pamela had with him, then we'd have been on to the Milo Nash connection sooner. Skinner said it scared the life out of Donald, realising that. If there was any life left to scare. He's on a downer, is Donald.'

'He's got a lot to carry,' says Jayden.

Behind them, the baby's crying ratchets up.

'I should go,' says Jayden.

'How's Cat doing?'

Jayden nods. Gives a small smile. 'It's tough right now. But we'll be all good.'

'Hey, look,' says Mullins. 'Once I'm back on my feet . . .'

He stops himself. Is it going to sound stupid coming from him? He's an officer of the law and all that; he can protect and serve with the best of them – *alright, with the middling of them* – but kids? Him? Front-line action? Not a bad thing to add to the CV though. His dating CV. If he ever has a date.

'Go on,' says Jayden.

'Babysitter,' he says. 'If you and the wife need a night out. Bit of time to yourselves and all that.'

'Yeah?'

'I might know one.'

73

The sign on the door of the Bluebird is flipped to 'Closed'. Cautious sunlight filters through the windows; shadows fade in and out. Ally accepts a mint tea from Sunita and checks her watch. Jayden should be here by now. She told him he didn't need to come, but he said he really wanted to.

It's the debrief. The first of its kind, actually, with a group of paying clients assembled. Sunita, Gideon and Connor. And Ray. He sits easily among this group. He and Connor are talking birdwatching: bitterns and spoonbills.

'Improbable-looking things,' laughs Ray. 'Ready-made caricatures.'

'A so-called friend of mine drew a caricature of me once,' says Gideon, leaning over. 'I could barely show my face in public afterwards. Suffice to say he's off the Christmas card list.'

Ally sits quietly. She knows it's just small talk, but the jollity feels jarring. Perhaps it's simply a reaction to the relief; Gideon said earlier that it's as if a great cloud has lifted from Porthpella. The village – and the Arts Trail – feels safe again. Wenna has hung even more bunting outside of White Wave. Spirits are light once more, even though Pamela Trescoe has been charged with two counts of murder and one of attempted murder.

And there is other wreckage.

Mullins is walking wounded. Saffron fought tooth and nail to save a life, her own broken wrist forgotten. Jayden is worried about Cat; Ally suspects he isn't feeling like they avoided a crisis this morning, but that they're in one still.

And Ally? Ally doesn't know how she feels.

The doorbell clangs and it's Jayden. She's so pleased to see him that she almost spills her tea as she gets up. The saucer clatters. It's Ray who reaches to steady it.

'Jayden,' she says. 'You're here.'

Sunita, Gideon, Connor and Ray break into clapping. Ally doesn't know where to look so she fixes on Jayden. He gives a half-smile; shakes his head. It doesn't feel like a victory, but given where they are, the dial has moved on the bad-news spectrum.

'Tell us how you did it,' says Gideon.

So, they do. Ally and Jayden describe each of the small fragments that, once assembled, completed a picture. They couldn't see it close-up, but when they stepped back, it came into sharp view.

'Skinner said that after they arrested her, Pamela boasted to him that she knew there was a bottle of cyanide in Billie Swann's old studio,' says Jayden. 'In Pamela's words, she said it was "just crying out to be put to good use".'

'My God,' murmurs Gideon.

'So Pamela killed Harrison so Donald Crosby would fall in love with her?' says Sunita.

'I think she was genuinely very concerned for Donald's well-being,' says Ally. 'She could see how deep his sadness went, and I think she wanted to try and—'

'Eradicate it at the source,' cuts in Ray. 'Not that simple though, is it? Because how happy is Donald Crosby now?'

Donald Crosby is not happy. Skinner said that it was like arresting a ghost.

'So poor Gina Best was collateral damage,' says Gideon. 'God, it could have been any one of us at that party, couldn't it?'

'We think Pamela somehow managed to intercept Harrison's cocktail from the barman,' says Jayden. 'She was dressed in black and white. All it would have taken is a few seconds to add the cyanide. And she probably held the glass stem with something as simple as a napkin.'

'How come Harrison didn't remember that it was Pamela who gave him the drink, when he was interviewed afterwards?' asks Connor. 'Or that Gina actually drank it?'

'Perhaps shock?' says Sunita. 'I should think a lot of that evening's events will have been scrambled.'

'And to a man like Harrison, Pamela would have been invisible,' says Ally. 'Her ordinariness was a disguise in itself.'

'So let me understand this,' says Gideon, 'after accidentally killing Gina, Pamela goes all out to murder Harrison the next night. And this time she gets her man. And she's so careful that the only thing linking her to the crime scene is her footprint.'

'Pamela got lucky there,' says Jayden, 'because that footprint was a match for Gina Best too, so the police didn't pursue it. If we hadn't already suspected Pamela, and Al hadn't spotted the Nikes in her shoe rack, we wouldn't have had much to go on at all.'

'Wow, she's artful,' says Sunita, 'to have evaded the police through it all.'

'Not as artful as she thinks,' says Jayden. 'Pamela couldn't have known that Gina owned Nike trainers in the same size. That was pure fluke. And her clever move for a fake alibi was quickly undone once it came under proper scrutiny. Skinner said the hospital CCTV shows her leaving, right, Al?'

'That's right,' says Ally. 'And coming back too. All within the timings of the murder.'

'Is that enough for a conviction though?' says Ray. 'Couldn't she claim to have been, I don't know, going for coffee?'

Ally nods. 'Absolutely, but she confessed everything once arrested. Skinner thinks the scene at the hospital broke her.'

'Oh Saffron,' says Sunita. 'What an incredible girl.'

'Pamela realised, too, that Donald was more devastated after Harrison's death than before it.'

'So it was all for nothing,' says Ray. 'Her grand gesture.'

'And what about Milo?' asks Connor. 'Could he identify her as the driver that hit him?'

Ally shakes her head. 'Apparently not. The impact came out of nowhere.'

Just like it had come out of nowhere – almost – for Pamela too. Skinner said Pamela had confessed to wanting to take the focus away from Donald's history with Harrison and put it back on an Arts Trail grudge. But she hadn't decided how. She was driving home and recognised Milo Nash walking along the lane. Her headlights picked him out and it was a split-second decision to attack him. He was simply in the wrong place at the wrong time.

'The police are confident they'll match trace evidence at the scene with Pamela's vehicle,' says Jayden.

'And Lara?' says Connor. 'The worst she did was mess around with spray cans and send creepy emails?'

'Pose as the killer, you mean,' says Gideon, 'and strike fear into all of our hearts.'

'I think Lara should pay for the surf school commission to be redone as soon as Milo's back on his feet,' says Sunita.

'As her Porthpella Swann song?' says Gideon. 'Sorry, couldn't resist. But seriously, you don't think Lara will stay here, after all this? Especially if it was her mother's casually strewn toxic chemicals that provided the first murder weapon.'

371

'It could set her on a different path,' says Jayden, 'with the community too, right? We don't always know what people are struggling with.'

'So Porthpella's a place that forgives and forgets, is it?' asks Ray, one eyebrow raised.

Ally can hear the scepticism in his voice. She feels rather sorry for Lara Swann.

'I think Porthpella is a place for second chapters,' she says.

To which Ray quietly replies, 'I like that.'

Sunita smiles. 'So do I, Ally. And I believe it too. I'll reach out to her.'

'Well, look,' says Gideon, 'all I know is that the Shell House Detectives absolutely came up trumps. And the Arts Trail lives to fight another day. Albeit without our principal potter . . . Ally, Jayden, you've done it again. This place that's so special to us all, you've made us feel safe once more. Wrongs righted. Justice served.'

'Gid?' says Connor, kindly.

Gideon takes a deep breath. His eyes blur with tears. 'I know. I'm waffling. But . . . Ally and Jayden, somehow you've taken a terrible thing and given us some kind of . . . glimmer. Of optimism. Perhaps the police would have got there on their own eventually, but all I know is that you two good people act, when the rest of us look the other way, and I think that's . . . special. God knows, this world is full of suffering, but very few of us step beyond our own doorsteps when it comes to truly helping. Now, I'm not casting myself as the mayor of Porthpella or anything like that . . .'

'Oh, I don't know,' says Sunita, with a tender smile, 'I think you'd make a fabulous mayor, Gideon.'

'. . . but Ally and Jayden, our little corner of the world is extraordinarily lucky to have you in it. And I hope you know that.'

Ally feels a swell inside her chest, a rising tide of emotion. Jayden drops his arm around her, and by the look on his face, she knows he's moved too.

She thinks of how much he's got on his plate – and how much he's still given to this investigation. She's hit by the sense that it could all end at any moment: that Jayden could seek greater security for himself and his family; or an offer might come along without him even looking, just like it did last summer with the task force in Plymouth. But whatever he does, she'll wish Jayden nothing but the best. And know that, astonishingly, she had the best herself for a while.

He winks at her; says quietly, 'Nice one, Al.'

Gideon holds out his hand to be shaken, then changes his mind and goes in for hugs instead. 'Now, who do we make the cheque out to?'

As Jayden answers, Ray catches Ally's arm.

'This is for you,' he says, passing her a letter. 'But don't read it now.'

74

Saffron stares at the newly whitewashed wall of Mahalo. The words *who's next?* are gone. So too is all the colour and light of Milo's remarkable work.

She turns away. According to this wall, it's as if the artist was never here at all.

Broady is out on the water, taking a lesson. After she gave her statement, he came to fetch her from the police station. He looked so weird in there, with his square shoulders and sun-bleached hair; neon boardshorts and flip-flops. Broady doesn't belong in a place that deals in strife. But when he turned to look at her, his face said otherwise. Because she'd gone to the hospital to see Milo without telling him.

Strife City.

There's something going on, isn't there? he asked her in the car on the way home.

No, she said truthfully. Then, also truthfully, *But I think . . . I've thought about it.*

They drove on to Porthpella in silence. And Saffron held on to all her tears – the shock of the fight with Pamela; the turmoil of emotion – until she was on her own again.

'Yo, Saff!'

She turns to see Mullins, shuffling along in the sand. He holds his coffee cup up.

'Don't rush back. Your mate makes a mean latte.'

'Ha ha. Well, she trained with the best.'

'How's the wrist?'

Mullins is at her side. He's wearing aftershave and a box-fresh rugby shirt that still has creases in it.

'It hurts. What about you and your tailbone?'

'Fighting fit, me.' He nudges her. 'I heard what you did.'

She looks up at him, eyes wide. 'Did you?'

'Saving Milo Nash. What did you think I was going to say? Saff, you bossed it. Took Pamela down single-handed – literally! You should be buzzing.'

She shakes her head.

'Let me guess . . . Surf God doesn't love that you're the town hero? Saving someone else's skin?'

Her eyes fill with tears. She goes to wipe them away, then remembers her plaster cast. She uses her other hand instead.

'Saff, I was joking.'

'Yeah, I know. Just . . . there's kind of more to it.'

And Mullins is looking at her like he might just get it.

'You fancy Graffiti Boy, do you?'

'I didn't say that.'

'And Surf God knows it, does he?'

Broady's actual words were: *If you're tempted, then we might as well already be over, Saffron.* And she doesn't think it's that simple. Or maybe it is? What she does know is that she hates feeling like the bad guy. She's never been the bad guy before.

'Problem is, Saff, you always go for the wrong people.'

'And what would you know, Mullins?' she laughs. 'Go on, what other kind of wise advice have you got for me?'

But he's not laughing with her. Mullins stuffs his hands in his pockets and sighs. It sounds like the creaking of a ship's bow.

'You're right. What would I know? Free agent, me. Keeping it that way too.'

He turns, raising his hand in a quick wave, then starts to make his way back up the beach.

'That it?' she calls out. 'No more advice?'

Saffron has the uncomfortable feeling that she's offended him.

He stops. His foot scuffs the sand. 'I got nothing, Saff.'

'I reckon you've got more than you think.'

He looks up, his face a question. Then he walks towards her. For the freakiest moment, she thinks he's going to try taking her in his arms, film-star style. But, instead, he says, 'Just . . . do me a favour. Don't settle. Okay?'

Then he's off up the beach before she can say anything back.

75

Donald rests his temple against the smeary bus window. He closes his eyes and feels every bump and jolt as it crawls its way along the lanes towards Porthpella. Every bump and jolt in his mind as well as his body.

Donald has been charged with obstruction and released on bail. Meanwhile, Pamela is under lock and key.

If you'd asked him yesterday if Pamela was a good person, Donald would have said yes, without hesitation. She kept her capacity for extreme violence ever so well hidden. All Donald can think is that she believed she was doing the right thing; that she was so sure of this that she lost all perspective. And of all the emotions he's feeling now – *news flash, Donald is feeling* – high among them is bewilderment. Bewilderment that he, of all people, inspired such passion. People do not write ballads about men like Donald. They don't compose sonnets. And they certainly do not kill in the name of love.

It was Pamela who told the detectives that she'd gone to Donald's house and admitted the murders to him. And it was Pamela who said that Donald had suggested Milo was a liability, planting the idea in her mind. Donald doesn't think she was going out of her way to implicate him, simply that when she knew the game was up, she stopped caring.

So the love she claimed she had for him had a limit after all.

Which is, in fact, reassuring. Because even without the killings – *how glib, to put it like that* – Donald does not want to be loved to that sort of fever pitch. Not by anyone, even a sane person.

Not least because he doesn't have a hope in hell of returning it.

As the bus judders to a stop, Donald's head bumps against the window. He opens his eyes and sees a young mum struggling to board, her pushchair loaded with groceries. She holds her squalling baby, a little red-headed thing, in her arms. Donald hears the tension in her voice – as frayed as old rope – as she speaks to the driver, digging in her purse for her fare, clattering the small change into the plastic scoop. Then she plonks down next to him.

He shifts up as much as he can, but the woman and the baby are still painfully close. He holds his breath; he cannot make himself smaller. The mum kisses the top of her child's head, murmurs something he can't catch. But he knows the words are kind.

Tears sting the back of Donald's eyes. *Oh Kitty.*

Experiencing an unfamiliar bolt of resolution, he takes his phone out of his pocket. Perhaps one good thing can come of this wretched mess. When was the last time Donald saw Annabel? And those children of hers? The strange thing is that there's already a message from Annabel waiting for him. As if the threads are still connected after all.

He clicks on it, expecting banality. A basic check-in.

Hi Uncle Donald. I know this is out the blue, but I just found out that I'm the sole beneficiary in Harrison Loveday's will. It's the last thing I was expecting. Last thing I wanted. Though I'd be lying if I said the money wouldn't come in handy. I don't know how to feel about it – and I thought that you, of all people, might understand that. It'd be good to catch up sometime. Annabel x

Donald bites down hard on his lip.

What does it mean? That Harrison wanted a relationship with his daughter, in death if not in life? Or is this why Harrison came to Cornwall? To tell Annabel that what's his is hers. Perhaps even to apologise. And if that were the case, would Donald have thought any differently of him?

No. This gesture alters nothing essential. Donald cannot change how he feels. He is, as Pamela would say, wilful, in this regard.

But perhaps he can draw a line under it.

The bus crests the hill above Porthpella, and the countryside opens up before him. Dark clouds crowd the sky, but just beyond the rooftops of the village there's a parting. A sliver of light, finding its way in.

It would, he thinks, make for a good painting.

76

'Ally, I was just thinking about you.'

Gus knows better than to imagine that the moonstone flint intel proved to be the nail in Pamela's Trescoe's coffin. But at least his photographic mission got him back in Ally's good books.

He opens his door yet wider and asks if she and Fox would like to come in.

'I'm sorry I was prickly yesterday,' she says, staying on the doorstep. 'It was unfair of me.'

'And I'm sorry I went about it the wrong way.'

He's picked over what he said to her; every darn word of it. He hopes he's misremembering slightly and that he didn't come over quite as peevish as he thinks he did.

'Of course you were right to talk to the police, Gus. And you did, by the way. See Ray, I mean. But he wasn't going to Sea Dream. He was going to The Shell House. Only I wasn't there, and he didn't tell me.'

'Why didn't he tell you?'

She gives a brief shake of her head, and he feels the rise of the green-eyed monster again. *Hopeless.*

'I think I probably owe you another apology too,' he says.

'You really don't.'

'A few, actually. See, I've been a little rattled by Ray turning up here. This part of your life that, well, I know nothing about.'

'I was a little rattled too,' she says with a small smile.

Oh God, what sort of rattled?

He ploughs on: 'Ally, I'd got so used to it being the two of us. And that's not to presume, my goodness, that's not my style at all . . . not like . . .' He stops himself, but not quite in time. 'What I mean is, we're such friends, Ally. Pals, aren't we?'

'We are.'

He sees her take a breath, and it seems to fill her whole frame. She looks so lovely, he thinks, with the light sunshine splashing her cheeks.

'But the ebb and flow,' she adds, 'of you and me. Sometimes . . . I don't understand it.'

'If you mean in November, if that's what you're talking about, I did want to stay. When you asked me that night, I wanted to stay more than anything.'

And what a relief to have it out in the open.

'I felt rather ridiculous,' says Ally. 'Like I'd crossed a line I didn't think was there . . .'

'I didn't think you were ready.'

She blinks.

'Ally, I knew you weren't. And the last thing I wanted to do was push you . . .'

Gus can see her processing this: his sensitivity, his consideration. But her face doesn't quite end up where he thought it might.

'*You* knew I wasn't ready?'

'I found Bill's clothes in your wardrobe. Not just a special jumper or . . . a wedding shirt, but . . . lots of things. Lots of his clothes. All hanging there, just like he was . . . alive still.'

She gives a barely perceptible shake of her head.

'Why were you looking in my wardrobe?' she asks quietly.

Relief? Talk about short-lived.

He tries to laugh. 'Well, remember what that godawful Roland Hunter had me down as. A peeping Tom, wasn't it?'

He laughs again, but his face is already falling. It is, he thinks, sliding all the way to the floor.

'Ally,' he says, 'it was stupid of me. It was when we had that breakfast – you know, with the croissants. When you were in the middle of the vineyard case. I was looking for Fox. He'd run off, and there he was in your bedroom, and . . .'

He runs out of words. And is met by silence.

'I can't erase him, Gus,' she says eventually.

'I would never ask you to.'

How big of me.

He tries again. 'Of course you can't, Ally. No one could, in your shoes. I mean, I still think about Mona . . .'

'Do you?'

'Mostly that I wasted the best years of my life by being with her.' He rubs at his head. 'Look, everything I'm saying and doing seems to be coming out wrong. The trouble is our friendship is so dear to me. The thought of ruining it . . . And then Ray comes in. Firing on all cylinders. And you don't seem to mind the attention. You seem to enjoy it, in fact. It threw me. Because all this time I thought you were still in love with Bill, and then this Ray . . .'

He realises she's stopped looking at him. Her hand tightens on Fox's lead.

Oh God.

'Ally,' he says.

'I do still love Bill,' she says. 'I always will.'

'Does Ray know that?' He bats it back quickly, too quickly, in the bittersweet satisfaction of being right. Only now he feels like he's standing on a cliff edge. Like he's got a bloody death wish. He braces himself.

'I have no idea, Gus,' she says. 'Because I wouldn't presume to know what anyone thinks. Not about something so personal.'

And he's in freefall.

Ally says something about needing to get back to Fox. Or perhaps *for* Fox, because her dog is right there beside her. The truth is, Gus isn't really paying attention, not anymore. *The fool I am.* But she's lifting her hand in the approximation of a wave and then she's on the path, and he's calling out that he's glad she caught Pamela, brava, Shell House Detectives have done it again.

And his favourite person in the world disappears into the dunes.

Fool.

Gus's phone pings in his pocket. He pulls it out because he thinks it might be her. Though why would Ally be emailing him, approximately thirty seconds after he was so clumsy? So unthinking. So . . .

Not Ally, but a Marissa Fallon. The name doesn't mean anything to Gus and he's about to shove his phone back in his pocket and get back to feeling dreadful, when he takes in the first line of the message.

> Thank you for sending me *The Deathly Spires*. I
> enjoyed the first three chapters and . . .

He gasps. An agent. Of course.

But his other rejection emails didn't begin in this way.

Gus hesitates, his finger hovering over the message. If he clicks on it, he'll have to read it in its entirety – and his fate will be cast. At least as regards Marissa Fallon.

But what about Ally?

He looks down the dunes. Ally is a figure in the distance now. She is all but gone.

Gus takes a breath – and opens the email.

77

Jayden quietly lets himself into the house. He said he needed an hour and he's been gone fifty-three minutes. Not that that makes him a hero or anything, but if it'd been seven minutes over the hour instead of under, he'd be feeling seriously bad.

That's how fine the line is at the moment.

It was Cat who told him to go and do the debrief with Ally at the Bluebird. *Really, I'm fine*, she said. Then, again, *It's your job, Jay. It's important.* And this time it was without any undercurrents. He added those all by himself.

He stands in the hallway. It's dead quiet.

It's mid-afternoon, a time of day that he knows, for Cat, can feel never-ending. In a dream world, naps would be happening, but Jazzy's been dropping hers lately, and Benji? Benji runs by his own clock.

'Jayden, dear.'

His mum-in-law treads quietly down the hall. She holds a finger to her lips.

'They're upstairs, fast asleep. All three of them.'

'All three of them?'

'Cat and Benji went up. Then Jasmine said she wanted to snooze too – while looking about as wide awake as anyone I've ever seen – but, well, we all know there's no dissuading Jasmine. But I just checked and . . . they're all out for the count.'

Sue lightly touches his cheek.

'You look tired too. Why don't you go on up?'

'I don't want to wake them.'

Sue smiles; gives a brief shake of her head. 'Cat has something to tell you. And don't look like that, love, it's a good thing. A wonderful thing.'

So Jayden pulls off his shoes and pads upstairs. There's probably more to talk about with Sue, because his mum-in-law is adamant that Cat never called upstairs to say she was going out. But maybe she just didn't hear her. Or perhaps that's sleep deprivation for you – Cat can't keep track of what she did or didn't do. But a doctor's appointment will be the next thing – Cat agreed to that – then perhaps a referral. Jayden saw a flyer once for a group in Penzance, a bit like Saffron and Broady's Blue Project, but for maternal mental health. Admitting you're struggling, and asking for help, can be a really hard thing to do; Jayden knows that better than anyone.

His own guilt? That sits heavy. Because while they've been pretty much fifty-fifty on it all, why didn't he make it sixty-forty? Or seventy-thirty? Or any other combination that would have let Cat breathe deeper; so when she closes her eyes to sleep, she can actually sleep.

Okay, so they've had a murder case on their hands these last few days, but . . . he could have stepped back.

The truth is, at the time, he didn't want to. He wanted to be all in.

He thought he could do it all, that's the thing. Be everything to everyone. Jayden's sense of duty has always loomed large. Duty to his family, the husband he is, the father he is, but a duty to himself and Ally too. Doing his best as a detective. Duty pulling him in different directions.

How does he get this right? Would it be easier if he was on a payroll? If he had a boss? A shift pattern? If his work was undeniably work, not something that – to some; to Cat? – looks like a hobby.

Gideon's words at the Bluebird mean more to him than the pay cheque – and he knows they do to Ally too – but it's a good thing he's earning this time. They can't always guarantee it though. When someone like Shaun Tremaine – from their last case, up at the vineyard – needs helping, they're not going to turn them away, are they? That's not Shell House.

Jayden's mind buzzes with this uncertainty.

The name Kitty Crosby is lodged in his head too; a running base note. Because this was a story that started nearly half a century ago. A vulnerable woman, an arrogant man – the tragedy of a mother taking her own life by walking into the sea. Donald's grief, and his resentment of Harrison, sat heavy. And Pamela? Pamela wanted to fix that. And was prepared to go to the worst possible extremes to do it.

Kitty Crosby.

Jayden doesn't want to think about Kitty dying – the whys, the hows, the what-ifs – but he knows he has to. That, too, is his duty.

Their bedroom door is ajar, and he nudges it quietly open. All three of them are in his and Cat's big bed. His wife on her side, her arm curled protectively around Benji. Benji in his snow-white romper suit, the back of his head dark as night; his tiny curls. Jazzy on the other side of Cat, arms thrown wide in her classic starfish pose, face tipped to the sky without a care in the world. One of them – at least one of them – is emitting a snore so quiet it's a purr.

Jayden watches for a moment, then has to get in on it. He slides himself carefully on to the bed, on the other side of Benji; drops a kiss on his warm head. He feels Cat shift. She opens her eyes, smiles a sleepy smile.

'Jay,' she says softly.

'Hey.'

'I wish you'd been here . . .'

Fifty-three minutes, I was fifty-three minutes. And you said I was okay to go.

'I'm sorry,' he starts to say, 'I—'

'Jay, he smiled. Benji smiled for the first time. It was amazing. So amazing.'

Jayden props himself up on one elbow. Cat's eyes are full of tears. Happy tears.

'He really smiled?'

'It was the most beautiful thing ever.' She glances at the still-sleeping Jazzy. 'Since Jazz, obviously.'

'Obviously.'

'I didn't know how much I needed to see it,' she says. 'Oh Jay, I'm so sorry you missed it.'

Would he have liked to see his son smile for the first time? Of course he would. But Jayden's got a feeling that this little man will have smiles to spare. That now he's started, he won't stop.

His heart swells.

Love, relief, a little nick of fear at the intensity of it all; how this feeling – all this – can be joy and pain in basically the same breath. Jayden realises he can't speak, even if he wanted to. His hand finds Cat's, and they each hold on tight. Like they're on a life raft; waves lifting, path uncertain. Beside them, Jazzy laughs in her sleep. At the sound, Benji's eyelashes flicker, then his eyes are open wide. Bright as a skyload of stars.

'Oh, hello, Benji Weston,' murmurs Cat. 'Now, have you got a smile for Daddy?'

78

It's nightfall. The tide is way up high, and from the veranda of The Shell House it sounds as if the waves are coming right this way. There's a stiff breeze blowing, and Ally is bundled up in a big coat. Fox is inside in his basket. She's on her own out here, in this outermost house.

A lonely spot: that's what the email from John Smith, from Lara Swann, said. But 'lonely' and 'alone' are two quite different things. And Ally doesn't feel lonely.

Tonight, the solitude is a particular relief.

Her fraught exchange with Gus stayed with her all the way into the evening. To know that he went looking in her house – not snooping as such; *snooping* would be too unkind a word to use – and then made a judgement, an assumption, about the most private part of her life, stung like a weever fish.

And he presumed her feelings for Ray too. When she doesn't even know them herself.

But Ally's upset has ebbed, and it is now replaced by reflection.

It's easier to think out here. The sky is full of stars. Fast-moving clouds scud across the crescent moon; it comes and goes with a magician's flourish. Flashes of silver illuminate the ever-shifting surface of the water.

Ally feels very small. The cacophony of human lives cut down to size.

She holds Ray's letter in her hand, the one he gave her at the Bluebird. She still hasn't opened it. It didn't seem right. With Gus's words still high in her mind, she knew the colours would mix unfairly.

At least it makes sense of why he wouldn't stay at The Shell House that time. On the one hand, the thought is freeing. But that Gus's good intentions should feel insulting is perhaps evidence in and of itself. No one likes to be second-guessed. Ally knows their platonic bond is rock-solid, their cherished friendship ocean-deep. But a romantic bond? That's far more delicate. She felt the blaze of it last summer. My goodness she felt it then. But Gus never heard the words she whispered in the ICU. What they have is a handful of moments, jewel-bright but scattered over time. Perhaps so scattered they hardly count.

You and this Gus guy, you're together? That was how Ray said it. And her hesitation was obvious.

There has been so much hesitation.

Ally looks down at Ray's letter, and suddenly tears it open.

Ray's penmanship has flair; it's angular, distinctly masculine. She stops at this:

> *Life moves in mysterious ways. Death too. This trip was nothing like I imagined except for one part. You, Ally. No, that's a lie. You are far better. I'd love the chance to say that to you face-to-face. I leave Porthpella tomorrow, but I'd love for you to come to Suffolk. I'd love us to sketch and walk like the old days. Just like the old days . . .*

The subtext of that ellipsis. Ally suspects that if Ray were Evie's age he'd have added a winking emoji. She's grateful that he isn't – and that he didn't.

She reads the rest of the letter, then looks out at the night. She feels absurdly alive.

The black air is full of the sound of the waves. Far out, the moonlight plays off the water, the glitter making her eyes burn. God knows Ally has days when, more than anything, she wants to wind the clock back too. But then there are the days when she lives wholly in the here and now. When she feels like she has everything she could ever want – or at least ever plausibly have – right here in the dunes. She misses Bill with every atom of her being, she loves him unendingly, but she's not lost here without him. Not anymore.

Is it the beachcomber in her, who now sees the glint of possibility on the shoreline? The allure of something, of someone, who has travelled a great distance – *forty-seven years, Al* – to wind up on these shores.

She imagines what it would be like to pack her sketchbooks and take a slow drive to Suffolk. The invitation is to stay at Ray's cottage, but his cat might take issue with that – so perhaps Fox is the reason that Ally might seek a local bed and breakfast. Or one of those tarred-weatherboard fisherman's huts she's seen pictures of: stilted legs and pointed roofs.

It might be an adventure, mightn't it?

Before she can change her mind, Ally goes into the house. She takes her car keys, and bends down to stroke Fox; the old boy doesn't wake. Then she closes the door of The Shell House and heads out the gate. Into her car and along the sandy track, her headlights playing off the lunar landscape. As she nears All Swell, she slows. Some nights, in midwinter, hers and Gus's are the only lights on in the dunes. She looks up at the window where she knows his desk is, but he's not sitting there tonight. *Dear Gus.* They still have things to say to one another. Or perhaps, for now, it has all been said.

Ally drives on towards the village. The road ahead is gleaming.

Epilogue

1980

Kitty Crosby stands with her feet in the sand. For once, her loud, relentless thoughts are drowned out by the roar of the waves. The whooping, looping cries of seabirds. The whistle of the wind in her ears. For Kitty, it's so quiet.

She's kicked off her shoes and wears only a light dress that blows against her thighs. Her arms and legs are dotted with goosebumps. She tips her head back and sucks in a breath.

No. Bigger. Deeper. She tries again.

She can't believe she's all on her own for once.

Baby Annabel is sleeping, and Kitty's mother is watching her. Kitty said she was going for a walk and then hurried away over the clifftops before anyone could stop her. Fleet-footed; propelled by the call of the sea. A turn of speed that surprised her.

The weight of Kitty's responsibility is crushingly heavy. How are the other mothers all so strong? An unsolvable mystery. Some days Kitty feels like a butterfly shell, so delicate that she'll shatter at the slightest touch. And there is no other half. She is all on her own.

Perhaps, in time, Annabel will become her other half; perhaps, deep down, she already is. A dimple-cheeked, plump-wristed companion, with obstinate curls and eyes as dark as rockpool pebbles. Undoubtedly, her daughter is made of stern stuff. Perhaps this is Annabel's father's genes, though Kitty would rather not think about that. She now knows that as soon as Harrison Loveday left her bed, she was as good as dead to him.

She hopes her daughter never experiences the feeling of being made worthless. She only wants Annabel to believe in herself; to know her goodness and strength. Though what place does Kitty have, preaching that message? Some days she feels so fragile, one onshore gust might whip her over the clifftops; so porous that every wave that crashes over her corrodes her a little more. She is a perpetual disappointment to her hard-working mum, her sad-eyed dad, her brother Donald, who gets so tongue-tied when she cries, he doesn't know what to do with himself. Kitty is a disappointment, surely, to her daughter too. Kitty is certain that, if she were capable of thought, Annabel would think that, of all the mothers, she drew the short straw. Perhaps that's the message in her wailing. The fury in her pink cheeks.

Why did it have to be you, Mama?

The truth is, though, Kitty loves her daughter more than anyone. Far more than she loves herself. One day she hopes she'll grow into the mother her daughter deserves. She just needs to keep on keeping on. Day by day. Hour by hour. Minute by minute.

This morning, Kitty experienced a few moments of joy. *Joy.* She didn't recognise it at first, because it was such an unfamiliar sensation. Annabel finished feeding, and instead of falling asleep, she swayed in Kitty's arms – milk-drunk, happy as the cat that got the cream – and sent her mama the sweetest smile. A trickle of milk at her lips; her dark eyes glowing. And Kitty melted; actually melted.

I made you, she whispered. *Not him, me. And I'm looking after you. Not as well as I should be, but we're muddling through, aren't we? The two of us.*

She kissed her darling girl and told her she would never, ever leave her, no matter what.

This resolution is unfamiliar too. Because there have been moments – sometimes many of them, as closely strung as beads on a necklace – when Kitty has felt such despair that she has wanted to go. To make it all stop, once and for all. Much as she has guarded this terrible secret, she wonders if those around her suspect it. Most days she has been too tired to care. But today? Today she would like to tell them – her mum, her dad, her brother – that her heart knows hope.

She moves towards the water. As she steps over the tangle of weed on the strandline, something catches her eye: a tiny open mouth.

A cowrie.

Kitty has always thought of them as a gift for the observant. She hasn't found one for a long time. She picks the shell up carefully; it's so small, so perfect. She darts back to her shoes and drops it inside one to keep it safe. Perhaps it'll be a good luck charm, passed from mother to daughter. Maybe one day, when Annabel is all grown up, Kitty will even tell her about the day she found it. How she felt a sea change and was so grateful she could cry.

Kitty turns back to the sea and feels its electric pulse. The waves are wild but beautiful. The wind screams in her ears. It's not enough to stand and watch. She wants to lose herself to sensation, just like she did as a child, running into the sea with her sweet brother beside her, jumping those walls of water, screaming with glee.

To feel fearless again. And free.

Her mum will no doubt tut when she returns; wring out her sodden dress. But Kitty will take her hands and thank her for holding her together these last months. And then she'll kiss her daughter, and whisper about the tiny, perfect cowrie that will one day be hers. A secret of the sea.

Then perhaps Kitty will sleep well tonight.

ACKNOWLEDGEMENTS

I owe a lot of people a lot of thanks, but first, I'm grateful to you, the reader. If this was your first visit to Porthpella, I do hope you'll be back. And if you've been here since the beginning, well, I can't thank you enough for that.

Next, thank you to my wonderful agent, Rowan Lawton, at The Soho Agency. I'm so appreciative of everything you do. Thank you also to Eleanor Lawlor and also to Helen Mumby on the TV side.

The day I signed with Thomas & Mercer, I really landed on my feet. Thank you to my editor Vic Haslam – you're the best champion I could wish for. Together with the fantastic Laura Gerrard, my stories always feel in such safe and loving hands and are always better for your combined editorial input and out-and-out enthusiasm. Thanks also to the wider team at Thomas & Mercer, including the eagle-eyed Gemma Wain, Rebecca Hills, Maisie Lawrence, Victoria Pepe and Sammia Hamer. One of my favourite parts of the process is seeing the super-talented Marianna Tomaselli's cover illustration, and with The Arts Trail Killer we have another absolute beauty.

While the writing life is often solitary, I'm lucky to have an amazing band of friends who offer solidarity, inspiration and kindness at every turn. You know who you are – and I hope you know how grateful I am too. Particular thanks to Lucy Clarke, who has read the first draft of every Shell House book so far, including this one.

The first people I dial in a crime writer's emergency are my CSI friend Zoe and my police constable friend Oli. Thank you for telling me how it's done in the real world. Any inaccuracies are, as ever, down to me.

Thank you to my husband, Robin Etherington, and my son, Calvin. Bobby, we first discussed this novel while lazing in a rooftop pool, surrounded by stunning Alpine peaks. It sure kickstarted the writing process in style (and does it *have* to be a one-off?). You and Calvin are the best pair of people I could ever hope to share this life with.

Thank you, too, to the rest of my family – the Halls, the Green-Halls, and the Etheringtons – for your unending love, support and enormous strength. And your artistic inspiration! Among our number we have painters, illustrators, quilters, knitters, feltmakers and carpenters, and I feel very lucky to have always been surrounded by such a creative lot. This book – with all of its arty escapades – wouldn't exist without your influence.

While I was working on The Arts Trail Killer my lovely mother-in-law, Hazel Etherington, passed away. Always a voracious and sharp-eyed reader of murder mysteries, I remember awaiting her feedback on the very first Shell House book with bated breath. Luckily, she gave it the thumbs up. I'm sad that she never got to read this latest, especially as the first time we ever met – in Arundel, twenty-five years ago – the annual Gallery Trail was underway, and she was exhibiting her paintings. This book is dedicated to Hazel's memory, with love – and cold white wine.

ABOUT THE AUTHOR

Photo © 2022 Victoria Walker

Emylia Hall lives in Bristol with her husband and son, where she writes from a hut in the garden and dreams of the sea. She is the author of the Shell House Detective Mysteries, a series inspired by her love of Cornwall's wild landscape. The first, *The Shell House Detectives*, was a Kindle Top 10 Bestseller, with the rights being optioned for TV. *The Arts Trail Killer* is her fifth crime novel. Emylia has published four previous novels, including Richard and Judy Book Club pick *The Book of Summers* and *The Thousand Lights Hotel*. Her work has been translated into ten languages, and broadcast on BBC Radio 6 Music. She is the founder of Mothership Writers and is a writing coach at The Novelry.

Instagram: @emyliahall_author

X: @emyliahall

Follow the Author on Amazon

If you enjoyed this book, follow Emylia Hall on Amazon to be notified when the author releases a new book!
To do this, please follow these instructions:

Desktop:

1) Search for the author's name on Amazon or in the Amazon App.
2) Click on the author's name to arrive on their Amazon page.
3) Click the 'Follow' button.

Mobile and Tablet:

1) Search for the author's name on Amazon or in the Amazon App.
2) Click on one of the author's books.
3) Click on the author's name to arrive on their Amazon page.
4) Click the "Follow" button.

Kindle eReader and Kindle App:

If you enjoyed this book on a Kindle eReader or in the Kindle App, you will find the author 'Follow' button after the last page.